WITHOUT FEAR OR FAVOR

ALSO BY ROBERT K. TANENBAUM

FICTION

Infamy

Trap

Fatal Conceit

Tragic

Bad Faith

Outrage

Betrayed

Capture

Escape

Malice

Counterplay

Fury

Hoax

Resolved

Absolute Rage

Enemy Within

True Justice

Act of Revenge

Reckless Endangerment

Irresistible Impulse

Falsely Accused

Corruption of Blood

Justice Denied

Material Witness

Reversible Error

Immoral Certainty

Depraved Indifference

No Lesser Plea

NONFICTION

Echoes of My Soul

The Piano Teacher: The True Story of a Psychotic Killer

Badge of the Assassin

Gallery Books
An Imprint of Simon & Schuster, Inc.
1230 Avenue of the Americas
New York, NY 10020

First Gallery Books hardcover edition August 2017

GALLERY BOOKS and colophon are registered trademarks of Simon & Schuster, Inc.

For information about special discounts for bulk purchases, please contact Simon & Schuster Special Sales at 1-866-506-1949 or business@simonandschuster.com.

The Simon & Schuster Speakers Bureau can bring authors to your live event. For more information or to book an event, contact the Simon & Schuster Speakers Bureau at 1-866-248-3049 or visit our website at www.simonspeakers.com.

Manufactured in the United States of America

10 9 8 7 6 5 4 3 2 1

Library of Congress Cataloging-in-Publication Data
Names: Tanenbaum, Robert, author.
Title: Without fear or favor : a novel / Robert K. Tanenbaum.
Description: First Gallery Books hardcover edition. | New York : Gallery Books, 2017. | Series: A Butch Karp-Marlene Ciampi thriller ; 29 | Identifiers: LCCN 2017013580 (print) | LCCN 2017020319 (ebook)
Subjects: LCSH: Karp, Butch (Fictitious character)—Fiction. | Ciampi, Marlene (Fictitious character)—Fiction. | Conspiracies—Fiction. | BISAC: FICTION / Mystery & Detective / Police Procedural. | FICTION / Legal. FICTION / Thrillers. | GSAFD: Suspense fiction. | Legal stories.
Classification: LCC PS3570.A52 (ebook) | LCC PS3570.A52 W58 2017 (print) | DDC 813/.54—dc23
LC record available at https://lccn.loc.gov/2017013580

ISBN 978-1-4767-9322-1
ISBN 978-1-4767-9323-8 (ebook)

WITHOUT FEAR OR FAVOR

A Novel

ROBERT K. TANENBAUM

Gallery Books

New York   London   Toronto   Sydney   New Delhi

To those blessings in my life:
Patti, Rachael, Roger, Billy,
and my brother, Bill
and
To the loving Memory of
Reina Tanenbaum, my sister,
Truly an angel

ACKNOWLEDGMENTS

To my legendary mentors, District Attorney Frank S. Hogan and Henry Robbins, both of whom were larger in life than in their well-deserved and hard-earned legends, everlasting gratitude and respect; to my special friends and brilliant tutors at the Manhattan DAO, Bob Lehner, Mel Glass, and John Keenan, three of the best who ever served and whose passion for justice was unequaled and uncompromising, my heartfelt appreciation, respect, and gratitude; to Professor Robert Cole and Professor Jesse Choper, who at Boalt Hall challenged, stimulated, and focused the passions of my mind to problem-solve and to do justice; to Steve Jackson, an extraordinarily talented and gifted scrivener whose genius flows throughout the manuscript and whose contribution to it cannot be overstated, a dear friend for whom I have the utmost respect; to Louise Burke, my publisher, whose enthusiastic support, savvy, and encyclopedic smarts qualify her as my first pick in a game of three-on-three in

ACKNOWLEDGMENTS

the Avenue P park in Brooklyn; to Wendy Walker, my talented, highly skilled, and insightful editor, many thanks for all that you do; to Sarah Wright and Cynthia Merman, the inimitable twosome whose adult supervision, oversight, brilliant copyediting, and rapid responses are invaluable and profoundly appreciated; to my agents, Mike Hamilburg and Bob Diforio, who in exemplary fashion have always represented my best interests; to Coach Paul Ryan, who personified "American Exceptionalism" and mentored me in its finest virtues; to my esteemed special friend and confidant Richard A. Sprague, who has always challenged, debated, and inspired me in the pursuit of fulfilling the reality of "American Exceptionalism"; and to Rene Herrerias, my coach at Cal, who believed in me early on and in so doing changed my life, truly a divine intervention.

PROLOGUE

TELEVISION CORRESPONDENT PETE VANSAND GROANED AS HIS driver turned onto Centre Street and they saw the seething crowd in front of the Criminal Courts Building. Both sides of the street swarmed with agitated people, as if someone had stirred up an ants' nest in Lower Manhattan. Everywhere he looked, people were shouting—some actually shrieking in their excitement—adding to a cacophony of outraged honking as yellow cabs, delivery trucks, and passenger cars tried to navigate around pedestrians who darted back and forth across the street.

The angriest and loudest voice blared from the small grassy park opposite the massive gray edifice. A short, cadaverous-looking black man on a bullhorn urged the crowd. "What do we want?" He cupped his ear to hear the response.

"JUSTICE!" the crowd screamed.

"When do we want it?"

"NOW!"

On the sidewalk in front of the building, a cordon of black-uniformed riot police in helmets and carrying clear polycarbonate shields stood shoulder to shoulder in a large semicircle. Their job was to keep the mass of amped-up demonstrators and curious on-lookers a safe distance away from a bevy of microphones that news crews had arranged at the top of a small flight of stairs leading to the entrance. More officers, in both uniforms and plainclothes, patrolled the sidewalk outside the human barrier, on alert for danger.

"*Jesucristo!*" swore Vansand's driver, Julio Escobar, who doubled as his cameraman. "Going to be hell to park, and I got to carry that heavy-ass camera. Looks like the freakin' circus is in town, man."

"More like somebody left the doors open on the Bellevue psych ward and the inmates got out," Vansand muttered.

"Good for ratings." Escobar shrugged with a sigh.

"Not for us if we don't get set up in time."

"I'm not the idiot who sent us on that fluff story to Coney Island."

"Stupid news director," Vansand agreed. He was growing more agitated as traffic slowed to a crawl.

"WHAT DO WE WANT?" the speaker bellowed.

"JUSTICE!" the crowd screeched.

Even with the windows of the van rolled up to keep out the op-pressive summer heat, Vansand recognized the strident baritone of the man on the megaphone as that of Reverend Hussein "Skip" Mufti, an "activist" Baptist minister from Harlem known more for his inflammatory politics than his work in any church. The journal-ist scowled. He thought he had an "understanding" with the reverend for exclusivity on interviews, but Mufti had been enjoying the current crisis by eagerly accepting every invitation from the national news shows that had flocked to Gotham. *He'll come crawling when the big dogs are gone and I've got the best soapbox in town*, Vansand thought. *Ol' Hussein likes his expensive dinners and bottles of wine on the station's credit card, but he's going to have to do some serious ass kissing to get back on my good side.*

Vansand checked his Rolex. It was five minutes until two o'clock, when New York County District Attorney Roger "Butch" Karp was due to announce his decision on whether to charge an NYPD officer for shooting an unarmed black teenager a month earlier. And Karp was known for being on time. The district attorney was also known for his dislike of press conferences and the media in general. But he'd had little choice this time. The streets had been roiling ever since the shooting. A young Asian police officer, Bryce Kim, claimed that the teenager, Ricky Watts, surprised him on the stairway of a tenement in Harlem and fired a gun at him. Kim shot the teen, who had then staggered down four flights of stairs before collapsing and dying outside the building.

According to Vansand's sources at the NYPD, there was little hard evidence that a shot had been fired at the officer. No gun had been found on the teenager, nor had the crime scene investigators found a bullet or shell casing from any gun other than the officer's. Only the officer's partner and one elderly woman reported hearing two shots. A number of other witnesses, however, had come forward contending they'd heard only a single shot. Even before the shooting, the city was tighter than a 42nd Street hooker's skirt. A

3

week earlier, a police officer had been executed at a park in Harlem by members of a group calling itself the Nat Turner Revolutionary Brigade. That was when Vansand got his first call from someone who called himself "Nat X," who then met with him in an abandoned building in Harlem and allowed his film crew to record his statement "as the founder of the Brigade." Wearing a handkerchief to hide his face, and disguising his voice, the self-described revolutionary had declared that the shooting was "a justified act in the war between the police and the black community."

Needless to say, the police were on edge after that and so was the community. So when Ricky Watts was shot by Officer Kim, the scene at the shooting had threatened to explode into chaos. Agitators who arrived even before the ambulance had accused the police of, in the words of Mufti, "a revenge assassination of an unarmed and innocent young black male" in retribution for the cop's murder. It didn't help that the police who responded shortly afterward were looking to knock heads. Only the professionalism of their sergeants and commanders kept more violence from erupting.

However, since then, several "peaceful" demonstrations organized by Mufti and others under the banner of the Black Justice Now movement had devolved into riots that included burned police cars and looted businesses, as well as assaults against police officers, the media, and onlookers. Mufti publicly decried the violence and called for restraint, but always with the caveat—when the television cameras were rolling—that ultimately the police were to blame for "waging war on young black men."

A week before today's press conference, the New York City

Council—of which Mufti was a member—passed a resolution urging Karp to "act with alacrity to right a terrible wrong that caused an innocent young man's senseless death and restore the public's trust in the New York Police Department and District Attorney's Office." Karp had responded through his spokesman that the "officer-involved shooting" was still being investigated and that no charges would be filed "unless and until the evidence warrants it, and a grand jury has returned an indictment." The statement, or more accurately Mufti's denouncement of the statement, set off another round of violent protests.

The national media, sensing a story that fit their narrative of out-of-control, racist police officers gunning down innocent black men, flocked to Gotham, and Mufti seized the moment. He'd shrugged off his gentleman's agreement with Vansand and latched on to and further sensationalized the massive media circus response. Making the rounds, he'd complained that Karp was stalling for time so as "not to anger his friends in the New York Police Department, who want this to all blow over."

Others in the Black Justice Now group had used even less restraint and accused the district attorney of plotting a cover-up with the NYPD brass. Nat X had arranged another interview with Vansand. "The oppressors of the white state have carried out an open season of murder against black men. Therefore, they, and anyone who supports them, white or black, are legitimate targets of the Nat Turner Revolutionary Brigade."

As if that wasn't enough, three police officers, including a lieutenant, had been arrested and charged with murdering one of

Mufti's colleagues, Imani Sefu, and the attempted murder of Mufti himself. The reverend's clout with activists and the media nationwide had skyrocketed, and he was enjoying every minute of his near martyrdom.

Vansand knew Karp was stuck between the proverbial rock and a hard place. Even though he'd moved swiftly to indict the officers, Mufti and others had been even quicker to exploit the accusations as proof that the system was racist and corrupt. And no matter what decision Karp reached regarding the Ricky Watts case, one side or the other was not going to like it, and the city would be rocked with violence and, perhaps, the further spilling of blood. But Vansand also saw it as a much-needed personal opportunity.

Graduating college with a television journalism degree some twenty-five years ago, Vansand, whose real last name was Potts, had been tall and handsome in that innocuous television sameness, with a pleasant voice. He landed a job working as a weatherman for a station in Des Moines. Popular with female viewers, he'd worked his way up from weatherman to weekend anchor to the daily evening news anchor, and he even won a regional Emmy for coverage of a tornado that had wiped out a small farm town. The actual reporting had been done by others, and he'd just supplied the face and voice for the script. But it was enough to get the attention of *RealNews*, one of the big network television newsmagazines.

RealNews had made him a star on the national scene, where he'd become known for his "ambush" journalism and willingness to slant stories in whichever direction he perceived would give him the best ratings. But that was all in the past. He'd fallen prey to the ravages of age, which moved at an accelerated pace in the TV news business. Seemingly overnight, he developed a paunch around his midsection and a wattle beneath his once firm chin that along with the puffiness under his eyes had resisted the best efforts of a plastic surgeon.

Two years earlier, *RealNews* had let him go with a retirement party and the Rolex, which reminded him daily of when he'd commanded that kind of money and prestige. He missed both, though he landed what most television desk jockeys would have considered a prime job with a New York City station. The owners hoped his name and former national prominence would result in better ratings, even if he was getting a little long in the tooth. They'd created the "Vansand Action Team" that consisted mostly of himself and Escobar and dispatched him for "special reports" that ranged from hard news to that day's hot-dog-eating contest at Nathan's in Coney Island.

He dreamed of the story that would get him back to the big time, where he could then fade gracefully to television news dotage. *Like they do at* 60 Minutes, he thought ruefully but with some hope. He firmly believed that could happen, now that the story was New York City on the brink of the worst riots since Los Angeles exploded in 1992 after the Rodney King decision. He knew he wouldn't be able to keep it all to himself; it was getting too big, and the national media, including *RealNews*, had more resources and time to devote to it. But he was determined to do whatever it took to stay out in front.

Although he'd been disappointed that Reverend Mufti had been about as loyal as a prostitute at a Shriner convention, it was no great surprise. But Vansand had something the other news teams didn't: Nat X. Several times since the Ricky Watts shooting he'd called in advance to tell Vansand and Escobar where to position themselves for the best footage of the scripted violence that erupted during the protest marches. Just that morning, Nat X had told him that "something big is going to go down at Karp's press conference."

"Like what?" Vansand had asked, thrilled at the insider information.

"Ain't going to tell you, my man," Nat X replied. "Can't trust no white man with that kind of information. But I got it set up for you. Make sure you take Oliver with you and keep the camera rolling on him."

Vansand had frowned. Oliver Gray was his intern, a young black journalism student at NYU whom Nat X had asked Vansand to take under his wing a week earlier. "He's the cousin of a friend of the female variety," Nat X had said, "if you know what I mean. She's going to be grateful, I mean really grateful, if you do this for me. He'll act as a middleman between me and you, too."

"Well, I don't know," Vansand had responded. "I don't have an intern budgeted and I don't know if the station . . ."

"Figure it out, Pete," Nat X told him. Then his voice grew cold. "I'd consider it a personal favor, but if you can't do it, I'm sure some other television station could use a bright young man like Oliver."

So Vansand had met the young man at the station. Thin and scholarly-looking, Oliver Gray seemed nice enough. Well-spoken and polite. The station hadn't objected to Vansand taking on an unpaid intern, and Gray had tagged along with the Vansand Action Team all week.

That morning when Vansand arrived, Gray was already waiting for him. The young man seemed excited and nervous at the same time. He repeated Nat X's promise that "something big" was going to happen at Karp's news conference. The newsman had gone into the morning's news-planning meeting crowing about the scoop he anticipated. But the news director insisted the team cover the hot-dog-eating contest first. "We need something light between all the heavy stuff," the director, who wasn't even as old as Vansand's son by his second wife, said. "You'll have plenty of time to get back for the press conference."

However, the director had not counted on a traffic jam coming back over the Brooklyn Bridge that had Vansand cursing as Escobar pulled up to the area of the street that had been cordoned off for the news vans. All the spots were taken, and a beefy traffic cop waved for them to keep moving even after Escobar pointed to the MEDIA sign in the front window.

"Pull up to the joker, and I'll give him the old Pete Vansand charm," Vansand said.

Escobar did as told. Rolling down his window, Vansand smiled at the cop. "Hi, Officer, WZYN News here. We're a little late arriving, so can we squeeze in behind the other news vans?"

"No room, move on," said the man, whose name tag identified him as Officer McKinnon. "You guys were all told to show up an hour ago."

"How about one for the home team? I'm Pete Vansand."

"I don't care if you're the mayor of County Cork. Move along or I'll have your vehicle towed."

"Oh, for Christ's sake," Vansand swore. "The press conference is about to start. Come on. I'm sure you've seen me on the evening news and special reports by the Vansand Action Team."

Officer McKinnon leaned over and studied Vansand's face as if seeing him clearly for the first time. He smiled, his Irish blue eyes twinkling. Vansand smiled back, relieved. But then the cop frowned and shook his head. "No, don't believe I've ever seen your mug," he said. "But you're on the evening news? Well, I'll tell the missus when I get home tonight that I met a famous man. Now move along."

Vansand slumped. "Fucking moron," he muttered.

"What was that, Pete, old buddy? Was there something you wanted to say to me?" Officer McKinnon smiled again, only this time there was nothing friendly about it.

"I was just saying what a paragon of the law you are," Vansand replied before turning back to Escobar. "Oliver and I will get out here and take the camera. Go find a place to park and then come find me."

"You sure?" Escobar asked, looking in the rearview mirror at the young intern, who was staring out at the crowd on the street. "It's damn heavy. Plus the union won't like it."

"Oliver can handle it," Vansand replied. "Can't you?"

Gray turned back toward the other two. He seemed to be sweating despite the air-conditioning. "Um, yeah, sure," he said. "I can help."

"Right," Vansand said. "And what the union doesn't know won't hurt them, right?"

Getting out of the van under the watchful eye of McKinnon, Vansand opened the side door for Gray, who picked up the camera with a grunt and stepped out. Returning the cop's glare, the pair walked back down the block to the cordon of police officers and the site of the scheduled press conference. Vansand led the way up to a police captain who was standing behind his men. "Pete Vansand," he said, holding up the credentials. "WZYN. This is my intern, Oliver Gray." Gray held up the press card issued to him by the station.

"You're late," the captain said, but tapped the shoulder of his man in front of Vansand. "Let them through."

Vansand passed through the police line and walked to the area on the side of the steps reserved for the press. But there he ran into a roadblock of his fellow journalists, none of whom were willing to let him move closer to the podium with the camera.

"Come on, you print guys don't need to film anything," he complained to a *New York Post* reporter blocking his way.

"Pound sand, Vansand," the other reporter said with a smirk. "You want a better seat, show up early. You television bastards always think you deserve special treatment."

Vansand gave up. "There's no dealing with idiots," he said to Gray. He pointed at the camera. "Have you learned how to use one of these yet at NYU?"

Gray shook his head. "I haven't taken the class yet. Sorry."

Vansand shrugged. "No problem. I'll do it myself." He reached for the camera. "The union would probably go even more ballistic if I let a journalism student shoot footage anyway. Going to be bad enough if they find out I did."

Suddenly there were shouts from the crowd on the other side of the police line. "There's Karp," someone yelled. "Quit protecting racist cops, Karp!"

Across the street, Reverend Mufti's chants gained new momentum. "What do we want?"

"JUSTICE!"

"When do we want it?"

"NOW!"

Vansand shouldered the camera and started filming just as a short, balding, pear-shaped man wearing a plaid vest and round wire-rimmed glasses stepped up to the bank of microphones. Behind him stood a tall, rugged-looking man with close-cropped, pewter-colored hair—Butch Karp. On the side of the podium closest to the press corps, a large, broad-shouldered black man scowled out at the press and crowd. He appeared to be some sort of bodyguard and was clearly not happy with the circumstances.

"Good afternoon, I'm Assistant District Attorney Gilbert Murrow," the pear-shaped man said. "District Attorney Karp will be issuing a statement in a moment. There will be no follow-up questions. Thank you."

With that, Karp replaced Murrow at the podium. If anything, he looked even less pleased than the bodyguard to be speaking to the press. "Good afternoon," he said. "Due to the lawlessness that has swept the streets of our city since the officer-involved shooting of a young man, Ricky Watts—"

"Murder, you mean!" someone in the crowd yelled. This was met with shouts of agreement, but Karp pressed on.

"Since the incident, the New York Police Department has conducted its investigation with its usual professionalism and thoroughness. The detectives involved in that investigation have now passed on their report to my office. I, personally, have tasked the NYPD detective squad attached to the District Attorney's Office to continue that investigation so that a determination can be made as to whether charges are warranted against the officer. That investigation has not yet concluded and therefore no decision has been made. When . . ."

As his words sank in, an angry murmur rose from the crowd. "He's going to let the pig off!" a woman screamed.

"No justice!" a large black man bellowed and pressed against the wall of riot officers.

"When that decision is made," Karp continued, "it will be according to the rule of law, and without fear or favor to either party, which every citizen has the right to expect from the County of New York District Attorney's Office. That includes police officers."

"Everybody except an unarmed black boy!" a protester yelled.

"Although this investigation will continue as long as necessary to establish the facts, I'm told by Detective Clay Fulton, the chief of the DAO squad"—Karp indicated the large man Vansand had assumed was his bodyguard—"that he expects it to come to a conclusion soon. I ask that the good citizens of our city exercise patience and restraint and allow the system to work."

"You're stalling, Karp!"

Across the street in the park, Mufti, apparently made aware of Karp's statement, picked up the speed and increased the angry tenor of his demands. "WHAT DO WE WANT?"

"JUSTICE!"

"WHEN DO WE WANT IT?"

"NOW!"

Karp looked at the media cameras. "Thank you. That is all."

As the angry crowd pressed up to the cordon of police, Mufti changed his chant. "NO GUN, NO EXCUSE!"

"NO GUN, NO EXCUSE!" the crowd responded.

Looking through the viewfinder on the camera, Vansand wondered what Nat X was referring to when he told him that something big would happen. *So far all I've got is what everyone else has*, he thought, miffed.

Then he felt a tap on his shoulder. "Excuse me, Mr. Vansand." The newsman recognized the voice of Oliver Gray.

"Keep the camera on me," Gray said, and moved past him toward the podium. He then shouted, "KARP!"

From off to his right in the media crowd, Vansand heard someone yell, "GUN! HE'S GOT A GUN!" Only then did he realize what he was seeing in the viewfinder. As Gray advanced toward the podium, he raised a handgun and pointed it at Karp. The journalist also realized in that split second that because he was farther toward the podium, the other television cameras had to turn to film Gray, which meant they couldn't capture the gunman and Karp at the same time. But he had both in his viewfinder, almost as if he was looking over Gray's shoulder.

It all happened so quickly—Gray's shout, the realizations, the screams of the panicking members of the press—that Vansand didn't have time to react, just film. Nor could Karp do anything but frown as the gun was leveled at him. Fulton was the only one to react, moving to get between the shooter and his target as he reached inside his suit coat. But he was too late.

There was the sound of a shot—so loud that Vansand jumped, but not so much that he missed filming the bullet slam into the district attorney's chest. That shot was followed by another and another impact. Karp fell back before the big detective obscured his view. A gun had materialized in Fulton's hand, and for a moment Vansand thought the detective was pointing it at him. But when he fired, it was Gray who was struck and knocked back; a second shot drove the young man out of the viewfinder and to the ground.

People were scattering all around him when Vansand heard more shouts and reeled around. It took him a moment to refocus the camera on the protesters across the street. Many of them were standing with clenched fists raised in the air as Mufti shouted into the bullhorn.

"WHAT DO WE WANT?"

"JUSTICE!"

"WHEN DO WE WANT IT?"

"NOW!"

Vansand felt someone tug on his sleeve. It was Escobar, his face flushed with excitement. "Holy shit, you get that?"

"Oh, yeah," Vansand said. "I got it all." He handed the camera to Escobar and stepped toward the podium, where a half dozen people including the black detective and a petite brunette woman surrounded the fallen district attorney.

With that scene behind him, he turned to his cameraman. "Roll on me in five, four, three, two, one . . . Pete Vansand reporting to you from the Criminal Courts Building in Lower Manhattan, where District Attorney Roger "Butch" Karp has just been shot by a gunman, an NYU journalism student named Oliver Gray. More on that exclusively on WZYN this evening. Pete Vansand signing off."

Vansand made a signal for Escobar to quit filming. He grinned. "Let's get that on air as soon as possible. Then, Julio, *mi amigo*, you can rent a tuxedo," he said, "because we'll be going to the Emmys!"

1

A month earlier

NYPD OFFICER TONY CIPPIO FELL FOR THE MOVE WHEN the teenager dribbling the basketball feinted left and then drove to the right, passing him, before going in for the easy layup. The ball rolled off the backboard and dropped through the hoop with a soft rattling of the chain net.

Cippio shook his head and high-fived the smirking teen. "Lucky shot," he teased. "Bet you can't do it again."

"Sheee-it. I can do that all day long on you, Slo-Mo." The teen looked around at his buddies, who laughed at his nickname for the cop.

Cippio laughed with them. "Yeah, probably." He was twenty-eight years old and had been on the force for three years. He'd also been a pretty good basketball player on his high school team on Long Island and in community college. But these playground wizards who learned the game on the courts of Marcus Garvey

17

Park, an oasis of grass, trees, playgrounds, and a pool in the middle of Harlem, were something else. The kid who'd just made him look like he was playing underwater was thirteen, maybe fourteen years old and could have beat anybody on his former teams.

It didn't help that he was in uniform and weighed down by his wide belt with its accoutrements of handcuffs, Taser, and handgun as well as a bulletproof vest on an evening when it was still ninety degrees with 75 percent humidity at six o'clock. *Oh, who you kidding,* he thought, *he'd have beat you with that move if you were wearing your birthday suit and he was handcuffed to a boulder.*

But Cippio hadn't asked to play with the teens to show off his basketball skills. The brass at Harlem's 25th Precinct were big about patrol officers connecting on a personal level with the community. "Get out of the cars and show them what nice guys you bums are," the duty sergeant had said with a grin.

So even though he knew it would feel like he was playing in a sauna while wearing a wet suit, Cippio parked his squad car on 120th Street and got out when he saw the teens on the court. "You coming?" he'd asked his partner, Eddie Evans, an older black officer with twenty years on the force.

"No, you go right ahead, Larry Bird," Evans had said, smirking as he shook his head. "I'll stay right here and keep an eye out for bad guys while you're off making a fool of yourself with those mini–Michael Jordans out there. Just don't pull a muscle in your groin, or your wife will blame me for your poor performance between the sheets."

"Don't be worrying about my performance," Cippio replied with a laugh. "Fran's plenty happy, and I got two kids and another one on the way to prove it."

"You sure they're yours?"

"Up yours, Evans. Just because you've been put out to pasture by Gloria doesn't mean the rest of us have been."

"Hell, that woman can't get enough of me, which is the reason I'm going to park my big black rear end right here and rest up so that I can keep that smile on her face."

"Uh-huh," Cippio said. "Just try not to let anyone steal the car with you in it. You're already enough of an embarrassment to the department."

Cippio popped the trunk of the car and took out the brand-new basketball he'd purchased the previous evening.

"What you got there?" his partner had asked when he'd brought it to work that afternoon.

"Just a little something for my homies in the park. Last time I played hoops with them, they were using a ball that looked like it was about to pop."

As Cippio walked across the street into the park toward the basketball court, he noticed the three black men sitting on a picnic table off to one side. They appeared to be in their late twenties or early thirties and were watching him. They didn't look friendly, and this made Cippio nervous. Relations with some members of the black community were strained following several highly publicized officer-involved shootings around the country that spring. While in a couple of these instances even other cops were questioning whether the shootings were justified, it didn't seem to matter what the facts were, or that in several prominent cases it turned out that the "victims" had been violent felons. The media was all about playing up the narrative that racist cops were running amok and shooting innocent, unarmed black men. The story line had been picked up by so-called community leaders, including Reverend Skip Mufti in Harlem, who never missed a chance to bash cops whether to the press or speaking as a member of the New York City Council.

As he glanced at the hard-eyed men, Cippio had more reason than most cops to be cautious. In the Italian-American Cippio family, there were only three honorable careers for a male: become a priest, join the military, or join the force. Most chose the latter, but it came with a price. He'd had an uncle and a brother killed in the line of duty, the first answering a domestic violence complaint and the second running into the World Trade Center to rescue civilians after the 9/11 attacks.

However, Cippio was determined to not show his nervousness. He nodded and smiled at the men, neither gesture returned, before stepping onto the basketball court. There he was welcomed with a little good-natured ribbing and genuine appreciation for the new basketball by boys too young to be caught up in the politics of hate.

A half hour later, the young officer announced that he had to leave. "And just when I was about to go on a shooting streak."

"A missing streak, you mean," said the teen who'd beat him with the layup. He reluctantly handed the ball back to the officer.

"You keep it," Cippio said. "It's the neighborhood ball. You take care of it, but everyone gets to use it. Right?"

The teen's face lit up. "Yes, sir, I'll take good care of it." He held out his hand. "Thank you."

Cippio shook the teen's hand. "It's Tyrone, right?"

"Yes, sir, Tyrone Greene. Remember that name, you can say you knew me when I'm in the NBA someday."

"Tyrone Greene, eh? I'll remember. I hope you play for the Knicks, and then you can get me courtside seats. Just remember, my name's Tony Cippio. I'll expect to pick up my tickets at will-call your first game."

The teen smiled again. "You got it."

Cippio began walking back to his squad car, but he hadn't gone far when he heard a voice behind him. "Officer Tony." He turned to see Tyrone trotting up to him, the basketball under his arm.

"Yeah, Tyrone?"

"Did you see the men over by the picnic table when you was coming here? . . . No, don't look at them," the youth said, turning in another direction as if still talking about the basketball game. "I don't want them to know I'm talking about them."

Cippio caught on and followed his gaze to the basketball court. "Yes, I saw them. What about it?"

Tyrone passed the ball back and forth between his hands. "They don't like police officers," he said.

"Yeah, they didn't seem real friendly," Cippio said. "I can't help that, but I hope you like police officers. Most cops are good men, and you can count on them, like you can count on me. There're always a few people who aren't going to like us, but I can't spend a lot of time trying to figure out why not."

"No, you don't get it," Tyrone said. "I mean they *really* don't like police officers. They tell me and my friends that the police are making war on black people and that they're here to protect us. They say we need to join up with them. My older brother, Maurice, went to one of their meetings and he said they was talking about shooting police."

Cippio frowned. "Do you know their names?"

Tyrone laughed as if the police officer was teasing him, but his eyes were serious. "No. Not really. The leader calls himself Nat X."

Cippio pretended to playfully reach for the ball. "You know where he lives?"

"All over the place, on couches and shit. He's not from around here. My brother said he's from the West Coast. He just showed up a few weeks ago and started having meetings. He says he's here to help us, but me and my friends don't like him; he just wants us to be all angry and do bad stuff. We don't listen to him, but some people do. Just be careful near them, okay?"

Cippio nodded. "Yeah, okay. Thanks, Tyrone. I think you're more of a man than someone like that any day. I appreciate you letting me play some hoops with you."

The youth stepped back with a wide grin. "You call that playin' hoops? My granny plays better than that. But you can come back."

As Cippio made his way back to the squad car, the three men at the picnic table got up and began to walk toward him. "Evening, gentlemen," he said, all of his senses on alert.

"What you doing harassing them little niggers, White Meat?" the tallest of the group said, his face set and his eyes dark and hard.

"Just playing a little ball," Cippio said, aware that the other two were spreading out around him.

"Uh-huh," said the tall man, apparently the leader by the way the others seemed to be waiting for him to act. "Making friends with the little niggers while they's young so you can shoot 'em easier when they get older. That it?"

Cippio looked him over, taking mental notes. Pockmarked face. Scar above his right eye. Retro-Afro hair. Thin but muscular. "I've never shot anybody. Now if you'll excuse me, I have to get back to my patrol car." He made a move to go around the leader, but one of the other men stepped in his way. Cippio's eyes narrowed. "You're impeding a police officer. If you don't want to be arrested, move out of my way."

The larger man lifted his chin defiantly. "Make me move, White Meat."

"You ain't wanted in this neighborhood," the leader said.

"It's my job," Cippio replied, and reached for the radio microphone on his shoulder, praying that Eddie Evans, sitting in the squad car fifty yards away, was watching.

"Not no more it ain't," the leader said, stepping back. As he did, he reached behind his back and pulled a gun from his waistband and pointed it at the officer's chest.

Cippio had just enough time to note that the stainless steel .45 caliber revolver had a mother-of-pearl pistol grip. The first slug from the Teflon-coated, armor-piercing bullet tore through his Kevlar vest and partially severed a blood vessel leading into his heart. He turned as he fell and lay on his stomach, mortally wounded.

The leader leaned over and grabbed Cippio by his shoulder and turned him over onto his back. The officer lay gasping, bubbles forming in the blood on his lips. "Please, I have children," he croaked.

"And now they ain't got no daddy." The shooter aimed at the officer's head and pulled the trigger again.

There was a shout, and the three men looked in the direction it came from. A black police officer was running toward them with his gun drawn.

The leader snapped off a shot in his direction, but the officer didn't swerve or deviate. He sighted down his gun as he ran but didn't pull the trigger.

"Let's go," the leader yelled. They all took off, running past the stunned teenagers on the basketball court, their game stopped, their lives forever changed.

Tyrone Greene left the others and ran to the fallen officer. "Officer Tony! Officer Tony!" he cried, kneeling down to cradle Cippio's bloody head. He looked up with tears running down his face as the officer ran up.

"This is a ten-thirteen, I got an officer down," Eddie Evans screamed into his microphone. "Get me an ambulance! Now, goddamn it!" He gently touched the teen's shoulder. "Move aside, son, let me help him."

Tyrone Greene did as he was told but remained on his knees next to the officer, who applied pressure to the chest wound. "Please, God, don't let him die," the teen sobbed.

"Come on, Tony, stay with me, man," Evans urged his partner. "Fran needs you. The kids need you. I need you."

However, no prayers or pleading helped. As the cop and the teen knelt side by side, the light left the dark eyes of Officer Tony Cippio; he gasped one last time, shuddered, and died. His partner continued CPR, but it was no use. He put his arm around the shoulders of the sobbing teenager. Together they shed tears. Then Evans cupped his hands on the side of Cippio's head. Leaning down toward him, Evans pledged, "Tony, no matter how long it takes, I will find the killers and ensure that they get their justice."

2

BUTCH KARP LOOKED AT THE TAN FEDERAL AGENT WITH A crew cut sitting across from him and tapped the manila file folder lying on the mahogany desk between them. "Okay, Espy, from what I understand, this group"—he flipped up the front cover and glanced at the first page—"the Nat Turner Revolutionary Brigade, has been making threats against law enforcement based on the media-driven false narrative that cops are running amok, gunning down innocent black men and not being held accountable."

Espy Jaxon nodded. "That's about the gist of it. I'm bringing this to your attention now, just like I did Chief DeCasio at the NYPD, because of a credible threat to law enforcement in New York City."

"How credible?"

Scratching at his short pewter gray hair, Jaxon shrugged. "We don't know much about this particular group other than we believe they're responsible for a series of armed robberies and at least one bank job in San Francisco that included the attempted murder of a police officer who was moonlighting as a bank guard. There seems to be some affiliation to other black nationalist groups in the Bay Area, including one thought to have pulled off the fatal shooting of two officers in San Jose last month. The Brigade, as they're now affectionately known by those of us watching out for them, made statements through the media praising the murders—called them 'casualties of war' and the only way to protect the black community from the police."

"Given today's political climate, that probably goes over well with the demagogues like our own Reverend Mufti who, if I remember right, labeled the murders 'regrettable but inevitable' the night it happened," a short, pear-shaped man standing near the bookcase on the other side of the room chimed in.

The speaker was Gilbert Murrow, technically an assistant district attorney, but he didn't try cases and instead served as Karp's office manager and spokesman for his media-averse boss. He looked more like an accountant with his wire-rimmed glasses and penchant for plaid vests and pocket protectors, but he was sharp and media savvy. "So you think they're coming to New York?"

"From what we understand, they're already here," Jaxon replied. "One of our sources in Harlem sent us a printed 'revolutionary manifesto' calling on the black community to, in their words, 'spread the flames of righteous revolution' from coast to coast."

"If I can ask," Murrow said, "what is your interest in all of this? I thought you ran a small independent counterterrorism agency, taking on Islamic extremists and such. Are these guys tied to ISIS or Al Qaeda?"

"Not that we know, Gilbert, though there is always the concern that these domestic terrorists—which is really what they are—will link up with some foreign group like ISIS. But the rhetoric coming out of the Nat Turner Revolutionary Brigade is more black liberation nationalist—secular and race-oriented—than theological ideology based on an extremist interpretation of the Qur'an. However, if both groups see a mutual benefit to their goal of accomplishing political change through violence in the United States, then they may be willing to forget any differences and work together.

"As for why I and my people are involved, as you probably know, we were created to be independent of other federal law enforcement and counterterrorism agencies. We . . . I . . . answer only to one person, whose name I can't divulge but he keeps the others off our backs so that we can operate freely. Even the White House isn't clear about our function, and so far we've flown enough under the radar to avoid interference from that direction.

"We do jobs the others may consider to be too big, or too political and bureaucratic to handle, or when there are questions of how the others are doing their jobs. We've uncovered some people within those agencies actually working against the national security for political or personal reasons. To be honest, we were asked to look into this because the current leadership of the Department of Justice and the FBI are too worried about politics to want to appear to be targeting black 'activists,' which is how they categorize even those with the most violent tendencies."

Jaxon turned back to Karp. "As for how credible this particular threat is to law enforcement in New York? We're worried that they're escalating—both in the rhetoric and with this shooting of officers in the Bay Area."

Whatever Jaxon was going to say next was interrupted by a knock on the door and the appearance of Clay Fulton. In the days that followed, Karp would think repeatedly about the timing of Jaxon's visit and Fulton's angry face.

"Excuse me," the big detective said, nodding to Jaxon. "Nice to see you, Espy." Turning to Karp, he said, "There's been an officer-involved shooting in Marcus Garvey Park; one officer was killed."

Karp frowned. While the shooting of a police officer in New York City was a significant event for the DAO, and one that he would monitor closely, it was not unheard of and would not have necessitated an unannounced visit from Fulton. There had to be something else.

"It appears to be more than the normal line-of-duty shooting," Fulton said. "Apparently, the suspect had been making threats to shoot police officers as a political statement. According to witnesses, the officer was confronted by three men—black, mid- to late twenties, early thirties—in Marcus Garvey Park. He'd gone to play basketball with some of the local teens while his partner waited in the car."

Karp and Jaxon exchanged glances. "We were just talking about this possibility."

"Yeah, and with what's been happening around the country, I'm thinking it's going to blow up in our faces," Fulton said. "The media will be all over it. I'm driving up to Harlem now and thought you might want to join me."

"Absolutely," Karp replied. "Who's there from the office now?"

"Kenny Katz picked it up. He was the ADA on call."

THIRTY MINUTES LATER Karp and Fulton arrived at Marcus Garvey Park, which stretched from 120th Street to 124th Street, between Mount Morris Park West and Madison Avenue. The first thing he noticed was the large gathering of police officers at the entrance, far more than would have been needed to secure the area or investigate the crime scene, which would mostly be done by plainclothes detectives and CSI technicians.

Those gathered recognized him as he exited the car. "Go get 'em, Butch," one of the uniformed police officers shouted. "Don't let these murdering scumbags get away with this!"

"Frickin' animals!" someone else yelled, and others joined in.

"They deserve a hot one in the head! Make 'em pay, or we will, Butch!"

Anger and a desire for revenge tinged their voices and was writ large on their faces. He nodded to a couple of officers he recognized but kept moving with Fulton into the park.

The crime scene was taped off, surrounding a bright red stain on the sidewalk. Karp looked around. He noted the basketball court and the teens who stood numbly watching. Here and there, outside the crime scene tape, small knots of locals gathered and talked quietly or stood solemnly off by themselves. While most appeared sad or worried, not all were friendly, and he wondered if any were there to report back to the killer.

"Where's the officer's partner?" Karp asked.

"Over there, name's Eddie Evans." Fulton pointed to a uniformed black officer sitting with his head down on the hood of a car parked on the grass. Several officers stood near him, one with a hand on his shoulder.

As Karp approached, the other officers stepped back. "Officer Evans," he said, extending his hand, "I can't tell you how sorry I am for what happened here today. You okay?"

The officer looked up, and Karp could see his eyes were red and welled with tears. "No, sir, no, I am not," Evans said quietly. "But thank you for asking. This is my fault, you know."

Karp furrowed his brow. "How do you mean?"

"I should have been with him. That's what a partner does, he's got your back. But I was too damn lazy." Evans shook his head. "Tony didn't have a mean bone in his body. He just wanted to play ball with some kids, show them that a police officer could be their friend." He gestured toward the crime scene tape. "Then this happens."

"I know it's natural to want to shoulder the blame," Karp said, "but I don't see how this one falls on you. From what I understand, he was murdered in cold blood, no warning . . ."

"Yeah, but this wasn't no confrontation out of the blue," Evans growled. "Those animals were waiting for this. A chance to kill a cop when his guard was down . . . and his partner wasn't paying attention. Tony was in the wrong place at the wrong time; he didn't do nothin' to deserve this. Now he's got a widow and a couple of young kids with another one on the way, who won't ever know their daddy, or what a good man he was."

"I expect that you and others who knew him will make sure his children hear about that," Karp said.

"I will, but it's not the same." Evans wiped at his eyes. "Don't worry about me, but go check on that kid over there. He warned Tony about the killer and saw it all go down."

Karp followed his gesture to a nearby picnic table. He saw Assistant District Attorney Kenny Katz listening in as a detective talked to a young teen, while another teen and an older woman looked on.

Again, the others stood back when he approached and knelt down on one knee to come face-to-face with the young teen. "Hello, I'm Butch Karp, the district attorney here in New York County," he said. "I'm sorry this happened and that you had to see it."

The boy looked at him and nodded but didn't say anything. He seemed to be trying to hold himself together.

"This is Tyrone," the woman said and patted the other boy on the shoulder. "And this is Maurice. I'm the boys' grandmother, Nevie Butler."

Karp stood and held out his hand, which the woman shook. But when he tried to offer it to Maurice, the youth looked away.

Turning his attention back to Nevie Butler, Karp asked, "I know this has been a trying day, and that Tyrone has already been questioned by Mr. Katz and Detective MacCallum here, but would you mind coming down to the DAO and letting me take a statement from Tyrone?"

Butler looked around nervously. "I want to help, Mr. Karp, don't get me wrong. But there's people around here who would not be happy about Tyrone talking to the police."

"He ain't got to say nothin' to you," Maurice suddenly spat.

His outburst earned him a smack to the back of his head from his grandmother. "Show some respect, Maurice," she said, then looked back at Karp. "Somebody's been filling the heads of young men like Maurice here with hate and anger. I'm old and it don't matter what happens to me, but I have to look out for these boys. Maybe tomorrow, if you wouldn't mind, we'll take the subway down to see you when nobody's watching."

Karp nodded. "I understand and that would be fine." He handed her a business card. "That has my direct line on it. Call when you're on the way."

As the old woman and her grandsons walked away, Karp wondered who it was that was filling young men's heads full of "hate and anger." And what they had to do with Tony Cippio and Espy Jaxon's warning.

3

ANTHONY JOHNSON JR. TOOK THE STAIRS TWO AT A TIME TO the sixth-floor apartment. He could feel the blood pumping through his body like an electric current, pulsing brightly with each heartbeat. Every breath made him feel stronger, more alive than he'd ever felt before.

The moment he looked into that cop's eyes and heard him beg for his life—"I have children"—felt like the moment before sexual release. Then pulling the trigger had consummated the ecstasy of killing another human being. And not just any man, *a fucking cop*. Not only that, but now he was a hero. He'd done what he loved to do anyway, only now everybody was going to look up to him.

He enjoyed making people suffer. Felt empowered by taking a life, which he'd done five times already. Two were members of a rival gang when he was just thirteen years old. He'd ambushed them as they sat on the front porch of a neighborhood home. Anthony had known them since grade school, and they were surprised when he pulled the gun and shot them in their heads as they tried to get away. Knowing there'd be few consequences because of his age, he'd openly bragged about the killings until his arrest.

Then, less than a month after his release from eighteen months in juvenile detention, he murdered an old woman in her home. Woke her up in the middle of the night, then raped her as he smothered her with a pillow. That one got him tried as an adult, but the San Francisco District Attorney's Office had let him plead out to sexual assault and burglary. It cost him two years in prison, but he'd made good use of that time by getting indoctrinated by black nationalist inmates so that when he got out he had a cause to go along with his viciousness.

Shortly before coming to New York, there'd been a crack whore who complained and hit him when he told her that he wasn't going to pay for the services she'd just rendered. He slit her throat, watching, fascinated, as she bled out. But no one cared about a hooker, and there'd been no consequences. In fact, it had been the best killing until the cop.

Had the motherfucker's life in the palm of my hand. The thought jumped into Johnson's hyped-up brain just as he reached the sixth floor. Standing there to catch his breath, he relived the moment, pulling the trigger of an imaginary gun pointed at an imaginary cop on the ground. The real gun—a Smith & Wesson .45 revolver with a mother-of-pearl handle—was tucked into the waistband of his pants beneath his sweatshirt, the stainless steel cold against his skin. *I made him afraid. Made him whine like a bitch.*

Johnson could hear that the party had already started in the apartment. Someone had cranked up the gangsta rap. He smiled as he grabbed the doorknob. Whatever bitch he ended up with that night, she was going to pay. His sexual appetite was going to be insatiable . . . and rough. He opened the door and walked in.

A cloud of marijuana smoke greeted him as two men and two women turned to look at him. They smiled as one. The women, sisters named Rose and Lupe, started throwing him come-hither looks. They didn't know what he'd done—he'd sworn the men to secrecy on pain of death—but they knew it was something special.

"It's my maaaaaaaan," bellowed one of the men, Big George, a three-hundred-pound behemoth who acted as his bodyguard. The giant crossed the room and they engaged in the ritualistic hand-shaking with an extra measure of respect that hadn't been there that morning when Big George had questioned if he was "all talk and no action."

They hadn't known each other long, only since Johnson had moved to New York City from the Bay Area a few weeks earlier to live with his cousin, Ny-Lee Tomes, the third man in the room. Making up for his lack of intelligence with a natural tendency toward violence, Big George had been taken with Johnson's anticop rhetoric. He had a rap sheet as long as his massive arms and no love for law enforcement.

Johnson had recruited Big George, and along with Tomes began holding a series of clandestine meetings with some of the younger men and teenagers in the neighborhood, preaching the black nationalist gospel. But when the revolution seemed to be composed of nothing more than angry speeches, Big George had started questioning Johnson's place as the Nat Turner Revolutionary Brigade's leader in New York City.

"I knew you could do it all along," Big George said, cementing Johnson's supremacy.

Johnson smiled. Secretly he was afraid of the police. His father had been a retired police officer when he'd impregnated Johnson's mother. He'd left them when his son was eleven, but not before he let the boy know, "I see right through you. You're an evil little bastard and no good is going to come of you." Johnson had shrugged. No matter how much the old man beat him, he continued to set fires and torture small animals, and he lied as easily as he breathed. There was a word for it that he learned as he got older and counselors, especially in juvie, tried to reach him: "sociopath". He wore it like a badge of honor.

After he got out of prison for raping the old woman, he'd joined up with the New Black Panther Party in the Bay Area, read *The Autobiography of Malcolm X*, and adopted the language of exclusionary black nationalism. Smart and a natural when it came to expressing his ideas, especially among his poorly educated peers, he enjoyed his growing reputation as a firebrand and "activist," even speaking at several rallies on college campuses. But he soon got bored with "just jawing"; in his opinion, the Panthers weren't violent enough. They talked too much about getting political and not enough about taking the fight to the streets, particularly against cops.

When he started complaining about the lack of real action, leaders of the group frowned. Then when he and a couple of cohorts formed the Nat Turner Revolutionary Brigade and carried out a series of robberies, they let him know that he was no longer welcome in the Bay Area. So he decided to take his show to New York City, where his mother's sister and her son, Ny-Lee Tomes, lived. He'd get a fresh start and recruit "soldiers" for his terrorism, preaching to young black men that they were at war with white societies and that killing cops was justified as an act of war.

"You've seen it on the television," he preached to small groups of five or six. "Cops are killing young black men, just like you, and they're getting away with it because the entire justice system is set up by whites. They will kill you if you don't kill them first. Show no pity, because you won't get any."

He was psyched to be practicing what he preached. The cop in Marcus Garvey Park was just the first of many in the coming race war in which he and the Nat Turner Revolutionary Brigade would play a major role.

"That was cold the way you did that pig, Anthony, cold . . ." Ny-Lee was about to go on in his effusive praise until he caught the look on his cousin's face. "I mean . . ."

Johnson pulled the .45 from his waistband and pointed it at his cousin as he pulled back the hammer. "How many times I got to tell you, you dumb nigger, it's Nat X! And you shut your mouth!"

"Yeah, yeah, Tony . . . Nat X. Yeah, Nat X. I'm sorry, man, don't shoot me!" Ny-Lee shrieked.

Johnson was somewhat mollified by the terror in his cousin's eyes. He looked over at Big George, who was smiling, and then the two women. The older one, Rose, who was Ny-Lee's girlfriend, looked scared. But her sister, Lupe, appeared to get off on his show of force; her eyes glittered with excitement. He smiled and uncocked the gun and put it on the table next to the couch as he settled down next to Lupe. "I ain't gonna shoot you. We blood. But you keep your damn mouth shut."

Tomes grinned and wiped the sweat off his forehead. "That's right, we're blood. You're Nat X. What you say goes!"

Lupe scooted closer to Johnson and put her hand on his knee. "You're all man, aren't you," she said. "What you do?"

"Never you mind, girl," Johnson replied as he put his arm around her shoulders, his eyes fastening on her ample bosom. "I'm just a soldier doing what needs to be done to protect our people. But you're right, I'm all man."

Big George fetched a couple bottles of beer from the cooler and brought one to Johnson. "You ain't just a soldier. You're a general . . . the motherfucking general of the Nat Turner Revolutionary Brigade."

Johnson winced at the new disclosure but he wasn't as ready to threaten Big George about saying too much in front of the women. Instead, he smiled and took a long pull on the beer before offering the bottle to Lupe.

Two hours later, Johnson grabbed his pistol and stood up, holding out a hand to the girl. He'd had a half dozen beers and had been smoking pot, so he staggered a little before saying, "Been a big day. Think the 'general' needs a massage from Private Lupe."

Rose got up from where she'd been snuggling with Tomes and grabbed her sister by the arm. "No way," she said. "She's only sixteen and she ain't going nowhere with you."

Johnson sneered as he put the gun in his waistband and looked at the younger girl. "You sixteen?"

"Yes, but I'm mature for my age," Lupe replied, turning angrily to her sister. "Stay out of my life, you old ho."

Rose slapped her but was immediately knocked to the ground by Johnson. "Don't get up, bitch," he warned, putting his hand under his sweatshirt where the gun resided.

"Hey now, cuz," Tomes said weakly.

Johnson's eyes grew large at the challenge, and he turned on Tomes with a snarl. Big George also got up from his chair and started for the smaller man. "Hey now what?" Johnson demanded. "You going to let your bitch give me orders? Tell my girl what she can and can't do?"

Tomes looked down at Rose, who was picking herself up off the floor. Her lip was split and blood dripped into the carpet. He shook his head. "Nah, she don't mean nothing by it. Just sisters being sisters."

Johnson's eyes narrowed, but he released his grip on the gun. Then he smiled. "Yeah, sisters being sisters. But bros before hos, right? Now me and little sister going to go to bed, so y'all keep it down out here, right?"

Big George laughed. "Yeah, we keep it down, while you getting it up!"

"Yeah, bros before hos," Tomes echoed. He reached down to help Rose up, but she angrily shrugged off his hand.

"That's good, that's good," Johnson said. "Get some rest. We got a meeting tomorrow night and need to plan some strategy."

Big George laughed again and raised his beer. "Now you talking. Now it's getting goooood!"

4

BUTCH KARP SMILED AT HIS WIFE, WHO APPEARED IN THE mirror as he fixed his tie. It was early in the morning, and the sun drenched the bedroom of their Crosby Street loft. They were getting ready for Officer Tony Cippio's funeral. Marlene smiled back and said, "It's always been a dangerous job, but something has changed. This targeting of police officers . . . these cold-blooded executions . . . they take it to a whole new level."

Karp took a moment to consider her comment. He'd been targeted by assassins in the past, too, but then it was always something personal between him and the would-be killer. This was different. Police officers with no direct connection to the killers, except the uniform they were wearing, were being gunned down without provocation or warning. But he'd seen a version of it before, and so had she.

"You're forgetting when the Black Liberation Army split off from the Black Panthers in the sixties and starting shooting cops, trying to provoke a race war," he pointed out. "Same sort of rhetoric, same kinds of responses from the so-called leaders of the community, trying to spin it so that the police are 'responsible' for the violence against them."

Marlene frowned as she applied her lipstick in the mirror. "I guess so," she said, patting a stray hair back into her tight black curls. "Maybe it's the reaction from the public that's different. I think there used to be more respect for the police."

"I think most people are still horrified. But you're right, there has been a cultural shift since the sixties toward the police," Karp said. "God knows, I've seen it in courtrooms. Juries used to believe police officers when they testified, but now it's flip-flopped. There's a tendency to view anything they say on the stand with suspicion."

"No other group gets branded by a few bad apples like cops do."

"Except maybe lawyers," Karp replied with a slight smile. "But seriously, I think people believe that the police need to be held to a higher standard of conduct. As a society we've authorized them to carry and use weapons on other citizens, so long as it is within the bounds of their employment and the law. That's a pretty heavy responsibility, and the consequences of a rogue cop stepping over those boundaries with lethal force is certainly worse, more final, than an accountant misfiling a tax return or a lawyer not responding to a motion on time. But yeah, you're right, the vast majority of police officers joined up because they want to help their communities. Now the inflammatory rhetoric and media exploitation have made every legitimate traffic stop a potentially deadly ambush by some unbalanced person who believes the lies. It's changed the nature of the job for police officers irrevocably."

"Sounds like a summation, counselor," Marlene said.

"I hope I get to use it someday on whoever killed Tony Cippio."

They locked up the apartment and went downstairs to meet Detective Clay Fulton, who arrived in a long black limousine for the ride uptown to Harlem, where Cippio's funeral procession would start outside the 25th Precinct on 119th Street. NYPD Chief Nick DeCasio also joined them for what would be a long, slow procession down Fifth Avenue, through the Queens-Midtown Tunnel, and onto the Long Island Expressway to Deer Park, Long Island, where Cippio would be buried next to his brother, who had died on 9/11.

Fifth Avenue was already lined row after row with police officers in full dress uniform, who snapped to attention and saluted when, led by the Emerald Society Pipes and Drums, the car bearing Cippio's body rolled past. As they passed, Karp studied the faces of the officers. Some just looked dazed, but many appeared grim and angry. There was a tension in their body language that made him uneasy. There was a true sense of urgency to find the killer.

Behind the rows of officers, residents and tourists had also gathered to watch the funeral procession. Most were respectful and some of them had tears rolling down their cheeks, waving as if saying goodbye or simply holding a hand to their mouth. In Harlem, most of those faces were black and the vast majority seemed sad, a few even crying. But here and there small groups held up antipolice signs or raised clenched fists as they shouted slogans behind the wall of police officers who withstood the provocation in stony silence. Karp wondered how long that patience would hold.

Someone calling himself Nat X had appeared on a television interview claiming responsibility for Cippio's execution, calling it an "act of war by the Nat Turner Revolutionary Brigade on behalf of the oppressed black community." The man wore a balaclava mask and black ball cap that hid his features; he'd also spoken through a voice changer. Without much hope, Karp asked Gilbert Murrow to request a copy of the unedited version of the interview, as well as to talk to Peter Vansand, the journalist who'd conducted the "exclusive." As expected, both requests were turned down. The long ride to Long Island gave Karp plenty of time to think about the murder of Tony Cippio, and no one seemed to feel like talking much anyway. DeCasio was a man of few words in the best of circumstances, but he'd sat stone-faced and silent, staring out the window, as did DeCasio's wife and Marlene.

As the procession crossed 110th Street, Karp noticed Tyrone Greene standing at the corner holding a new basketball in his hands and crying. His grandmother stood behind him with her hands on his shoulders. Karp recalled their meeting at his office the day after Cippio was murdered.

NEVIE BUTLER HAD called in the morning, saying she could bring the boys in that afternoon.

"When I get off work. I'm a nurse's aide at an old folks' home—they call it 'assisted living' now, but there ain't much living going on there."

Karp had offered to send a car or pay their cab fare, but she insisted on taking the subway, explaining, "Folks around here won't talk as much."

Karp asked Fulton and ADA Kenny Katz to be present at the meeting. Tyrone had apparently opened up to Katz somewhat following the shooting, and he thought a familiar friendly face might counter his and Fulton's, two big men with countenances that could make dogs howl. "We'll meet in the conference room," he said.

Karp's receptionist, Darla Milquetost, had shown the three in when they arrived. "Please have a seat," she said, pointing to the chairs around the table. Butler and Tyrone sat, but Maurice remained standing. "I ain't sitting down with the po-lice," he said sullenly.

"Maurice, sit your insolent butt down," his grandmother demanded, glowering at him.

Karp interceded as he and Katz sat, too. "It's okay," he said. "He can stand if he wants. Actually, Maurice, I'm the district attorney, but Clay Fulton is a detective with the NYPD. We're just trying to piece together what happened at Marcus Garvey Park yesterday when the officer was killed, and we want to locate the man or men who did this."

"I ain't got nothing to say to you," Maurice replied, and stuck his hands in his pockets. "Y'all just out to kill black men. We have to fight back to defend ourselves."

47

"MAURICE!" Butler scolded. She turned to Karp. "He's been getting his head filled by evil, ungodly men preaching hate and violence. I apologize, Mr. Karp."

"No need to apologize. We're not here to force Maurice to talk if he doesn't want to." Karp turned to Tyrone. "But would you mind if I ask you a few questions?"

Tyrone looked at him, then his grandmother, who nodded, and back to Karp. "Am I in trouble?"

The question surprised Karp. He smiled and shook his head. "Not at all. From what I heard, you acted very bravely and tried to help Officer Cippio."

At the mention of the officer's name, the boy's eyes filled with tears and he hung his head. "He was a nice man. He gave me . . . us . . . a new basketball. I warned him not to go near those men."

"I want to ask you about those men," Karp said. "But let's start at the beginning and sort of walk us through what happened, starting with how you met Officer Cippio."

Taking a deep breath, Tyrone began. He told them how Cippio had started showing up to play basketball. "At first we thought he was just doing it for show, but I think he liked to play with us. He was pretty good, too, even though I called him 'Slo-Mo.'" The boy grew silent and tears fell on the table.

Karp leaned toward Tyrone. "I'm sure he'd like to be remembered that way by you."

Tyrone looked up and smiled slightly. "Yeah, he was funny and he cared about us," he said, but grew serious again. "I told him to stay away from those men."

"Let's talk about them. Why did you warn him?"

Tyrone shrugged, looking at his brother, who scowled. "'Cause they been talking bad about the police in the neighborhood. They've been saying that the police is the enemy. Maurice went to one of their meetings—"

"You what?" Nevie Butler turned angrily toward her grandson. "When I get you home . . ."

"Shut up, Tyrone," Maurice shouted, and started to advance toward his brother. But Fulton, who had positioned himself behind the younger boy, stepped forward. His face said all Maurice needed to stop in his tracks.

Tyrone shook his head. "I ain't lying for those men, Mo. They ain't our friends. Officer Tony was my friend." He turned back to Karp. "Maurice told me they talked about shooting police."

Karp narrowed his eyes and looked over at Maurice, who flushed and hung his head. "Do these men have names?"

"I know one of them who used to live near us," Tyrone said. "His name is Big George. He's a giant and he's mean, but I don't know his last name. He wasn't the guy with the gun, just with him. The guy with the gun calls himself Nat X, but that's not his real name."

"How do you know that?"

"Because he told us he was just using that name because of Nat Turner, who he said led a slave uprising a long time ago that killed a bunch of white people in someplace like Virginia."

"So were Nat X and Big George two of the men you were warning Officer Cippio to stay away from?"

"Yes, them and another guy. They were sitting on a picnic table, watching us. I told Officer Tony that they were bad, and he said he'd be careful." The boy's head swung slowly back and forth. "It didn't matter. He tried to walk past them, but they got in his way."

"How do you know that?"

"I was watching. He was walking back to his car, but they saw him and got up from the picnic table. Then they got around him. He tried to get past, but Big George stepped in front of him. That's when . . . that's when . . . the other one with the gun shot him."

Tyrone led Karp through the horror of watching the officer gunned down in cold blood. Karp had already seen the statement from the Medical Examiner's Office and expected the ballistics report soon; he wanted to know how the boy's recollection of events would match the facts.

Karp asked, "Have you seen Nat X close up?"

Tyrone nodded.

"Can you describe him for us?"

"Yeah. He tried to talk to us on the basketball court. He's kind of tall and skinny. He's got little, like, craters all over his face and a mark above his eye." The boy touched his skin above his right eye.

"A mark? You mean a scar?"

"Yeah, a scar that looks like part of a circle."

Karp noted the boy's eye for detail. Eyewitness accounts, especially in a traumatic situation, were often inaccurate. To ensure trustworthiness, information needed to be corroborated by other relevant facts, or other witnesses, but some were better than others, and Tyrone seemed to have exceptional recall. "Did you see the gun he used to shoot Officer Cippio?"

Tyrone nodded. "Yeah, I seen it pretty good," he said. "He was still holding it when he ran past us. It was all silver and had a white handle."

"A white handle?"

"Yes, a shiny white handle."

"Do you know much about handguns, Tyrone?"

The boy looked at his brother and then his grandmother. "Some." He shrugged.

"A child can't grow up in Harlem without seeing guns," Butler explained. "It's a shame, but it's also the truth."

Karp nodded. "I couldn't agree more, it's pretty sad. So is there anything else you can tell me about this gun, Tyrone?"

Tyrone bit his lip. "Well, it wasn't a semi."

"You mean a semiautomatic?"

"Yeah. It was more like a cowboy gun."

"A cowboy gun?"

Katz, who had brought his laptop to the meeting, interjected. "Give me a few minutes and I can create a photo gallery of different kinds of handguns on my computer."

Karp nodded. "Let's take a break," he said to the others. "I'll get together with Kenny. And if he wouldn't mind, Detective Fulton can get you something to drink from the vendor across the street. Would anyone like a soda or coffee?"

Tyrone brightened. "You got orange soda?"

"Do you have orange soda, please?" his grandmother said with an arched eyebrow.

"Do you have orange soda, please?" the boy repeated after her.

Karp laughed. "A man after my own heart. I think that can be arranged. Would you care for anything, Mrs. Butler?"

"Just water, thank you."

"Sure." Karp turned to the older boy. "Can we get you something, Maurice?"

He shook his head. "No," he said abruptly until he saw the look in his grandmother's eyes and added, "Thank you."

"Then we'll start again in about twenty minutes."

After they left the three visitors in the conference room, Karp turned to Fulton. "Hope you don't mind I volunteered you to run for sodas? I want to see what kind of magic Kenny can whip up here on the fly."

"No problem," Fulton replied. "I wouldn't mind getting a little fresh air and a soda myself. Orange for you, too?"

Karp smiled. "You know me too well." He pointed to the door leading to his inner office. "After you, Kenny."

Twenty minutes later, Karp and Katz walked back into the conference room. They were accompanied by another man, whom Karp introduced as Hal Sherman, a stenographer who had worked for the DAO for twenty years. Fulton had already distributed an orange soda to Tyrone and a bottle of water to Nevie Butler. Maurice sat on the floor in a corner of the room.

Katz sat down next to Tyrone and opened his computer, though he didn't let him see it just yet. Karp pushed his yellow pad toward the boy and offered his pen. "Kenny is going to show you a dozen photographs of different handguns," he said. "The photographs are all numbered. But I don't want you to say anything, or write anything down, until you've seen all of them. You can ask Kenny to go back to see any or all of them again. Then, when you're ready, if you see a gun that looks like the one the man who shot Officer Cippio used, I want you to write the number of the photograph on the pad. Think you can do that?"

Katz turned the laptop toward Tyrone and began to slowly click through a dozen photographs of handguns. "Let me know if you want to go slower or back up," he said as the boy studied each with his brow furrowed.

Karp noted that after a few photographs Tyrone's facial expression changed. But no one said anything until they got to the end and the boy reached for the pen.

"Do you want to see any of them again?" Katz asked.

"No, I'm good," Tyrone replied, and wrote the number 4 on the pad.

"Are you telling me that Number 4 resembles the gun Nat X used to shoot Officer Cippio?" Karp asked.

"Yes, sir, looks just like it." Tyrone pushed the pad and pen back to Karp.

"Please write your initials and today's date next to the number," Karp said. "And Mrs. Butler, would you please do the same thing and place your initials and date right below Tyrone's?"

After they did as requested, Karp turned to the stenographer.

"For the record, Number Four is a stainless steel, forty-five-caliber revolver with a mother-of-pearl grip."

A few minutes and a few follow-up questions later, Karp told Tyrone, "You've been a big help." He turned to Butler. "When we catch the people who did this, we will probably need Tyrone to testify at the trial."

"I understand. We'll have to cross that bridge when we come to it."

Karp nodded. "Is there anything you need from me now?"

The woman shook her head. "No, sir. We'll catch the subway back home."

"If you need anything, or you think of something I should know about, you have my direct line. Please call me."

"And mine," Fulton added, handing out two of his own cards.

"Thank you, we will," Butler replied. She looked at her older grandson. "Let's go, Maurice. You have some explaining to do when we get home."

As the boys left the room, Butler pulled Karp aside. "I'll be having a discussion with Maurice about these men. He's a good boy, just a little mixed up. I 'spect he'll come around shortly."

When she was gone, Fulton said, "Tyrone is pretty observant. Right caliber. A revolver explains the lack of shell casings. That mother-of-pearl looks like an after-market grip, not something you'd normally find on that gun. A little unusual for a shooter like this."

"Might be a good thing for us," Karp remarked. "If we can find it and the man who pulled the trigger."

"What about Maurice?"

Karp thought about it for a moment, then smiled. "Mrs. Butler's a good woman. Let's see what she comes up with."

Laughing, Fulton nodded. "Yeah, I had a grandma like that . . . wasn't no way she'd have put up with me giving the po-lice lip. I suspect he's in for a tough time when she gets him home."

Whatever Nevie Butler had said to her older grandson, so far it hadn't produced any new information. They still didn't know who Nat X was or where he was living. Nor had Fulton's discreet inquiries in the neighborhood turned up a "Big George."

MARLENE SQUEEZED KARP'S hand as the NYPD Emerald Society Pipes and Drums began playing "Amazing Grace." He glanced sideways at her and saw the tears rolling down her cheeks. She was staring across the grave to where Officer Tony Cippio's young widow sat sobbing in her black dress, her hands on her pregnant stomach, her father-in-law's arm around her shoulders. The Cippios' bewildered and frightened children squirmed in their seats off to her other side, trying to make sense of their mother's bereavement and this strange, sad gathering.

Karp leaned over slightly so that his shoulder rested against Marlene's for support. Sitting across from Tony Cippio's widow and children, Karp thought it was time to pull young Maurice Greene in and let Fulton put the fear of God in him. A dangerous killer was on the streets, and not just dangerous to cops. Karp worried about the safety of Tyrone Greene and his grandmother. Somebody brazen enough to kill a police officer in front of witnesses might later decide to eliminate those witnesses.

Fulton had talked to Mrs. Butler about it, but she didn't want any additional police presence in the housing project where they lived. Not even plainclothes. "People around here can sniff out a police officer from a block away," she'd told the detective, who relayed the conversation to Karp. "Rightly or wrongly, a lot of folks around here aren't real happy with the police, and I'd be worried they'd say something to this Nat X if it looked like Tyrone was cooperating with you. I'll rest easier when you catch him."

Marlene had told Butch that she didn't blame Nevie Butler but had an idea about who might be able to keep an eye on them without drawing a lot of attention. As the funeral service came to a close, Marlene squeezed his hand again. "I feel so sorry for him, too," she whispered.

He followed her eyes back across the casket to the big man who sat with his arm around Fran Cippio: her father-in-law, Vincent Cippio Sr., a retired NYPD sergeant, was well known to Fulton.

"Went to the academy with him," Fulton told him. "Tough story. Old-time cop family. Lost a brother and another son—one of the nine/eleven heroes—in the line of duty. Lost his wife last year to cancer . . . now this. I feel for the guy."

"How's Tony's wife doing?" Karp asked.

"Rough sledding. Two young ones and another on the way. Apparently she lost her folks in a traffic accident when she was young. She and Vince will need to lean on each other."

"If there's anything we can do," Karp said.

"Yeah, I'll let you know." Fulton nodded. "The NYPD Patrolmen's Benevolent Association has a Widows' and Children's Fund to help out. We take care of our own."

Karp caught the edge in Fulton's voice. It surprised him a little bit. They'd met shortly after Karp joined the New York DAO out of law school and Fulton was a rookie patrolman. They'd been through a lot together, and Fulton was the epitome of calm and cool no matter what was going on around him. His bitterness now was unusual.

"You okay?"

Fulton started to nod his head but stopped and shook it instead. "No. I'm not okay. I've had too many friends killed in the line of duty. Too many good men, and women, who got up in the morning and put on the uniform or grabbed the badge, but then didn't make it home that night. But to have a young father shot down just because he was wearing the uniform? . . . So no, I'm not okay. A lot of the guys aren't okay. I'm pissed off, and so are they. It's not just the killer, either. The public is buying this bullshit that racist cops are on the rampage. They don't care that good cops are being murdered. I'm worried that someday there's going to be a backlash."

There wasn't anything Karp could say except, "I'm with you on this."

"I know you are, Butch, and it's appreciated."

The three made their way over to offer their condolences first to the widow and then to Cippio's father. "We just wanted to tell you again how sorry we are for your loss," Karp said, shaking the man's hand. "We'll catch this guy."

Vince Cippio nodded. "And when you do, make him pay."

"I promise, justice will be done."

As the grieving family turned to speak to other well-wishers, Fulton looked at Karp. "You ready to go?"

"Yeah." Karp turned to Marlene. "Sure you don't want us to drop you off?"

"No, thanks. I've got to see a man about a dog. I'll catch a cab." She stood on her toes to kiss him on the cheek.

Karp frowned. "I don't want to know where you're going, do I?"

"You're so perceptive."

Shaking his head, Karp looked at Fulton. "Let's go before she breaks down and tells me. I sleep better when I don't know."

Leaving the cemetery, Karp noticed a group of four uniformed police officers standing in the parking lot. He recognized one of them as Tony Cippio's partner, Eddie Evans; the other three, all white, seemed to be consoling him.

At least that's what he thought at first. But the more he watched, the more it seemed that there was some tension between the other three and Evans. One of the white officers, in particular, an older cop, seemed to be doing most of the talking.

"What do you make of that?" Karp nudged Fulton and nodded toward the group.

Fulton frowned. "Don't know. The older guy I recognize as a lieutenant in the Homicide Bureau, Jack Gilliam. We're not particularly fond of each other."

At the same time, one of the other white officers saw them looking and said something. The others stopped talking and looked. Gilliam turned back to Evans and patted him on the shoulder, and the three white officers left.

Fulton frowned. "Like I said, there's a lot of anger out there."

"I hope cooler heads will prevail," Karp said. "We've got our work cut out for us."

"So we do, Mr. DA. So we do."

5

THE TWO BLACK TEENAGERS FIDGETED AS THEY WAITED IN the shade of the abandoned Harlem tenement building. Even though shadows were starting to grow long as the evening progressed, the air hung oppressively hot and humid. But that wasn't the sole reason sweat dripped from their faces and their shirts clung to them like wet rags. They were waiting for a man who promised that on this day they'd earn the respect that had eluded them all of their lives. But at what cost?

The teens had been best friends since meeting in the third grade at the Frederick Douglass Charter School of Harlem and they were now seniors at Weyland High School for Gifted Students in Mount Vernon. Their education alone brought them closer, but it also reinforced their separateness from their neighborhood peers.

Most of the local teens attended the public high school, which was only a few miles from Weyland as the pigeon flies but worlds away in terms of expectations. The students at Weyland, a magnet school for gifted minority children, worried about grade point averages, senior projects, and applying to college. Their counterparts in the public high school worried about survival.

Set on the grounds of a former estate built by a nineteenth-century sugar baron, Weyland's campus was lined with trees and carefully manicured lawns and gardens. A private security firm patrolled the campus to keep the students safe. The classrooms were fitted with the latest technology and run by well-paid teachers who had competed to land a job there. Upon admission to the middle school, each student received a new laptop computer, which was replaced by a newer version when they graduated to the next level. Students were expected to go to college after graduation and "make something of their lives."

Meanwhile, surrounded by a hard-featured landscape of concrete and asphalt, the public school students—those who hadn't dropped out—passed through metal detectors just to enter the deteriorating buildings. Inside, the hallways were patrolled by NYPD officers and the classrooms were supervised by jaded, poorly paid union teachers who did little to control their unruly, and sometimes violent, charges. Most of the teachers were just putting in their time until retirement; those who did care had to battle Kafka-esque, inept bureaucratic system to reach the rare students not so beat down by the environment that they kept trying. Even then, few people outside of that rare teacher, and perhaps the students' families, expected them to succeed at anything—such was the nature and cruelty of low expectations.

The two teens took a bus to Weyland, which they also had to take back each day to the hood. They wore school uniforms of blue jacket, gray trousers, starched white shirt, and blue-and-white-striped tie. Some of their counterparts also wore uniforms of a sort, defined by the color claimed by one gang or another.

Encouraged by parents who knew that education was their sons' way out of the circumstances of their birthplace, the two teens were bookworms, devoted Harry Potter fans, nerdy in both their speech and their choice of clothes when not in uniform. Neither of them was athletic in a culture that judged young men on their ability to play sports or their hard exteriors.

It was a tough way to grow up. The segregation inevitably led to bullying, which had escalated from having their schoolbooks knocked out of their hands to actual assaults. But it was the words that hurt the most, the accusations of "trying to be white," and the lack of respect.

Things would have been worse had it not been for Maurice Greene, one of the few friends they had in the neighborhood. It was him they were waiting for before walking to meet the man who was going to change everything. They'd known Maurice from the playgrounds of their childhood; he was one of the few who didn't hold their opportunity to better themselves against them. Maybe that was because he was a star on the public school basketball team and drawing the interest of college recruiters.

"Think Maurice is going to show?" DeShawn Lakes asked. He was tall and thin, light-skinned, with an oval face and large green eyes that bugged slightly.

The other teen, Ricky Watts, shrugged and pushed his black-framed glasses up his broad nose. He was nearsighted, short, and built like a pear. "I don't know. I talked to him on the phone last night and he said he'd be here. But he's been hard to reach ever since his little brother saw that cop get shot. He told me his grandma is keeping him on a tight leash."

Lakes nodded but felt a knot in his stomach. Maurice was the one who'd brought them to a meeting with Nat X, the revolutionary. He'd teased them when he first told them about the meetings, which he called "community self-preservation discussions."

"I don't know," Maurice had told them. "Maybe you ain't black enough to hear the truth."

He'd winked and laughed when he said it, and they knew he was kidding. But they'd heard similar accusations all their lives and it stung. They insisted that they were "black enough" and asked to attend.

AT THE FIRST few meetings, Nat X had talked a lot about black pride and African contributions to the world. "Contributions," he'd argued, "that have never been recognized, or have been appropriated, by the oppressive white culture." But as the meetings went on, the man's rhetoric grew angrier. The only way for the black community to realize its full potential was to cast off the yoke of whites and form a separate black nation. But that, he added, could happen only by "taking up arms against the oppressor class and their servants, the police."

This had gone on for about a month with meetings held two and even three times a week. The meeting place was never the same and Nat X never told them his real name. He was always in the company of a huge violent criminal they knew as Big George, and another man he sometimes called Cousin Ny-Lee. The last couple of meetings had also been attended by a young man named Oliver Gray, who described himself as a "black radical Socialist" and told them that Nat X reminded him of Che Guevara. He seemed a little unbalanced despite his calm demeanor, so they avoided him and his call for "assassination and a bloody uprising."

At first, Nat X had derided the two teens and their educations. "You is being groomed to be a couple of house niggers, that's all," he said as both boys blushed in shame. "You know what a house nigger is? Back in the day, house niggers got special privileges the field niggers didn't get. They got better food than the other slaves. They got taught manners and how to speak. And they got to eat and sleep in the master's house. They thought they was better than the field niggers."

With Big George standing behind him with a menacing scowl on his face, Nat X had walked up until his face was only a few inches from theirs. "But at the end of the day, they was still just black slaves . . . property. They weren't better than the field niggers; in fact, they was worse because they forgot who they were and where they come from. Is that what you want? To be house niggers? To forget who you are and where you come from?"

"No, sir," they'd said in unison.

Nat X stepped back and nodded. "That's good. That's real good. Someday soon, you may be asked to prove it. Are you going to be ready?"

"Yes, sir," they'd replied, which earned them a handshake from Nat X and a smile from Big George.

As the weeks passed, Lakes and Watts noticed that there were fewer familiar faces at each meeting. "He's weeding out the weak and those he doesn't trust," explained Maurice, who seemed increasingly caught up in Nat X's rhetoric. "He thinks you two got promise."

The secondhand praise had done wonders for their self-esteem. A black activist, someone who was trying to protect their people from an oppressive culture, thought they had promise. Respect was a powerful drug, and it had nudged them farther into the fold.

Still, it all seemed like mostly talk until the evening they got a call from Maurice, who told them someone shot a cop and his little brother saw the whole thing. In Marcus Garvey Park. When Lakes asked who did it, Maurice suggested it was Nat X, Big George, and Ny-Lee. He swore them to secrecy. Soon enough the story was on the news, and the boys were shocked. It didn't seem like that cop was doing anything wrong. "He was just playing some basketball with some kids," Lakes insisted.

"WHERE'S MAURICE?" NAT X asked suspiciously. The boys were standing outside a tenement building where Nat X had told them to meet him. They shrugged. Watts said, "He said his grandmother was watching him like a hawk. I guess his little brother was there when . . . when . . . well, you know. They had to go talk to the district attorney and everything."

Nat X's eyebrows rose and he looked over at Big George. "Is that so? What he tell the DA?"

"He said he refused to talk and he was only there because his grandma made him go," Lakes said, leaving out any mention of Tyrone Greene answering questions.

Nat X smiled. "Yeah, well that's good. Can't have traitors among us, can we?" He reached around and pulled out a gun from underneath his sweatshirt. Both boys had seen guns before, but this one was something special. Silver with a shiny white handle.

"That's mother-of-pearl," Nat X said with pride as he pointed at the grip. He held it out to Lakes. "Go ahead. Take it."

Lakes tried to act like holding a large handgun was nothing new to him. Then he passed it to Watts, who seemed even more impressed as he sighted down the barrel.

"Yeah," Nat X said. "You like that? That's power. The only kind of power the white man understands." He winked. "That there is a cop killer. Those bullets? They go right through a Kevlar vest like it was butter."

The teens looked at the gun with renewed awe. This was the gun. Watts returned the gun to its owner.

"So let me ask you a serious question," Nat X said. "Are you ready to strike a blow for your people? You going to be heroes of the revolution? Or are you going to be house niggers?"

The teens looked at each other. They were scared and also felt backed into a corner. In some small way, both were tired of being bullied, and they saw this as their chance to become neighborhood heroes to those same kids who ridiculed them daily. They looked at Nat X. "We're ready," they said in unison.

Nat X grinned. "That's good. That's real good. See, I told you," Nat X said to his companion. "These two are straight-up soldiers in the Nat Turner Revolutionary Brigade." His eyes narrowed.

"Let's go."

"Where we going?" Lakes asked.

"You'll find out when we get there."

The four hadn't made it more than a few blocks when a car pulled over to the curb just ahead of them. A large man, almost the size of Big George, got out.

"DeShawn, what the hell are you doing out here? You're supposed to be home studying," the man said.

"Who the hell are you?" Nat X said with a scowl.

"Who am I?" the man replied. "The name's Jonas Lakes, Reverend Jonas Lakes. I'm this boy's father. Now who the hell are you?"

Nat X held out his hand. "Just a friend—call me Nat."

Reverend Lakes ignored his hand. "You ain't no friend of mine. And what do you want with these two boys here? I see you, Ricky Watts. Your mom isn't going to be happy hearing you're walking around with this sort of trash."

"Hey, watch what you're saying, old man," Big George growled and started to advance. But Nat X grabbed him by an arm.

"I don't appreciate that," he said to the reverend. "But I ain't got time to deal with you now." He turned to DeShawn. "Looks like you need to go home and study like a good little house nigger."

"Watch your mouth, trash," Reverend Lakes warned, but he stopped and his eyes narrowed when Nat X reached menacingly behind his back. "Oh, I see how it is, tough guy. Well, come on, De-Shawn, and you, too, Ricky. I'll drive you home."

DeShawn left the group and walked toward his father. But Ricky hung back. "I'm staying," he said.

"That's right, he's his own man," Nat X said. "DeShawn, you and your daddy just run along."

"Yeah, run along, old man," Big George repeated.

Reverend Lakes hesitated, then shook his head. "Get in the car," he told his son.

As they drove away, Nat X turned to Watts. "I'm real proud of you standing up for the cause."

Watts blushed and smiled. "I'm all in."

A few minutes later, the three men were standing at the entrance to an alley next to a tenement building. Nat X looked around, but there was nothing much to see, just a Dumpster about twenty feet down the alley, but no people. He nodded at the building.

"I've been watching this place for a while. And every night about this time, two cops start at the top of the building and walk down the stairs." He pulled out the silver revolver and wiped it off with a handkerchief. "They won't be expecting you," he said, and held out the gun to Ricky, using the cloth to avoid leaving his fingerprints.

"You . . . you . . . you want me to shoot them?" he said, blinking hard behind his thick glasses.

"You said you were ready," Nat X replied, his voice firm. "Did I make a mistake and pick a boy to do a man's job?"

"No, I'll do it," Watts said. He swallowed hard as he held out his hand and took the gun. The weight of it seemed to give him courage.

Nat X smiled. "Good. I knew I could count on you. Just go in that door over there and up a couple of flights and set yourself up on one of the landings. Be ready, and when they come around the corner, they won't be expecting you . . . that's when you do it. Boom boom and it's over. If they're still moving, shoot them in the head. Then get your ass out of there and we'll meet you."

Watts nodded and tucked the gun under his shirt. He walked resolutely to the entrance.

6

As the two officers emerged from the hallway onto the ninth-floor landing, the older one stumbled. "Ah, damn," Liam Conway said. "Bum knee. I should be riding a desk, not doing sweeps in a piece-of-shit tenement in Harlem with a rookie."

An obese man whose prodigious belly folded itself over his equipment belt, Conway looked around the stairwell with distaste, making a face as if he'd swallowed something particularly loathsome. The only light was supplied by a small grimy window four feet above the floor, but it was enough to see the graffiti-covered walls and the trash on the floor. He sniffed. "Bah, smells like every junkie in the building pissed in here. Bunch of fucking animals."

The "rookie," Officer Bryce Kim, didn't say what he was thinking. His partner was a racist who had nothing good to say about anybody who wasn't white. He even made little remarks about Kim's Korean ancestry and didn't hesitate to use "gooks" and "slants" to refer to Asians. He was also a lousy cop who'd never made it past patrolman due to his tendency to rough up suspects, and a history of "minor" transgressions like being on the take and demanding sex from hookers. Each time Conway had landed in hot water, though, the police union had saved him.

Now the brass were trying to get him to take early retirement by giving him lousy assignments. Such as walking a beat in one of the most crime-ridden neighborhoods in the city with a rookie partner he obviously disliked based on his race, and the fact that Kim took the job seriously.

"Come on, Conway," Kim said. "Let's get this over with."

In response, Conway bent over and winced as he rubbed his knee. "You go on ahead. I'll catch up as soon as I work this kink out."

Kim knew that the delay had nothing to do with Conway's knee. In addition to all of his other foibles, his partner couldn't make it through a shift without draining a pint flask of bourbon. He usually showed up for work with alcohol already on his breath, and when they first started working together he'd made a joke of his frequent nips "for medicinal purposes." After Kim complained to the desk sergeant, who happened to be a friend of Conway's, the boozy officer was more circumspect when he took his "medicine," but he hadn't stopped.

Kim knew Conway wanted him to go elsewhere so he could have a drink. He shook his head and shrugged before starting down the poorly lit stairs. The sounds of the residents emanated from behind the apartment doors. Children laughing or crying. Adults arguing. Doors slamming. Loud music blaring. But still he was conscious of his own heavy breathing, aware that if anything happened, he had no real backup.

Not every hallway had a working lightbulb. Most of the light from nearby streetlamps was blocked by surrounding buildings. The gloom that enveloped the hallways and stairwell got to Kim.

Every cop working in the city, especially Harlem, was on edge after the Cippio shooting. This guy, Nat X, who'd claimed responsibility, was still out there, threatening more executions. There was no way of knowing whom he'd target next.

Kim unfastened his holster and drew his 9 mm despite knowing it was against departmental policy. His nerves almost got the best of him as he came to the top of the flight of stairs above the fourth-floor landing and was surprised by a sudden movement. A woman smoking a cigarette near the open window gave a little cry when she saw him and scuttled back through a door that had been left ajar. He realized that he'd raised his gun.

No wonder she was frightened, he thought. He was about to re-holster when there was more movement at the bottom of the next flight of stairs. It took him a moment to realize what he was seeing. In the shadows stood a young black man. He was short, pear-shaped, wearing round, wire-rimmed glasses, and he looked scared. Only then did the police officer see the silver-colored gun in the young man's hand.

There was a flash and a deafening roar when the youth pulled the trigger. And almost on top of that, a second blast when, reacting defensively, Kim raised and fired his weapon. For a moment, both young men stood there as if surprised by the sudden violence that had erupted between them.

Kim ducked back up the stairs. In shock, it took him a moment to realize that his assailant had missed. He listened. There was the sound of someone stumbling down the stairs below him and shouts from other parts of the building. One of those shouting was his partner.

"Kim! Are you okay?" Conway called down.

"Yeah, I'm good," Kim responded. "Suspect's heading for the street."

Up above, Conway called it in on his radio. "This is a ten-thirteen. Officer in distress. Shots fired. We need backup NOW!" Kim could hear him laboring down the stairs, and then his florid face poked around the corner. He was holding his gun out, his hand shaking. "Jesus Christ, Kim, what the hell happened?"

"I . . . uh . . . I came around the corner and this kid, he had a gun. He tried to shoot me."

Down below they heard the heavy door leading out onto the streets burst open. "He's getting away," Kim said. He stood up and began moving down the stairs.

"Wait for backup," Conway insisted.

"There's blood here," Kim replied. "I think I got him. I'm going down."

"Dammit, wait," Conway replied, but his partner was gone.

Kim went cautiously, following the trail of blood. He paused briefly at each floor, half expecting to see the gunman waiting, before pressing on. On the second floor, an older black woman and several children stood with the door open to the stairwell.

"Get back inside," Kim ordered before proceeding. They retreated, slamming the door behind them.

Reaching the ground floor, Kim hesitated. The gunman was obviously wounded, but he didn't know how badly. *He might be waiting for you*, his brain cautioned him. But he steeled himself and kicked open the door.

Whatever he expected to see, he wasn't prepared for what he found. A trail of blood across the sidewalk led to the prone body of the shooter. He wasn't moving.

An extremely large black man knelt at the suspect's side and looked up as Kim approached. "You killed an unarmed boy," he said loudly.

"Back away," Kim told him, his gun trained on the body on the ground.

"He ain't got no gun!" the large man shouted as he stood up.

People were starting to gather, so the man repeated himself. "This cop just shot a black kid who ain't got no gun!"

"That's not true," Kim replied, frowning. "He had a gun."

"Liar," the man shouted again and held up his hands, which were covered in blood. "There ain't no gun."

The crowd began to murmur and tried to move closer. "You're right," a woman yelled, "there ain't no gun!"

Conway appeared from the doorway, his gun drawn. "Back off," he shouted at the gathering group of onlookers. He walked over to the figure on the ground and felt for a pulse.

Meanwhile, Kim radioed for help. "I need an ambulance!"

"Won't do any good," Conway said. "He's dead." He looked at Kim. "What the hell?"

"He had a gun. He shot at me!"

Looking back down at the body, Conway's lips twisted. "There's no gun now."

"Murderers!" screamed the large black man. "The cops murdered this boy!"

Others in the crowd took up the cry. "Murderers!"

Conway looked at the mob that was growing and getting angrier by the moment. "Better call again for backup," he said. "This ain't going to be pretty."

7

KARP SMELLED THE GIANT BEFORE HE SAW HIM. HE WAS talking to Dirty Warren, who owned the newsstand in front of the Criminal Courts Building, when he was assailed by the odor of a body that had not experienced a shower in months, if not years, and breath that hadn't been exposed to toothpaste in that time, either. It nearly made him gag, but then he smiled.

"Good morning, Jacob," Karp said as he turned to greet the bear-like man who stood behind him with one large grimy finger inserted half its length up his nose.

"'ood aper-oon, 'ister 'arp," the Walking Booger replied with a small bow.

Although Karp could understand the impaired speech from years of experience with the local sidewalk denizen, he knew his large friend struggled with a speech impediment exacerbated by rotten and missing teeth. This man was possibly the largest human

Karp (who at six-foot-five was no slouch himself) had ever seen. The Walking Booger was swaddled in a makeshift array of soiled, unwashed layers of clothing, including several coats, despite the already rising heat index. In fact, very little skin was showing except on his extremely filthy hands. A dark mane of hair covered his head, neck, and most of his face so that only his small, beady, bright eyes could be seen twinkling through the fur.

"Hi, Booger . . . fucking twat whoop whoop," said Dirty Warren, who suffered from Tourette's syndrome. "Everything . . . whoop . . . okay you know where? . . . Piss shit!"

"Eber-ree-ting is 'kay," the giant replied without removing his finger.

"Good. David asked me to . . . butthole bitch oh boy ohhhhh boy . . . keep you company tonight," Warren said. "Because of the . . . whoop whoooop . . . riots."

"'ood," Booger said. The hair on his face moved in such a way that Karp assumed he'd smiled. "I 'ike 'ompany. Bye, 'arren, bye, 'ister 'arp." With that, the giant shuffled off, the crowd on the sidewalk parting like a school of herring trying to avoid close contact with a shark.

"Well, that was short and interesting," Karp said. "By David, I don't suppose you mean David Grale?"

Warren arched an eyebrow. Former Catholic social worker–turned–serial killer, David Grale lived in the tunnels and warrens beneath the city of New York. He was the acknowledged King of the Mole People, thousands of homeless people who scavenged a living on the surface but lived in darkness with several million New Yorkers above them largely oblivious of their existence.

If there was a redeeming feature to Grale's murderous ways, it was that he killed only vicious criminals—murderers, rapists, and terrorists. He'd once been a co-worker at a soup kitchen for the poor with Karp's daughter, Lucy, which was how they'd all initially become acquainted. In the years since, Grale had appointed himself guardian of Karp's family and was especially close to Marlene and Lucy.

Despite his reservations about vigilante justice, Karp couldn't help but be grateful for the several occasions when Grale had saved not just his wife and children from killers but also the inhabitants of Gotham—even if they never knew his role in preventing terrorist attacks. But the last few times Karp had met him, Grale seemed to be sinking farther into madness, convinced that he was fighting a battle between good and evil. The madness and his lifestyle appeared also to be taking their physical toll on him; he looked haggard, his skin pale and waxy, his eyes sunken, and his chest consumed by a wet cough that Karp thought might be tubercular. Still, he commanded a network of street people—like Dirty Warren and the Walking Booger—that had better communications than the NYPD.

"Maybe," Warren said with a grin. "But aren't you . . . oh boy whoop whoop . . . the top law dog in New York County?"

"Technically, yes," Karp replied. "Why?"

"Well, you think I'm going to . . . bastard ass . . . admit to hanging around a maniacal killer like . . . whoop . . . David Grale?"

Karp laughed. "Good point."

Warren smiled, then said, "Hey, I got a . . . whoop whoop . . . trivia question for you."

Karp rolled his eyes. They'd been playing movie trivia for years while exchanging good-natured jibes, and Warren had yet to stump him. "I hope it's better than your last few feeble attempts."

"Pride before fall . . . son of a bitch . . . Karp. Okay, okay . . . asswipe nuts . . . here it is. Who said, 'If we'd made love last night I'd have to stay. Or you'd have to leave'? That's all you . . . oh boy oh boy . . . get."

Karp pretended to be stumped. He rubbed his chin with his hand and looked up at the bright blue sky.

Warren peered at him through his smeared Coke-bottle glasses as he hopped from foot to foot. "I think . . . whoop oh boy . . . I finally got you," he said with a grin. "Didn't we have a steak dinner bet on—"

"I believe it was the character of John Book, played by Harrison Ford, in the movie *Witness*," Karp said, laughing as Warren's smile evaporated. "He was talking to Rachel Lapp, a young Amish woman played by Kelly McGillis. Rachel's son had witnessed a murder in Philadelphia and . . ."

Karp stopped talking and looked at Warren, who was wiggling his eyebrows. "Are you trying to tell me something? Does this have something to do with your conversation with Booger?"

Warren shoved his glasses farther up his beak-like nose. "I don't know . . . damn bastard . . . what you're talking about." Then he giggled.

Shaking his head, Karp patted Warren on the shoulder. "I got it . . . too much information. I have to go. How about a couple newspapers for me?"

"You can't . . . whoop . . . handle the truth," Dirty Warren said, handing over the morning editions of the *New York Times* and the *New York Post*.

"What is this a two-fer? Jack Nicholson in *A Few Good Men*," Karp said, and glanced at the front pages of both papers. The headlines led with the officer-involved shooting the night before in their usual low-key way.

The *Post*:

Cop Guns Down
Unarmed Teen!

The *Times*:

NYPD Officer Shoots Black Teen
in Tenement Stairwell

*Victim Said to Be "Exceptional Student"
at Charter School; No Gun Found*

Both papers also featured stories about the riot that broke out shortly after the shooting. Several vehicles, including one NYPD patrol car, were burned, a dozen people were arrested, ten were sent to the hospital, and two police officers had to be treated at the scene. The officer involved, Bryce Kim, had been identified.

"Scary stuff," Warren noted.

"Hopefully cooler heads will prevail," Karp replied, feeling like he was falling back on that old expression more often than he would have liked.

"Is there . . . whoop whoop . . . any such thing as 'cooler heads' anymore?"

Karp handed Warren a couple bucks for the papers. "That's a good question, my clever friend, and one I don't have the answer to right now. I'm running late, thanks for the newspapers and the trivia. Try to come up with something a little tougher next time."

"Screw you, Karp," Warren replied with a smile.

Karp shook his head. Sometimes he was pretty sure that not all the curse words that rolled out of the little news vendor's mouth were a result of the Tourette's.

Inside the courts building, Karp rode the elevator to the eighth floor, where his office was located. In the reception area, Darla Milquetost looked up from her filing and nodded toward his inner sanctum. "Clay Fulton and Espy Jaxon are waiting."

Karp found both men seated in front of his desk and deep in conversation. "Hello, gentlemen, sorry I'm late," he said. "I stopped to get copies of the newspapers." He handed one to each of the men, who glanced at the front pages and then exchanged them.

Turning to Fulton as he sat down at his desk, Karp asked, "So what do we know?"

The big detective scowled. "Not a whole lot. The officer, Bryce Kim, was a rookie. He's a second-generation Korean immigrant; family owns a little grocery store in Chinatown. They've already received threats thanks to the media identifying them. NYPD has an extra presence on the street, but that won't stop some lone nut. Officer's been placed on administrative leave. His story is that he and his partner, a real piece of work named Liam Conway, were doing a sweep in the building when he saw the deceased—one Ricky Watts—at the bottom of a flight of stairs. He says the deceased shot at him and he returned fire."

"Kim's story check out?"

"Depends who you talk to. Kim's gun was fired once. His partner, Conway, says he heard two shots, one on top of the other."

"He didn't see what happened?" Karp asked.

"Apparently, he was 'delayed' while Bryce went ahead," Fulton said. "A woman, Martha Motumbo, elderly, lives in the building with her two grandchildren, and she said she heard two shots as well. She opened the door to the stairwell when she heard somebody—apparently the deceased—stumble by. She saw Bryce in pursuit. He told her to return to her apartment. That's what she did until contacted by detectives last night.

"Deceased was a seventeen-year-old student at Weyland School for Gifted Students in Mount Vernon but lived with his mother in Harlem. Smart kid. No record, not even juvie."

"So what was he doing there?"

Fulton shrugged. "Good question. Nobody there knew him."

"You said depends who you talk to."

"Yeah, several other witnesses came forward and said they only heard one shot," Fulton said. "But if the guns were fired simultaneously in a stairwell where the sound would have echoed, it might have been difficult to distinguish two shots."

"But no other gun was located?"

Fulton shook his head. "No. If there was one, it was gone."

"And no eyewitnesses to any of this?"

"Just Kim and Watts." Fulton dug a small notebook out of his shirt pocket and flipped it open. "One witness, a George Parker, says he was standing outside the building when he heard one shot, then Watts staggered out the door, crossed the sidewalk, and collapsed on the curb. He claims that Watts had nothing in his hands, no gun, no weapon of any kind."

"What about the crime scene techs? They find anything?"

Again, Fulton shook his head. "Nothing yet, though they're still processing the scene. But nothing was found in the hall or stairwell. No shell casing, no marks on the walls."

"Possible that the bullet could have exited the building through a window?"

Fulton allowed himself a slight smile. "Now you're thinking like a detective. I wondered that myself and went over there before coming here." He handed Karp a manila envelope.

"Here are a few initial photographs," he said. "The first one is the front of the building, shows the door the deceased exited. You can see the crime tape around where he collapsed. The second shows the stairs. I stood where Kim said the deceased was standing and looked up. There's a window where Kim was standing—I circled it on the photograph—but it was closed, as it is there, and there's no indication that it was struck by a bullet. Crime scene tech who was there when I showed up said it was closed when he arrived the night before, too. I talked to the building superintendent and he said those windows are supposed to be kept shut to help keep dirt and insects out—fat chance in that hellhole."

Karp laid the photos back down. "How's Kim doing?"

"Pretty shook up," Fulton replied. "But he's more worried about his parents right now." The detective started to say something else but stopped.

"What is it, Clay?"

Fulton sighed. "Everybody—cops, I mean—is on edge from the Cippio shooting and all this inflammatory bullshit that's flying around. Looks like Kim let some of it get to his head, too. He admitted that he had his gun already out when he confronted Watts. That's a violation of departmental policy. I don't know, but that stairwell is pretty dark, and maybe he was a little spooked and thought he saw Watts holding a gun."

Karp nodded. "Well, keep me updated. Obviously, this blew up pretty quick last night. The demagogues and the media are all over it. Reverend Mufti was on the news this morning calling it a 're-venge killing' for Cippio's shooting. And that ass—that fine example of journalism, Peter Vansand, gave our suspect, Nat X, a soapbox to call for a general uprising. There's a planned Black Justice Now 'peace march' starting in Marcus Garvey Park tonight. I have a feeling it's going to be anything but peaceful."

"The brass at NYPD are thinking the same thing," Fulton said. "Crowd control will be out in force, but that only goes so far."

Karp refrained from saying that he hoped cooler heads would prevail, though he thought it as he turned to Jaxon. "I suppose you're wondering why I asked you to drop by?"

"Well, I figured it wasn't just to get the latest on the Nat Turner Revolutionary Brigade and this guy, Nat X," Jaxon replied. "I could have told you that over the telephone, and it's not much."

"You're right," Karp said. "I have a favor to ask." He looked at Fulton. "Did you bring it?"

"I did." Fulton reached down beside his chair and retrieved a locked satchel.

"What's in the bag? Or don't I want to know?" Jaxon asked.

"Please, take a look," Karp said.

As Jaxon opened the satchel, Fulton handed the agent another manila file folder and explained, "You're looking at touch DNA samples gathered from the officer's clothing at the Cippio crime scene and later the Medical Examiner's Office. The papers contained in the file explain each individual sample."

Jaxon looked up, puzzled. "I don't understand."

Karp nodded. "I'm trying to anticipate what I might run up against in court when we catch the killer. Given today's climate of distrust, and accusations that law enforcement—particularly at the local level—is racist and willing to bend or break the rules to protect officers and unfairly prosecute 'innocent' people, I'd like to ask if you can get this tested for me. It's being tested in the NYPD labs, but we'd like a second opinion from another laboratory."

Jaxon leaned back in his seat. "I'll be happy to help, but why not get the DOJ and the FBI involved?"

Karp's lips twisted. "I've considered that. I know you were a special agent in charge of the bureau here in New York and that you still have friends there. But let's just say that in today's climate, I don't trust the hierarchy in either the DOJ or FBI. They have an agenda that comes down from on high, and it is not a pro–law enforcement one."

Jaxon nodded. "I don't blame you. I know from talking to those 'friends' you mentioned that they aren't too happy with the higher-ups, either. It seems that justice has been politicized."

"There's also a release in the folder," Karp went on. "I'd like you to sign and date the form, indicating exactly when and from whom you received these samples."

Jaxon smiled and shook his head. "That's my friend Butch, always a few steps ahead of everybody else."

Karp laughed. "Hopefully, I'm not running toward a cliff."

A few minutes later, after Jaxon left the office, Karp looked at his friend Detective Fulton. "I'd give anything to know why Ricky Watts was in that tenement."

"It's the million-dollar question," Fulton responded. "And given what happened last night after the shooting, and what I suspect is going to happen tonight, the sooner we find an answer, the better off this city will be."

8

Lieutenant Jack Gilliam nudged the man sitting next to him drinking a beer at Farrell's Bar & Grill in Brooklyn. "There he is," he said.

"You sure about this?" said a third man, sitting across the table.

"I'm not sure of anything," Gilliam growled. "I'm just going to feel him out now that things have ramped up."

"But he's . . . you know . . ."

"Black? Yeah, I know, but he's also a cop," Gilliam replied. "A cop whose partner just got gunned down in cold blood. Then these so-called activists, like that piece of shit Mufti and his loudmouth pal with Black Justice Now, Imani Sefu, go off on that bullshit that a totally unrelated shooting was revenge. Like that gives them the right to riot. Six more cops were hurt during that 'peace' march the other night, and one of them's still in a coma. Evans is black, but he's a cop and he can't like this any more than we do."

Gilliam stood as Evans made his way over to them. "Hey, Eddie, good to see you," he said, extending his hand. He pointed to the seat next to him. "Take a load off. You remember Joe Satars and Johnny Delgado?"

Evans nodded to the other two. "Been a while since I've been over to Brooklyn, much less Farrell's," he said. "It still a good cop bar?"

Delgado laughed. "It's the best. Lots of cops and firefighters. A great place to hook up with uniform chasers; they all know where to find us."

"We call him 'Don Juan' Delgado," Gilliam joked. "But it is a good place to hang out with guys who know what it's like to put on the uniform."

"You married?" asked Delgado, who obviously spent a lot of time combing his wavy dark hair and working out at the gym. "I know a few girls in here who like older guys."

"Hey, who you calling old?" Evans laughed, then held up his left hand to show the gold band. "But yeah, married twenty years. Two kids."

"That's good, that's good," Delgado replied. "You could be like Joe here. He's been married more times than Larry King, but then they sober up and divorce him."

"Fuck you, Delgado." Satars was a tall, pale scarecrow of a man with a sour expression.

"Get you something to drink?" Gilliam asked.

"I'll take a beer," Evans replied.

Gilliam made a motion for a draft to a waitress standing over next to the bar. He turned back to Evans. "Hey, sorry things got a little testy the other day at Tony's funeral."

Evans looked at Satars. "Yeah, well, your boy here made it sound like I let Tony's shooter get away."

"I just asked why you didn't take the shot . . ."

"There were kids . . ."

"Yeah, well . . ."

"Knock it off, Joe." Gilliam gave Satars a hard look before turning back to Evans. "Sorry, Eddie. Sometimes my friend here acts like he watches too many cop shows on television instead of just being a cop." He paused and gave Satars another meaningful look. "No one who knows shit blames you for not shooting when there were kids and other people around. We're all just hot because of what happened to Tony."

Evans continued to glare at Satars but relaxed when his beer arrived. "No one is hotter than me," he said. "I loved that guy."

Gilliam patted him on the back. "No one doubts it. Good kid, too. I worked with his dad some when I was on patrol. Good man all around, a crying shame he's lost two boys now to terrorists."

"Hey, I lost a partner, too," Delgado said. "A junkie stabbed him when we were walking a beat in the Bronx."

Evans took a sip of his beer. He was quiet for a moment, then shook his head. "That would be almost easier to take than this. Don't mean any disrespect, it must have been tough on you, too. But I think I could handle it better if he'd been stabbed by a junkie, or shot during a holdup, or a thousand other things that happen to cops every day. But this . . . this waiting for him to get done playing basketball with kids, and then shooting him down for no reason. There's just something different about it."

"The world is changing, brother," Gilliam said.

"Damn straight," Delgado added. "They're hunting cops, and it's goddamn time we do something about it."

Gilliam made a motion to Delgado, who sat back and picked up his beer. "What do you hear about Tony's shooter?" Gilliam asked Evans.

"Not much. You got anything?"

"A little," Gilliam said. "I've been checking in with Homicide over at the Two-Five. I heard they got some touch DNA from the perp off of Tony's shirt. And a pretty good physical description from that kid."

"Tyrone."

"Yeah, Tyrone. Apparently, his grandmother took him straight to the DA's office, so I haven't seen the report. But they're looking for this guy Nat X who's been bragging about it on television."

"That son of a bitch Peter Vansand could help us catch him," Delgado spat.

"But he won't," Satars hissed. "It would violate his 'journalist's ethics,' whatever the fuck that means."

"I'd like to stick his ethics—" Delgado began, but Gilliam silenced him again with a look.

"As I said, we're all tired of it," Gilliam said. "And it's not just the nutjobs like this Nat X. These so-called activists like Mufti and Sefu are stirring them up, making it seem like killing cops is something good for the black community."

"I heard one of them was arrested at the riot the other night for assaulting a cop," Evans noted.

"Yeah, this punk Sefu, whose name apparently means 'sword of faith' or some mumbo jumbo like that; real name is Todd Reade, a former community college rabble-rouser, started the Manhattan version of Black Justice Now. He's cooling his heels in the Tombs on the assault rap."

Evans frowned. "He didn't make bail?"

"Apparently he hasn't tried," Gilliam said. "He's playing up the 'political prisoner' bit."

"Anybody talk to him?"

"The guys from the Two-Five tried. No go."

"Somebody ought to make him," Satars snarled. "Him and Mufti are no better than terrorists, and we should be treating them like that."

Evans was quiet for a moment. "So why'd you ask me to come here tonight?"

Gilliam put down his beer. "We're thinking we need to start sending our own messages. Knowing how you felt about Tony, I thought maybe you'd want to join us."

"And do what?"

Delgado piped up. "These guys like Mufti and Sefu do a lot of lying about cops. We'll be sending them strong messages very soon."

Evans frowned. "What do you mean, messages?"

"Eye for an eye," Satars said.

Gilliam looked around and then leaned toward Evans. "We don't want this to be a white-versus-black thing. We want this to be cops standing up for other cops. That's why we want you to join us. Maybe with the right people, this goes nationwide, every department."

"We put the fear of God in a few of these loudmouths who make psychopaths like Nat X into heroes, and turn this thing around," Delgado added.

"You in or out?" Satars asked.

Evans looked from face to face to face, then raised his beer. "I'm in."

The other three raised their glasses. "Here's to the thin blue line," Gilliam toasted.

"To the thin blue line," the others echoed.

9

Big George waited in the dark outside for an hour until he saw Ny-Lee Tomes leave the building where his girlfriend, Rose, lived with her sister, Lupe. He followed Tomes, waiting for the right moment. He knew the routes Tomes took when he returned to the apartment he was currently sharing with Nat X, and had a place in mind for what he intended.

Then one more visit and we all done, the big man thought with satisfaction. He was looking forward to it. In that, he and Nat X were alike: they both enjoyed hurting other people. He didn't know about all this "black nationalism" that Nat X spouted, but it sounded good. He didn't like white people, unless it was to rob and rape them, and he hated the cops, so any talk about killing them met with his approval. But he would have been happy to kill anybody, even black folks, as he didn't like most of them much, either.

In his mind, Ny-Lee Tomes was a punk who stood between him and something he wanted. He'd had his eye on Rose since meeting her and couldn't understand why she'd reject a real man like him over a skinny little nobody like Ny-Lee. Well, one way or the other, when Ny-Lee was out of the picture she'd be made to see the light.

All of his life he used his size and propensity toward violence to intimidate other people and get what he wanted. It had started with kids in school; he would take their lunch money and bully them on the playground. When he was fifteen, he'd been sent to jail after he beat one of his mother's many boyfriends almost to death with a crowbar. Not that he cared that much about his mother—hadn't even cried when she OD'd on heroin a year later—but the man had looked at him funny and got a cracked skull as a result.

When he got out of jail, he'd been recruited by one of the many gangs in the neighborhood. But he was more of a loner and didn't go for all that gang love shit, nor did he like being subservient to the group's hierarchy. So he'd gone his own way, and when they tried to force him back in, he'd killed two of them. He had been left alone ever since.

In fact, he hadn't thought much of Nat X when he showed up and started talking about how he was going to take over Harlem and lead a revolution. But Nat X had treated him with respect, even telling him his real name, and he'd been caught up in the idea of a violent revolution, especially as it involved killing cops. Nat X had promised him that he'd be a general in the Nat Turner Revolutionary Brigade. "You'll have any bitch you want, as many as you want," the man had promised. That sounded good, and Big George, while no scholar, was smart enough to know that his violence could use some direction.

Still, there'd come a point after a few weeks where he grew tired of all the meetings and talk with other young men and teenagers. He decided to challenge Nat X for leadership, if for no other reason than to impress Rose. But then his man had shot the cop. *And that was damn cold*, he thought as he followed along behind Ny-Lee Tomes. *Got to give props for that.*

Nat X had impressed him again when he talked that kid into shooting a cop, even though it didn't turn out exactly the way he'd planned. They'd waited in the alley until they heard the shots, Big George and Nat, and figured the kid had ambushed two of the pigs. Instead, he staggered out the door, blood gushing from a chest wound. The kid collapsed dead in the gutter.

Nat X had immediately grabbed the gun out of the kid's hand and put it in his own waistband under his sweatshirt. "You stay here," he told Big George, "and when people start showing up, yell that the cops killed an unarmed kid."

There was only one hitch. Just as Nat X was about to walk off, they noticed a haggard white woman poking her head around the corner of the alley next to the building. Who knew where she'd been before they saw her, but she was looking at them now and had to have seen Nat X take the gun.

"I'll take care of this," Nat X said to Big George, and yelled at the woman, "Hey, come here." But her face disappeared and Nat X had to run after her as she fled down the alley.

In the meantime, a crowd gathered, and Big George had played up his role so well that there'd been a riot. A few days later, he'd fired up the crowd even more when he was invited to speak at the "peace rally" in Marcus Garvey Park. He'd surprised even Reverend Mufti when he'd called on the assembly to "burn it down," and they responded with an all-out riot.

He got his lick in, too. When he saw a cop chase down and try to arrest the leader of the Black Justice Now crowd, he jumped the officer from behind, ripped his helmet off, and battered his head into the sidewalk until the man was unconscious. Newspapers said the cop was still in intensive care, and that made him feel proud.

Later, Big George got to thinking about the woman in the alley and worried she might say something. But Nat X had blown off his concern. "I tried to catch up to her, but she disappeared down some dark hole," he said. "Doesn't matter, she's just some homeless old hag. No one would listen to her if she did try to rat us out." But Nat X didn't blow off the matter of Tyrone Greene witnessing the shooting of Cippio. It wouldn't take much to get a kid to talk.

Then Maurice Greene had showed up at Ny-Lee's apartment. "Well, little man, where you been?" Nat X had asked. He was smiling but his voice was hard.

"My grandmother's been making me come home straight from school and not letting me go out," Maurice replied. "Not after my little brother was at the park and saw you . . ."

Nat X's face hardened. "Saw me what? He didn't see shit."

"Yeah, no . . . I know he's just a kid," Maurice stammered. "But he talked to the district attorney—"

"What he tell him?" Nat X interrupted.

"Just what he saw. And about your talks in the neighborhood."

"What else?" Nat X lifted his sweatshirt to partly reveal the silver revolver. "And don't you lie to me."

"I wouldn't," Maurice replied, obviously frightened. "He described you a little bit."

"Your little brother talks too much."

"He don't mean nothing by it," Maurice said. "He's just a dumb kid."

Nat X stood up from the couch he'd been sitting on and walked over to Maurice until their faces were only inches apart. "Yeah? And what about you, Maurice? Your grandma tells you what to do. Did she tell you to talk to the district attorney, too?"

Maurice swallowed hard. "She wanted me to, but I didn't tell them anything."

Glaring at the teen, Nat X asked, "You hear about what happened to your friend Ricky Watts?"

"I heard he got shot by a cop," Maurice replied, his eyes welling with tears.

"That's right," Nat X agreed. "Shot in cold blood. Didn't even have a gun. We're at war, you hear me, boy?"

"Yes, sir."

"People get killed in wars. And you better remember that. You talk to DeShawn? I ain't seen him, either."

Maurice shook his head. "No. He's not answering his phone."

Nat X nodded. "Well, if you do talk to him, you remind him of what I just told you. People get killed in wars, and he needs to keep his mouth shut. Or Big George here might be paying y'all a visit. Understand?"

"Yes, sir."

Big George noticed that Maurice's visit seemed to rattle Nat X. He started talking about leaving town and going back to the Bay Area, to "get things going there." He acted like it was all part of the plan, but Big George thought he was getting nervous. Nat X had been on the television a lot with that Vansand, and even though he'd been careful not to show his face and had disguised his voice, he worried that the newsman might try to set him up.

Nat X said he would leave Big George in charge of the Brigade in New York while he was gone. Big George wondered aloud if his absence might make the younger sister Nat X had been bedding, Lupe, available.

"No, I'm taking that ho with me," Nat X said with a laugh. "Nights get cold around the Bay. But if you play your cards right, I think Rose can be your woman."

"What about Ny-Lee?" Big George asked.

Nat X looked thoughtful as he took a long drag on a joint. "I think maybe Ny-Lee needs to have an accident. He keeps making too many mistakes, like telling people my name. I think if the cops ever grabbed him, he'd sing like a bird."

It had taken Big George a moment to catch Nat X's drift, then he raised an eyebrow. "But he's your cousin."

Nat X shrugged. "I hardly know him. He's just the kid of my mother's sister. You're more my blood brother than he is."

Big George had liked that. He didn't have any brothers or sisters, at least none he knew about. After that, he'd have done just about anything for the leader of the Nat Turner Revolutionary Brigade.

"There's some loose ends that need to be tied up around here," Nat X had said. "Ny-Lee, Maurice, DeShawn. I think they all know too much. And maybe Rose, when you're done with her. I've even been working on a surprise for the fucking district attorney—what's his name?"

"Karp," Big George said.

"Yeah, Karp. I ain't happy he's taking his sweet time to charge that cop for shooting poor ol' Ricky!"

Big George was impressed. Shooting cops was one thing; taking on the DA was another. "What you got planned?"

"Never you mind," Nat X replied. "Better for you if you don't know. But if Oliver Gray needs some help sometime, you'll know it has to do with this. Catch my meaning, bro?"

BIG GEORGE CERTAINLY had caught his meaning, especially about tying up loose ends, which was why he was following Nat X's cousin. When Ny-Lee was just about to reach an alley entrance he'd selected, he called out.

Ny-Lee jumped like someone had shot at him. He turned with his eyes big as saucers. But when he saw Big George, he relaxed. "Hey, man, what you doing in this neighborhood?"

"Just visiting a friend," Big George responded with the obligatory handshakes. "Saw you walking ahead of me and hurried to catch up. Where you heading?"

"Just back to the apartment," Ny-Lee said, then grinned. "That Rose, she about wears me to a frazzle. I need to get me some sleep."

"Well, then I don't suppose you'll be wanting any of this fine blow." Big George pulled a small vial of cocaine out of his pocket.

Ny-Lee's affection for the drug was well known, though he rarely had money for it. "Well, now you put it that way. Maybe a snort or two and a couple of cold ones would hit the spot. I said I was tired, but not *that* tired," he said with a grin.

Big George also smiled. "Yeah, that sounds good. Let's duck into the alley so we don't get spotted."

Ny-Lee guffawed. "Ain't nobody in this neighborhood going to care. And who's going to fuck with you anyway?"

"Just the same," Big George said. "Nat X wants us to lay low. He's worried the cops will be looking for us and doesn't want us to draw attention to ourselves."

Ny-Lee cast a glance over each shoulder and nodded. "That's good thinking," he said, and led the way into the alley.

When they reached a spot in the shadows, Big George fumbled the vial of coke and dropped it on the ground. "Oh, shit, you see it?" he asked.

"Yeah, it's right here." Ny-Lee bent over to pick it up. He never saw the lead-weighted sap that cracked his skull and drove him into the ground. And he was still barely conscious when Big George rolled him over and straddled him with his plate-sized hands around his neck. He woke up just long enough to feel his windpipe crushed before returning to the blackness.

Big George retrieved his vial of coke from the clutched hand of the dead man and got up. *One more visit, and I'll do a little snort myself*, he thought.

TEN MINUTES LATER, Big George was standing in the doorway of an abandoned building across the street from the small walk-up where Nevie Butler lived with Maurice and Tyrone. He'd tried the door of the building and it gave with just a little force. Inside was nothing but empty rooms and rats. Perfect for his needs. He took out his cell phone and dialed a number.

"Maurice," he hissed, "you know who this is. Come outside. I got a message for you from Nat X. Come alone."

It took several minutes for the teen to come out the door and slowly walk down the steps. He looked nervously both ways.

Big George whistled to draw Maurice's attention and then stepped farther back into the shadows of the doorway. The teen crossed the street and approached him.

"What's up?" Maurice asked, trying to sound less nervous than he obviously felt.

"Time's up," the giant replied. "For you, your grandma, and brother, too."

Maurice turned to run, but Big George was faster than he looked and was on him in a flash. His massive arm went around the boy's neck as he pulled him into the building. He'd kill him there and then go across the street to deal with the other two. The stranglehold had the desired effect, and Maurice slumped to the ground, unconscious.

Big George was about to finish him off just like Ny-Lee when he became aware of a horrendous odor, and a snuffling, shuffling sound behind him. He whirled and found himself facing what looked like an enormous bear in human clothing standing next to a much smaller man. "Who the fuck are you?" he snarled.

"Well . . . shithead bastard whoop whoop . . . my name's Warren, Dirty Warren to my friends, which you definitely are not," said the smaller man. "And this here . . . oh boy oh boy . . . is Booger. Oh, and by the way, fuck you, too."

"'eah, 'uck you," the bear-man said.

"Goddamn, he smells bad," Big George complained. "Get out of here and forget you ever saw anything, or I'll kill both of you."

"I'm afraid we can't do that and . . . whoop nuts balls . . . I'm afraid you won't be going anywhere, either," Dirty Warren said. "You see, we were just making sure you didn't hurt the boy until . . . oh boy oh boy son of a bitch . . . someone else got here."

"You got a worse mouth than me, motherfucker," Big George said. "But it won't make no difference—two of you, three—'cause I got my little friend here." With that, he pulled a gun from his waistband.

Booger, or the Walking Booger, as he was called, started to come at him, but Warren put a hand on his arm. "Wait, Booger, he wants this one himself . . . whoop."

Despite the gun in his hand, Big George felt a chill run up his spine. "Who you talkin' about, fool," he snarled. But the chill didn't dissipate; instead it seemed to grow and was punctuated by a voice, cold and dispassionate, behind him.

"Me," was all it said.

Without knowing why, terror gripped Big George's heart as he turned to meet the threat. He was surprised that the voice's owner was so close. He found himself looking into the pale and haggard face of a man whose sunken eyes burned with madness. "Repent," the apparition whispered.

"What the fu—" Big George gasped as something pierced his enormous stomach and sliced up into his rib cage, then down, where it cut first left, then right. He tried to raise his gun, but the odiferous monster behind him held his arm in a grip so tight he couldn't move.

The apparition stepped back, watching Big George whimper as he felt his intestines slide out of his body just before he fell to the ground.

"Good evening . . . oh boy ohhhhh boy . . . David," Dirty Warren said to the apparition, who had bent over his prey to wipe the blood off the blade of his long knife. "Glad you showed up . . . asswipe bitch . . . though I'm sure Booger could have handled him."

"I'm sure of it, too," David Grale replied. "But better that this demon's blood is on my hands. Now I would guess that the danger has passed and we may all retire for the night."

"Good . . . whoop whoop . . . I was getting hungry," Warren said. "'ooger 'ungry, too."

"Then enjoy your dinners, my friends," Grale said just as a groan escaped from the teenager lying on the ground. "I suggest we leave quickly."

When Maurice Greene woke up, he felt something warm and wet and sticky on his face and hands. He sat up, and in the half-light of a streetlamp outside, saw the prone body of Big George. Then he noticed that he was sitting in a pool of the dead man's blood.

That's when he started screaming.

10

CLAY FULTON REACHED INSIDE HIS JACKET AND FELT FOR the security of his holstered 9 mm as he waited at the bottom of a flight of stairs leading to the sixth floor. Not that he thought he was going to need it. Lined up on the stairs above him and on the landing outside an apartment rented, according to the building's superintendent-landlord, to one Ny-Lee Tomes, eight heavily armed members of an NYPD Emergency Services Unit prepared to execute a no-knock warrant.

Earlier that morning, as he'd briefed the unit, Fulton impressed upon them the importance of taking the occupants of the apartment alive, if any were present. "I don't want any officer to hesitate if it means protecting himself or a fellow officer," he'd said. "But there's a lot at stake and we need defendants, not bodies."

There was no need to elaborate. Every officer knew that with the city on a razor's edge because of the shootings of Tony Cippio and Ricky Watts, the last thing Gotham's nervous citizenry needed was another riot. Some were just looking for an excuse; to them, Nat X was a hero. It didn't help that his take on black liberation theology to justify a war on police, along with Reverend Mufti's passive-aggressive rhetoric rationalizing his actions, had been picked up in the media's narrative. Just the night before, Nat X had made another appearance on Peter Vansand's television program, in which he'd predicted his own death at the hands of the police. "They will not take me alive," the man in the mask had warned. "Even if I tried to surrender, I wouldn't live long enough to see a trial."

Now, Detective Fulton and his boss, DA Butch Karp, hoped that with his capture, they could prove him wrong and expose him and his cause in open court.

THE EVENTS THAT led to the ESU readying to enter Ny-Lee's apartment had begun the night before, when Nevie Butler called him at his home as he was relaxing in front of the television with his wife. He'd given Mrs. Butler his direct line when she brought her grandsons to talk to Karp, instructing her to call him "anytime" if there was an issue.

Apparently, there was an issue—he could hear someone screaming hysterically in the background as Butler tried to explain why she was calling. "Detective Fulton, I am so sorry to trouble you at this hour," she said calmly, considering what she was about to impart. "But I'm afraid we have a problem, a bad problem. A man just tried to kill my grandson Maurice. I'm not quite clear what happened after that because Maurice is beside himself, but apparently that man is now dead."

Fulton sat up. "Did you call the police?"

"No. I thought I should call you first. Given the circumstance, I wanted to talk to somebody I could trust. What do you want me to do?"

"First, are you safe?"

Butler hesitated. "As safe as we can be in this neighborhood behind a locked door. But I'm scared, though I'm trying not to let the boys see that I am."

"Where is the man who tried to kill your son? Is he there in the apartment?"

"No, he's apparently in an abandoned building across the street. It used to be a clothing store, but it's empty now. All I know is that Maurice got a phone call last night, and when I wasn't looking, he sneaked out of the house. I was about to go out looking for him when he came running back in hollering and looking like he was being chased by ghosts. He told me that some man named Big George—I'm guessing it's the same man that Tyrone mentioned to you and Mr. Karp—had knocked him out, but when he woke up, the man was dead. My boy's got blood all over himself."

As the woman talked, Fulton walked to his bedroom and changed into his work clothes. The mention of Big George had him on high alert. It didn't surprise him that whoever killed Tony Cippio would try to silence any witnesses—that's why he and Karp had offered extra police presence. But if not the cops, who'd saved the boy?

"I'm on my way," Fulton told Butler. "But it's going to take me a half hour to get there. In the meantime, I'm going to have marked patrol cars sent to your address from your local precinct because they can get there faster. I'll make sure that the officers are told not to contact you; they'll be outside for your protection and also to check on the man across the street and if necessary protect any evidence there. Are you sure you're okay?"

"Yes, but please get here faster because this isn't going to be a secret for long."

"I'm afraid that can't be helped. But we will protect you and the boys. How is Maurice now? Was that him I heard when I called?"

"Yes," Butler said. "He was hysterical. He's calmed down some now, but he's curled in a ball and won't talk to me."

"I'm sure he's in shock," Fulton said. "So I'm also going to ask for a paramedic to come to your apartment to check on him. Okay?"

"Yes, please, I don't know what to do for him."

After repeating that he was on his way, Fulton hung up and called Karp, filling him in on what he knew.

"I'll leave right away and meet you uptown," Karp said.

"You'll probably beat me there. Be careful. Apparently Big George is no longer a threat, but we have no idea who killed him or why. And we don't know where Nat X is."

With a blue light on top of his car, Fulton drove as fast as traffic would allow from his home in Brooklyn to Harlem. As he pulled up, he noted the police presence and the ambulance parked in front of a dilapidated walk-up that he surmised was the Butler residence. He also saw that the building across the street had been cordoned off with crime scene tape as investigators came and went. A crowd had gathered at both ends of the street beyond the police barricades.

Fulton walked up to a uniformed police captain. "Detective Fulton with the DA's office," he introduced himself. "I got the call from the woman inside, Nevie Butler. How's it going?"

"Reminds me of the bad old days of Fort Apache in the Bronx," the captain replied. "A lot of hostility out here, Detective. It looked like it might get out of hand earlier, but Mrs. Butler came out and told the crowd that everything was okay and for them to go home. Most are still here, but it seemed to calm them down a little bit. Meanwhile, other than letting her know we're watching the entrances to the building, we've left her alone as instructed."

"What about across the street?"

The captain made a face. "Pretty messy. We got an unknown stiff, black male, somebody gutted him like a tuna at the Fulton Fish Market. Crime scene techs and an assistant medical examiner are in there doing their thing. Here's your boss."

Fulton turned to see the tall figure of Butch Karp walking toward him. "Hey, Butch, where do you want to start?"

Karp nodded toward the abandoned building. "The paramedics are checking on Maurice now. He's in a bad way, and I'm not sure we're going to get anything out of him tonight. So let's see what we got and then check on him and Nevie."

The crime scene was still being processed when they entered the building. Walking carefully, a photographer was taking pictures of a large pool of blood that surrounded an enormous young black man who lay in the middle of it.

"Hi, Al," Karp said to the NYPD photographer, whom he'd known for several decades. "What do you have . . . other than the obvious?"

"Just trying to get a good photo of some imprints in the blood," Al said. "In addition to the deceased, it looks like we have at least three others. One I'm assuming is the kid from across the street; you can see where he was lying down, his handprints, and tennis prints. Then there's those large prints there; they're rather indistinct, as if whoever stood there wraps his shoes or feet in rags. Then there are these I'm photographing now. Look like boots—hobnailed boot imprints, you can see the nail heads, sort of old-fashioned. He and the deceased were apparently standing face-to-face. The other big guy, the one with the rags on his feet, was behind the deceased when he went down."

"Ugh! What's that smell?" Fulton asked. He'd been at enough crime scenes to recognize the sweet, slightly metallic scent of fresh blood and the stench when a victim's entrails have been sliced open, but this was different. "Smells like something rotten."

Karp didn't answer, though a funny look had passed across his face. Instead, he turned to a detective who was looking at a wallet. "What do you have, Detective?"

"Looks like the deceased was one George Washington Parker, age twenty-seven, late of 110 West 151st in Harlem," the detective responded. "At least that's according to his government-issued identification card. No driver's license."

Karp looked at Fulton with a raised eyebrow at the mention of the deceased's name. "Big George," he said, then turned and walked over to a woman who was talking into a tape recorder. She stopped speaking when he approached.

"Hi, Gail," he greeted Assistant Medical Examiner Gail Manning. "You were on call tonight."

"Yeah, I'm basically on the 'gun and knife club' shift these days. But I like it. It gives me time to be with the grandkids during the day while their mother and father work."

"So which is it," Karp asked, raising an eyebrow, "gun or knife?"

"Other than the obvious, I'll know more when I get the body downtown for an autopsy. But, as you can see, he was essentially disemboweled by what I'm guessing was an extremely sharp and large blade of some sort. I didn't want to move him too much until we're ready to bag him and go, but there appears to be one entry wound with several tracks, one cut up, starting just below his navel, then back down and cutting left and right. He's basically lying on top of a pile of his intestines. That takes strength and technique from whoever did this."

Having seen enough, Karp and Fulton left the crime scene and walked across the street. They knocked on Nevie Butler's door.

"Good evening, Mr. Karp, Detective Fulton," she said, her voice trembling. "This is all so horrible."

"Good evening, Mrs. Butler, we're glad you called," Fulton responded. "We're here to help and get to the bottom of this. Where are your grandsons?"

"They're in their rooms. Tyrone is scared, but he's okay. Maurice, however, is a mess. He hasn't said a word after he stopped screaming and told me what happened. Just sort of has a terrified look on his face. The paramedic is with him now, says he's in shock and they want to take him to the hospital."

"What can you tell us?" Karp asked.

"Well, he says he got a call from Big George saying to meet him across the street," Butler said. "And I know he snuck out of the apartment when I was taking my bath. He says that this Big George told him he was going to kill him and me and Tyrone. And that's all he remembers until he woke up next to a dead man with blood all over."

Nevie Butler stopped for a moment, and her eyes welled with tears. "Mr. Karp . . . you don't think . . . that my grandson killed that man, do you?"

Karp shook his head. "We can't be sure until our investigation is complete, and I've had a chance to talk to Maurice, but we believe that someone else killed the man across the street. Do you have any idea who else might have been involved?"

"No, no idea." She shook her head.

At that moment, a paramedic came out from a back bedroom. "How is he?" Karp asked.

"In shock, traumatized, showing classic signs of PTSD," the paramedic said. "Nonverbal. He started to get agitated so we gave him a sedative. We'd like to move him to Bellevue for psychiatric evaluation."

"Can I talk to him?"

The paramedic shrugged. "You can try, but I don't think you're going to get anywhere right now between his state of mind and the sedative."

As the paramedic predicted, Maurice either couldn't or wouldn't cooperate. He just looked at them blankly when they entered the room and then closed his eyes.

The paramedic and his partner arrived with a gurney. "Okay to take him?"

After assuring Nevie Butler that she and Tyrone would be kept safe with a police presence and that Maurice would be well cared for, Karp and Fulton left the scene. But instead of going home, they went to the Criminal Courts Building, where they worked the rest of the night.

In the ensuing hours, the dominoes continued to fall. The police had gone to the apartment listed on the deceased's identification card. The current tenants, who had been living there for several months, said they didn't know anyone named George Washington Parker, or Big George, but that the last tenant had left the place a mess.

The homicide detectives working the scene also called in and confirmed that the dead man's telephone proved that he called the number for Maurice Greene that evening close to Gail Manning's estimated time of death.

A quick check revealed that George Washington Parker had a

rap sheet with convictions ranging from armed robbery and aggravated assault to manslaughter. "He's basically bounced in and out of the system since he was a kid," Fulton said. "And those are only the charges that stuck. He was a suspect in a dozen more, including murder."

A big break came after Fulton suddenly left Karp's office and returned ten minutes later. He was smiling grimly. "I knew there was something familiar about the name George Washington Parker," he said, "but I couldn't quite put my finger on it. Then I remembered where I heard the name. George Washington Parker, same address, was the first witness to reach Ricky Watts, the kid shot by Officer Kim. I called the detective working the case and asked him to read me the report. According to Parker, he was outside the tenement when he heard a single shot and then Watts staggered out the door and collapsed at the curb. He stated that Watts didn't have a gun."

"Quite the coincidence," Karp remarked.

"Yeah, and the detective told me that Parker was also involved in inciting the riot that night."

Karp thought about the implications. "So we have Tyrone Greene placing Big George Parker, if this is the same guy, with Nat X at Marcus Garvey Park when Tony Cippio was shot. We also have Parker at the building where Ricky Watts was shot by an officer who claims that Watts shot first. And now Parker shows up and threatens to kill Maurice Greene, his brother, and grandmother, but is instead disemboweled by a person or persons unknown."

"What do you want to do next?" Fulton asked.

Karp thought about it for a moment. "Let's put together a photo lineup including George Washington Parker and see if Tyrone Greene can pick him out." He picked up the telephone and called Bellevue to speak to the psychiatrist evaluating Maurice Greene.

Two hours later, the district attorney and the chief of his detective squad made their way to Bellevue's psychiatric ward. After speaking to the psychiatrist, who asked them to keep the questioning short, Karp and Fulton entered the room where Maurice Greene lay in a bed, with his grandmother sitting in a chair next to him. "Maurice, do you remember who we are?" Karp asked.

Maurice nodded. "Yes, sir," he answered, which was a good sign.

"We'd like to ask you some questions about what happened last night," Karp began, "but first I'd like you to look at some photographs and let me know if any of them look familiar to you."

Karp handed the file containing the photo lineup to the teenager. It took him only a few moments before he closed the file. "Number three, that's Big George," he said.

"Do you know him by any other name?"

"No, just Big George."

"Was he the man who attacked you last night?"

"Yes. He said he was going to kill me, Tyrone, and my granny. He put his arm around my neck and I guess I blacked out because the next thing I know I"—the boy stopped talking and choked up—"the next thing I know I woke up and I could feel something sticky on my face and my hands. It was dark so it took me a minute to see him—"

"See who?"

"Big George. He was lying on his stomach. His eyes were open but he was dead."

"Did you see anybody else?"

Maurice hesitated and then shuddered. "I thought I saw something in the shadows at the back of the room. It moved and I started to scream and got up and ran back across the street. I don't remember much else." He trembled.

"Maurice," Karp said, "just a couple more questions. How do you know Big George?"

Maurice took a deep breath, held it, and let it go with a sigh. It was obvious he was conflicted, but at last he said, "I know him from Nat X."

Karp and Fulton looked quickly at each other. "Nat X?" Karp asked, to keep him going.

"Yeah, Big George was sort of his bodyguard. I attended some meetings."

"Do you know Nat X's full, or real, name?"

Maurice shook his head. "No, he never told us."

"Do you know Ricky Watts?"

This time the teen's eyes filled with tears; he had a hard time answering. "He was my friend," he blurted out. "I've known him since elementary school before he started going to that charter school. But we stayed friends."

"Did Ricky Watts know Big George and Nat X, too?"

Maurice nodded as his face flushed and tears crept from his eyes. "Yeah, he went to some of the same meetings I did." He started to cry.

Karp waited for him to pull himself together, then said, "Maurice, I know this isn't easy, but I need to find Nat X."

Maurice turned his head to the side so he wouldn't have to look at Karp.

"Maurice? Do you know where we can find Nat X?"

The teen turned back to look at him but remained quiet until his grandmother prodded him. "Maurice, son, you answer the man," she said gently. "I know you made promises, but promises to bad men are bad promises. This man sent his evil friend to do you harm, and to harm your brother and me. He's not somebody you should protect."

Maurice looked at his grandmother and finally spoke. "I'm not sure," he said. "But I could sometimes find him living at his cousin's apartment."

"What's his cousin's name?"

"Ny-Lee Tomes. He lives on the corner of 134th and Malcolm X Boulevard, Browning Apartments, sixth floor."

And that was how Fulton found himself at the end of a line of the Emergency Services Unit, which most police departments referred to as a SWAT team, waiting to bust into an apartment where they hoped to find a cop killer. But first other members of the unit were quietly evacuating apartments on either side and above and below the target in case bullets started to fly.

They were just about ready to go when a woman's scream from inside the apartment made the decision for them. "Go! Go! Go!" shouted the officer in charge of the unit.

Team members swung a battering ram twice at the door before

the doorjamb shattered. They stepped back as other officers, their guns raised, swarmed the room.

"Police officers! Hands where we can see them! Get down!" they shouted to some unknown person.

Fulton entered the apartment, where a woman sat on the floor with her hands above her head looking at a television and moaning. Meanwhile, the other officers moved quickly through the apartment.

"Clear!" they shouted as they went from room to room until they determined there was no one else present.

The woman was crying, "Oh, Ny-Lee, Ny-Lee . . . what did they do to you?"

"Where's Ny-Lee?" Fulton asked.

The woman pointed at the television screen. A news crew was broadcasting from the street where the police had an alleyway cordoned off with crime scene tape. "We are standing outside of an alley," the reporter said, "where an hour ago the body of a man identified as Ny-Lee Tomes was found stuffed in a Dumpster. According to a police source who asked not to be identified, the victim appears to have been strangled and his neck broken."

"Miss," Fulton said, squatting in front of the woman, "what's your name?"

She sniffled. "Rose Torres."

"Miss Torres, how do you know Ny-Lee Tomes?"

"He was my boyfriend. We was going to get married." She began to cry. "I came over this morning when he didn't answer his phone. He always took my calls, no matter what."

"I'm sorry for your loss," Fulton said. "Do you know who might have wanted to harm Ny-Lee?"

"Oh, yeah," the woman said, her face suddenly contorting with anger. "I know who did this. It was Nat X. Maybe he had his thug Big George do it, but it was Nat X who had it done. I hope he rots in hell."

11

KARP FINISHED SHAVING AND EMERGED FROM THE BATH-
room, where he found Marlene standing at the island in their
kitchen watching the morning news.

He hadn't talked to her since getting the call from Fulton two
nights earlier that brought him to the scene of Big George Parker's
demise.

The pace had picked up after Fulton called and told him about
the events at Ny-Lee Tomes's apartment and then escorted Rose
Torres down to the office. That had set off another round of interviews and strategizing. By the time they wrapped up, it was midnight. He'd gone home, crawled into bed, kissed his sleeping wife
on the cheek, and fell into exhausted slumber until the alarm went
off at six.

"Good morning, stranger," he said. "What's on the tube?"

Marlene smiled at him over her cup of coffee and shrugged.

"Where shall I start? Maybe the ESU raid in Harlem yesterday that may or may not be tied to a gruesome murder the night before, which may or may not be tied to the shooting of a police officer in Marcus Garvey Park."

"Somebody's talking too much, and it better not be coming out of my office," Karp growled.

"The news guy quoted a 'highly placed' source in the NYPD," she said. "No need to take a rubber hose to Gilbert Murrow."

"Not that he minds the television cameras, but Gilbert's not a rat," Karp said with a smile of his own. "But that reminds me, I've been meaning to ask you about that gruesome murder."

"Oh? And what could I add to what you don't know already?" Marlene asked innocently.

"After Tony Cippio's funeral, you told me that you needed to go see a man about a dog . . ."

"Yes, and you thought it best not to inquire further," Marlene replied pointedly.

"Right," Karp replied. "And maybe I still shouldn't, but this grue-some murder happened across the street from two witnesses in the Cippio case. The 'victim' apparently tried to murder the older boy but was stopped by an assassin."

"Sounds like a Good Samaritan intervened."

"I guess, if Good Samaritans haunt Harlem at night gutting violent three-hundred-pound thugs."

"Times change."

"Uh-huh." Karp wasn't surprised by his wife's reaction. She'd once worked for the New York DAO in the sex crimes unit; it was where they met. But after a letter bomb exploded, blinding her in one eye, followed by years of dealing with serial killers, terrorists, and various other violent characters, she was somewhat jaded. In fact, from time to time she'd met violence with violence and had even owned a VIP security service. Marlene straddled the line between justice and vigilantism, which time and again threatened their marriage. Karp was by the book, and though that crisis had passed and she seemed to have put most of it behind her, he knew it was never that far from the surface.

"Well," he continued, "if I didn't think the coincidence too great, I'd say this, um, Good Samaritan has all the earmarks of your friend David Grale."

"*Our* friend David Grale. He's certainly saved our bacon, and the lives of our children, as well as the citizens of this misbegotten city, enough times to be considered *our* friend."

Karp knew his wife had a point, even though David Grale was a serial killer who had dispatched numerous criminals. "Okay, our friend David Grale. But vigilante justice is still against the laws I'm sworn to uphold."

"Didn't you say this violent thug . . . Big George Parker . . . was trying to murder the witness? I believe the use of lethal force to protect oneself or others from death or serious bodily harm constitutes self-defense."

"You're probably right in that regard," Karp conceded. "But from a prosecutor's standpoint, I would have liked to talk to Big George before a homicidal religious fanatic flayed him like a tuna."

"I'm sure," Marlene agreed. "But perhaps Big George left this

Good Samaritan no choice but to render him harmless. And I think we both know that this particular Good Samaritan might not have the same goals when dealing with killers as the district attorney of New York County. I believe his goals might be to kill them all and let God sort them out later."

Karp caught the edge in Marlene's voice and decided not to press the issue. "In any event, I'm not shedding any tears over Mr. Parker. And I'm glad this 'Good Samaritan' just happened to be in the neighborhood in time to save a teenager's life."

Marlene put her coffee down and walked around the end of the island to stand on her tiptoes and kiss her husband. "Think you're going to be late getting home tonight?"

"I hope not," he said, then wiggled his eyebrows suggestively. "What have you got in mind?"

"Well, the boys are staying with a friend tonight." Marlene giggled, referencing the couple's twin boys, Isaac and Giancarlo. "So I was thinking about throwing together chicken cacciatore and pairing it with a bottle of Chianti, followed by a bubble bath with candles and—"

"I'll be home by seven," Karp interrupted with a laugh and kissed her again. "Now I've got to go, or I might never leave."

Karp waved away the unmarked police car and its occupant at the curb who provided security. The temperature was already rising and it might be the only opportunity for a walk that day in New York, and he enjoyed the walk from Crosby Street to 100 Centre and the Criminal Courts Building. He needed the time to absorb what had happened over the past few days. It felt as if events were moving inexorably toward a conclusion, but he was still missing major pieces to be sure of the outcome.

None too soon, either. The mayor and the City Council were trying to pressure him in regard to indicting Officer Bryce Kim. The city was on edge after the riots, and many of the denizens of Gotham didn't understand what the holdup was when the media and demagogues like Reverend Mufti made it clear that a white cop had used unnecessary deadly force against an unarmed black teenager. Mufti used his position on the Council to further the false narrative, as well as decry the "unjust incarceration of political prisoner" Imani Sefu, while accusing the DAO of "stall tactics."

Karp could not have cared less about what any of them said about how he conducted his business; he was not going to be rushed into indicting anybody based on politics, particularly now that new evidence was coming to light that questioned the narrative about the death of Ricky Watts. But he was conscious of the impact of these wild claims on innocent citizens, as well as the police officers on the front lines during the rioting, and knew that he needed to move as quickly as possible to put all the pieces together.

It came down to finding Nat X—this Anthony last name unknown, if Rose was right—and, if possible, the silver, white-handled revolver. *But where is he?* Karp wondered.

Arriving at 100 Centre Street, Karp walked over to the newsstand where Dirty Warren was involved in a conversation with the Walking Booger. Each of them greeted him in his own inimitable way.

"Hello, gentlemen. Could I trouble you for the morning

newspapers?" Karp said, trying to ignore the pungent aroma of Booger, a scent he was reasonably sure was the same as Fulton had commented on two nights earlier over the body of Big George Parker.

"Sure . . . whoop nuts tits . . . Karp," Warren said. "Seems to have been . . . oh boy ohhhh boy . . . plenty of interesting news lately."

With the little man peering up at him through his filthy glasses, Karp decided to play along. "Always is in Gotham," he said. "That reminds me, where were the two of you a couple of evenings ago?"

Warren and the Walking Booger exchanged an amused glance. "I believe . . . fucker son of a bitch . . . I was at home reading a good book," Warren said.

"I was 'aving 'inner at the 'aldorf 'otel," Booger added, causing them both to break out in gales of merriment.

Karp shook his head and laughed. "Well, that's good, because it can be dangerous wandering the streets. I wouldn't want you two upstanding citizens getting into any sort of trouble."

"I told you coppers . . . oh boy ohhh boy . . . would never get cuffs on me," Warren replied in his best gangster imitation.

Karp rolled his eyes. "Edward G. Robinson in *Little Caesar.* And not a very good impersonation, I might add."

Warren and Booger both guffawed. "I'll . . . asshole whoop whoop . . . work on it next time."

"By the way, have either of you seen David Grale lately?"

"David . . . whoop . . . who?" Warren said, furrowing his brow in mock confusion.

"'avid 'oo?" Booger repeated.

"Never mind, you dirty, double-crossin' rats," Karp said with a laugh.

"James Cagney in *Blonde Crazy* . . . oh boy ohhhh boy . . . 1931!" Warren shouted and high-fived Booger.

"Not bad, Warren, not bad," Karp said.

As he turned to leave, he wondered what the rest of the day would hold.

It started off well enough with a visit from Reverend Jonas Lakes, who arrived in his office with Fulton and a very frightened-looking DeShawn Lakes.

"I believe my son has something to say to you," Reverend Lakes said. "And I believe I might have something to add to his story."

Two hours later, with more pieces of the puzzle in place, Karp had a visit from Fulton, who said he'd just heard from a distraught Rose Torres. "Apparently, when she got home after leaving here yesterday, her sister was nowhere to be found," the detective said. "That in itself wasn't unusual, though she was, of course, worried because of what happened to Ny-Lee, and because Lupe was hooking up with Nat X. When her sister didn't come home this morning, she snooped around a little in her room and discovered that Lupe had packed her things and flown the coop."

"On the move with Nat X?" Karp stated more than asked. He was thinking about the news reports and a fugitive deciding New York City was getting too hot for comfort.

"Looks that way," Fulton said.

"It may be too late," Karp said. "But let's get a BOLO out to the airports to be watching for Lupe Torres. If they're traveling together, he might have false identification, but maybe she didn't have time to get any."

The day got even better after lunch as he was talking to Fulton and connecting evidentiary dots on one of his ubiquitous yellow pads. "Mr. Karp, I have Mr. Jaxon on line two," receptionist Darla Milquetost announced over the intercom.

"Thank you." Karp leaned forward to punch the correct button on the machine. "Hello, Espy, where have you been hiding?"

Jaxon laughed. "Avoiding the Big Apple, that's for sure. But I have some news that I think will make your day."

"You're starting to sound like Clint Eastwood in *Dirty Harry*," Karp said. "So make my day."

"Have you heard from the NYPD lab about the touch DNA found on Tony Cippio's shirt?"

Karp furrowed his brow. "No. I know they're a little backed up. So give, the suspense is killing me."

"Well, after excluding his wife and his partner, our lab was left with genetic skin cell and sweat markers from an unidentified male. We put it in the National Crime Information Center database and got a hit."

Karp felt his heartbeat starting to rise. "Don't keep me waiting, Espy," he pleaded.

"It picked up on an Anthony Johnson, age twenty-five, last known place of residence San Quentin State Prison, where he was doing time for sex assault and burglary. As you know, it's routine to take DNA swabs from every incoming inmate in many states, including California, and then put the information into the database. It appears Mr. Johnson has been doing some traveling."

"That's great, Espy," Karp said. He quickly filled Jaxon in on what had been happening over the previous few days, including Rose's recollection of a party on the night of Cippio's murder and her boyfriend slipping up and referring to Nat X as "Anthony."

"Any word on where he went after San Quentin?" Karp asked.

"Nothing yet," Jaxon replied, "though I have feelers out with some former colleagues in the bureau I trust. But he was picked up for the sex assault in Oakland."

"Thanks, Espy. For a fed, you sometimes do good things." Hanging up, he looked over at Fulton, who'd been following the half of the conversation he could hear. "Know anybody with the Oakland Police Department?" Karp asked.

"As a matter of fact, I do. Want to fill me in on why you're smiling like the proverbial cat that ate the canary?"

"Hmmm? Oh, I was just thinking about dinner tonight. But let me tell you why I asked about the Oakland PD."

An hour later, Karp's evening plans burst faster than the bubbles in Marlene's bathtub when he got a call from Gilbert Murrow. "Apparently the correctional officers at the Tombs made a 'mistake' this morning and left Imani Sefu out in the yard with a white supremacist," his aide-de-camp said. "A lifer called Tiny Adkins, who was here from Attica for resentencing on a manslaughter case. Not only that, but somehow Adkins was carrying a shiv that he used to stab Sefu thirty-nine times before the guards could pull him off. Sefu was dead on the scene."

"A transfer? How the hell did he get a shiv into the Tombs?" Karp demanded.

"Sharpened toothbrush with a rubber glove wrapped around one end for a handle."

Karp groaned. He was sure that Adkins had just lit the fuse on the powder keg that was New York City as soon as news of the murder hit the streets. The previous evening, Reverend Mufti had appeared on Vansand's program, demanding that the charges against Sefu be dropped, as "he acted in self-defense to protect himself from brutal treatment by law enforcement," and that he be released with an apology. Now the only way he was getting out of jail was in a body bag.

An hour later, it was all over the television newscasts, as were calls by Reverend Mufti for people to protest "this heinous assassination and the questions that have come to light." Karp called Marlene and delivered the bad news. "I better stay here," he said. "Tell the boys to keep off the streets, and you, too. I'll have extra patrols outside tonight . . . I'm sorry, babe."

"That's okay," Marlene replied. "The chicken cacciatore will be here tomorrow, and the boys are in Mount Vernon and won't be back for several days. I'll save the bubble bath until Clark Kent has some time for Lois Lane."

Karp had barely hung up when his telephone rang again. It was Eddie Evans.

"Mr. Karp, I think I better come talk to you. It has to do with Imani Sefu."

12

Reverend Hussein "Skip" Mufti exited the dark limousine and walked quickly up to the entrance of the brownstone on 73rd Street on the Upper East Side. He inserted a key in the door and waved to the driver, who flashed his lights and pulled away.

Sitting in an unmarked police car across the street a little ways down the block, Vince Cippio Sr. scowled. "Pretty ritzy neighborhood for a mistress," he said to the man sitting next to him in the backseat.

Jack Gilliam laughed. "He makes a hundred and fifty thousand as a city councilman, but that's not half of it. The guy's crooked as a meth addict's teeth. If you're a businessman and want something done in Harlem—like get a development plan through the so-called land use committee or a liquor license or a gun license—you're going to be laying out some serious dough for

Mufti's retirement account. He's worth millions and can afford to keep his girlfriend happy and far enough away from his wife to be safe."

"So why don't you just nail him for extortion and malfeasance?" Cippio asked. "Seems like that would be a hell of a lot easier than what you got planned."

Gilliam shook his head. "The feds have been after him for years. But the guy's slick. He's stashed the cash somewhere untraceable, probably offshore . . . It's all pretty subtle, like holding out with his buddies voting for some project, then suddenly changing his vote. Or asking for favors without any evidence of money changing hands. Point is, if the feds can't get him, we sure as shit aren't going to with the City Council watching every dime that goes into the department."

"Besides," Joe Satars said from the front passenger seat, "he'd just claim he was being persecuted by racist cops, and the press would come to his rescue. We're going to send these dumb monkeys a message they can't possibly miss. Not after the little incident in the Tombs the other day."

"Dumb monkeys?" Cippio repeated with a scowl.

Gilliam rolled his eyes. "Ignore the racist dumbass," he said. "Joe, how many times have I got to tell you this isn't about your prejudices. It's about the war on cops."

"It sure as hell ain't the Little Sisters of the Poor," Satars retorted. "You got your reasons to hate 'em, I got mine."

"Your reasons are why Eddie Evans didn't throw in with us," Gilliam pointed out. "And we could have used his help."

"Evans? You mean Tony's partner?" Cippio asked. "What's he got to do with this?"

"We were thinking he might join our little club," Gilliam said. "Seeing as how him and Tony were close."

"If they were so close, he should have been with his partner, and maybe nothing would have happened," Johnny Delgado, the driver of the car, remarked.

"Kind of makes you wonder if he was in on it," Satars added.

"I swear to God, you two, if you were any dumber, you'd be a couple of sticks," Gilliam said. "Evans is a good officer. It was a bad situation."

"Just saying that sometimes race is thicker than the blood cops bleed every day to protect people who don't give a damn," Satars said.

"And I'm just saying to keep your yap shut."

The men were quiet for a minute before Cippio spoke again. "So how's this going to go down?"

"Well, our friend the reverend is learning right about now that his girlfriend is not at home," Gilliam replied. "He'll be calling her in five, four, three . . ."

The cell phone next to Gilliam rang.

"You going to answer that?" Cippio asked.

Gilliam shook his head. "No. You see, what that horny little bastard doesn't know is that Miss Lucinda Barnes, age nineteen—"

"And one fine-looking piece of brown ass," Delgado interjected.

"As I was saying, Miss Lucinda Barnes, an illegal immigrant from

Jamaica, was arrested this afternoon with a kilo of cocaine in her possession. She was quite distraught . . .

". . . especially since Joe and Johnny planted the coke in her apartment when she was out yesterday. My two associates here work in narcotics, so procuring the necessary contraband was no problem. Nor was convincing Miss Barnes to accept our offer to leave the country and return home rather than spend the flower of her youth in the Bedford Hills Correctional Facility for Women."

"What if she changes her mind and says something?" Cippio asked.

Satars and Delgado laughed. "Jamaica is the violent crime and murder capital of the Caribbean," Delgado said. "All sorts of bad things can happen down there to an attractive young woman. We have friends with the Kingston Police Department; Joe and I take little vacations down there all the time. They'll look in on her for us."

"You got it all figured out."

"You okay with this?" Gilliam asked, giving him a look. "You can back out now and no one will think less of you. We're doing this for Tony."

Cippio shook his head. "Nah, like I told you the other day. I hold this guy and that asshole Sefu responsible for the murder of my son. They stirred the hatred up; no different than pulling the trigger themselves. I want blood for blood. I didn't know you guys were taking care of things, but I'm grateful that somebody is. I've lost two sons to fucking terrorists, and if I can stop one more father from having to go through what I've gone through, then I'm good with this and what you got done with Sefu."

"That was easy," Satars boasted. "Tiny Adkins is one of the most dangerous and notorious white supremacists in the system, and he runs the meth trade inside the joint. He was only too happy to do us a favor so long as the guards don't check his girlfriend too closely when she comes to visit—if you know what I mean. And I got a cousin works in the Tombs, all he had to do was leave a sharpened toothbrush in Adkins's cell and let them both out in the yard at the same time."

"I thought we weren't going to talk about it," Gilliam growled.

"Ah, what the fuck, Adkins won't talk. He knows he's not getting out and he likes being the big man on the inside," Satars said, "and Vince here, he's one of us."

"You can trust me," Cippio agreed. "Like I said, these guys as good as pointed the gun at my boy's head. Good riddance. But what about the bodyguard in the limo?"

"He comes back promptly at midnight," Gilliam said. "When the reverend doesn't show, he'll go check on him. After that, a friend of ours with the One-Nine Precinct will oversee the investigation."

"Think we'll get away with it?"

"Oh, I'm sure his pals will have their suspicions, and there'll be a hullabaloo," Gilliam said. "But the investigation's going to say suicide. You'll see why in a minute . . . Hold on a moment while I text the reverend." He picked up the cell phone from the seat and began tapping on the screen, speaking as he typed. "I want one million in my account . . . or . . . photos in nightstand go to *Times*."

"What photos?" Cippio said when Gilliam looked up.

"A couple of weeks ago, we put a camera in the bedroom," Delgado replied. "I tell you, for an old bastard, the guy can go to town." He laughed, as did Satars.

"I don't get it. We're just going to blackmail him after all this?" Cippio said, scowling. "I thought—"

"Don't worry," Gilliam said. "You'll get your revenge. The photos are just part of the cover-up. Let's go."

"You going to send that?" Cippio said, nodding at the phone.

"In a minute," Gilliam said, as he and the other two cops got out of the car. Cippio followed them.

Delgado and Satars walked quickly across the dark street. They hesitated under a streetlight, looking around, then disappeared around the side of the building. Gilliam popped the trunk of the car and pulled out a bag. He motioned to Cippio, and they followed the others to the emergency exit at the back of the building.

Using a skeleton key, Satars opened the door. "No camera," Gilliam whispered, pointing to where a security camera would have normally been placed. He then pressed Send on Lucinda Barnes's cell phone.

The men made their way up the stairs to the fourth floor, where a quick scan showed that no one else was present. Satars again slipped the key in the lock, and they swiftly entered the apartment and made their way to the bedroom.

Sitting on the bed, holding a set of photographs and looking dumbfounded, was Reverend Mufti. He looked up. "Who are you?"

Gilliam didn't speak, just reached into the bag and pulled out a length of rope with a noose on one end. At the same moment, he raised a Taser and shot Mufti, who flopped onto the floor and lay there twitching.

Delgado stepped forward and yanked the reverend to his feet. Satars arrived from the kitchen with a chair while Gilliam threw the rope over an exposed beam in the ceiling.

As he was coming to, Mufti realized what was happening. "No, wait!" he cried out. "I can pay you. Look in my suit pocket. The little notebook. It's all my accounts at a bank in the Grand Caymans. There's plenty to go around."

Instead, Satars stuffed a sock in Mufti's mouth, and then the two younger cops lifted him onto the chair. Gilliam threw the noose around the desperately pleading man's neck and pulled it tight, tying the other end around a leg of the bed.

"Want to do the honors?" Gilliam asked Cippio, nodding at the chair.

"Yeah, sure," Cippio said, but instead of kicking the chair out from under Mufti, he pulled a gun from the holster beneath his jacket. "You're under arrest."

"You fucking bastard," Delgado said as he started for Cippio, but he backed off as the barrel swung to point at his face.

"What is this, Vince?" Gilliam asked. "I thought you wanted to avenge Tony?"

"Not like this," Cippio said.

"Fucking nigger lover," Satars spat, but whatever else he was going to say was interrupted by a deep voice behind them.

"You want to repeat that to my face?" Detective Clay Fulton said as he entered the room. Behind him a half dozen detectives from the DA's Office followed with their guns drawn. "Get on your knees and keep your hands where I can see them!"

Cippio removed the noose from around Mufti's neck and helped him step down from the chair. The reverend's eyes were still wide in fear. "They tried to lynch me," he said, pointing a shaking finger at the three rogue cops as they were being cuffed.

"Yes, sir," Fulton replied. "It appeared that way. I'd like you to come down to the station to give a statement."

"What? So you can do me like you did Imani Sefu?"

"No, sir. You're not under arrest. We'd just like to get your statement, then you'll be free to go," Fulton explained.

Mufti was silent and then the realization came over his face. "You knew they were going to do this, and you let them almost do it."

"We knew they planned something," Fulton said, "but we didn't know what. Mr. Cippio here is a former police officer, and he was our guy on the inside. He wasn't going to let you be harmed, and we were listening the whole time."

"A wire? I told you not to trust this son of a bitch," Satars angrily reminded Gilliam.

Gilliam's broad face was red with anger as he turned to Cippio. "You turned on your fellow officers for a piece of trash like this, a man who advocates killing cops? What would your sons say?"

Cippio leaned over until his face was a few inches from Gilliam's. "My sons? Don't talk to me about my sons. My sons wouldn't have wiped their shoes on scumbags like you. You dishonored everything good they stood for; you don't deserve to wear the uniform they died in. It's too bad they won't be able to tell you that themselves, because where you're going after they pull you out of prison in a box is straight to hell."

Fulton placed a hand on Cippio's shoulder. "It's okay, Vince. Your sons are proud of you, and so is every cop who wears the uniform for the right reasons." He turned to his men. "Get this trash out of here."

13

THE RAGGEDY WOMAN SCURRIED ALONG THE DARK STREETS, casting frequent fearful glances over her shoulder and peering anxiously into the shadows as she passed alleys. This wasn't her usual part of town; she preferred north of Central Park, in Harlem, even though beneath the layer of grime she was white. It just seemed that most of the people there didn't look down on her as much as they did in the wealthier parts of Manhattan like Chelsea, the Village, or here on the edge of SoHo.

Actually, the woman wished she didn't have to wander at night looking for the—she stopped and looked at the note she'd scribbled on the palm of her hand—*Housing Works Bookstore . . . near Crosby and Prince.* But she'd seen something and her conscience was guiding her feet. Oh, she tried to ignore it, forget about what she'd seen. She told herself that nobody would believe her anyway and that it would be dangerous to talk. Not just because of what she saw, and who was involved, but because a street person talking to the authorities might get her killed just as a matter of principle. Snitches couldn't be trusted.

Yet not doing anything ate at her, reminded her of what she had been, not who she had become. She'd known the truth and had said nothing. In the meantime, people had rioted and people had been hurt. She blamed herself, and sleep, which she never got much of in the best of times, rarely lasted more than an hour or two before she'd wake up with it on her mind.

Tormented, she'd finally gone to talk to her spiritual counselor, though he was a far cry from the Catholic priests she'd known as a child. The man she sought out for his guidance wasn't ordained or even a graduate from a seminary or school of theology. He was just someone who cared about the poor and forsaken, interested in the priesthood but eventually rejecting it to pursue evil men as their judge, jury, and executioner. The King of the Mole People. David Grale.

Although she preferred to live aboveground, at least until the bitter winds of winter chased her below the streets, she knew she could find him in the large underground cavern that was the principal "city" of the Mole People. No one knew exactly how many hundreds of people, many of them entire families, lived in what was once going to be a part of the New York City subway system, hollowed out but since abandoned. The area was close enough to where the track eventually ran for the electricians and engineers among them to tap into the electricity without draining enough to be noticed.

David Grale ruled his kingdom from there, at least when he wasn't out on the streets where, legend had it but few knew for sure, he hunted and killed evil demons in the shape of men. He sat in a large throne-like chair recovered from some Dumpster, on a large shelf above the main floor that originally had been intended as a station platform. He was like some mad Shakespearean king with his pale haggard face, burning cavernous eyes, and hooded robe. He held court there, hearing the complaints and requests from his subjects, passing judgment, making ultimate decisions for the group.

Grale's moods were as difficult to predict as the man himself. He could be kind and gentle, a father to his flock. Or he could be an insane despot, harsh and unbending, especially when dealing with others' "sins"—whether in the outside world or among his people, where breaking the rules could get one exiled and committing the crime of rape or murder could mean death.

However, on the day she'd finally worked up the courage to approach his dais, he smiled and greeted her like an old friend, inviting her to sit in the chair next to him. "What's troubling you, my child?" he asked. "I can see it in your face."

She hesitated, afraid that if she started, there would be no turning back. "I saw something that I should report to the police," she said. "But I'm afraid."

"What are you afraid of?" Grale said, furrowing his brow.

"People. People involved in what I saw. But also just people. You know my story."

"We all come with stories," Grale replied. "You're safe here. Now what is it that you saw?"

The woman had looked into his deep brown eyes, saw the madness that lurked around the edges but also the humanity in their centers. So she told him.

When she finished, Grale bowed his head in thought. "We don't tell each other how to live our lives here. As long as you live by the rules and do no harm to others, each person is left alone to wrestle with his or her own conscience. I do know your past. But these are evil men and evil times; good people need to stand up to them."

The woman trembled. "I'm afraid."

"I understand," Grale said. "I can tell you that there is no danger from one of the men you saw, the big one. But there are a lot of forces at work here, and not just one man, so I won't tell you there is no danger."

"Couldn't you tell them?" she pleaded.

Grale reached out and stroked her cheek with a long, bony finger. "You, better than most, know I can't. Nor should I."

The woman began to cry. "I can't do it alone."

Looking at her thoughtfully, Grale said, "What if I introduced you to someone, a friend, someone I would trust with my own life, to guide you through this? She would see that you are safe."

The woman felt doubt. "Why would she do this for me?"

Grale smiled. "Because it would be the right thing to do. And because she is a good person, someone put here by God to fight the forces of darkness. If you like, I will get a message to her and the two of you can meet. You can decide then if you want to continue on this path."

So the meeting had been arranged at this bookstore known for helping people with AIDS find housing. She'd taken the 4 train to Houston Street and walked the few blocks, sure that she was being followed and that some bogeyman would jump out of the shadows at any moment. But at last she came to the bookstore, where she stood looking up at the entrance.

She considered turning away. But the voice that had been talking to her from the past wouldn't let her. The next thing she knew she was opening the door and walking into the bookstore. The musty scent of old books and strong coffee from the little café in the back reassured her.

As she made her way toward the back, a petite, dark-haired woman sitting in a chair reading looked up. "Judy?" she asked and smiled. "Judy Pardo?"

"Marlene Ciampi?"

"That's me," Ciampi said, rising. "Can I get you a cup of coffee?"

"Yes, thank you, that would be nice."

Fortified with their drinks, Ciampi led the way back to a private cubicle. "So, do you want to tell me what this is about?"

Pardo started slowly. That day. The alley. The two men and the teenage boy. The gun. The man who chased her.

When she finished, Ciampi was quiet for a moment, studying her. "You know you need to come forward," she said. "Probably testify."

Pardo hung her head and started to cry. "I don't know that I can."

Ciampi leaned forward and put her hand on the woman's arm. "People's lives depend on it. A bad man is out there on the streets. And that boy died because of him."

Pardo was suddenly conscious of the ragged clothes she wore. The dirt on her hands and her unkempt hair. "I'll be humiliated," she cried. "I've been to jail for drugs . . . heroin . . . and something else I'm even more ashamed of."

"There are a lot of things in my life I'm not very proud of," Marlene said.

"Looking at you, I doubt it was something like this," Pardo said. "I've also been arrested and convicted for prostitution."

"Are you still involved in the life?"

Pardo started to shake her head but then shrugged. "I'm not now. But I've quit before, and the heroin always gets me back into it. I do good for a while. Even work jobs. But something goes wrong. I have a bad day, or my boyfriend leaves me, or I just think about the life I had and where I'm at now, and I'm right back out there doing whatever I need to do for another hit."

"Do you want to quit?" Marlene asked gently. "You know as well as I do that's the first step. If you go forward with this . . . telling somebody what you saw, and I think you should . . . you're going to need to get clean. If you want, I can help get you into a place where you'll get help and you'll be safe. But are you ready?"

Pardo sat still for a moment, then nodded. "I'm ready. And I'm ready to do the right thing."

Ciampi smiled and held up her cell phone. "Excuse me for a moment. I need to make a call." She walked around the corner of a bookcase.

When she reappeared, she said, "We're good. I've called a cab to take us to the East Village Women's Shelter. It's a high-security shelter that offers drug rehabilitation as well as life skills that you need to get back out there. You'll be safe and you'll be surrounded by a lot of people who are going through, or have already gone through, what you are."

Pardo smiled. "It sounds nice."

"Good, it's settled, then," Ciampi said. "Just one more thing. I want to stop by my apartment. I want you to meet my husband."

"That's kind of you, but why?"

"Because he's the district attorney of New York County and he's the man you need to tell your story to." Marlene looked the other woman in the eye. "If you're not ready, that's okay, but we're only a couple of blocks away. And there's no time like the present, right?"

Pardo bit her lip, then nodded her head. "If you say so, but there's something else I didn't tell you. Something important."

"And what's that?"

"I used to be a cop."

14

"**WHAT DO WE WANT?**"

"Justice!"

"When do we want it?"

"Now!"

Karp could hear the chanting from the park across the street rising up to his office on the eighth floor of the Criminal Courts Building. A sea of humanity ebbed and flowed, snarling traffic, swirling around the makeshift stand in the park where Reverend Mufti shouted into his bullhorn. The crowd pressed against a cordon of police officers in riot gear who stood in front of the entrance.

The crowd and its ringmasters had been gathering since noon, waiting for the press conference. They were expecting to hear that Karp was going forward with an indictment against Officer Bryce Kim for the shooting death of Ricky Watts. But they were going to be disappointed, and that would mean trouble.

"I don't like this," Fulton said, coming over to stand next to Karp as he peered down. "There's a lot of anger out there, and you're going to be exposed in a way we can't protect you. We don't even know where this Anthony Johnson, aka Nat X, is, or any of his followers. But it's not just about them, either; all it takes is one lone nut who thinks he's striking a blow for the cause."

Karp looked at his friend. "I don't think we have to worry about Johnson today. Ambushing an unsuspecting cop is one thing. Even talking some kid into trying to shoot an officer or, if what we're hearing out of Oakland is right, raping and strangling old women in their beds at night is more his style. But showing up here, trying to do something in front of a few hundred police officers who are ready for him and would like nothing better than to take him down? Nah, he doesn't have the cojones for that."

The chanting outside grew louder. Across the office, where he was standing next to the massive bookcase, Gilbert Murrow shook his head. "I can't believe that Mufti is leading the protest. You'd think after Clay and Vince Cippio saved his butt, he'd be a little grateful."

After Eddie Evans called and said he wanted to talk about the death of Imani Sefu, he'd met with Karp and Fulton and told them about the meeting at Farrell's Bar in Brooklyn. "I don't think it was an accident that Sefu got left alone in the exercise yard or that Adkins had a weapon," he said. "I think it was a setup, and I think they've got plans to go after others, maybe Mufti."

After giving it some thought, Karp asked Evans if he'd be willing to wear a wire and meet with the three officers again. "I would,"

Evans said, "but I don't think they'd trust me after the way I left it, at least not enough to say anything. But I thought you'd ask, and I do have an idea."

The plan was to ask Vince Cippio Sr. "That's a lot to ask a man who just lost his second son in the line of duty," Karp said.

"That's why I think he'd do it," Evans said. "Tony was a great cop. In addition to that he had a lot of integrity, wouldn't so much as accept a free cup of coffee on a cold day. The reason why he was playing basketball with a bunch of kids on the day he got shot was to show them what a police officer is supposed to be. And that apple definitely did not fall far from the tree. He talked a lot about his dad's influence on him as an officer and a man. I don't think Vince is going to be too happy with a bunch of vigilante cops using his son's death as an excuse to commit murder."

So Evans and Fulton had gone to see Cippio who, they later told Karp, had grown more visibly angry the more he heard. He insisted that he be wired.

As it turned out, Cippio had almost waited too long before stopping the hanging. "I have to admit," he'd said later when they all met back in Karp's office, "I wanted to see Mufti sweat. He has no idea how his words hurt those of us who have lost people we love to murderers who are encouraged by inference, if not calls to action, to attack police officers."

Fulton laughed. "Well, he did more than sweat. He needed a change of underwear before he came down to the office to give a statement."

Whatever Mufti felt after the attempt on his life was foiled, it wasn't gratitude. He immediately went to the press with a full account, including a dramatic reenactment for Vansand's program. He said the plot was "proof that something evil lived in the heart of the New York Police Department, as well as police departments across the land." The only mention of his saviors was to note that "if not for the actions of a black officer, I would have been martyred."

Nor had he let up after Karp indicted Gilliam, Delgado, Satars, and Adkins for the murder of Imani Sefu, and the three officers for the attempted murder of Mufti. "What else could the district attorney do with the eyes of this city and the world upon him?" the reverend pontificated on one of the national Sunday-morning news shows. "Let us see how he proceeds not only with these cases, but the murder of an unarmed black teenager, Ricky Watts, by a police officer."

Now with Mufti inciting the crowd gathering in front of the Criminal Courts Building, Karp was going to have to appeal to a mob for patience. "Grateful?" he responded rhetorically. "His brush with 'martyrdom' has only increased his platform and standing. This attempt on his life by the thin blue line, or whatever they were calling themselves, had the opposite effect of what they intended. If police officers would commit murder to silence Mufti, that must mean he's speaking the truth: cops are running amok, killing innocent black men. And now they want blood—not just those three idiots, but Bryce Kim's as well. Mufti's eating this up."

"Maybe you should say that there's evidence supporting Kim's story," Murrow said. "And that it's tied to the murder of Tony Cippio."

Karp shook his head. "We've been over this. We don't know

where Anthony Johnson is, but wherever he is, I don't want him to think we're on to him, or know his real identity. And until we can find him and bring him to trial, everything else will just be interpreted as stalling and play into the hands of Mufti and the media."

Turning away from the window, Karp looked at the half dozen yellow legal pads on his desk. They represented his notes on the Cippio and Watts cases: what he had, what he didn't have and needed. Every day it seemed that a new piece of the puzzle was added. First Jaxon had come through with a DNA match to Anthony Johnson. Then it was Maurice Greene and DeShawn Lakes. Then the other evening when Marlene returned from "going to see another man about a dog" with Judy Pardo in tow.

Each piece alone didn't amount to much, yet together they were creating a solid case. He was still missing the two most important pieces, however: the killer and a silver, mother-of-pearl-handled .45 revolver. But as of that morning, he believed they were so close he could practically write his opening statement for the trial.

Earlier that morning, he'd barely walked in the office when Fulton had appeared at the door. The detective held up a file folder and grinned.

"What's that?" Karp had asked.

"The Holy Grail," Fulton replied. "Actually, it's the police report on that beef Johnson did in Oakland that Jaxon told you about. Only it wasn't just a sex assault. He murdered an old woman, but the DA let him off with the lesser pleas. I told you I have a friend with Oakland PD, and he just sent a copy of the case file. Pretty grim stuff—what he did to the victim—but the most interesting information to us at the moment is the list of items stolen from her apartment, put together by her son."

Karp smiled. Fulton loved telling detective stories and Karp knew he was building to the climactic moment. "And on that list was . . . ?" he asked, playing along.

"Drumroll, please," Fulton said, stretching out the moment. "A stainless steel, forty-five-caliber Smith & Wesson Model 460 with an after-market mother-of-pearl grip. Apparently, her husband was a small-town police chief and it was given to him when he retired. It was registered, so we have the serial number."

"We need that gun," Karp said.

"Working on it," Fulton replied. "It's an unusual piece. Expensive, too. There's a chance he'll try to get rid of it and sell it to one of his cronies, and it will turn up in some other crime. Or maybe he'll try to pawn it, and we'll get lucky. NYPD has a notice out to all the pawnshops in the city, and all the Bay Area PDs are doing the same there in case he returns. Jaxon said he'd get it into the national crime computer. So let's hope we get lucky."

"We just need to buy a little more time," Karp said, as much to himself as the others. He looked at his watch and sighed. "Okay, let's go get this over with."

"I'm with Fulton on this," Murrow said. "I wish you'd reconsider. I can just go give a statement on your behalf. Nobody wants to shoot me."

Karp shook his head. "That just plays into their narrative—that I'm hiding out, stalling for time, hoping it will all pass over. I've got to go show my face, even if it's just to say nothing much is new."

"You know how I feel," Fulton said. "But if you're going to do this, it's simply to deliver the message and get the hell out of there. No questions and answers."

"Okay, okay." Karp held up his hands in mock surrender. "I already gave in to your rules of the game. We'll play it your way, but we're going to play it."

Seeing the look on Fulton's face, Karp added, "Look, guys, nothing I'd like more than to take the private elevator down, avoid the crowd, walk home while the sun is out, kiss my pretty wife, and relax for a few hours. But I got a job to do, and part of that is trying to reassure the people of this city that we're out there trying to protect them, not hiding."

Fulton nodded. "I hear you, Butch. I know where you're coming from. I've spent my whole life trying to do just that. I'm just worried about a friend."

Holding out his hand, Karp said, "I've never had a better friend, Clay, or met a man I trusted as much. You're more than a friend, you're my brother, and you always will be."

The big man's eyes welled up as he shook Karp's hand. "Feeling's likewise, but all this talk is giving me the heebie-jeebies."

The moment was interrupted by a large sniffle. They both looked over to where Gilbert Murrow was wiping his nose. His face flushed when he saw them watching.

"Murrow, are you crying?" Fulton asked with a smile.

"Absolutely not," Murrow denied, pushing his glasses back up his nose. "I was just interrupting this love fest or we're going to be late."

The three men took the elevator down to the lobby, which had been cleared of most of the public. However, Marlene was waiting near the elevator bank.

"You didn't need to come," Karp said. "This is going to last all of five minutes."

"I wanted to show my support." Marlene nodded toward the doors. "It's getting pretty wild out there."

Karp looked beyond the door. He could see the bank of microphones waiting for him, and beyond them, the assembled press, and beyond them, the black-uniformed riot police and the sea of angry faces.

"Then the sooner we do this, the better," he said, and led the way out of the door.

"There's Karp," someone yelled from beyond the wall of police. "Quit protecting racist cops, Karp!"

"WHAT DO WE WANT?" Reverend Mufti's voice boomed from across the street.

"JUSTICE!" the crowd responded.

"WHEN DO WE WANT IT?"

"NOW!"

Karp looked up, above the crowd at the bright blue sky beyond the roofs of the city. He closed his eyes for a moment and thought about his family. His sons. His daughter. The woman at his side, his wife, Marlene. About their sometimes crazy, always exciting lives together. *I'd do it all again*, he reflected, then wondered as he heard Murrow introduce him, *Why the morose thoughts?*

Karp took a deep breath and let it out as he stepped up to the podium next to Fulton, who stood glaring out at the crowd. "Good afternoon," he said. "Due to the lawlessness that has swept the streets of our city since the officer-involved shooting of a young man, Ricky Watts—"

"Murder, you mean!" someone in the crowd yelled. This was met with shouts of agreement, but Karp pressed on.

"Since the incident, the New York Police Department has conducted its investigation with its usual professionalism and thoroughness. The detectives involved in that investigation have now passed on their report to my office. I, personally, have tasked the NYPD detective squad attached to the District Attorney's Office to continue that investigation so that a determination can be made as to whether charges are warranted against the officer. That investigation has not yet concluded and therefore no decision has been made. When . . ."

As the words sank in, an angry murmur rose from the crowd. "He's going to let the pig off!" a woman screamed.

"No justice!" a large black man bellowed and pressed against the wall of riot officers.

"When that decision is made," Karp continued, "it will be according to the rule of law, and without fear or favor to either party, which every citizen has the right to expect from the County of New York District Attorney's Office. That includes police officers."

"Everybody except an unarmed black boy!" a protester yelled.

"Although this investigation will continue as long as necessary to establish the facts, I'm told by Detective Clay Fulton, the chief of the DAO squad"—Karp nodded toward Fulton—"that he expects it to come to a conclusion soon. I ask that the good citizens of our city exercise patience and restraint and allow the system to work."

"You're stalling, Karp!"

Across the street in the park, Mufti began bellowing into the bullhorn again. "WHAT DO WE WANT?"

"JUSTICE!"

"WHEN DO WE WANT IT?"

"NOW!"

Karp looked at the media cameras. "Thank you. That is all."

As the angry crowd pressed up to the cordon of police, Mufti changed his chant. "NO GUN, NO EXCUSE!"

"NO GUN, NO EXCUSE!" the crowd responded.

Just as he was beginning to turn away from the media and the crowd, Karp heard someone shout his name from down the steps. He thought it was someone in the media and though he'd said he wasn't going to answer any questions, he hesitated. That's when he saw him: a thin, young, well-dressed black man who separated himself from the rest of the media and stood pointing something at him.

"Gun! He's got a gun!" someone yelled.

Karp frowned. He sensed, more than saw, Fulton start to react. Then there was a flash, and something struck him in the chest harder than he'd ever been hit before. *I've been shot*, he thought as he began to fall back. Then there was a second blow.

As he lost consciousness, he heard another shot, closer than the first two. Marlene screamed his name. There was an intense pain in his chest and then nothing. His heart stopped beating.

15

Moto Juku jumped when the cell phone on the coffee table started buzzing. He looked at caller ID and frowned. "It's Georgi from the pawnshop," he said to the young black man sitting next to him on the couch.

"Answer it on speakerphone," his companion said, taking another puff on the joint they'd been smoking before passing it to the teenage woman next to him. "But I'm not here."

Juku nodded and answered. "'Sup?" he asked.

"What's up? What's up? You tell me what's up," the agitated voice of the pawnshop owner boomed into the tiny apartment.

"What do you mean?" Juku replied.

"I'll tell you what I mean. Cops are visiting every pawnshop in the Bay Area, including mine, looking for a certain gun."

"What gun?" Juku asked, though he knew what the caller was

referring to—a stainless steel .45 caliber revolver with a mother-of-pearl handle.

Anthony Johnson had shown the man the gun two weeks earlier when he'd come to his apartment in the Tenderloin district of San Francisco. The implication was that he was a thoroughly dangerous man.

"Don't play stupid with me, Juku," the pawnshop owner, Georgi Gregorian, snarled. "The gun your pal, Nkama, or whatever the hell his real name is, talked me into taking under the table and delaying sending the serial number in like a law-abiding establishment. Now I know why. It's hot, and by that I mean hot enough that they're going shop to shop. They got the serial number, make, and model. And they're making it clear that if we don't say anything—and get caught—they are going to make life a living hell."

Johnson tugged on Juku's arm and whispered, "Ask him if they were looking for anybody in particular."

"They mention anybody by name?"

"No. What? You think they're going to tell a pawnshop owner why they want this gun? Now I got a hot gun in my safe, and my ass is grass if they catch me with it, but I can't sell it to anybody legit with this kind of heat. And if I sell it to some creep who uses it for a crime, and he gets caught and rats on me, I'm doubly screwed. So where is he?"

Johnson shook his head violently. "He's not here," Juku answered.

"Yeah, well, you tell him he's got an hour to get his ass down here and pick this thing up, or I might have to call the cops and suddenly 'remember' that I gave a 'friend of a friend' a private loan. I'm not going to prison again for your asshole pal."

Juku looked at Johnson, who shook his head as he rubbed his thumb and forefinger together to indicate he didn't have the money to reclaim the gun. "I don't think he has that kind of money."

"I don't give a rat's ass," Gregorian said. "He can bring me what he's got and owe me the rest. I'll take a personal note from you, Juku, since you're the one who got me into this mess. Or you can give me your vinyl record collection and we'll call it good."

Johnson nodded. "Okay, yeah, I'll tell him," Juku said.

"You do that," Gregorian replied and hung up.

Juku told Johnson, "You got to go get that gun, or he'll turn us both in."

Johnson accepted the joint from his bleary-eyed girlfriend and took a hit and let it out before answering. "I guess so. But I'm not," he said. "You are."

"Me?" Juku felt the blood drain out of his face.

"Yeah, everybody knows you in this neighborhood, including the cops," Johnson replied. "Nobody's going to care if you go into a pawnshop and pick up something."

A young woman entered the room from the bedroom. "He'll do no such thing," she said to Johnson. "He's not going to get mixed up in anything criminal. In fact, we want you out of here!"

Johnson leaned back into the couch and hiked up his sweatshirt so that the small semiautomatic handgun in his waistband was visible. "Well, now," he said. He smiled but his eyes were cold. "Seems like your woman is telling you who can be your friend."

Juku gave his girlfriend a look. "Stay out of this, babe," he said, and turned to Johnson. "You did say you were only going to stay for a couple of days, and it's been almost two weeks."

IT HAD BEEN a surprise when Anthony Johnson, with his teenage girlfriend, Lupe, had turned up at Juku's fourth-floor, one-bedroom apartment. He didn't know him all that well and was surprised that Johnson even knew where he lived.

They'd met earlier in the year at a club where Juku, whose real name was Mike Sakamoto, was DJ'ing the music. At the time, Johnson, who'd let it be known that he'd just been released from San Quentin, seemed to be pretty cool. He talked a lot of black liberation theology which, as a Japanese-American hipster, Juku thought interesting from a philosophical point of view. They'd hung out some, done a little cocaine, smoked some grass, hit the music scene together. It had been kind of exciting to have a former hard-core gang member and, if Johnson's boasts were to be believed, a killer as part of his "posse."

Still, the novelty had grown old. There was only so much rhetoric about the coming race war and shooting whites down in the streets that Juku, who looked and acted a lot younger than his fifty-odd years, was comfortable hearing. So he'd been just as happy when Johnson quit calling or showing up at the clubs he worked.

Juku didn't know he'd gone to New York City "to visit my cousin" until after he invited the couple in. A couple of beers and a few hits of pot later, after Lupe got up to go to the bathroom, Johnson had confided, "I was wondering if we could crash here for a couple of days? I'm waiting on some money I'm owed, and Lupe's pregnant."

"She seems a little young," Juku's girlfriend, Monique, said.

"Old enough," Johnson said with a laugh.

Monique scowled at the answer, but she was the one who insisted—because of the girl's condition—that they stay "for a day or two until you can get a place of your own." The apartment was tiny, but they'd put an air mattress in the living room for the couple to sleep on.

However, a day or two had turned into more than two weeks. The money just kept getting delayed, "but I'll get it soon," Johnson insisted.

In the meantime, Johnson and Lupe rarely left the apartment. They just lay around all day, smoking pot and watching television.

One thing that had changed since Juku had seen Johnson last was that the latter's black liberation rhetoric had increased in intensity and violence. "You ought to understand where I'm coming from," he argued once when they'd been discussing the Black Justice Now movement. "You're Asian. Whites treated your people as subhumans, too, though nothing like the African man. And someday, when the race war starts, you're going to have to choose sides."

One evening, as they were watching the news, a story came on about the district attorney of New York City being shot by an assassin at a press conference during a protest. When the broadcaster said that the DA had been taken to the hospital in critical condition, Johnson laughed and clapped his hands.

Noticing the confused looks on the faces of his hosts, Johnson explained. "The man's a racist. When we were there, a cop shot an unarmed black kid—murdered him in cold blood, no doubt about it—but the DA, his name is Karp, won't do nothing to cops. So I guess now the tables is turned. Good."

Johnson had changed the channel and didn't bring up the subject of the DA again. Juku, who rarely paid attention to the news, didn't inquire further.

One of the rare times Johnson did leave the apartment was with Juku, whom he'd asked to take him to a pawnshop. "I need somebody who'll give me something righteous for this," he said, waving the silver revolver around before sticking it in his waistband. "But has to be somebody maybe willing to look the other way and not register it with the police."

Even though Johnson promised to "throw a little cash" his way, Juku wasn't happy when they took Johnson's battered old Lincoln to a pawnshop Juku had had some dealings with in the past. He had a massive collection of vinyl LPs that he'd kept in immaculate condition, which the owner, Georgi Gregorian, coveted and hoped that someday Juku would not redeem. Gregorian had a reputation for bending the rules . . . for a price.

He looked over the revolver, then put it back on the counter. "It's a nice weapon," he said. "What do you want for it?"

"Fifteen hundred," Johnson said. "It's worth twice that at least."

"Not to me, it's not," Gregorian replied. "I'll give you a thousand."

"Oh, man, that's robbery," Johnson complained. "Shit . . . Okay.

So long as you don't feel a need to report the serial numbers to the po-po."

Gregorian frowned and raised an eyebrow when he looked over at Juku. "I see," he said. "Well, in that case, I'll give you seven fifty for the risk. Take it or leave it."

Johnson cursed and pleaded, but the pawnshop owner wouldn't budge. He finally agreed. "But don't sell it off. It's special to me."

Scooping up the cash, Johnson left the store with Juku trotting after him. "I thought you said that white motherfucker was a friend," he complained. "Someday oppressors like that be looking at the wrong end of a gun."

He'd never offered Juku any of the money. And when asked if he would be moving out soon, he started to get belligerent. "I told you I can't until my money comes in," he said. "You wouldn't want to throw a pregnant girl out on the streets, would you?" He made sure that his hosts knew that in spite of pawning the revolver, he still had a small semiautomatic .380.

Now Juku found himself stuck between an angry pawnshop owner and a self-professed killer, all over a gun. He didn't like guns, particularly those in the hands of former gang members and possible killers.

"Tell you what, Motor Joker," Johnson said with a sneer. "You go pick up the gun, and me and the bitch will clear out of here."

That's how Juku found himself walking into the Bay Area Pawnshop just as the sun was setting. Georgi Gregorian looked up and scowled as he approached. "Where's your friend Nkama?" he asked.

"He sent me," Juku replied. "Just give me the gun so I can get the hell out of here."

"You got cash?"

"He gave me two hundred bucks . . ."

"Damn, you're short," Gregorian said. "But I want that gun out of here. Give me the cash and you can sign a note for the other five fifty, plus a hundred interest, that's six fifty. Your friend's a son of a bitch."

"All I know is he's holed up in my apartment with some pregnant teenager from New York, along with my girlfriend. I want him gone, too."

"You worried he might do something?" Gregorian asked.

Juku nodded. "He's got another piece and he's paranoid as shit," he said, putting the money on the counter. "Just get the gun so I can get out of here."

Gregorian picked up the money. "Wait here." He disappeared through a doorway.

A few seconds later, instead of Gregorian, a large black man emerged from the back room with a gun pointed at him. He was followed by two more men, also with their weapons leveled at him. Two others rushed in the front door.

"POLICE! HANDS UP!" the large black man shouted.

"Don't shoot! Don't shoot!" Juku screamed as he was thrown against the counter and frisked by one of the other officers. He was then spun back around, though the officer kept an iron grip on his arm.

"Where's Anthony Johnson?" the black man asked.

Juku felt faint. "He's at my apartment."

"Which is where?"

"On Turk Street," Juku replied. "He won't leave."

"How do you know him?" the detective demanded, still pointing his service revolver at him.

"He used to come into a club where I DJ'd a few months ago. He just got out of San Quentin and talked a big game. Then a couple weeks ago, he showed up with his girlfriend, Lupe, and asked if he could crash for a few days. But every time I ask him to leave, he threatens us."

The man nodded. "What's your name?"

"Moto Juku . . . well, that's my stage name. It's Mike Sakamoto."

"I'm Detective Clay Fulton, New York Police Department. These other gentlemen are detectives with San Francisco PD." Fulton held up a photograph. "You recognize this man?"

"That's him, that's Anthony Johnson."

"Do you know him by any other name?"

Juku thought about it. "He called himself Deme Nkama or something like that when he pawned the gun. But I've never heard him use it any other time."

"Ever heard of anybody named Nat X?"

Although the detective's face was impassive, Juku could feel the tension in the other man's body. He shook his head. "Sorry, no. I'd tell you if I had. I just want that guy out of my life."

Fulton thought about it, then asked, "Do you think you could get him to come out? Maybe if you said Mr. Gregorian would only take a note from him personally?"

Juku shook his head. "I don't think so. He's paranoid and hasn't hardly come out of the apartment for two weeks. I think he'd know something was up."

"And if he does, then we may have a hostage situation," Fulton said to the other officers. He motioned to them to step out of Juku's earshot. Whatever he said, one of the officers hurried outside while talking on his radio.

Fulton returned to where Juku was nervously waiting. "I can't guarantee I can get him out of your life, we may need you to testify against him."

Juku's eyes got big. "What did he do?"

"I'm not at liberty to say," Fulton said. "Like I said, I can't say he'll be out of your life if you're needed at trial. But with your help, I think we can get him out of your apartment. Does he have a car?"

"Yes, an old Lincoln parked right across the street."

"Perfect."

"Please, my girlfriend . . ."

Everybody turned when the officer who'd left returned and nodded. Fulton smiled. He called to the back room, "Where's the gun?"

Another detective appeared and held up a bag containing a silver-colored handgun with a mother-of-pearl grip. "Right here," he said.

"Anything?" Fulton asked.

"Nope, wiped clean. No prints."

"How about the cartridges?"

"Partials." The detective held up another bag with six bullets. "Maybe something."

Fulton pointed at the gun. "Let me have it, please," he said, and picked up the backpack Juku had arrived with and put both on the counter.

"What are you doing?" Juku asked.

"Anthony Johnson asked you to come get the gun," Fulton said. "You're going to take it back to him as soon as a little something I asked for arrives. Now let me tell you how this is going to go down."

Forty minutes later, Juku returned to his apartment. He found Johnson standing at the window looking out on the street.

"Where the hell you been, Juku?" Johnson demanded.

"He had other customers and made me wait until they were gone," Juku replied. "He wasn't happy about getting two hundred bucks."

"Fuck him," Johnson said. "You get it?"

Juku held up the backpack. "Yeah. I had to sign a note to get it back. But just leave and we'll call it even."

Johnson snatched the bag out of his host's hands and unzipped it. He grinned as he pulled the revolver out and snapped the chamber open, spinning it to see that it was loaded. "There's my baby," he cooed.

"You got what you want, now leave," Monique said.

Johnson glared at her and walked over waving the gun. "You know what, bitch, you got a big mouth."

"Yeah, bitch," Lupe parroted. "You got a big mouth."

"Hey, get the fuck out—" Juku began to say as he tried to step between his girlfriend and her antagonist. But Johnson clubbed him to the ground with the gun.

"Shut the fuck up." Johnson leaned over and put the barrel of the gun against Juku's head. "You want me to pull the trigger, Jap boy?"

Monique screamed. "No, please," she begged. "I'm sorry. I'm just afraid of guns."

Johnson looked up at her, his eyes bright, insane. But then he laughed and the madness subsided. "Afraid of guns? Smart girl." He put the gun in his waistband. "But don't worry, we'll leave in a day or two."

Suddenly, a car alarm went off outside. Scowling, Johnson went over to the window and looked out. "What the fuck? Some home-boy is trying to break into my car." He rushed out of the apartment.

Reaching the street, Johnson pulled the revolver from his pants and held it at his side as he walked over to a large black man who had gained entry to the Lincoln. "Step back, motherfucker," he said. "I want to see your face before I blow your fool head off."

The man backed out of the car with his hands up. But when he turned around, it was Johnson who looked confused. "I seen you before," he said.

"New York City," Fulton replied. "I'm a cop, and you're under arrest for murder." He reached inside his jacket for his gun.

"Fuck you, pig," Johnson said, and pulled the trigger. But instead of the explosion of a hammer striking a shell to send a bullet on its way into the cop's brain, there was a dull click.

"Dummies, dummy." Fulton pointed his gun at Johnson with one hand and wrested the revolver from the killer's grip with the other. "Get on the ground."

Other police officers came running up. But as Johnson started to follow the command to get down, one of his hands began to reach for the pants pocket where the .380 waited. He stopped when he felt the cold steel of the detective's gun on the top of his head.

"Go ahead, asshole, please," Fulton said quietly, hopefully. "I *want* you to go for whatever you got in that pocket. There's nothing I'd like better right now than to blow your brains all over the street."

Johnson's arms went back out to the side and he lay flat as another officer frisked him and removed the gun. He looked across the street and saw his former host and the two women emerging from the building, escorted by uniformed police officers.

It dawned on him then that he'd been betrayed. "I'll get you, Juku!" he screamed. "I'll get you!"

Juku shook off his police escort and walked over until Fulton intercepted. "Fuck you, Johnson," Juku said. "You're going away, and I'm going to help put you there."

"Don't worry about him," Fulton said. "Somebody's waiting for him back in New York who will make sure the only way he gets out of prison again will be in a pine box."

16

PETE VANSAND YAWNED IN THE BACK OF THE COURTROOM. Bored and tired of sitting on the hard wooden bench, he could hardly keep his eyes open as the district attorney waited patiently for a prospective juror to answer his question.

"Mrs. Fenton, would you please tell us your thoughts about how police officers interact with residents and business people in the black community?" Karp had asked the middle-aged black woman.

Her first response was to nervously glance at the court security officers standing at the back doors, and then he caused those in the courtroom waiting for her answer to chuckle when she asked, "Will I get in trouble if I say something that might not be nice?"

Karp smiled and shook his head. "No, no. Your honest, deeply held thoughts are what this process is all about. It's the only time we'll have to share our thoughts during these proceedings. So what would you like to say?"

The woman hesitated and fidgeted in her seat. "Well, I . . ."

"Come on, get on with it," Vansand muttered under his breath. Jury selection for *The People of the State of New York v. Anthony Johnson* had been going on for two weeks, and there was one more seat to fill. The voir dire, the questioning of the prospective jurors, had been mildly interesting as Karp and the lead defense attorney, Margarite Nash, jockeyed for advantage. But Vansand was ready for the grand finale of what he considered *his* story—one of those rare times when the journalist was actually part of the story, and he intended to reap the benefits.

It had been eight months since that fateful day when his intern, Oliver Gray, had surprised them all by attempting to assassinate Karp and dying in the process.

The district attorney had been saved only by a bulletproof vest that absorbed the impact of the two bullets that struck him. However, if what Vansand had heard was true, the blow from one of the bullets had actually stopped his heart. Karp had been in cardiac arrest when the detective who'd been at his side scooped him up like he was no more than a child, put him in a police car, and administered CPR all the way to Bellevue Hospital. It was there that Karp had come back to life on an emergency room table.

After the attack, Vansand had been questioned by the police about Gray, but he'd mostly played dumb. He said the young man had applied for a job, and he'd taken him on as part of his station's effort to afford opportunities to minority students. He said he had "no indication" that Gray was a radical bent on murdering the district attorney of New York, or any warning that Gray was planning something. He made no mention of the fact that Gray had been forced upon him by Nat X.

Hiding behind media shield laws that allowed him to protect his sources, Vansand refused to answer when asked by a police detective if he knew whether Nat X and Anthony Johnson were the same person. Privately, he was sure of it, but he'd invoked his journalistic privileges, and the disgusted detective had given up trying to get anything more out of him.

As he'd gushed to his cameraman on the day of Karp's shooting, Vansand had parlayed being in the right place at the right time, and in the company of the would-be assassin, into a regional Emmy Award. He'd been sorely disappointed that his story failed to win a national Emmy, losing out to a reporter who'd covered a mass shooting by an ISIS sympathizer in California.

However, that disappointment had paled in comparison to his frustration that the national news shows had yet to offer him a full-time gig. They kept putting him off, saying they'd talk about it "when this case is over . . . In the meantime, do you have anything new for us?"

At first, he'd been able to keep up with the demand, including an exclusive interview with Johnson, who had been transported from California to the Tombs. In the interview, Johnson denied being Nat X, "though I can sympathize with his cause." Vansand had gone along with the subterfuge. In fact, he was Johnson's main conduit to the media. Several other journalists, including some of the big names in the business, had tried end runs on him, promising his source all sorts of things under the table. But Vansand had put an end to that when he informed Johnson, and then the public, that the two of them had landed a seven-figure deal with one of the big New York publishing houses for a memoir they would co-author.

Margarite Nash had given him some preferential treatment, especially after he'd run with several of her story "suggestions," and she'd used her attorney-client privileges to slip messages to him from Johnson without the police seeing them. But she courted the national news teams, too, especially as time had gone on.

The streets had quieted after the assassination attempt on Karp. Even the most vociferous of his detractors, including Reverend Hussein "Skip" Mufti, whose own brush with death at the hands of rogue police officers had launched him into activist superstardom, had toned down the rhetoric, though not without caveats. He'd issued a statement that while it was "regrettable" that the district attorney had been attacked, and that Oliver Gray felt the need to resort to violence, "it is in some ways understandable that a 'troubled' young man might strike out at a symbol of the oppression he'd been born into, no matter how inappropriate that act may have been."

At the same time, Mufti denied that his own inflammatory rhetoric contributed to Gray's attack or the riots that preceded it. "I am the messenger, not the message," he proclaimed in an interview for Vansand's feature story on the assassination attempt. "I am merely giving voice to what so many other of my people are feeling."

The activists ramped back up when Johnson was extradited to New York and arrived proclaiming his innocence and labeling himself a "victim of a system dedicated to silencing its critics." Johnson had soon been indicted for the murder of NYPD Officer Tony Cippio and, in a move that caught everyone off guard, the attempted murder of Officer Bryce Kim. The indictment for the second charge read that Johnson had "acted in concert" with young Ricky Watts—supplying him with a gun and encouraging him to use it to shoot a police officer.

Mufti went ballistic over the second charge. He appeared on all the Sunday-morning news shows, including a new New York program hosted by Vansand, where he accused the DAO of "shamefully using the death of Officer Cippio to sweep the murder of an unarmed black male under the rug of an unrelated case."

There'd been a protest that night, with demonstrators showing up outside 100 Centre Street in front of the Manhattan House of Detention for Men, otherwise known as the Tombs, located in the northern sector of the Criminal Courts Building. They shouted and waved signs such as FREE ANTHONY JOHNSON and DON'T SHOOT THE MESSENGERS.

The gathering turned ugly after Mufti arrived and protesters began sitting in the middle of Centre Street, blocking traffic. Television news crews had been on the scene and broadcast images of the police dragging the demonstrators out of the way. But things didn't get out of hand until Vansand's news team showed a clip of three police officers violently taking a large young black man to the ground. The newscast didn't bother to note that they edited the scene prior to the takedown, when the young black man attacked an officer with a baseball bat, sending the officer to the hospital with a cracked skull and broken arm. Soon reports of small but violent demonstrations erupting in various neighborhoods throughout the city began filtering into the newsroom.

The next day, Johnson had contributed to the circus when he refused to participate in the legal process as he was being formally charged in court and asked if he wanted an attorney appointed for him. Instead, he'd stood up and shouted, "I am a political prisoner and as such do not recognize the legitimacy of these proceedings." He then shut up and sat back down, refusing to answer any more questions from the judge or the Legal Aid lawyer there to assist him.

Johnson changed his tune somewhat when Nancy Kershner, the judge assigned to the case, informed him that a trial would be scheduled and go forward "with or without your participation. I'll leave you to determine the consequences of that." After thinking about it for a minute, he'd responded, "I won't allow my voice for the liberation of my people from the yoke of white tyranny to be suppressed. Therefore, I have decided to represent myself against the oppressor."

However, even that stance didn't last long. The following day, Schmendrick, Fritz, and Schmidt, one of the top criminal law firms in the city, announced that it would be engaging its "full weight, experience, and resources to prevent this travesty of justice" and had agreed to represent Johnson. In addition to a reputation for throwing lavish cocktail parties attended by the stars of stage and film, athletes, lobbyists, and politicians, they were known for taking on liberal causes pro bono so long as there was a lot of publicity involved. Rumor was that the firm had wealthy benefactors both in the city and nationally who sponsored the firm's causes célèbres for political reasons.

The firm revealed that its latest "star" attorney, Margarite Nash, would be heading up the defense team. Tall and beautiful, if somewhat severe-looking with her long blond hair pulled tightly back in her signature bun, Nash was the daughter of one of Vermont's wealthiest power couples. Growing up, she'd attended only the finest prep schools, got her undergraduate degree from Bryn Mawr, and then graduated magna cum laude from Yale Law. Now in her late thirties, she basked in the limelight of her celebrity status, having never met a television camera or print journalist she didn't love. "Some of them quite literally," was the joke around the New York Press Club.

When the indictments were first announced, the media had engaged in varying degrees of eye rolling and faux outrage. The television broadcasters, including Vansand, openly smirked and scoffed at DAO spokesman Gilbert Murrow's oft-repeated mantra that the DAO would not comment "except to say that we will let the evidence speak for itself at the trial."

The *New York Times*, having admitted in the previous election cycle to giving up any attempt at objectivity in its news columns, saturated its front page and main city page with what were essentially anti-DAO opinion pieces. They skirted the issue of fairness by quoting defense-friendly and anti-law-enforcement sources, often anonymously, knowing that District Attorney Karp would not respond in kind.

Meanwhile, the *New York Post* ran pretty much any rumor that came across the transom on its front page in large, stacked head-lines punctuated by exclamation marks. Again, most of the inflam-matory content in the paper was attributed to unnamed "inside sources"; it didn't seem to matter to either paper that the sources, if they even existed outside of the reporters' fantasies, were invariably wrong and/or one-sided.

Margarite Nash made sure they all had plenty to quote. How-ever, she was more than just a pretty face or a media whore. She was smart, tough, arrogant, and expensive—at least when the cli-ents were wealthy. She also knew how to use the media attention she sought, declaring on the day she took over the case that the charges against her client were "outrageous."

"They are simply more proof, as if we needed it," she complained at a hurriedly put together press conference, "that the powers that be in New York County, as well as this country, want to silence the voices of dissent and quash the notion of justice for the black community—especially if those voices are challenging the racist monolith of law enforcement."

No wallflower outside the courtroom or press conference, she'd even managed to get herself arrested several times in the past for her "causes." And those now included another demonstration ar-ranged by Mufti to protest an appellate court decision overturning a motion she won before Judge Kershner to split the two charges against Johnson into separate trials.

After Kershner granted her motion, Nash had confided to Vansand over martinis at Bemelmans Bar on the Upper East Side that she'd made her motion "because the prosecution's case is stronger when taken as a whole. Viewed separately, the juries won't see the connections." She said that she'd have a better chance if she could try them separately. "And that, by the way, my dear Petey," she'd purred, pulling him by his necktie so close he could feel her breath on his lips, "is off the record. At least for now." He'd swallowed hard and nodded.

However arrogant and manipulative Nash was, she didn't always get her way. After Kershner granted Nash's motion, Karp's office had filed a writ of mandamus asking the appellate court to promptly hear arguments to overturn that decision. As he had unsuccessfully argued before Kershner, the district attorney persuaded the appellate panel that the murder of Officer Cippio and attempted murder of Officer Kim were both part of a "common scheme, plan, and design by the defendant to assassinate police officers."

Karp went on to argue that "it was all part of the defendant's delusional ideology that leads him to believe that he is at war with the police and civil society. Therefore, the assassination of Cippio and attempted murder of Kim are consistent with the defendant's evil plan." The appellate court had agreed with Karp and directed trial judge Kershner to keep the cases joined and move them forward to trial.

Seething at the setback, Nash had joined the demonstration the next day outside the Criminal Courts Building and was arrested along with a dozen other protesters for blocking the sidewalk. She then shocked even Vansand after she got out on bail by tweeting, "No wonder Nazi Karp was shot. Sic Semper Tyrannis #freeanthonyjohnson."

Even Nash's bosses were apparently displeased with the "poorly worded" message and Latin reference to what John Wilkes Booth had shouted after assassinating Abraham Lincoln. The tweet had been quickly removed from Nash's account, but not before it had gone viral and hundreds of thousands of people—many of them potential jurors—had seen it. She'd later that day issued an apology of sorts through the law firm's public relations team, explaining that "I believe so deeply that an injustice is being done to my client that I allowed my emotions to get the better of my judgment."

Karp did not respond to her tweet or apology. "There will be no comment," Gilbert Murrow said when Vansand called.

Still, as the months dragged on leading to the trial date, the activists and the national press began to lose interest, taking their bullhorns and cameras elsewhere. Occasionally some event tied to the case would cause a flare-up. The most notable of those had been when Murrow sent out a press release announcing that NYPD Lieutenant Jack Gilliam had pleaded guilty to the murder of Imani Sefu and the attempted murder of Reverend Mufti. The tersely worded statement noted that Gilliam had agreed to testify against his co-conspirators, Joe Satars and Johnny Delgado, both of whom had pleaded not guilty.

It made little difference to the activists, including Mufti, that an investigation coordinated by the NYPD and DAO had uncovered the truth behind Sefu's death and saved the reverend's life. Nash, who repeatedly ignored the judge's gag order, issued her own statement, contending that Gilliam's admission of guilt and the charges against the other two "just prove that a cancer resides in the body of New York City law enforcement, as well as law enforcement throughout this country, that seeks to destroy its critics by any means possible."

Mufti, who didn't like falling out of the spotlight, called for a demonstration in the park across from the courts building, but the day had been bitterly cold and the event sparsely attended. A few demonstrators were arrested when they tried to take over the entrance to the District Attorney's Office on the Leonard Street side of the building. The small crowd was summarily removed by the police, which didn't generate the expected media coverage.

Otherwise, the case slowly ground forward as Nash and her law firm's army of attorneys, clerks, and secretaries flooded the DAO and court with motions, including demands that the charges be dropped for a lack of evidence and because of "the outrageous conduct of the New York district attorney, the defendant has been denied a reasonable and fair bail." Most of these pro forma motions were rejected by the court.

At last, eight months after Johnson's arrest, with winter and spring battling for supremacy in Manhattan, jury summonses were sent out to several hundred Manhattanites to appear as prospective jurors in the case of *The People of the State of New York v. Anthony Johnson.* Then seventy-five of them at a time were directed to go to Part 38 Supreme Court New York County, where Judge Kershner was presiding. From this venire group, the court clerk called twelve names and told them to be seated in the jury box.

When Kershner asked Karp to proceed, he introduced himself,

Nash, and Johnson. He explained that Johnson had been indicted by a grand jury for the murder of Officer Tony Cippio and the attempted murder of Officer Bryce Kim. After reading the indictment to the prospective jurors, he listed the witnesses he expected to call during the People's case in chief. "Defense counsel, Ms. Nash, has also provided me with a list of witnesses whom she may call. If you are familiar with any of these people, please let us know during the course of questioning."

Facing the jury box, Karp continued. "A jury of twelve will be selected one at a time beginning with seats one through six in the front row of the jury box, going from my left to right, and then seats seven through twelve in the back row. The first juror selected and sworn in will be the jury foreman. There will also be four alternate jurors, who will hear the testimony but will not take part in the deliberations unless one or more of the twelve jurors cannot perform his or her duties."

Turning slightly so that those prospective jurors in the box and in the gallery could see him, he concluded, "Judge Kershner will instruct you as to the law that applies in this case. But you are the fact finders, the sole arbiters, who will decide this case based upon the evidence from the testimony that is offered from the witness stand and whatever exhibits Her Honor places in evidence. In coming to your final decision, you will do so without fear or favor to either party."

Judge Kershner then invited Karp to begin the questioning, the voir dire, of the prospective jurors seated in the jury box. It was clear to Vansand that Karp wanted jurors who would fall in line with his pro-law-enforcement spiel despite his call for "fair, reasonable, open-minded jurors."

As expected, Nash's questioning leaned toward finding jurors who had a dim or skeptical view of law enforcement. She obviously wanted people of color on the jury while challenging the presence of white jurors, particularly if they seemed "law and order types" or well-to-do and educated.

Vansand wasn't surprised by her blatant anticop line of questioning and attempts to seat a favorable jury based on race and socio-economic status. Her task was easier than that of the prosecution.

"All I have to do is find one juror who will vote for acquittal, and we're in hung jury country," she gloated during another two-martini lunch following several days of jury selection. "I'd love to get a black woman from Harlem on the jury. Want to know why? A black woman, especially one from a low-income neighborhood, is likely to either know of someone with a kid who has had a run-in with law enforcement, or have a child herself who has. The maternal instinct comes out, and she is likely to give the benefit of the doubt to a young black man being unfairly treated."

She laughed. "Meanwhile, Karp has to find twelve for a unanimous verdict. Try to find twelve people in Manhattan who agree on anything."

Karp had to combat not only the obviously pro-defense/anti-cop prospects whom Nash favored, using up several of his peremptory challenges in the first few days whenever Kershner, a former ACLU lawyer, wouldn't dismiss a prospective juror for cause. He also had to counter preconceptions created by popular culture that focused on corrupt law enforcement as a central theme. One female juror insisted that she knew how to judge evidence because she'd watched a lot of *Law & Order*–type shows and expected the real police to conform their procedures to those of Hollywood cops.

It was rough going at times for the DA; an older white man proudly proclaimed himself "a card-carrying member of the Communist Party USA" and admitted that he wanted to see the institutions of American government overthrown.

"Who do you see as the guardians of those institutions?" Karp asked.

"Why, the police and the military," the man replied, his tone making clear that this should be evident.

"So is it fair to say that you are not a supporter of police in general?" Karp asked.

"Of course I'm not," the man scoffed.

"Then of course it follows that you believe that police officers lie?"

"That's putting it mildly, Mr. DA," the man said, rolling his eyes.

Karp looked at Kershner. "Your Honor, I would like to approach the bench on the sidebar on the record regarding this prospective juror."

"By all means," the judge replied.

When Karp and Nash reached the side of the dais out of hearing of the jurors, he said, "Your Honor, based upon the answers given by this prospective juror, it is clear to the People that he is unfit to serve given the nature of his expressed bias toward police."

"All he's doing is speaking the truth," Nash responded. "Then again, that's not the type of person the prosecution wants in this case."

Karp was about to say something, but Kershner interrupted him. "Just a minute, Mr. Karp, let me get the prospective juror over here on the record." She turned to the man and said, "Mr. Mannheim, would you please join us."

When he walked over, the judge asked, "Notwithstanding how you answered Mr. Karp's questions, do you believe that you can be fair and impartial in this case?"

Mannheim smirked. "I believe I can. I'll listen to all the evidence before I reach any conclusion."

Karp shot back, "Well, Mr. Mannheim, can you explain what part of your alleged brain is going to be fair and impartial regarding the police when you just said they're a pack of liars?"

"Typical of a bourgeois district attorney, trying to intimidate me just because I was being honest and forthright," Mannheim sputtered.

"No, Mr. Mannheim," Karp replied. "It is your blatant hostility and biases that would preclude you from sitting on any jury and rendering a fair decision. Your Honor, I renew my application to have this man dismissed for cause."

"Mr. Karp," Kershner said, "the court believes that Mr. Mannheim can be fair and impartial in spite of some of the comments he's made responding to your aggressive approach. Mr. Mannheim, you may return to your seat."

"In that case," Karp interjected, "I will use one of my peremptory challenges, and I want him removed from the courtroom so that he doesn't contaminate any of the other jurors."

"Very well," Kershner said. "Mr. Mannheim, you are excused from these proceedings. Please leave."

At last it had come down to one more seat to fill. So far the jury was composed of seven white jurors—three women and four men—a Hispanic male, and three black men.

Karp had only one peremptory challenge left when Mrs. Fenton, the middle-aged black woman, was called. A single mother raising two young boys, she lived in East Harlem and ran a small boutique there. She'd described her living situation as "scraping by" and said she worried about her sons in the crime-riddled neighborhood.

When Karp told her that he wanted her honest response, she said, "Well, I have to say, Mr. Karp, that I do think there are some issues between the police and the black community. I think sometimes the police jump to conclusions when they see a black person, especially a young black man, that they might not with a young white man."

"Have you had any personal problems with the police or know someone who has, whether it was a perceived problem or a real one?"

The woman nodded. "Not me personally. But I know some people through my church who have had problems with police officers."

Karp walked over to the rail of the jury box until it was just him and her talking. "Mrs. Fenton, what schools do your sons attend?"

"My boys are ten and twelve and attend a charter school uptown."

"Have they had a good experience?"

Fenton smiled. "Yes they have, sir."

"Why did you send them to a charter school and not a regular public school?"

"Mr. Karp, I was fortunate to be able to get my boys into that school. There are fifty thousand other children on the waiting list to get into charter schools in this city. I want them to get a good education so that they can get into college and someday be somebody. The public schools are too violent and dangerous. I don't want my boys bullied and pushed around or called names for trying to study and get good grades. I work all hours sewing the dresses and shirts and blouses I sell in my store, trying to put a little aside every day for their college funds."

"Thank you very much, Mrs. Fenton," Karp said. "Now, is there anything you'd like to ask me?"

Mrs. Fenton shook her head. "Only that I hope I don't have to answer any more questions," she said, which brought a laugh from everyone else in the courtroom.

"None from the People." Karp smiled. He turned to the judge. "Your Honor, Mrs. Fenton is acceptable to the People."

"Well, then, it looks like we have a jury," Judge Kershner said. "We will proceed with opening statements tomorrow morning at nine." She turned to the twelve jurors. "I'm going to turn you over to my chief court clerk, Al Lopez, and he will take you through what to expect and what is expected of you. So I'll leave you with this admonishment. Please do not discuss this case with anyone, including your closest family members and friends, the other members of the jury, or the media. Do not watch television news reports about this case, or read newspaper or magazine articles about it. If someone should approach you and try to talk to you about the case, do not answer their questions and report this contact to Mr. Lopez at your earliest convenience. Mr. Lopez, please escort the jury from the courtroom."

"About time," Vansand muttered again as the jurors left. He stood up and looked around. There weren't any other reporters in the courtroom. They all thought jury selection was too boring to cover, and they'd certainly been right—not much happened, at least nothing that would make the national television news executives sit up and take notice of him. He could feel his opportunity slipping through his fingers. He needed something big.

Leaving the courtroom, he was met out in the hall by his cameraman. "Anything worth filming?" Escobar asked.

Vansand let out a sigh and shook his head. "Nothing to get excited about. We can maybe run some old footage—find a way to work in the Karp shooting—but otherwise we don't have much." He thought about it for a moment, then nodded toward the elevators. "Let's swing by the DA's office and see if anything is shaking there."

As they reached the eighth floor, two women were leaving the district attorney's office and heading for the elevator. He recognized one of them as Judy Pardo, who was on the prosecution witness list. Nash had shown him an old mug shot of her and described her as "a former cop–turned-prostitute" who was a major issue for the defense as she connected Johnson to the shooting death of Ricky Watts.

An interview with her might make the national news, he thought, *especially right before the trial. But she's probably not going to cooperate.* "Get off first when we get to the lobby and be ready to film," Vansand whispered to his cameraman. He smiled and held the door for the two women. "Going down, ladies?"

The smaller woman frowned when she saw him but nodded. "Yes, thank you." The other woman seemed to recognize him but didn't speak. He waited until the doors had closed, then turned to the taller woman. "Are you Judy Pardo?"

"You don't have to reply," the smaller woman said to her companion before turning to him. "Leave us alone, please."

"I just want to ask a few questions," Vansand replied. He moved into position so that when the doors opened in the lobby, Escobar got out first and turned the camera to the reporter and the women.

"Ms. Pardo, is it true you're a former police officer?" Vansand said loudly as he jumped in front of the women.

"No comment," the smaller woman said as Pardo held her hand up in front of her face. "I told you to back off. You're already way out of line. Now get the hell out of our way."

As the women attempted to go around him, Vansand pursued them. "Have you been arrested for drugs and prostitution?"

Judy Pardo's shoulders slumped and she slowed, but the other woman grabbed her by the elbow and propelled her forward. "Don't answer," she said.

"Who talked you into testifying, Ms. Pardo?" Vansand yelled. When there was no reply, he added, "Once a whore, always a whore, right?"

This time Pardo stopped and faced him. "I guess you would know, Mr. Vansand," she said before turning back and leaving the building with the other woman.

Vansand laughed as he looked at his cameraman. "You get that?"

"Yeah. You do know that was the district attorney's wife with her," Escobar said.

"Really?" Vansand smiled. He nodded toward the door. "C'mon, let's see where they go. I know the defense has been trying to find out."

"Why do they want to know?" Escobar asked as they ran outside and hailed a cab.

Vansand shrugged as they got in. "I guess Margarite wants to question her before the trial. Johnson asked me to find out where she is living. He's my ticket back to the Bigs, and I'm not going to ask too many questions." He tapped on the glass to get the driver's attention. "You see those two women getting in the cab up the block? I want you to follow them."

17

AFTER THE JURY HAD BEEN IMPANELED, KARP AND HIS CO-
counsel, Kenny Katz, had gone back to his office to continue the
ongoing process of witness prep.

"So you're happy with the jury?" Katz had asked.

Karp thought for a moment, then nodded. "Yeah, pretty happy. I
mean, in some ways it's always a crapshoot. You hope you've picked
people who will be fair and judge the evidence on its merits, not their
personal beliefs or whatever hocus-pocus the defense attorney is going
to try to conjure up. But you can't always account for someone who
makes a decision based on emotions, or even the chance that someone
slipped onto the jury by saying all the right things and hiding their
true agenda so that they can make a political point by ignoring the evidence and the law. That's why when I thought we might have someone
like that—such as our favorite Communist, Mr. Mannheim—I asked
to speak to the judge at sidebar so the other jurors couldn't hear."

"I thought that was to keep his opinions from tainting the others," Katz said.

"It was in part," Karp agreed. "But it was also to prevent anyone else with an agenda from knowing what to say, or not say, to get selected as a juror."

Karp considered such conversations teaching moments for his young protégé, just as his own mentors had brought him along when he was a rookie assistant district attorney. Katz was a quick study who was already working major cases, including several homicides, though nothing this complicated or as politically charged.

Katz had been a law student at Columbia when Islamic terrorists had crashed airliners into the World Trade Center. He dropped out of law school and joined the Army and became a Ranger. He'd served three tours of duty, two in Afghanistan and one in Iraq, earning his sergeant's stripes, two Bronze Stars, and a Purple Heart in the process.

When he left the Army, he returned to law school and graduated magna cum laude. But instead of going into a more lucrative branch of law, he applied for the only job he ever wanted, as a prosecutor with the New York DAO. In that, Karp saw a lot of himself and, seeing the young man's brilliance, toughness, and work ethic, he took him under his wing, often having him sit second chair during the toughest cases in order to learn on the job.

Katz's question about the jury had spilled over into Karp's philosophy on jury selection, which included such minute details as the way prospective jurors dressed when they came to court. "This is serious business," he said. "Not only are we on a solemn, sacred search for truth and justice for a slain police officer, a man's life is at stake. We want people who will take it all seriously. If they show up in a T-shirt, old jeans, and flip-flops, that's not the sort of person we want on the jury."

"You're not concerned about black jurors? I mean given today's climate and the nature of this case?" Katz asked.

Karp shook his head. "Not at all. In fact, in a way it's an advantage. We're still looking for the same sort of juror regardless of race. But these so-called progressives, like Nash, see all black people as one big homogenous group who all think and act alike. Plus, they're never going to kick a black juror off because of how it would look if they said a black person couldn't be fair."

Katz nodded. "Yeah, the jury foreman, Al Maxwell, seems real solid. Army sergeant, combat vet, Purple Heart. I saw a lot of guys like him when I was in-country. There's something about sharing a foxhole that tends to make you forget about race; all that matters is that the guy next to you has your back. Not always, maybe—there's racism in the military, just like there is in civilian life."

"Which is something he acknowledged," Karp pointed out.

"I was a bit worried about him when you asked if he'd ever had any experiences with the police in which he felt he'd been treated unfairly because of his race, and he came back with that story about 'driving while black' in Newark. It sounded like that cop was a real asshole."

"Yeah, but Maxwell isn't just a combat vet," Karp said. "I don't know if Nash even noticed that on his first tour to Afghanistan, he was an MP, an Army cop. He knows there are good cops and bad cops, but that most are doing the best they can in a difficult job under stressful circumstances. He's not going to hold the actions of one bad apple against everybody else in the barrel. He was also well-dressed and well-spoken. And when he got out, he used his GI Bill benefits to go to college and started up an Internet security company. Did you notice what he said when I asked him how he would describe himself?"

"Yeah, it was American first, and a proud veteran who had served his country honorably second," Katz said. "He was obviously proud that he'd worked hard to make something of himself and didn't make excuses when things didn't go his way. It wasn't until Nash asked him if he was involved in the black community that he discussed his pride in being deacon in a Baptist church and an African American. I loved it when he talked about his efforts to trace his ancestors back to slavery on a Georgia plantation and before that to West Africa. I'm a little surprised that the defense didn't try to get him off the jury, especially because he was going to be the foreman."

"No way," Karp said. "All Nash saw was a black man and all she heard was that he'd had a bad experience with the police and that his ancestors were slaves. She sees a caricature, not the man under the skin. And she couldn't very well kick the first black man seated off the jury; she'd have been drummed out of every liberal cocktail party in New York for the rest of her life. The same with the other black men."

Katz laughed. "How about Mrs. Fenton? She thinks there are issues between the police and the black community."

"Right, and a lot of it drummed up by the so-called activists and the complicit media," Karp said. "But the police have always got to be vigilant about how they go about their jobs. We allow them to carry weapons and, when lawful, use deadly force; with that comes extra responsibility. That sort of power is bound to attract a few bad apples, bullies like Satars and Delgado or a guy like Gilliam who thinks that badge puts him above the law when something happens he doesn't like. The point is we don't pretend these issues don't exist; we acknowledge them and deal with them, as we are with those three numbskulls. But this case isn't about racist cops and black activists. And for that reason, Mrs. Fenton is the best of the lot."

"Why do you say that?"

"She's a small-business owner," Karp said, "which makes her a great judge of character and demeanor. Every time someone comes into her business, she has to make snap judgments: Is this guy going to buy something, or is he going to rob me? She also understands the value of honesty and makes important decisions every day that affect her bottom line and life."

"Nash didn't seem to care that her kids go to a charter school."

"Well, for one thing, it's a neighborhood charter school, not out in the white burbs, and going after her would be attacking every single black family—what did she say the waiting list is now, fifty thousand?—that wants to get their kids into a charter school instead of subjecting them to the war zones otherwise known as the failing and violent New York City public schools," Karp said. "Again, Nash just sees a struggling black single mom with two kids who knows people whose children have been in trouble with the law. It fits her narrative. But they're the ones judging people by the color of their skin, not the content of their character, to quote MLK."

Karp urged Katz to stay on top of the order in which the prosecution witnesses would appear. "You know the parade I expect to call, so make sure they're called in an orderly fashion."

⚜ Then the discussion had turned to Judge Kershner. Anorexically thin and frail with overly large eyeglasses—a sort of younger version of Supreme Court Justice Ruth Bader Ginsburg, Kershner had butted heads with Karp several times when she was the lead attorney with the New York ACLU. She was also a social climber among the liberal elite in New York City, courting invitations to cocktail parties and events, always with an eye on an eventual appointment to the federal bench.

Karp had never tried a case in front of her, but she had a reputation for favoring the defense. In fact, when some of the younger ADAs in the office heard that she was going to preside over the Johnson case, they'd rolled their eyes and predicted a long, uphill battle. But Karp quashed that at a Monday-morning bureau chiefs meeting with a story from his college basketball career.

"We were feeling sorry for ourselves at the half because the ref wasn't giving us the calls," he told them. "But my old coach had one response: 'Score more points, stop them from scoring, and take the ref out of the game.' We are going to score so many points and stop them from scoring during this trial, that the judge won't be able to throw the game, even if she wants to."

Now Karp went into more detail on how he planned to counter

a defense-leaning jurist. "We are going to prepare for this case like we've never prepared in the past."

"You've always emphasized preparation as the key to successful prosecution," Katz noted.

"Yes, but we're going to double and triple that. I want you to prepare a legal memo, a mini-brief, on every potential legal issue that might arise, no matter how insignificant or unlikely it might seem. If it comes up during the trial, we're going to have it at our fingertips to hand to the judge. We're not going to get in a war of words and argue semantics with the defense—that's what Nash wants. Let them howl at the moon all they want, we're going to put the law in front of the judge in black and white and force her to make her rulings based on that. She's not going to want to be overturned by an appellate court; she wants a seat on the federal bench, and she's not going to get it if she gets reversed for ignoring the law, especially in the trial of a cop killer."

Karp reminded Katz that they knew what the defense was all about. "We've seen it before. The Big Lie—say it enough times and hope the jurors will buy it—combined with the frame defense. Goes back to the old law school courthouse saw for defense attorneys: If your case is weak on the facts, try the law. If your case is weak on the law, try the facts. And if your case is weak on the law and the facts, try the district attorney. The facts aren't on her side and she doesn't have a legal case. As long as we stick with the game plan, we'll take her apart like Grant took Richmond."

"Nice imagery." Katz laughed. "Are you going to want me to file these legal memos as pretrial motions for the judge to rule on?"

Karp smiled and shook his head. "No. Only if necessary to counter defense arguments, regarding the admissibility of evidence, for example," he said, and then explained how he planned to lay a trap for the defense, which left Katz grinning.

Their conversation about Judge Kershner ended with Katz complaining about her refusing to excuse Mannheim. "After everything he said about the police, it was clear he wasn't going to be fair and impartial."

However, Karp had surprised Katz by somewhat defending Kershner's decision. "Yes, she should have cut him loose for cause, but judges don't like dismissing jurors for cause because it's an appealable issue. Again, the last thing Kershner wants is to have a verdict overturned because the appellate court doesn't like a decision she made during jury selection. So put it on the lawyers—me, in this case—to get rid of some clown like Mannheim."

THE FOLLOWING DAY started with Judge Kershner admonishing the jurors that they were to consider only the evidence such as they heard it from sworn witnesses and any exhibits she accepted into the record. "What the lawyers say is not evidence," she stressed.

After that, she had invited Karp to give his opening statement, which he kept simple, laying out a general outline of the facts of the case, as well as what witnesses and other evidence he intended to present. He did take the opportunity to "respectfully add to Her Honor's definition of what evidence jurors could consider" by pointing out that they could note "demeanor when determining the credibility of a witness."

Standing at ease in front of the jurors, he then touched on the "frame defense" and how Nash would have no choice but to attack the prosecution's evidence "lacking any evidence of her own to the contrary. But you'll see that, barring a crystal ball, which, obviously, does not exist, there is no way that my office, no matter how venal or contemptible Ms. Nash may deem it, could have created the voluminous trustworthy, corroborated, and dovetailing evidence you will be given."

Karp spoke calmly and matter-of-factly, looking into the eyes of each juror as he moved along the jury box rail and without the histrionics that Nash was certain to display. He'd save any righteous indignation he might want to channel for his summation, when it would count.

"And when this trial is over, the People will have proved that the defendant, sitting in this courtroom over there," he said, turning quickly to point at Johnson, who ducked his head at the suddenness of the accusatory finger, "brutally executed, in cold blood, Officer Tony Cippio—the father of two young children, and the loving husband of a pregnant wife—as he lay on the sidewalk, mortally wounded and begging for his life. He then attempted to murder Officer Bryce Kim by callously and indifferently persuading a promising young man, Ricky Watts, to commit this heinous crime, handing him his mother-of-pearl-handled, forty-five-caliber revolver. You will see that weapon here in evidence."

Returning to the prosecution table, Karp looked again at the jurors for a long moment and then concluded, "And we, the People, will prove this assassin's guilt not just beyond a reasonable doubt, but beyond any and all doubt. Thank you."

After Karp took his seat, Kershner asked Nash if she wanted to present an opening statement. "I do, Your Honor," said Nash, who was dressed in a gray suit and a figure-hugging white blouse. She walked toward the jury, shaking her head before she looked up.

"Ladies and gentlemen, you will see that the State's case is nothing more than a shameless, dangerous conspiracy to silence critics of law enforcement in New York County . . ."

Margarite Nash paced like a caged animal in front of the jury box as she delivered her opening remarks, her voice dripping with well-rehearsed contempt. "And as you will hear, they will stop at nothing, including murder, to achieve that goal."

"So, what exactly are the facts—the FACTS—in this case? Well, we know that a young police officer was killed in Marcus Garvey Park during some sort of confrontation with several individuals. We have no idea what this confrontation entailed. Whether he said or did something to provoke the attack, we'll never know, but tragically his death was the result. And why won't we know?"

Nash smiled sardonically. "Because the police couldn't find the real killer. In fact, they had no information except the guess of a traumatized teenager who witnessed the incident from a distance." She held up a finger as if to scold. "But that didn't stop the NYPD or the District Attorney's Office from settling on a suspect . . . someone whom they knew had spoken out against police brutality in the past. Someone whom they knew was visiting New York City and had been asked to speak at several gatherings of young men about standing up for their rights and their communities. But such talk is dangerous, so when they needed a suspect for the death of Tony Cippio, they had the perfect fall guy."

This time she was the one who pointed at Johnson, sitting in his button-down Brooks Brothers shirt, tie, and slacks, but he'd been warned, and instead of ducking he shook his head sadly. "They had my client."

As Nash pointed, Karp turned to look at the defendant, whose face was the picture of aggrieved injustice. Glancing behind the defendant, he noted the packed gallery that included Reverend Hussein "Skip" Mufti and his bodyguards. "That's right," members of the gallery spoke aloud. "You tell them, sister."

As his counterpart spewed venom, Karp kept his expression bland and his focus on the jurors to see how they were reacting to her accusations and tone. They were all attentive, but their faces betrayed various emotions from concern to studious concentration to angry scowls, though whether the latter was due to Nash's words or her tone was impossible to know.

In general, he wasn't worried about how the jury took the opening remarks. The trial had a long way to go, and they had not yet heard any of the evidence, or closing statements, when he'd get a chance to put all the pieces together for them.

Karp spotted Pete Vansand in the gallery. He didn't show it on his face, but he felt a flash of anger remembering Marlene's account of the run-in with the journalist and his cameraman when she was escorting Judy Pardo back to the East Village Women's Shelter. The same man who helped a would-be assassin get past the police at his press conference and then filmed the murderous plot. His distaste for Vansand's ethics had only grown when Murrow showed up in his office a few months after the event with a newspaper photograph of Vansand smiling as he accepted the Emmy for his story on Karp's near miss with a killer.

The man had been a patsy for the defense ever since, and a mouthpiece for Johnson and Mufti. Now he capped it off by harassing a witness who was already frightened and not looking forward to the humiliation she would suffer on the witness stand.

However, there was nothing Karp could do about Vansand, and he wasn't going to let his aversion to the man distract him. He resumed watching the jurors as Nash described the People's case as "a shotgun approach to justice . . . pull the trigger and send as many little pellets as you can out there, hoping that one or more hit something that will resonate with you."

More than an hour after she began her opening statement, most of it repeating herself in a variety of ways, Nash wrapped up. "The prosecution and their henchmen the police have three goals. The first is revenge, plain and simple—they want blood for the blood of Officer Tony Cippio. It doesn't matter to them if they convict the right black man so long as it's a black man—the same sort of mentality as a KKK lynch mob in the South, just string up the first black man you see."

Nash's eyes narrowed. "As bad as that is, the other two reasons are, to me, even worse. One is to obscure the murder of two young black men—Imani Sefu and Ricky Watts—at the hands of New

York police officers. It's a bait and switch, people: 'We don't want you to look over there at what the police did, we want you to look over here at this young man whom we've chosen as the sacrificial lamb.' The other is to silence a courageous and outspoken critic of the racist monolith of law enforcement, and they will stop at nothing, including, as you will see, murder."

Nash walked over to the defense table and stood behind Johnson, placing her hands on his shoulders. "This is nothing more than a classic attempt to frame an innocent man by any means possible. And we'll be asking you to send a message that we refuse to live in a police state by finding Anthony Johnson not guilty of these outrageous charges."

When Nash sat down, Kershner looked at Karp. "Are you ready to call your first witness?" she asked.

"I am, Your Honor." Karp nodded to Detective Clay Fulton, who was standing next to the door in the side of the courtroom that led to the witness waiting room. "The People call Vincent Cippio Sr."

18

KARP WAITED UNTIL THE FATHER OF THE SLAIN POLICE OF-ficer was sworn in and eased his large frame into the chair on the witness stand. When the man was settled, he asked, "Would you please state your name and spell it."

"My name is Vincent Cippio . . . that's V-I-N-C-E-N-T C-I-P-P-I-O."

"And do you sometimes go by another name?"

"Yeah, most people call me 'Vince' or 'Sarge.'"

"Why 'Sarge'?" Karp asked.

"When I retired I was a sergeant in the New York Police Department. That's what my guys called me and it stuck, I guess."

"How long were you with the NYPD?"

"Thirty-five years, all with the Seven-Three Precinct in Brooklyn."

"And you were a sergeant how much of that time?"

"About thirty years."

As Cippio spoke, he kept his eyes on Karp or the jurors. He knew he couldn't risk looking at the defendant. "I know if I look at him in the courtroom," he'd told Karp in the witness waiting room that morning, "and he has that smug look on his face that I've seen on television, I'll want to rip the bastard's throat out. It will be all I can do to not go off on him just knowing he's there."

"Have you received any commendations during your career?"

Cippio half shrugged his broad shoulders. "I received the Medal for Valor and a few others."

"The Medal for Valor . . . NYPD's third-highest award for heroism," Karp said.

"Objection," Nash said as she smiled condescendingly and rose to her feet, taking a moment to straighten her tailored gray jacket. "Your Honor, what is the possible relevance of this line of questioning?" she asked, as if dealing with a prosecutor just out of law school. "The witness supposedly is here to testify as to the identity of the deceased, his son. However, the district attorney is launching into this irrelevant tour of family history to inappropriately play on the jury's emotions."

Karp turned slightly to address the judge, though he made it a practice to never put his back to the jurors. "Your Honor, as she has through the media prior to this trial, counsel at least implied during her opening statements that she would attempt to impugn the character of New York police officers as a class of people, including the victim and members of his family. I am merely establishing for the jury the sort of officer the witness was during his long and stellar career."

"And now the district attorney is making speeches," Nash shot back.

Judge Kershner's face twisted as she thought for a moment, then nodded. "The district attorney is correct that you implied that strategy and he has the right to address this with his witness. So your objection is overruled. However, Mr. Karp, please move on."

As he walked toward the witness stand, Karp said, "You just testified that you were always assigned to the Seven-Three Precinct in Brooklyn, which for the jurors is referred to by the public as the Seventy-Third Precinct, correct?"

"Yes."

"That's a pretty rough precinct, is it not? A lot of homicides and violent crime?"

"Yeah, about as rough as it gets. But there's a lot of good people there, too, just trying to get by. I made a lot of friends working at the Seven-Three."

"Are you aware of the racial makeup of the population served by the Seven-Three?"

"It's basically a minority community, mostly black."

"Sergeant Cippio, as a police officer, did you interact with civilians differently based on their race or ethnicity?"

Cippio shook his head. "People's people. Every group has its bad apples, but for the most part if you treat other people with respect, you get respect back."

Karp nodded. The whole delving into the background of a victim's family member wasn't something he normally did, and he found the entire exercise of having to "prove" the sergeant's exemplary career to be distasteful. But it had been necessitated by Nash's statements to the media, as well as her comments during pretrial hearings and jury selection, that implied that even the victim's police officer father was a racist bent on seeing a black man convicted whether or not he was guilty.

Asking hard questions of a grieving family member would normally be akin to playing with fire for a defense attorney. But she was counting on a change in climate for how the public viewed law enforcement.

"Sergeant Cippio, would you describe for the jurors your family's history with the New York Police Department."

"There's been a Cippio with the NYPD since 1920, when Alphonse Cippio, a second-generation American, joined the force. Typical New York Italian family. Basically, males are expected to become cops or priests or join the military, though there's been a few black sheep who went to medical school or started a business," he added with a smile.

"Is there a reason for that?"

Cippio shrugged. "I guess it's sort of a feeling of wanting to give back to the community that took our family in when we first came to this country. It's been passed down ever since. I remember my grandfather talking about it, and I certainly heard it from my dad. I talked about it with my sons since they were little . . ." He stopped and blinked his eyes several times. "I guess I sometimes now question the wisdom of that."

Nash stood up again. "Your Honor, this is all very touching, but I really have to object about the relevancy."

Without turning to look at her, Karp responded with a touch of anger. "Again, defense counsel has been the one throughout the proceedings leading up to this trial to make it clear this isn't just about defending her client; it's a wholesale indictment of all police officers. All I'm trying to do at this point is explain to the jury something about the character of the victim and what led to his being in Marcus Garvey Park on the afternoon he was brutally, cold-bloodedly executed by her client."

"Very well, Mr. Karp, a little more and that's all," Kershner replied. "Overruled."

Karp turned back to Cippio. "Have members of your family on the force been killed in the line of duty other than your son Tony?"

"Yes, my grandfather's brother, I guess he'd be my granduncle. He was killed by the Mob in the 1930s when he refused to take bribes from the Black Hand in the Garment District," Cippio replied. "And my brother, Dom, was killed responding to a domestic violence call."

Cippio paused and swallowed hard. "Then my first son, Vince Jr."—he stopped and had to collect himself—"he died on September 11, 2001. He was last seen running into Tower Two at the World Trade Center. He'd already brought two groups of people out and was going in for more when the building collapsed."

"And was he recognized for his bravery?"

Cippio nodded. "Yes, he was awarded the NYPD Medal of Honor."

"And that would be," Karp said, walking over to the lectern to study his notes on a yellow legal pad, "the department's top award for, and I quote, 'individual acts of extraordinary bravery intelligently performed in the line of duty at imminent and personal danger to life.'"

"Yes, sir," Cippio said with obvious pride.

"Specifically, the NYPD Medal of Honor is, and again I quote, 'awarded for acts of gallantry and valor performed with knowledge of the risk involved, above and beyond the call of duty.'"

"Yes, sir."

"He ran into that building knowing there was a good chance he would not be coming out?"

"Yes, sir." This time Cippio's response was hardly more than a hoarse whisper as he tried desperately not to crack.

"To try to save other people," Karp continued. "To protect and serve?"

"Yes, sir. That was my boy . . . ," Cippio said in a near sob. "That was both of my boys."

"And where is your son Vince Jr. buried?"

The question seemed to hit Cippio like a bullet to the chest. His shoulders slumped, his head hung, and his body shook. It took him a full minute to bring himself under control, and when he spoke, his voice was high and tight.

"We never received his remains . . . none were identified. Nevertheless, his mother and I made sure that he had a proper funeral with a Memorial Mass and placed a gravestone at the cemetery site on the family plot."

Karp gave Cippio, who was breathing hard in his grief, a few more moments to gather himself. "Tell us about your son Tony."

Cippio let out a deep sigh and shook his head. He smiled slightly. "He was a good kid, sensitive. He was always bringing some stray home. He has a dog, Wink, he found while on patrol, probably the scruffiest, most obnoxious mutt you'll ever meet. But he loved that damn mongrel, and it loved him right back. Even now, every time Wink hears the door open, he runs to see if it's Tony come home."

The man's voice broke as he said "home," and it took him a few moments before he could go on. "Tony was a good boy, believed in Jesus, knew his catechism front to back way ahead of the other kids, even his brother. We thought he might be a priest. But he met Franny in high school and it was love at first sight."

Pausing, Cippio looked back toward the gallery where his son's widow sat in the front pew behind the prosecution table. She dabbed at her eyes but smiled at her father-in-law.

"He was straight A's in high school, a pretty good basketball player," he continued. "But after what happened to his brother, we were hoping he wouldn't be a cop. Things were changing on the streets, worse than even the hard times in the sixties. No respect. Not from the criminals, not from the public. But after his brother died, there was no way you could stop Tony from joining the force."

"You mentioned that times were changing on the streets," Karp said. "Did you worry more about Tony than, say, Vince Jr. or your-self?"

Cippio nodded. "Back in the day, you might get in a shootout during a robbery or trying to apprehend some violent guy, even get shot by some hothead in a domestic violence dispute like my brother. But now a police officer pulls somebody over for a traffic violation and has no idea if it's a deadly ambush, some guys looking to shoot a cop for no better reason than he's wearing the uniform. They're hunting police officers and except maybe in the past with the Black Liberation Army—"

"Objection!" Nash shouted, jumping to her feet. "Your Honor, may we approach the bench?"

"Of course," Kershner said.

When Karp and Nash reached the sidebar at the judge's dais, the defense attorney hissed her objection. "This was discussed at a pretrial hearing, Your Honor. There would be no attempt to link my client to the actions of the Black Panthers or Black Liberation Army. I know this witness was admonished not to bring it up, and yet the district attorney, and Your Honor's compliance, with all due respect, led him down this path. I object and I move for a mistrial on the grounds that the witness's illegitimate and egregious ignoring of the judge's prior ruling will prejudice the jury."

"The witness simply made reference to a historical fact, and all of Ms. Nash's revisionism won't change it a bit," Karp responded. "The linkage to the defendant may well exist in his alleged mind."

Again Kershner's lips twisted as she considered the objection. "I don't see that this slip rises to the level of declaring a mistrial; however, I am going to sustain the objection and instruct the jury to disregard the witness's statement. And Mr. Karp, you will direct your questions away from this topic and onto the current matter. Am I clear?"

"Oh, this is very much the current matter," Karp replied.

"Very well," Kershner said with disdain. She shook her head and turned to the jury. "Defense counsel objected to a remark from the witness alluding to crimes that may have been committed by others more than forty years ago that have no bearing on this trial. You will disregard those remarks. I sustain the objection. Mr. Karp, you may continue."

"Thank you, Your Honor." Karp turned back to Cippio. "Sergeant Cippio, what sort of police officer was your son?"

"Objection. The witness was not his son's superior officer, nor did they ever work together," Nash said.

"Your Honor, if I may set the table for the foundational basis for this line of questioning," Karp said.

"Go ahead," Judge Kershner said tersely.

"Sergeant Cippio, in your role as a patrol sergeant, did you come into contact with a large number and variety of police officers, some of whom you supervised but some you didn't?"

"Yes, hundreds, probably thousands."

"And there were good officers and bad officers?"

"Yes, some were definitely better than others. Most were good."

Karp nodded. "I imagine that among the attributes of a good officer would be such qualities as knowledge of the law, perhaps expert marksmanship, courage might be another, and dedication to service. But what else might constitute a good officer?"

"Well, I'd say having good people skills," Cippio replied, turning to the jurors. "Police officers are placed in a lot of situations and have to deal with a lot of different people. So it helps to have the right attitude going in."

"And what is that 'right attitude'?"

"With the best officers it's that they want to help people; they see their role as protecting and serving their communities, just like it says on our patrol cars."

"And in your capacity as a patrol sergeant, you had the opportunity to note whether an officer had good people skills or did not?"

"Yes, many times."

Karp looked at Kershner. "Your Honor, I'd like to submit Sergeant Cippio as an expert in observing the demeanor of police officers and what differentiates a good police officer from a bad police officer, and ask you to overrule counsel's objection."

Kershner raised an eyebrow but nodded. "Overruled. The sergeant can speak to this matter."

Turning back to Cippio, Karp continued. "In your expert opinion, was your son, Officer Tony Cippio, a good police officer?"

Cippio nodded. "He was everything you would want in an officer. Brave, courteous, knew the law . . . But most of all he liked people and wanted to help. He wanted to make a difference in their lives. We often talked about the job, and even after a long week, he'd be all jazzed up. But usually it wasn't about some arrest he'd made or exciting event; usually it was something he did that made a difference in someone's life. He talked about wanting a better world not just for his kids but other people's kids, too. And he was an optimist; he thought he could turn around the way people seem to be viewing cops by showing them what a good officer was like. That's why he was playing basketball with those kids."

As Cippio spoke about his son, Karp glanced back at the defense table. Nash sat listening with her elbows on the table, her chin propped up on her fists, expressionless. Johnson slouched in his seat, looking around the courtroom as though almost anything else interested him more than the witness's testimony.

"Yes, he was a good police officer," Cippio said, and hung his head.

Karp gave him a moment, then spoke softly. "Sergeant Cippio, on the night your son was murdered, did you receive a telephone call from the New York City Medical Examiner's Office?"

Cippio nodded and wiped at his eyes. "Yes," he croaked. "I was asked to go to the morgue."

"Were you already aware of what had happened to Tony?"

"Yes. A couple of my guys had come over to the house to deliver the news so that I wouldn't have to get it from a telephone call or the television."

"Did you in fact go to the morgue?"

"Yes."

"I'm sorry, Sergeant Cippio, I know this is tough, but what were you asked to do at the morgue?" Karp asked gently.

"I was . . . I was . . . ," Cippio stuttered before pulling himself together and looking at the jury with a tear-stained face. "I was asked to identify the body of my son Tony."

"And were you able to do that?"

Cippio looked down again. A few of the jurors were now also wiping at their eyes and sniffling into tissues. "His face . . . his face was a mess because that animal shot him in the head. But he was my boy, my little Tony."

In order to give the witness more time, Karp walked over to the prosecution table and looked down at his yellow pad, which contained his notes regarding this witness. He then walked slowly back over to the witness stand to pour a glass of water from a pitcher and handed it to the grieving father.

"Thanks," Cippio replied. He took a sip and set the glass down before reaching for a tissue and blowing his nose. "I can go on."

"Sergeant Cippio, at some point after your son's execution, did you receive a visit from Tony's partner, Eddie Evans, and Detective Clay Fulton from my office?"

Cippio's face hardened. "I did."

"Can you please explain to the jurors the purpose of that visit?"

"Yeah." Cippio turned to the jurors. "Several police officers had tried to recruit Eddie to participate in a plan to murder a so-called black activist."

"Had they already carried out another such plan?"

"It was my understanding that they were suspected of arranging for the murder of a man named Imani Sefu, who was being held in the Tombs at the time."

"The Tombs? You are talking about the Manhattan House of Detention for Men located adjacent to this building?"

"That's correct."

"But it was your understanding that the officers intended to commit another murder and were trying to get Evans to go along with the plan?"

"That's my understanding, yes."

"Is Eddie Evans a black police officer?"

"Yes, he is."

"So why would these other officers try to recruit him to murder a black activist?"

Cippio shrugged. "Because he was my son's partner and they thought he might want revenge. Also, the leader, Lieutenant Jack Gilliam, told me later—"

"Objection, hearsay," Nash said.

Karp had anticipated this objection from Nash, even though it played to her Big Lie frame defense that Gilliam and his alleged fellow police conspirators were part of an effort by law enforcement to silence critics. But he responded, "Your Honor, I'd ask that the witness be allowed to answer. For the record, Lieutenant Gilliam will be testifying later to this same issue. It's important for the jury to understand and hear testimony regarding the entire nature factually of the transactional, contextual basis of the limited aspects of these acts." He then handed the court and defense counsel a legal memo prepared by Katz on point regarding this legal matter. He asked that it be marked in order People's Exhibit 25 for identification.

Kershner read the memo and looked at the defense table. "Ms. Nash, do you have any legal argument in response to the district attorney's legal argument?"

Looking like she'd been struck, Nash hemmed and hawed before she addressed the court. "Your Honor, I'd like to, uh, um, time to prepare my own memo."

"Well, do you have anything to say now in response?"

"Uh, no, um, maybe tomorrow I'll have a memo."

Judge Kershner just shook her head and said, "I'll allow it, Mr.

Karp, subject to your stated limited purposes. The witness may answer the question."

Karp glanced over at Katz, who had a wide grin on his face. He nodded to Cippio.

"As I was saying, Gilliam said he hoped that if Evans participated, it would convince other black officers to join in."

"So this wasn't just a whites-against-blacks conspiracy on the part of these other officers?"

Cippio frowned. "Well, I think two of them, Joe Satars and Johnny Delgado, are a couple of racist pieces of crap, excuse the language. But I think Gilliam had simply had it with these attacks on police officers. He told me—"

"Objection, hearsay," Nash said.

"Same argument, Your Honor," Karp replied. "Goes to foundation."

"I'm going to sustain the objection," Kershner replied. "You can ask this of Mr. Gilliam himself when he takes the stand."

Karp moved on. "Evans rejected their initial effort to recruit him?"

Cippio nodded and then explained how his son's partner became suspicious that the other officers had carried out their plan when Sefu was murdered in the Tombs. "That's when he contacted the DAO. Then Eddie and Detective Fulton came over to my place and asked if I'd go undercover."

"Why did you agree to help?"

Cippio's eyes narrowed. "Because I was a police officer sworn to uphold the law and protect people no matter what the color of their skin or what they said, even if I didn't like it. My sons were the same. But these . . . these pieces of crap, they didn't just commit murder, they tarnished the badge my sons and I and all those other members of my family wore with pride and with honor. I was happy to help."

Karp then led Cippio through the events leading up to and after the attempted murder of Reverend Mufti. As he prepared to finish his questioning, Karp asked, "Can I ask what you think personally of Reverend Mufti?" He looked back at the gallery, where Mufti's followers scowled though the reverend himself remained expressionless.

"Personally? I think he's a jerk," Cippio said. "I think he makes a living by playing on people's fears and prejudices. I think him, and other anticop blowhards, twist the truth and stir things up so that sooner or later some sociopath with a gun kills a cop because he's been persuaded that it's the right thing to do."

"Do you hold him responsible for the death of your son Tony?" Karp asked. Now Mufti was scowling angrily, too, though he also looked embarrassed.

Cippio turned to look at the reverend. "Maybe not specifically," he said. "I don't think he told anybody, 'Go kill Tony Cippio in Marcus Garvey Park.' But words have power and they can be used to make people do things that harm other people. So yes, in a way, I hold him and others like him responsible for the death of my son."

Karp let it sink in for a moment. "And yet you risked your life to save him and catch the killers of Imani Sefu."

"Yeah," Cippio said. "I did."

"Why?"

"Because once a cop, always a cop . . . I took an oath to protect and serve. It was the right thing to do. It's what my son would have wanted me to do."

Karp turned to the defense table. "No further questions. Your witness."

Nash quickly gathered herself and marched over to the witness stand. "Mr. Cippio," she said, "we are all sorry for what happened to your son."

"You don't sound sorry," Cippio retorted.

Stunned, Nash took a moment to recover. "Well, I am," she said. "But I also have a job to do and that's to save an innocent man from false accusations."

"I understand you have a job to do," Cippio agreed.

"Thank you. Now, Mr. Cippio, were you present in Marcus Garvey Park when your son was confronted and shot?"

"No, I wasn't."

"So you don't have any direct eyewitness knowledge as to what actually occurred before the shooting?"

"Correct."

Nash nodded and moved on to the undercover operation. "Would you say that the murder of Imani Sefu and the attempted murder of Reverend Mufti were racially motivated?"

Cippio shrugged. "I think Satars and Delgado are racists based on the things they said when I was around them. But Gilliam—"

"So these attacks were racially motivated?"

"In part, yes," Cippio agreed.

Nash crossed her arms as she strolled over in front of the jurors. "Are there a lot of racists in the New York Police Department?"

"I wouldn't say a lot. But like any part of our society, there are some."

"Are you a racist?"

"No, I am not," Cippio said with a frown.

"So you might not know the prevalence of racism in the department?"

"I guess not an exact number or percentage. But police officers work with all sorts of people of every race and ethnicity, and there are very few reported incidents."

"Might that be because people of color would be afraid to report these sorts of incidents to the police?"

"Only because of guys like Mufti," Cippio shot back.

Nash's eyes opened wide for a moment, then she scowled. "Isn't that a racist comment?" she accused.

"No, it's the truth. Guys like him have made people afraid of the police."

"It has nothing to do with the police themselves?" Nash suggested sardonically.

"There are bad apples in every barrel," Cippio conceded. "But good cops want to get rid of the bad cops even more than citizens do. They give us a bad name and make it even harder to do an already tough and dangerous job."

"So do you blame activists, like my client, Anthony Johnson, for the murder of your son?"

225

"Not exactly." Cippio leaned forward, his back straight and his demeanor ramrod firm, and looked right at Nash. "I blame activists for setting the scene. I only blame your client for the murder of my son because he pulled the trigger."

"Objection!" Nash blurted out. "Your Honor, I move to have that answer stricken from the record as nonresponsive and prejudicial."

As Kershner was about to rule, Karp didn't wait and stood up immediately and shot right back, "Ms. Nash opened the door and the witness slammed it shut with justification."

"I believe Mr. Karp is correct on this matter," Kershner responded. "Objection overruled."

Nash responded indignantly, "Well, then, I have no further questions."

Kershner asked Karp, "Do you have anything for redirect?"

Karp remained standing behind the prosecution table. "Yes, Your Honor."

"Please proceed."

"Sergeant Cippio, would it be okay with you if my office framed an innocent man for the murder of your son?"

"Absolutely not."

"And why not?"

"A couple of reasons," Cippio replied. "One, I don't want just anybody to pay for my son's murder. I want the actual killer caught and sent to prison for the rest of his life."

"And the other reason?"

Cippio shook his head and slowly, deliberately answered, "What cop would want anybody framed for murdering another cop when it means the real killer would still be out on the streets, maybe killing more cops? It just doesn't make any sense, does it, Mr. Karp?"

Karp nodded and smiled slightly. "Common sense and reasonableness are virtues of not only a good police officer but also of good citizens," he replied, looking over at the jurors. "Thank you, Sergeant Cippio. No further questions, Your Honor."

19

AFTER THE LUNCH RECESS, KARP LED OFFICER EDDIE EVANS step-by-painful-step through the events leading to the murder of his partner, Tony Cippio. A narrative that had many members of the jury, as well as the gallery—at least those sitting on the prosecution side of the aisle—in tears.

"I was sitting on my lazy ass in the patrol car when my partner needed me," Evans testified hoarsely. He choked up several more times as he described seeing the killer grab his fallen partner by the shoulder to turn him over. "He then stood up and shot Tony in the head."

Karp hated to do it to the officer, who he knew blamed himself for Cippio's murder, but he needed the details in order to do the "dovetailing" of the corroborating evidence he'd promised the jury in his opening statement. More would follow with other witnesses, the pieces interlocking, but it started with Evans.

Karp asked Evans if his partner had ever expressed any racist sentiments.

"Hell, no," Evans replied vehemently. "Tony was color-blind. We were more than just partners, he was my brother and I was his. He would have given his life for me, or anybody, really . . ." He looked up, and with tears streaming down his face, he continued, ". . . and I would have given mine. I wish, God, how I wish, I could do it all over again and have taken those bullets for him."

Wrapping up the direct examination, Karp questioned Evans about his meetings with Gilliam, Satars, and Delgado both at Cippio's memorial service and the bar in Brooklyn. "And can you tell the jurors what led to your suspicions that these three rogue cops were behind the murder of Sefu?" he asked.

"It was obvious he was one of the guys they blamed for Tony's murder and then the riots after that kid got shot by an officer . . . him and Mufti," Evans said, nodding toward the gallery where the reverend sat. "It was too much of a coincidence that Sefu ends up 'accidentally' being left alone with a violent white supremacist and that guy happens to have a weapon. So that's when I called your office."

Nash, in her cross-examination, asked Evans only a few questions about the murder of Cippio. They were mostly to establish that he was not able to make a positive identification of the shooter, nor had he seen the gun clearly.

"I could tell it was a revolver," Evans said, "but that was about it. It happened so fast, and I was running and calling for help."

At that point, Nash suddenly asked, "Officer Evans, is racism pervasive within the New York City Police Department?"

Evans frowned. "Pervasive? No. Are there racists in the department? Yes, like any other segment of our society. But to be honest, I run into it more often from people on the streets than I do from my brother officers. We like to say that blue trumps black and white once you put on the uniform."

"What about the white officers charged with the murder of Imani Sefu and the attempted murder of Reverend Mufti?"

"Those officers do not represent the majority of officers at the NYPD," Evans stated firmly.

"Nevertheless, a group of NYPD officers murdered one black activist, and conspired to murder another, because of their outspoken criticism of police brutality—"

"And they were caught and charged," Evans interrupted. "I believe that one of the officers has pleaded guilty and the other two are still awaiting trial."

Nash scoffed. "Do you have any doubt that those two are guilty?"

"I haven't seen the evidence, but they deserve their day in court . . . just like your client."

"Still, as you noted, one of them has pleaded guilty," Nash went on. "He's on the prosecution witness list to appear at this trial, probably part of whatever deal he worked out with the—"

"Objection," Karp interjected, rising. "Defense counsel speculates and isn't privy to whatever my office may or may not have done regarding the prospective witness. To be sure, once he appears on the witness stand, it will all become extremely clear."

"Sustained," Kershner replied. "Ms. Nash, please keep your questions on point."

Nash rolled her eyes and turned back to Evans. "Okay, let's stick with the *fact* that one white police officer has pleaded guilty to the murder of a black activist and the attempted murder of another black activist, as part of a conspiracy to silence anybody who speaks out against law enforcement. And if law enforcement is willing to murder black activists, why should these jurors believe they wouldn't stoop to framing another?"

"Objection, Your Honor," Karp said, more forcefully this time. "Defense counsel is giving speeches, not asking questions. Even if there was one scintilla of evidence to support what she just said, and there's not, the witness is in no position to answer a question like that."

"I'll overrule you, Mr. Karp. The witness may answer the question," Kershner said.

Evans shrugged. "I guess they'll just need to listen to the evidence and make their decisions from there."

"Even if that means convicting an innocent man the system wants to silence, just like Imani Sefu and Hussein Mufti?"

Evans stared hard at the defense attorney and shook his head. "I guess I just have more faith in the intelligence of jurors than you do."

Again, Nash looked stunned by a retort she hadn't expected. But she recovered. "Or maybe you're worried about what your white 'brothers' in uniform will say if you don't toe the line. No further questions."

Kershner raised her eyebrows at Nash's remark but said nothing to her. Instead, she asked Karp if he had anything for redirect.

"Just a couple questions," he said, then looked at Evans, who was obviously seething over the defense attorney's remarks. "Officer Evans, are you angry about the murder of your partner, Tony Cippio?"

"Yes. Angry and sad, and I feel guilty as hell that I wasn't there for him."

"Do you want to see someone brought to justice for his brutal, cold-blooded execution?"

"More than anything."

Karp pointed at Johnson. "Do you want to see that man pay for the murder of your partner?"

Evans scowled as he looked at the defendant. "If he's guilty, yes."

"And if he's not?"

Evans frowned as he returned his gaze to Karp. "Then no. That would mean the real killer got away with it. I can't think of anything worse than that."

"Thank you," Karp said. "No more questions, Your Honor."

"Ms. Nash, anything further?"

Sitting in her seat, writing notes on a legal pad, Nash didn't even look up as she shook her head.

"Ms. Nash, please answer so that the jurors, the court reporter, and I can hear you," Kershner said crossly.

Karp, who had returned to his seat, scribbled a fast note for Katz to see: "Slowly the tide turns."

Nash sighed loud enough to be heard throughout the courtroom. "No, Your Honor," she replied just as irritably as the judge. "I have no more questions for this witness."

"Very well." Kershner peered through her glasses at the clock on the wall of the courtroom. "It's two o'clock. It's a little early, but do you want to take our afternoon break now, Mr. Karp, or call your next witness?"

Karp stood to answer. "If it pleases the court, now would be good. My next witness is a youngster, and I'd like to look in on him before I call him to the stand."

"All right, court is in recess," Kershner said. "We'll reconvene in fifteen minutes."

As the jury was being escorted out, Karp walked over to the door leading to the witness waiting room and left the courtroom. He took just a few steps down the narrow interior hall and opened the door. Basically, the room was barren with a table in the middle and several chairs placed about.

Nevie Butler was sitting with Tyrone, who looked frightened. The woman brightened when she saw him. "Good afternoon, Mr. Karp. Did you come for Tyrone?"

"The court is in recess for fifteen minutes," Karp explained. "When we reconvene, we'll ask for Tyrone to be brought into the courtroom by Detective Fulton. I just wanted to check in to see how he's doing."

Butler stood. "I need to visit the little girls' room. So I'll leave you two alone if that's okay." She took her grandson's face between her two hands and looked lovingly into his eyes. "I am so proud of you. You're going to be just fine."

With that she turned and left. When the door clicked shut, Karp sat down across from Tyrone. "Are you okay?"

The young man shrugged. "Yeah, a little nervous I guess." He tugged on his shirt collar and tie.

Karp smiled. "It's natural to have some butterflies. Just answer the questions honestly and focus on what you know, what you observed, and you'll do well. If you don't know the answer to a question, or if you don't remember, just say so. All you have to do is tell the truth, Tyrone."

There was a knock on the door and Fulton poked his head in. "It's time."

Karp patted Tyrone on the shoulder as he stood. He then held out his hand, which Tyrone shook shyly. "Your grandmother is not the only person proud of you," he said. "I am, and so is Detective Fulton, and I know if Officer Tony was here, he'd tell you the same."

Although not all of the fear left Tyrone's eyes, his face relaxed and he smiled. "Thank you, Mr. Karp. I'm doing this for him."

Karp left and reentered the courtroom, taking his seat behind the prosecution table. After the jury returned, he stood and announced, "The People call Tyrone Greene."

Fulton opened the door, and the young teen entered and stood for a moment blinking at all the faces turned toward him. He looked like a frightened rabbit about to turn and run, but then his eyes caught those of his grandmother sitting in the row behind the prosecution table. As she smiled and nodded, he stood up straighter and walked over to where the court clerk beckoned.

Tyrone was sworn in and took the seat at the witness stand. Karp's telling the youngster that he was proud of him wasn't just lip service. There'd already been one attempt to intimidate, even kill, Tyrone and his family when Big George Parker met his fate.

And Mrs. Butler had reported a number of threats since the media released his name as a prosecution witness.

Marlene had assured him that her man with a dog was watching out for the family. And Clay Fulton said the precinct had stepped up patrols around their neighborhood. But he knew such precautions weren't foolproof.

Nevie Butler had refused to move to a safe house or take her boys out of school. "This is our home," she told Karp when he called to ask how they were doing. "And their schoolwork comes first. We are not going to be chased from here by cowards and bullies. Thank you, Mr. Karp, but we're staying. Besides, we got some good neighbors watching out for us. We know how to take care of our own around here."

Karp picked up a photograph from the prosecution table and walked to the witness stand. "Your Honor, the record will reflect that I am showing the witness this photograph marked People's Exhibit 31 for identification," he said, holding it up.

Karp handed the photograph to Tyrone Greene, who looked suddenly sad.

"Tyrone, do you recognize the person in this photograph?"

"Yes, sir, that's Officer Tony."

"Officer Tony. Do you know his last name?"

"Cippio. Officer Tony Cippio."

"And how did you know Officer Tony Cippio?"

Tyrone smiled, though his lower lip trembled. "He used to play basketball with us at Marcus Garvey Park."

"Who is us?"

"Just me and my friends from the neighborhood."

"How often did he play basketball with you and your friends?"

Tyrone looked up at the ceiling as if counting, then shrugged. "Maybe six times. He just showed up one day and asked if he could play."

"Was he a good basketball player?"

That made Tyrone smile and snort. "Not bad for an old white guy."

"Old?" Karp queried. "How old would you say he was?"

"Well, not as old as you."

The court burst out laughing. "Well, thank you for that reminder," Karp said, laughing, too.

The interplay had done its work by loosening up Tyrone, who was smiling. But he stopped when Karp walked across the courtroom to stand in front of the defense table and pointed at Johnson, who first glared at Karp but then smiled at Greene. "And do you recognize this man?" he asked.

Tyrone nodded but didn't speak. He blinked back tears as Karp gently reminded him that he needed to speak up so that the jurors could hear him. "Yes, he said his name was Nat X."

"Let the record reflect that the witness has identified the defendant," Karp said. Then he walked back toward the witness stand. "He told you his name was Nat X?"

"Yes."

"Was 'X' his last name?"

"I guess. That's all he told me and my friends."

"How do you know him?"

"He started coming around the basketball court. He wanted to talk to us about stuff."

"Yes, we'll get to that in a moment," Karp said. "Approximately how long ago did you first meet the defendant?"

Tyrone looked at the ceiling to think about that, too. "Two or three weeks before Officer Tony was shot."

Karp walked back to the witness stand and took the photograph from Tyrone. "Your Honor, I move to enter People's Exhibit 31 into evidence," he said as he walked along the jury rail showing the photograph to the jurors.

"Accepted."

Returning the photograph to the prosecution table, Karp said, "You mentioned that the defendant wanted to talk to you about 'stuff.' What kind of stuff?"

Tyrone fidgeted in his seat. "Stuff like how white people hate black people. And that we had to stand up for ourselves and other black people. He said there should be a black America and a white America."

"Did he say anything to you about police officers?"

Tyrone looked at the defendant and then back at the district attorney. "Yes, he said that we're in a war and that police officers were the enemy."

"Anything else?"

Tyrone frowned. "Yes, he said we had to protect ourselves from them and that they was enemy soldiers."

"How often," Karp asked, "did the defendant try to talk to you and your friends about the police being the enemy?"

"A few times," Tyrone said. "He invited us to meetings, but we didn't want to go."

"Why not?"

"We didn't . . . I didn't like . . . what he was saying. I ain't ever had any trouble with the police, and my grandma, she says they're our friends." Sadness washed over his face again. "Officer Tony was my friend."

"How did the defendant refer to you and your friends on occasion?" Karp asked.

Suddenly Tyrone looked angry. "Sometimes he called us names, like 'little niggers.' That's not a good word. We didn't like that."

"Do you know anybody who did go to these meetings?"

Tyrone nodded. "Yeah, my brother, Maurice, went. And he told me his friends DeShawn Lakes and Ricky Watts went, too."

Karp nodded. "How old are you, Tyrone?"

"I just turned thirteen."

"And how old is Maurice?"

"He's going to be eighteen real soon."

"How often did the defendant come to the park?"

"Sometimes every day. Then a couple of days would go by and we wouldn't see him, then he'd show up again."

"Did he come alone?"

Tyrone shook his head. "He was never alone. He was always with Big George and sometimes with another man I didn't recognize."

Karp walked over to the prosecution table and picked up another photograph, which he then showed to Tyrone. "Do you recognize the person in this photograph?"

"Yes, that's Big George."

"Did Big George have a last name?"

"Not that I knew."

"Your Honor, let the record reflect that the witness has identified a photograph, People's 32 in evidence, of George Parker as someone known to him as 'Big George,' and that he has seen Big George in the company of the defendant at Marcus Garvey Park on a number of occasions."

Karp and Nash had butted heads at a pretrial hearing over whether he would be able to get evidence about Big George Parker into the trial. Kershner had ruled that he could ask his witnesses if they knew the man and where they knew him from.

However, as Nash had demanded, he was precluded from discussing Big George's death at the abandoned house across from the home of Nevie Butler and her grandsons, his assault on Maurice Greene, and suspicions that he'd murdered Ny-Lee Tomes. The judge had agreed with the defense attorney that such revelations would be "too prejudicial" to the defense.

"Tyrone, did you see Big George at Marcus Garvey Park on the afternoon that Officer Tony was murdered?" Karp asked.

"Yes."

"Was he with anyone?"

"He was with Nat X and the man I didn't know."

"Just so the record is clear, when you say Nat X, that's the same person as the defendant, whom you previously identified seated right over here in this courtroom?" Karp pointed at Johnson.

"Yes, sir."

"So when you saw the defendant with Big George, what were you doing?"

"We were playing basketball."

"Where were Nat X, Big George, and the unidentified man?"

"They was sitting on a picnic table over near the 120th Street entrance."

"What were they doing?"

"Smoking dope and—"

"Objection."

"Sustained."

"Are you sure the three men you saw from the basketball court were those men?"

"Yes, they were there first and I walked right by them."

"Did Officer Tony arrive before or after you?"

"After. We were already playing when he showed up." Tyrone hesitated and shook his head sadly. "He brought us a brand-new basketball because ours wasn't any good no more."

"Did the defendant ever play basketball with you?"

Tyrone looked over at Johnson, this time with disdain. "No. He said basketball was just another way for white men to get rich off of black men."

"Did Officer Tony have that same attitude?"

"No." Tyrone smiled. "He said he was going to come watch me play in Madison Square Garden when I'm playing for the Knicks."

"But first you're going to play ball in college?"

"My grandma says she'll tan my hide if I don't graduate from college," Tyrone said, smiling at Nevie Butler as the spectators and courtroom staff laughed. "So I guess I'll have to go."

"Might be good to have a fallback," Karp said. His face grew serious. "I know this is going to be hard on you, but I need you to tell the jury what happened that early evening when Officer Tony Cippio started to leave the park after playing basketball with you."

Tears welled in Tyrone's eyes, but he sighed and did as asked, stopping to answer Karp's queries during the narrative, such as when he got to the part where he'd warned the officer about the men on the picnic table.

"And you said you described Nat X to Officer Cippio and to me as tall and skinny with a scar over his right eye." Karp showed a photograph to Tyrone and asked him to identify the person depicted.

"It's him," Tyrone said, pointing at Johnson. "You see the scar above his eye?"

"Have you seen this photograph before?" Karp asked.

"Yes, you showed it and some other photos of men to me. You asked me if I could identify the man who shot Officer Tony."

"And did you do that?"

"Yes, I picked that photograph."

"About when was that?" Karp asked. "Was there some sort of event that happened to fix the time in your mind?"

"Yes, it was after you got shot. I remember that."

"So almost two months after Officer Cippio was shot?"

Tyrone shrugged. "I guess. I know summer was over and I was back in school."

"And did I ask you to identify the man you saw shoot Officer Tony on another occasion?"

"Yes, sir. Me and my grandma and Maurice all came down to the jail. First me and then Maurice went into that little room and looked through the glass into another room at some men standing against a wall. They each were holding up a number. You said it was a one-way mirror and that we could see them but they couldn't see us."

"And did you identify the man you knew as Nat X from that lineup?" Karp asked.

"I knew him right away," Tyrone said.

The teen grew more emotional as he described seeing the confrontation between Tony Cippio and the men who got up from the picnic table. "I knew there was going to be trouble," he said, shaking his head back and forth. "I told him not to go near them. I told him they didn't like police officers."

"What happened, Tyrone?" Karp asked as he leaned on the jury rail.

Tyrone was silent for a full minute, wiping at the tears in his eyes. But when he looked up at Johnson, it was with hatred. "He shot him. He just shot him to death," the teen said angrily.

"Who shot Officer Tony Cippio?" Karp asked for emphasis.

"HIM!" Tyrone yelled, rising partly from his seat as he pointed a damning finger at Johnson, who glared malevolently.

For the second time that day, Karp walked over and poured the witness a glass of water. Tyrone had reacted exactly as he'd hoped, but now he wanted to settle him down.

He turned to the judge. "Your Honor, for demonstration purposes, I would ask that Assistant District Attorney Kenny Katz be allowed to assume the role of the victim. And that the witness be allowed to leave the stand for this presentation."

"Very well," Kershner said.

"Mr. Katz, if you would," Karp said, directing his co-counsel to the center of the court. He turned back to Tyrone and asked him to approach. They'd gone over it in his office so that Tyrone would know where to go.

"You've testified that Big George stepped in front of Officer Tony. So if I'm Big George and Mr. Katz is Officer Tony and he's facing me, where was the defendant?"

Tyrone stepped up behind Katz. "Right here."

"So demonstrate how the defendant shot the officer, please."

Tyrone raised his arm and pointed his finger at Katz's back. "BANG!" he yelled, loud enough to make some of the jurors jump.

Katz pitched forward and fell onto his face, then tried to rise.

"After Officer Tony fell to the ground, what happened?" Karp continued.

Tyrone stepped forward and grabbed Katz by the shoulder and turned him over. "Officer Tony sort of held his hand up and I think he was saying something, but I couldn't hear."

"What did the defendant do then?"

Tyrone again raised his hand and, standing over Katz's prone figure, pointed his finger at his victim's head and pulled the imaginary trigger. "BANG!" he yelled. "He shot Tony again in the head."

Katz fell back and lay still. The impact of the demonstration was so vivid the courtroom was dead quiet.

"You may return to your seat," Karp told Tyrone. "And you, too, Mr. Katz."

The jury was rapt now and hanging on Karp's every word, their eyes following him as he walked over to the prosecution table, where he picked up a paper bag. He returned to the witness stand. "Were you able to see the type of gun the defendant pointed at Officer Tony?"

"Yes, it was a revolver."

"Any particular color?"

"Silver."

"Was there anything else you noticed about the gun?"

"Yes, it had a shiny sort of white-silver handle on it."

"How could you tell that?"

"Because when Officer Tony was facing Big George, Nat X pulled up the back of his sweatshirt and I could see it sticking up out of his pants. And then again when he pulled it out and when he ran past us."

Karp reached into the bag and pulled out the stainless steel, .45 caliber revolver with the mother-of-pearl grip taken from defendant Anthony Johnson in San Francisco. "Did it look like this gun?"

"Yes, it looked like that gun."

Karp replaced the gun in the bag and set it back on the prosecution table. "Is there any doubt in your mind that the men you walked past when you arrived at the park—whom you identified as Nat X, Big George, and an associate of theirs—were the same men who confronted Officer Tony?"

"They were the same guys."

Returning one last time to the witness stand, Karp asked, "What did you do after you saw the defendant shoot Officer Tony twice, once when standing behind him and again in the head while Officer Tony lay defenseless on the ground?"

"I ran over to see if I could help. I held his head until the black policeman got there."

"Was Officer Tony still alive?"

"He was making some sounds like he was trying to breathe," Tyrone said, and stifled a sob. "Then he died."

As Tyrone cried, Karp looked at the judge. "No further questions."

Judge Kershner was silent for a moment and had to clear her throat before she asked Nash if she wanted to cross-examine the teen. The defense attorney seemed unsure at first but then gathered herself and walked swiftly to the witness stand.

"Good afternoon, Tyrone. May I call you Tyrone, since the DA did?" she asked.

"Yes, ma'am."

Nash smiled, though grimly. Karp knew she had to limit her questions; after all, her contention was that her client wasn't even present at the murder. So all she could challenge was Tyrone's identification as far as the scene and his conversations with Nat X, which is where she started.

"Did this Nat X ever try to get you to shoot a police officer?" she asked.

Tyrone shook his head. "No, he said we were at war with whites and the police were soldiers. And that we had to protect ourselves and our community. But he didn't say, 'Tyrone, go shoot a police-man.'"

"How far were you from the men sitting on the picnic table?" she asked.

"Pretty far."

"How far is pretty far?"

"I don't know," Tyrone said, frowning.

"Well, the size of a football field, one hundred yards?" Nash asked.

Tyrone thought about it, then shook his head. "No, not that far. Maybe twenty yards?"

Nash smiled. "That's a pretty good guess. What if I told you it was about twenty-five?"

"I guess," Tyrone said with a shrug.

"The man that you claim was my client, Mr. Johnson, you said he was wearing a sweatshirt," Nash said. "Was it a hoodie type of sweatshirt?"

"Yes. A black hoodie sweatshirt."

"And was he wearing the hood up or down?"

"Up."

"So this man you say you saw shoot the police officer from a distance of twenty-five yards, he was wearing a black sweatshirt with the hood up covering his face?"

"Not all of his face. And I saw him when I walked by before the shooting."

"And did you then watch him the whole time you were playing basketball?"

Tyrone scrunched up his face. "What do you mean?"

"I mean did you ever take your eyes off of the man you first saw on the picnic table?"

"Um, I guess I didn't watch him the whole time."

"So someone else could have taken his place?"

"Objection," Karp said, rising to his feet. "Sheer speculation, Your Honor, with no supporting evidence."

"Overruled, Mr. Karp," Kershner said. "I'll allow it."

"He was wearing the same black hoodie," Tyrone said.

"How do you know? Have you ever seen anyone else wearing a black hoodie?"

"Well, yeah, I guess so. But he was with Big George."

"Is it possible that Big George sometimes associated with other men who might wear black hoodie sweatshirts—?"

"Yes. But—"

"Please wait for me to ask you another question, Tyrone," Nash said sternly. "Now, did this Nat X ever show you a silver gun with a shiny handle?"

"No."

"So he never talked about killing cops and he never showed you this gun?"

"No."

"I see. And the next day you went to the district attorney's office and that's where this whole story was put together, right?"

"No," Tyrone said. "I knew what happened that night. You're twisting things around."

"Am I? Or is it the DA who twisted things around, put words in your mouth?"

"No, that's not what happened!"

"And these photographs you supposedly picked out of lineups, they were shown to you by Mr. Karp as well, weren't they?"

Again the youth looked at Karp, who couldn't offer any help. "Yes, he showed them to me."

"And lo and behold, you picked out the photographs of my client, a black activist who talked to you about the black liberation movement but never once talked about killing police officers or showed you that gun you just identified?"

"I saw what I saw," Tyrone said defiantly.

"Yes, of course you did," Nash said, "which was exactly what the district attorney wanted you to see! No further questions."

"Mr. Karp, redirect?" Kershner asked.

"Absolutely," Karp said, striding out into the courtroom and then up to the defense table, where he loomed over the attorney and her client. He pointed so that the end of his finger was close enough to Johnson that the defendant could have grabbed it if he dared.

"Tyrone, is this the man you saw shoot Officer Tony Cippio in the back and then in the head with a silver-colored revolver?"

"Yes, sir, I'm sure of it."

"Thank you," Karp said. "No further questions."

20

THE MOUSY LITTLE MAN WITH THE BAD COMB-OVER AND wearing a dark suit, narrow tie, and starched white shirt straight out of the 1950s peered through his Coke-bottle eyeglasses at the paperwork Karp had just handed him on the witness stand. He looked up. "I'm ready when you are," he said.

Dr. Sherman Offendahl looked the part of a mild, bookwormish scientist. However, Espy Jaxon had assured Karp that when it came to DNA expertise, the lead geneticist with the Armed Forces DNA Identification Laboratory was a "giant in the field."

"I had to call in some favors to get this guy on board," Jaxon had explained months earlier to Karp. "He's respected throughout the world, and above reproach, as is the Armed Forces Lab. So much so that some of the top labs regularly ask him to review their methods and discuss the latest technology with their people."

Karp started the DNA testimony when court convened the next

morning by calling Jaxon to the stand to quickly run through the events leading to his request to find a laboratory apart from the NYPD lab to test the touch DNA samples taken from the shirt of Tony Cippio. He'd expected Jaxon to take the samples to the FBI lab in Quantico, but his friend decided to use the Armed Forces facility.

Karp limited his questioning of Jaxon to establishing the chain of custody for the evidence. That included showing him the returned samples of the material he'd given the agent several days after the Cippio shooting.

"Agent Jaxon, are those your initials on the sample cards?" Karp asked.

Jaxon examined the documents and nodded. "They are."

Karp entered them as People's Exhibit 58. Nash hadn't even bothered to look at the documents and didn't object.

"Agent Jaxon, did I explain why I asked for federal assistance with DNA testing in this case?"

"I believe that there was some concern on your part because the victim was a New York police officer, and that given today's political climate, you wanted a second opinion, so to speak, on the evidence of whatever the NYPD crime lab reported so that there would be no question as to the legitimacy of the results. I requested that the Armed Forces Laboratory test the samples to avoid any such potential conflicts."

Nash declined to cross-examine Jaxon. As the agent stepped down from the witness stand, Karp glanced at Katz, who raised an eyebrow, smiled, and went back to making notes on a legal pad.

Karp then called Offendahl to the witness stand. After the judge accepted the man as an expert in the field of DNA, the district attorney handed him the reports. The scientist examined them and announced he was prepared to answer questions.

Karp began by asking him to first define DNA and what was meant by a "DNA profile."

"Ah, yes, well," Offendahl began, "DNA is short for deoxyribonucleic acid. Without going into a lot of scientific terminology, it is the genetic material that determines the makeup of all living cells, and many viruses. It is passed down from parents, who each contribute fifty percent, to a child. It is unique to an individual, except in the case of identical twins, who share the exact same genetic makeup. A so-called DNA profile are the small variations between unrelated individuals, which is why a profile is as unique as a fingerprint."

"Is DNA profiling absolute?" Karp asked.

Offendahl thought about it for a moment. "Sometimes we are asked to test genetic material that is degraded, such as over time or exposure to, say, sunlight or radiation. In that case, we sort of hedge our bets and offer a range, such as the likelihood of two people sharing the same profile to, say, one in a million or, as in the case of the samples I was asked to test for your office, one in a billion."

"Has there been much in the way of changes to the science of DNA profiling over the years, particularly the amount of genetic material necessary for accurate testing?" Karp asked.

"Oh, yes." Offendahl nodded. "DNA testing was first developed in the mid-1980s, and like any new science went through a period of growth and improvement. Right up until the mid to late 1990s, quite a sizable amount, comparatively, of genetic material—such as a large blood smear—was required. As time went on, however, techniques and technology both improved, and by the late 1990s that amount might need only be a drop of blood."

"And has the science continued to progress?" Karp asked.

"Indeed," Offendahl replied, obviously enjoying having an audience. "Modern-day DNA profiling, called STR analysis, is a very sensitive technique that requires only the tiniest speck of blood or saliva, even a hair root or a few skin cells."

"When might a few skin cells come into play?"

"Well, believe it or not, we human beings are constantly shedding our skin, sort of like snakes only not in large, contiguous pieces. Indeed, the average human being sloughs off about a million skin cells every day. Although some of the genetic coding in those dead cells is damaged and worthless from a testing point of view, most carry the DNA profile of the individual. So when someone takes off an article of clothing, skin cells go with it, or if someone touches something, particularly something like clothing, they leave behind those skin cells."

"Is that what is meant by 'touch DNA'?"

"Yes, in a lay sense."

"Is testing for touch DNA accurate and a scientifically accepted technique?"

"Absolutely. Of course, great care must be taken for the proper collection, retention, and forwarding of such material, but if all of that is done, it is very precise and accepted in courtrooms all over the world."

As he questioned the scientist, Karp looked from time to time at the faces of the jurors, noting their fascinated expressions. Modern jurors had been exposed to a lot of television crime shows, some better than others, and they expected these "*CSI* moments." In this case, he was happy to be able to provide them.

"Dr. Offendahl, have there been instances in the past in which individuals have either by accident, negligence, or deception rendered an inaccurate or misleading report on a particular DNA test they conducted?"

Offendahl frowned and nodded. "Unfortunately, yes. Just like in any other sort of police work, some individuals may be careless or even purposefully misleading about a test result for one reason or another."

"Is this common?"

Offendahl shook his head. "No, not at all. There are literally hundreds of thousands of DNA profiles conducted every year, and those are just the ones tested for law enforcement purposes. Obviously, millions have been completed since the science began to be used. And while there have been some high-profile instances of unqualified or even malicious individuals falsifying results, they are a tiny minority. They are quickly found out, and safeguards have been instituted, especially following these high-profile cases."

"Dr. Offendahl, you testified that you have conducted thousands of DNA profiles and testified under oath more than six hundred times regarding tests you've conducted," Karp said. "Has there been a single instance in which your work was found to be incorrect, or where you were successfully challenged for being inaccurate?"

"Not once," Offendahl replied.

Karp pointed to the exhibits Offendahl held in his hands. "Would you please describe for the jurors the reports I asked you to examine a few minutes ago?"

"Of course. They are both reports regarding touch DNA profiles taken from the shirt of the deceased, Officer Tony Cippio. One profile was conducted by the New York Police Department crime laboratory, and the other I conducted myself at the Armed Services Laboratory."

"How would you describe the results of the reports?"

"They are virtually identical, with some very minor discrepancies that can be attributed to the relative strength of the genetic sample," Offendahl said.

"And what might cause such a discrepancy?"

Offendahl pursed his lips and shrugged slightly. "Oh, for instance if you had a smear of blood, there might be more blood on one end of the smear than the other, so the relative strength of the genetic sample might vary. In these two instances, the discrepancies are so small as to be inconsequential."

"So by comparison, the results are similar enough to fall within the scientifically acceptable range of certainty?"

"Absolutely. Both laboratories examined the same genetic material."

"And was genetic material located on Tony Cippio's shirt?"

"Yes, as expected, there was material—blood, skin cells— matching the deceased's DNA."

"Any other material?"

Offendahl glanced at the reports and nodded. "Yes, that of five humans and one canine. Apparently Officer Cippio had a dog or at least petted one enough to have dog saliva and hair at several locations on the shirt."

Karp smiled and used the opportunity to remind the jurors of Vince Cippio's remarks about his son's penchant for picking up strays. "He did, indeed, named Wink . . . Were you able to identify the human DNA?"

Again, Offendahl referred to the reports. "Yes, as you would expect, four of the human profiles belonged to people close to the deceased: his wife, his two children, and his partner, Officer Eddie Evans."

"And the fifth?" Karp asked, walking over toward the defense table.

"The fifth was unknown," Offendahl said. "However, I entered the DNA profile into the FBI's DNA database, otherwise known as CODIS, for Combined DNA Index System, and I got a hit."

"A hit?"

"A match," Offendahl explained, "for a DNA sample for an individual who had lived in the San Francisco Bay Area of California."

Karp nodded. He had to tread carefully at this point because the rules of evidence prevented the prosecutor from referring to the defendant's prior criminal history in front of the jury unless the defendant took the stand.

"Do you know the identity of the individual who matched the DNA profile taken from Officer Tony Cippio's shirt?"

"I do." Offendahl nodded toward the defense table. "The defendant, Anthony Johnson."

"And did the New York Police Department profile agree with your conclusion?"

"Yes, as I said, they were for all intents and purposes identical. The NYPD profile was also a match for the defendant, Anthony Johnson."

Karp looked at Johnson, who rolled his eyes as if the entire testimony was boring him. "To what degree of scientific certainty is the touch DNA profile from both reports a match for the defendant?"

"There is a one-in-one-billion chance that two people could have that same DNA profile. In other words, beyond any and all doubt, the DNA taken from the shirt is a match for Anthony Johnson."

Karp looked at Kershner. "Your Honor, I ask that Assistant District Attorney Kenny Katz be allowed to play a part in another demonstration for the court, as well as your permission for the witness to step down from the stand."

"Go ahead."

Nodding to his co-counsel, Karp waited for Katz to reach the well of the court before turning back to Offendahl, who was now in front of the witness stand. "Dr. Offendahl, on what part of Officer Cippio's shirt was the DNA profile for the defendant located?"

"The top right shoulder and back area."

Karp nodded at Katz, who turned around with his back toward the two other men. "If Officer Cippio was shot . . . BANG . . . and fell forward onto his stomach"—as Karp spoke, Katz lay down—"can you demonstrate where on Cippio's shirt the defendant's DNA would be located?"

Offendahl stepped over Katz and reached down and across with his left hand, and grabbed Katz by his right shoulder. Without saying anything, Karp looked back at the jurors. Their eyes told him everything he needed to know. They had seen this before, when Tyrone Greene acted it out. He turned back to the scientist.

"Thank you, Dr. Offendahl. You may return to the witness stand. No further questions."

Nash rose to her feet but remained behind the defense table. "I only have a few questions, Dr. Offendahl," she said. "Of all those times you've testified under oath, how many times have you testified for law enforcement as opposed to how many times for the defense?"

"I've never counted."

"What about a percentage?" Nash insisted. "What percentage of the time do you testify for the prosecution compared to the defense?"

Offendahl shook his head. "Criminal case DNA testing is only a small part of what I do, but most requests for testing certainly come from the law enforcement side. But I don't really consider myself testifying 'for' or 'against' either side. I'm a scientist; I conduct research, apply the scientific method, examine the data, and reach a conclusion. Whatever that conclusion is—whether it's helpful to the prosecution or to the defense—I don't skew it for one side or the other."

"Nevertheless, you work for the government."

"I work for the government in many capacities. As I explained to Her Honor when we were discussing my bona fides, most of my work is with the identification of human remains, including our missing war dead or mass casualty victims, such as with the attacks on the World Trade Center on nine/eleven."

"And when you do work on criminal cases, it is mostly at the request of law enforcement?"

Offendahl sighed. "Yes, mostly."

Nash smiled. "No further questions."

"No redirect," Karp said. He knew that Nash was saving her attacks on the DNA evidence for when she called her own expert witness. But Offendahl was rock solid, a scientist who approached his work objectively and who had without fear or favor tendered his conclusion, which had corroborated that of the NYPD lab. He thought back to his decision to ask Jaxon to get a second opinion; he'd known even then that there was a good chance the defense would try to argue it was all a frame and the police couldn't be trusted. He wasn't worried about Nash's expert; he had a surprise waiting for her then, too.

In the days that followed, more pieces snapped together seamlessly. Karp called Assistant Medical Examiner Gail Manning to testify about the horrendous damage done by two .45 caliber cop-killer bullets. And how the killer had fired the first from nearly point-blank range into the victim's back and then stood over the dying man and fired down into his head.

Then he called an NYPD ballistics expert, Don Spicer, who began by testifying that the two bullets used to kill Cippio were .45 caliber. However, he said that both bullets, actually fragments of bullets, were too damaged for him to declare with "scientific certainty" that they'd been fired from the revolver taken from the defendant in San Francisco. He was able to say only that they were "consistent" with bullets he'd test-fired from the revolver.

Spicer also testified that the fragments were of the same make and type as four bullets given to him for testing by the District Attorney's Office. Even more damaging was his testimony about chamber marks on the two empty cartridge cases also found in the gun.

"Chamber marks are nearly microscopic striations, or scratches, on the outside of a cartridge when it is loaded or removed from the chamber," Spicer said. "Roughness in a chamber—invisible to the naked eye—causes these striations. Most chamber marks occur after a cartridge has been fired because the case expands under pressure against the walls of the chamber. Then, when the cartridge is pulled out of the chamber, the sides are scratched."

Spicer explained that just as every barrel of a gun is slightly different, causing "land and groove marks" on a bullet as it passes through, the striations are unique as well. He'd examined the spent cartridges under a microscope and noted on blowup photographs the unique markings on each. He then test-fired six similar bullets from the revolver and examined each of the spent cartridges. Two of them left "identical" marks to the previous spent cartridges. It was damning evidence.

Then, as his brother, Tyrone, had before him, Maurice Greene identified the defendant as the revolutionary he'd known as Nat X and testified that he'd picked him out of a photo lineup from his bed in Bellevue Hospital and then a standing lineup at the DAO.

He talked about the meetings he'd attended with his childhood friends, DeShawn Lakes and Ricky Watts, in which Johnson talked about casting off the yoke of white oppression and forming a separate black nation by "taking up arms against the oppressor class and their servants, the police."

Then DeShawn Lakes took the stand and identified the defendant as Nat X and corroborated what Maurice had said about the meeting. But he added the scene outside the tenement building with his best friend, Ricky Watts, when Nat X let them hold the big silver gun—yes, one that looked just like the revolver in the evidence bag. "He said it was a 'cop killer,' loaded with bullets that would go through a Kevlar vest 'like it was butter.'"

DeShawn testified about the day he and Ricky met up with Big George Parker and the defendant Johnson, aka Nat X, who asked them if they were ready to "strike a blow for your people . . . be heroes of the revolution? Or are you going to be house niggers?"

He'd been ready to go through with it, too, such was the romantic persuasiveness of Nat X. But then his father, Reverend Jonas Lakes, intercepted them and saved him from himself.

Reverend Lakes took the stand as well. He, too, had gone down to the DAO after Johnson was extradited from California and picked him out of the lineup as the man he'd seen in the company of his son and Ricky Watts.

"I should have stopped Ricky," he cried on the stand. "I should have picked that boy up and made him get in the car." But instead, he'd driven off in one direction while Watts was marched to his doom in another. "I will never forgive myself for that," he said, then looked at Johnson and added, "And God might, but I won't forgive you, either."

As each witness climbed onto the stand and added his piece, Nash was unable to stop the onslaught. Oh, she did her best to claim it was all part of the frame. Black teenagers frightened of the police, coached to say whatever the district attorney wanted. But each witness was placing a damning evidentiary tile in the mosaic that ultimately would depict the defendant guilty beyond all doubt.

Meanwhile, Karp enjoyed watching the smug and defiant visage of the defendant gradually evaporate until he took on the look of a caged rat waiting for the footfalls of his executioner. But there was more.

The testimony of Manning, Spicer, the teens, and Reverend Lakes had taken the rest of the day and part of the next. Then Karp called Judy Pardo, the cop-turned–drug addicted prostitute, seeking this one last shot at redemption. She was the one who could connect the murder of a police officer to the attempted murder of another. Karp had been looking forward to it.

21

Judy Pardo cast an appraising look at herself in the small mirror that hung from the back of the door to her tiny room at the East Village Women's Shelter. She was dressed in an olive green sweater and a knee-length gray skirt—hand-me-downs given to her by the staff but in nice condition and certainly better than the rags she'd been wearing when she arrived eight months earlier.

Girl, you've put on a few pounds, she thought. *Then again, you were too skinny—guess that's what a heroin habit and eating out of Dumpsters will do for you.*

However, it wasn't the clothes she wore, the weight gain, or even the haircut Marlene Ciampi had treated her to for her day in court that jumped out from the mirror. It was her soft chocolate eyes. Surrounded by lines from the hard life she'd lived, they were bright and clear. For so long whenever she'd bothered to glance in a mirror, they'd been clouded by drugs and the pain and humiliation common in a person whose self-respect was absent. It was good to recognize the person she once was staring back at her.

She owed it to Marlene, who'd brought her to the shelter, and to the staff, who'd stuck by her, even when she'd relapsed. Some of them formerly drug addicts themselves, they understood like no one else could the insatiable craving that heroin created. They also knew that it wasn't just the physical addiction she fought but also the underlying psychological issues that left her vulnerable to the drug's siren call.

Pardo took a deep breath and let it out slowly. She was afraid. Afraid of appearing as a witness at the murder trial of a man who seemed to have a lot of angry, violent supporters. And that didn't take into account that a street person who lived among drug dealers, pimps, gang members, and all other manner of criminal sociopaths had to be careful about being seen as a "snitch." Someone who was going to break the code of the streets and "rat" for the prosecution in one case couldn't be trusted not to do it again to one of them. The saying "The only good rat is a dead rat" didn't refer to the rodents who shared the streets and alleys with them.

The threat had lessened somewhat when she heard that David Grale had put the word out that anyone who harmed her would have to answer to him. For all of their bravado and savagery, there weren't many who wanted to cross the King of the Mole People. It didn't mean that someone wouldn't try, especially as she'd been warned that a "bounty" had been put on her head, presumably by Anthony Johnson's supporters. But so far no one had tried to collect.

However, it wasn't the potential for violence that frightened her the most. She had been living on the streets so long that it was simply an accepted fact that her life could end at any moment, even if she never came forward as a witness. She'd been robbed at the point of guns and knives, raped and beaten unconscious, and that didn't take into account the possibility of freezing to death, overdosing on drugs, or dying of starvation or disease.

No, what she feared more than violence or the other dangers of life on the street was the humiliation she would have to endure when she took the stand. She'd be laid open for the jurors, the spectators, the media, and, through them, all the world to see. Her face, her life story, her fall from grace would appear on the front pages of newspapers and on the evening news.

"Once a whore, always a whore." That's what the television reporter Pete Vansand had said to her a few days earlier when he ambushed her and Marlene in the elevator outside the district attorney's office. She forced herself to watch Vansand's report that night, listened to his sneering remarks about the "police officer–turned-prostitute." Of course, he left out her retort that it took one to know one; he, after all, was in charge of the public perception and wasn't going to be fair about it. She watched as a way to prepare herself for what she knew was coming, only it was going to be worse, much worse.

Vansand wasn't the only journalist who had attached himself like a leech to her sordid story. All the New York newspapers and television stations, even the national news, had picked up on it and apparently had no compunction that a lot of what they reported was inaccurate. They'd even located her family—her aging parents, her sister and brother—in New Jersey and harassed them for interviews, which they'd refused, and made them virtual prisoners in their homes. At least until the trial was over.

Satisfied with her appearance, Pardo looked around the room. It was just large enough for a twin bed, a chest of drawers, and a small desk. Two paintings of flowers hung on the off-white walls, and the tiny closet held the few articles of clothing she'd accumulated since moving in.

Soon after the trial she would have to leave, and the thought made her want to cry. The shelter represented the only real safety she had known for years. Only Marlene's intercession had allowed her to remain this long, especially when she'd relapsed during the first couple of months and tested positive for cocaine. But she was studying to be a sonographer, and in spite of some trepidation, looked forward to making it on her own, drug-free and healthy.

She didn't know how she could have made it without Marlene Ciampi. The district attorney's wife had not only found this safe haven for her and been at her side through the legal proceedings, she'd been the one to sign her up at the community college for the sonography classes and insisted on paying her tuition. "I sold a VIP security firm I started," Marlene had explained, "and that gave me more money than God, or at least enough to help a friend get on her feet."

Pardo really had burst into tears when Marlene said that; it had been a long time since someone on that side of the streets had called her a friend. And Marlene's husband, District Attorney

Butch Karp, had also treated her with kindness and compassion, starting with that first night when Marlene insisted they stop at the loft. He'd listened to her story without judging her or being condescending, and he treated her the same way the next day when she went to his office to give a statement.

Nor had he changed as the trial approached. Karp was the consummate professional, and under his trial preparation she almost imagined she was back on the police force, getting ready to testify. They had gone to the meeting room on the last day of jury selection, so he could go over a few items. He'd asked her if she felt ready for what was to come.

She'd been thinking about that for months. "I made a mess of my life, Mr. Karp—"

"Please, in the courtroom it's Mr. Karp, here it's Butch."

"Butch, then." She smiled. "I was saying I made a mess of my life, and it's been a long time since I followed through with much of anything other than where to get my next hit of heroin or a place to sleep out of the cold. So I know this isn't going to be pleasant, but I'll be damned if I'm not going to follow through."

Karp had nodded. "I appreciate that, and I can't thank you enough on behalf of a couple of people who aren't able to—Officer Tony Cippio and a teenager named Ricky Watts, as well as their families, and Officer Bryce Kim, who has had to live with this hanging over his head."

"Thank you . . . Butch . . . but when I was a young police officer on the beat, I always dreamed of doing something like this. You know, taking down a really bad guy and getting him off the streets.

I used to practice in front of a mirror how'd I'd answer questions from the witness stand, matching wits with the defense attorney, pointing to the defendant and saying, 'That's the guy, right there.' Then justice would be served and my community would be safer because of me."

She'd stopped and smiled. "I know it all probably sounds silly coming from a former hooker and heroin addict."

"Not at all," Karp said. "I think all good people would like to think that in the moment of truth, they'd come through for their friends and family and neighbors. And soon, you'll get your chance from the witness stand. In the meantime, there's that old saying from the Bible about how people in glass houses shouldn't cast stones. Personally, I don't know too many people, maybe none, who should be picking up rocks anytime soon."

Karp had left her in the meeting room to wait for Marlene, who wanted to escort her back to the shelter. But Marlene had been running late so it was bad timing that they'd run into Vansand and his cameraman on the elevator. *Once a whore, always a whore.*

Pardo shuddered and had to fight the feeling of panic. She put on her coat, picked up her purse, left her room, and headed out of the shelter. It was a little early; Marlene wasn't due for another ten minutes, but she thought that getting out in the brisk air would clear her head. She decided to walk to the corner where Marlene had said she'd pick her up.

"I have to run an errand in Brooklyn first," Marlene had said when she'd called that morning, "so I'll be in my truck. A big black four-wheel-drive Ford."

"Sounds like something a teenage boy would drive," Pardo had said with a laugh.

Marlene chuckled. "Exactly. I was always something of a tomboy growing up. I loved big trucks and fast cars. We'll have to go find some mud over in Jersey after the trial, and I'll show you what my baby can do!"

As she began to walk, Pardo noticed a black vehicle coming up from behind her out of the corner of her eye. She started to turn, thinking it was Marlene, though she expected her to come from the other direction. Turned out it was a black Cadillac SUV with dark-tinted windows that slowed as it pulled even.

Several events quickly unfolded. The Cadillac stopped suddenly and a heavily tattooed black man jumped out of the front passenger seat and opened the back door of the vehicle. At the same time, someone gripped her arm from behind and she felt something hard pressed against her back.

"Get in the fucking car, bitch," the man holding her snarled. "Move or I'll shoot your whore ass."

Out of nowhere, she recalled the words of her self-defense instructor at the Police Academy. "Never ever get in the car," he warned.

"What if they have a gun?" one of the cadets had asked.

"Even more important that you don't get in the car," the instructor answered. "If they're trying to abduct you in public, and they have a gun, chances are they're not going to pull the trigger and bring attention to themselves. But if they want you to get in the car, it's so they can take you someplace where no one will hear a shot. Fight like hell to stay out of the car."

He continued, "If you can get free, take off running. Again, they probably won't shoot. And if they do shoot, they probably won't hit you—most jackoffs with a gun couldn't hit the Brooklyn Bridge. And if they get lucky and you catch a bullet, chances are it won't be fatal. Stay out of the car and your odds of survival go up, or else get in the car, tuck your head between your knees, and kiss your ass goodbye."

So when the man propelled her toward the car, Pardo screamed and lashed out with one of her feet, kicking the man standing by the door between his legs. Not expecting the well-aimed blow, he gasped and sank to his knees. She then braced her feet—one on the seat and one on the side of the car—and pushed back as hard as she could. The move caught the gunman by surprise. He stumbled backward, and she was able to wrest her arm from his grip. She took off running.

"Come back here, bitch!" the gunman bellowed, and lunged after her.

Pardo had ten feet on her assailant but knew he'd catch her quickly . . . if he didn't shoot. She was trying to decide whether to turn and face him when a big black truck coming from the opposite direction suddenly accelerated, swerved across traffic, and struck the grille of the Cadillac, setting off the alarm and the air bags, rendering it, and the driver, incapacitated. The black truck passed. There was a shriek, a sickening thud, and then the sound of the truck crashing into the brick front wall of the shelter.

Whirling, Pardo was stunned to see Marlene open the driver's-side door and stumble out of the truck. She looked hurt, probably from the air bags that had deployed and struck her in the face and chest. The gunman looked worse, pinned between the partly destroyed wall of bricks and the crumpled front of the truck. He was obviously dead, with a grotesque look of shock and pain on his bug-eyed face.

That still left the man she'd kicked in the groin. He had lifted himself off the sidewalk and pulled a semiautomatic from his waistband, which he started to point at Marlene.

Pardo looked down. The gun of her original assailant lay in front of her on the sidewalk. She picked it up and aimed. "Don't move, or I'll blow your fucking head off!" she yelled.

Startled, the man turned his head and looked at her while still holding his gun on Marlene, who staggered against the truck. Then he laughed. "You old ho. You can't think straight, much less shoot straight."

A wave of doubt passed through Pardo, but then her eyes narrowed as she sighted down the barrel of the gun. "I'll have you know, I was third in my class at the Police Academy for marksmanship. I can still drop your fat ass from this distance. You want to take that chance, punk?"

The man scowled, then lowered the gun. He placed it on the sidewalk and put his hands up. "You'll pay for this someday, bitch."

"Maybe so," Pardo replied. "But not today. Today I'm living the dream."

22

Sitting at the prosecution table, Karp glanced at the clock on the wall of the courtroom: 9:15. Court was supposed to have started fifteen minutes ago with him asking Judy Pardo to take the stand, but he had no idea where she was.

Marlene had called forty minutes earlier saying she was approaching the shelter and would pick up Pardo and drop her off before parking. But they'd been a no-show. He started to wonder if his witness had developed cold feet. *Maybe Marlene's trying to talk her down*, he thought.

His case had been going well, with each piece of the puzzle falling neatly into place. The medical examiner, the ballistics expert, the teenagers, and Reverend Lakes had all testified as expected, and Nash had failed to make any headway against them. The only thing she could do was cast aspersions. Now all that remained was for Pardo to provide the lodestar evidence connecting the defendant to the attempted murder of Officer Bryce Kim. Then Karp would tie up the loose ends with his last few witnesses and rest the People's case.

"Mr. Karp?" Judge Kershner asked. "Perhaps we should move on to another witness."

Karp rose to his feet. "Just a few more minutes, please, Your Honor. I asked Detective Fulton to find out what's going on. I should hear from him shortly."

"Very well, five minutes and then call someone else or rest your case."

As he took his seat, Karp glanced over at the defense table. Nash was writing on a legal pad with a barely discernible smile. Johnson, on the other hand, was looking at him directly with a grin. The defendant winked.

He knows something about this, Karp thought. *I'm sure of it.*

Just then Fulton entered the courtroom and walked quickly over to Karp. They spoke for several minutes.

Karp looked over at the defense table, where Nash was now watching them curiously. Johnson had kicked back in his chair with his legs stretched out in front of him and his hands behind his head, which he bobbed as though listening to music that only he could hear.

Controlling his anger, Karp stood. "Your Honor, may we approach the bench at sidebar? This has to do with my next witness."

"By all means," Kershner said. "Ms. Nash, join us, please."

At the dais, Karp kept his eyes on the jurors, who looked perplexed, but he spoke so that only the judge, defense attorney, and court reporter could hear. "Your Honor, Detective Fulton just informed me that there was an attempt to abduct my witness, Ms. Judy Pardo, at gunpoint about forty-five minutes ago. She's okay and on her way to the courthouse now, but that explains her tardiness."

"I should say so," Kershner replied, shocked. "If this is true, it is extremely alarming."

"Indeed," Karp responded. "I'd also point out that Ms. Pardo was staying at a women's shelter, the location of which is kept secret for the obvious reason that the clients there are usually seeking to get away from abusive and oftentimes violent former husbands and boyfriends. We're not sure how these assailants—my understanding is there were three—learned the location, but we plan to get to the bottom of it." He gave Nash a hard look.

The defense attorney recoiled angrily. "If you're implying that I, or my client, had anything to do with this, I take great umbrage."

"Take it any way you want," Karp said. "And we had better not learn that this was connected to rumors we've been hearing about a reward being offered for information regarding the whereabouts of this witness. In any event, Your Honor, be certain I'll find out."

"That's outrageous," Nash retorted, and turned to the judge. "Your Honor, this witness is a drug addict and prostitute with a criminal record. I'm sure that she has consorted with all manner of nefarious criminals. It is likely that someone recognized her, or she herself gave out the address, and that *if* this attack occurred, it has nothing to do with this case. When this witness appears on the stand, I demand that nothing be said about this incident."

"Don't worry," Karp shot back. "We'll save it for another day."

"Well, just to be clear, Mr. Karp," Kershner said, "unless it is directly related to the case, I'm not inclined to allow any testimony about it. In the meantime, you say the witness is all right? Anybody else injured?"

"My understanding is that the witness is a little shook up but okay," Karp said. "However, the person who was bringing her to the courthouse has been taken to the hospital, suffering from a concussion."

"What about the kidnappers?"

"I'm told that one died at the scene. Two others are in custody. One of them was apparently knocked unconscious and has also been transported to Bellevue."

Kershner shook her head. "It sounds like the Wild West out there, Mr. Karp. How would you like to proceed at this point?"

"I'd ask that the court recess until after the noon break so that I can check on the status of the witness and give her a chance to collect her thoughts. It will also give Detective Fulton and me an opportunity to speak to the uninjured suspect and, perhaps, determine if there is a connection to this case."

The judge looked at Nash, whose lips tightened at the implied accusation. "Fine with me," the defense attorney said with a sneer. "It will give me a chance to lodge a complaint with the New York Bar about the district attorney's conduct."

"I'll look forward to answering that complaint, Ms. Nash," Karp responded.

AN HOUR LATER, Karp was in his office on the phone with Marlene, who complained about having a massive headache to go along with "feeling like someone used my arms and body as a heavyweight punching bag" due to the air bags in her truck.

"Well, you're doing better than Mr. Jason Fuqua, the man you crushed the life out of with that gas-guzzler of yours," Karp said. "Clay tells me he had a rap sheet for manslaughter, felonious assault, armed robbery, and sexual misconduct, and those are just the highlights. I don't think the good citizens of Gotham are going to miss him any."

"What about the other two?" Marlene asked.

"One has been tentatively ID'd as Martin Bell, formerly of San Francisco."

"No connection to anyone we might know there, I'm sure," Marlene interjected sarcastically.

"Well, as it turns out, he spent a few years in San Quentin about the same time as Anthony Johnson. Clay and I tried to have a word with him, but he lawyered up pretty quick. We don't know much about the driver; somebody named Bubba Smith, and yes, Bubba is his legal name. Apparently his headache is even worse than yours and we've been unable to speak to him so far. Any thoughts on how these guys knew where to find Judy?"

Marlene was quiet for a moment. "I have an idea. We might have been followed the other day. But it's something I may bring up with my friend with the dogs."

"I don't want to know," Karp said. "But I trust that this friend won't do anything to interfere with this trial."

"How could a man with dogs interfere with a trial when the great District Attorney Butch 'aka Superman' Karp is at the helm?"

"Again, I don't even want to know about your friend or his canines." Karp shook his head. "I don't know how you do it, Marlene, but once again you're in the middle of the action."

"Tell me about it," Marlene replied. "Or better yet, send aspirin and flowers, but to the loft; they're about to let me out of here."

"Done. I'll check in with you at the afternoon recess. And Marlene . . ."

"Yes, dear."

"I love you, and I'm glad you're okay."

"I love you, too. Now go get the bad guy."

Leaving his inner sanctum, Karp paused long enough to ask his receptionist, Darla Milquetost, to send flowers to his residence. "And put a box of chocolates with it. She asked for aspirin, but I think candy is a better bet."

"Anything you want to put on the card?" Milquetost asked.

"Yeah, sure, put 'From a secret admirer, Rin Tin Tin.'"

"How romantic," Milquetost said, and rolled her eyes.

Karp laughed. "Oh, and order a few sandwiches for me and the others, please," he said before walking into the meeting room where Fulton, Murrow, Katz, and Judy Pardo waited. "How are you doing, Judy?" he asked.

Pardo looked up from the coffee she was sipping. "You know," she said. "I'm okay. I was pretty panicked at first, but then the adrenaline kicked in and . . . well . . . I hate to say it, but I haven't felt this alive in a long time."

Fulton laughed. "Once a cop, always a cop."

Pardo smiled. "I appreciate you saying that, Detective Fulton, but it's not true. I lost my badge for good reason a long time ago, but maybe I got a taste again of what it was like."

"Nonsense," Fulton replied. "I talked to the detective on the case. He said you handled it like a pro." His face grew serious as he looked over at Karp. "She might have saved Marlene's life; the perp had the drop on her."

"It seems you can add me to the list of people who owe you their thanks," Karp said.

"Aw, shucks, Marshal Dillon," Pardo said, affecting a western twang. "'Twern't nothin' . . . But seriously, I'd probably be dead if Marlene hadn't shown up when she did. So I guess we're even."

"Obviously, these guys were trying to help Johnson," Murrow said. "Do you think Nash was involved?"

"I hope not," Karp said. "I really do. As arrogant and ideologically driven as she is, the system doesn't need any more blows; people are going to stop believing, and that's when we'll really be in trouble. Defense lawyers trying to knock off prosecution witnesses would be another nail in the coffin. In the meantime, let's turn our focus back to the trial." He looked at Pardo. "Do you think you can testify in about an hour?"

"Yes, I'm ready. In fact, I think in a weird way, having to fight for my life has made me more determined than ever to see this through."

Karp nodded. "I've met some tough characters in my time, starting with Detective Fulton and Kenny Katz, who between them have been blown up and shot more times than Arnold Schwarzenegger in a *Terminator* movie. But I don't think they have a corner on the market with you and Marlene around."

"Thanks," Pardo replied. "If I remember correctly, you took a couple for the team yourself."

"And that wasn't the first time," Fulton added.

"Okay, okay. If you folks can get past this tough love fest, what do I tell the press?" Murrow asked. "There was a television crew on the scene when they were still trying to get Marlene's truck off the one guy, and the others are clamoring for a comment."

"Same as we always tell them," Karp replied. "Come to court, that's where we do our talking, otherwise no comment."

"That will make them happy," Murrow said.

"The taxpayers of New York County don't pay me to please the media," Karp said with a smile. "Okay, then, I believe Ms. Milquetost is ordering sandwiches; let's have lunch and go over what's next."

An hour later, with Judge Kershner on her dais and the jury seated, Karp stood and nodded to Fulton. "The People call Judy Pardo."

As Pardo entered the courtroom, the spectators and members of the media in the gallery craned their heads to get a look at the cop-turned–heroin addicted prostitute they'd all heard or written or talked about. Such a buzz of muted voices rose from the benches that Kershner banged her gavel to bring order to the courtroom.

While Pardo was sworn in, Karp used the opportunity to see how Johnson was reacting. The defendant was glaring at Pardo, but he must have felt the eyes of his nemesis on him and turned to meet his gaze. Karp allowed himself the slightest smile, and was pleased to see the fear in Johnson's eyes before the killer looked away.

Karp began by asking Judy Pardo to talk a little bit about her upbringing. He wanted her to get comfortable with answering questions, looking at the jury as she did so, and he was also setting the stage for when he had to deal with less pleasant subjects.

"Well, I was born and raised in New Jersey and had a good childhood for the most part," she said. "Pretty typical Italian family. Dad was a plumber, mom was a stay-at-home housewife. Me, my sister, and brother all went to Catholic school."

"Were you a good student?"

Pardo hesitated. "Well, I tried hard. I'm dyslexic, though back then they called it 'slow learner,' and I had a hard time reading. Some of the other kids called me dumb, so my self-esteem took some hits."

"How did you compensate?"

"My mother worked with me a lot. And I had some good teachers who were patient and understanding. I don't take standardized tests well, but I do great with verbal testing."

"So you made it through high school?"

"And two years of dental hygienist school with a lot of hard work, tears, and frustration. But I got mostly A's."

"Are you still dyslexic?"

"Yes. It's not something that goes away with age. With a lot of time, I can read and write . . . slowly. You learn to compensate, but it's still there."

"Are you going to school now?"

"Yes," Pardo said with pride. "I'm studying to be a sonographer."

"Is it difficult?"

"Yes, there's quite a bit of reading material and I have to be able to look at results and interpret what I see. But we've come a long way in understanding dyslexia and helping people cope. Such as word recognition software my guardian angel bought for me."

Karp knew who her "guardian angel" was but left the statement alone and moved on to more difficult topics. "Was there an incident, or incidents, during your childhood that also affected your self-esteem?"

"Objection, Your Honor," Nash said. "This is more *Oprah* than court, with all due respect."

"Your Honor, please take this subject in connection with respect to the subsequent revelations of her character, which the People will disclose shortly through her testimony," Karp responded. "I suspect the defense will try to use it to its advantage. However, understanding Ms. Pardo's character will better enable the jury to determine the truth of her testimony."

"Very well, objection overruled, please proceed," Kershner said.

Pardo nodded. "Yes. My parents liked to have friends over for cocktails and card games. There was one friend of the family, we called him Uncle John, who was over a lot. He used to insist on 'tucking me in' when it was time for the kids to go to bed. And he used to touch me inappropriately."

"These touches were sexual in nature?"

"Yes."

"Did you tell anyone?"

"Not right away. I was only seven or eight when this was going on. He told me that I would get in trouble if I told anyone that he'd touched me down there."

"Did you eventually tell someone?"

"Yes, when I was nine, maybe ten, I told my priest."

"And what did he say?"

"He said it was my fault. That I must have 'enticed' Uncle John."

"How did you react to that?"

"I believed him," Pardo said with a shrug. "He was the priest. He spoke for God. I felt even worse about myself, though I didn't know what I should have done differently."

"Did you ever tell anyone else?"

Pardo nodded. "I eventually told my mom, and she told my dad."

"What happened?"

"I don't know exactly, but Uncle John quit coming to our house. I assume my dad said or did something to him."

"How do you think the sexual abuse affected you later as you got older, became a young adult?"

"A sexually abused child has a difficult time with boundaries," Pardo said. "I also dealt with a lot of depression in my teenage years and to this day, really."

"Did you and are you getting any help to deal with this?"

"Yes. I've gone to counseling since I was a teenager, though I haven't been much over the past ten years or so. But I'm seeing a counselor now, and a lot of that is coming to terms with what happened to me when I was a little girl."

Karp waited as Pardo poured herself a drink of water and took a sip, her hand shaking as she held the cup to her lips. "Ms. Pardo, did you at some point join the New York Police Department?"

The question caused the gallery to start buzzing again. This was the lead-in to what they'd come to hear. But they quieted down with a look from Kershner.

"Yes."

"Would you tell the jurors how that came about?"

"I was twenty-one and dating a police detective named Gary Proust," Pardo began.

"Excuse me for interrupting, how did you meet?"

"I answered an advertisement for a 'consultant' to work 'undercover' for a loss prevention firm," Pardo said.

"Which is . . . ?"

"A company that worked with other companies to cut down on their losses, such as employee theft."

"Whose company was it?"

"It was Gary's; he'd started it about five years before we met. It was supposed to be a sort of moonlighting thing in his off hours, but he probably spent more time on the company than he did police work. I met with him and it sounded exciting. He wanted me to work undercover, gaining people's trust and then busting them if we could catch them."

"Were there indications that not everything was on the up-and-up?" Karp asked.

"Yes," Pardo said. "Some of these theft rings were pretty big, stealing hundreds of thousands of dollars. Sometimes when we caught them, Gary would let them buy their way out of trouble—he called it a 'fine'—and we wouldn't report them."

"Why did you go along with that?"

Pardo took a deep breath and shook her head. "I guess I was young and stupid. He told me that it was the way things were in the 'real world.' He said the companies were covered by insurance, but if we turned these people in, their lives would be 'ruined' by criminal charges. He said lots of cops did things that weren't entirely legal or within the rules—like take money to patrol a little extra in a high-crime area or look the other way on drug deals, so long as the dealer was paying them off. He complained that he couldn't make it on his detective's pay—not with two ex-wives, three kids, and all the support he had to come up with every month. Plus, he liked nice things: cars, a boat at his place in the Hamptons, a condo in Midtown."

"And you believed him about this kind of widespread corruption on the police force?"

Pardo shrugged. "I was twenty-one when we met. He was quite a bit older, forty, and seemed really worldly. I didn't have a reason to doubt him."

"At some point did your relationship turn from professional to romantic?"

"He started coming on to me almost right away. But I wasn't interested, at least not at first. But he was charming, good-looking, and really sure of himself, and I found that attractive. He bought me flowers and nice dinners, even took me to Las Vegas once but was a gentleman and got us separate rooms. Eventually I gave in . . . I guess you'd say I fell in love."

"So at what point did you decide to become a police officer?"

"Well, I enjoyed the investigative and undercover aspects of what I was doing," Pardo said. "Gary would tell me stories about his work as a cop, and it sounded interesting and exciting. As I was saying earlier, I lacked self-esteem—which is probably why I was with a man twice my age—and I thought maybe being a cop would restore my lost self-confidence."

As Karp spoke, he moved along the jury rail, occasionally looking at the jurors' faces. In reality he was gauging their reactions to his witness, and so far they were attentive and obviously following the story. "Was there an issue, however, with becoming a police officer?"

"Yes. Before you can be considered for the Police Academy, you have to take a written exam, and there was no way I was going to pass that with my dyslexia."

"Did your boyfriend, Gary Proust, have an answer for that?"

"Yes, he knew someone who oversaw the testing. I went in and took the test, but to this day I have no idea what most of it asked. Most of it was multiple choice, so I guessed and filled in the little dots. I didn't write anything on the essay part. But two weeks later, I got a notice in the mail that I had passed."

"Did you think you were doing anything wrong?"

"Yes, but I told myself that I could make up for it by being a good police officer and helping people."

"How did you do at the Police Academy?"

"I struggled with some of the written work, but Gary helped me and, when necessary, got his friend involved. But in everything else—driving, physical fitness, knowing the law—I was at or near the top of my class."

"Did that include marksmanship?" Karp asked, allowing a little bit of a smile remembering her account of what she said to the gunman earlier that morning.

Pardo smiled back, relieved to have that inside joke to break the tension. "Yes, I was third in my class."

"So then, you are familiar with firearms?"

"Yes. We learned to shoot handguns, rifles, and shotguns."

"What sort of service weapon did you carry?"

"I preferred a thirty-eight-caliber revolver. It's sort of old-school—everybody else was packing semiautomatics, which hold more bullets and can be fired somewhat faster. But I was more accurate with the revolver . . . and I didn't think I'd ever need more than six."

"So you would know a revolver as opposed to a semiautomatic by sight?"

"Yes, of course."

"Would you be able to tell what caliber a weapon was by sight?"

"Well, obviously that would depend somewhat on how close I was, but even from a short distance I might have a good guess. Maybe not between a thirty-eight and a three fifty-seven revolver, which are very close—in fact, thirty-eight-caliber cartridges can be fired from revolvers chambered for a three fifty-seven, though the converse is not true. But it would be possible to tell the difference between a large-caliber revolver—such as a forty-five or a forty—and a smaller-caliber weapon, like a twenty-two."

Karp leaned against the jury rail. "Let me back up a little. So after the Police Academy, you applied to and were hired by the New York Police Department?"

"Yes. It was one of the proudest days of my life."

"I imagine it was also good for your self-esteem?"

Pardo beamed at the memory. "Yes. I remember like it was yesterday, the first time I put on the uniform. I didn't feel dumb anymore or like I was a slow learner. And I wasn't just Gary's girlfriend and employee. I was somebody."

"So was it all about the exciting nature of the job?"

"No. That was part of it, to be sure, especially for a twenty-four-year-old woman who a few years earlier was studying to clean people's teeth," Pardo said with a laugh. "But I think what I was looking forward to the most was helping people."

"How did the fact that you were a victim of sexual abuse as a child figure into that?"

Pardo looked at the jurors. "Maybe it sounds corny, but I really did think about being somebody a child could turn to if he or she needed help. Maybe not a sex abuse victim. Maybe just kids who needed someone to care about them."

Karp left the rail and strolled to the well of the court. "Ms. Pardo, have we met in my office to discuss this case, as well as your background?"

"Yes, several times."

"And during one of our conversations, did you tell me about a dream you had as a young officer . . . something you wanted to accomplish?"

Pardo laughed. "Well, like any young officer, you get tired of writing traffic citations and hauling drunks off to detox and maybe breaking up a brawl and writing them up for disorderly conduct. To be honest, most police work tends to be a little boring and routine, especially when I compared what I was doing to what Gary did as a detective working on major cases. So I had this little daydream about taking a bad guy—a really bad guy—off the streets so he couldn't hurt anybody else."

"Did you ever get that opportunity?"

Pardo's face fell. "No, not really. I made my share of arrests, including a liquor store robber who had a toy gun. But nothing really dramatic."

"How long were you an officer?"

"Two years."

"And during that time were you still dating Gary Proust?"

"For about the first six months after I joined the department."

"What happened after six months?"

"I was starting to have issues with his moonlighting," Pardo said. "I stopped working for him after I joined the department. In fact, I was learning that not everybody on the job, except maybe Gary's pals, took bribes or were corrupt. Yes, a few badge-heavy guys liked carrying guns and having power over people's lives. But most of the cops I worked with were in it for the same reason I was—to help protect the community."

"You didn't know it was wrong before that?"

Pardo hung her head. "I'd be dishonest if I said I thought it was all okay. I knew even before I got out of the academy that it was wrong. But I was young and in love, and I'll confess, I liked the money and having things that I couldn't buy when I was younger."

"What did Detective Proust do when you told him you didn't want to work for him anymore?"

"He laughed. Called me Miss Goody Two-shoes. Said fine, do what I wanted."

"But you continued in the relationship for another six months?"

"Yes. And I reaped some of the rewards of Gary's activities. He was still generous, bought me things, even proposed and gave me a beautiful engagement ring when I said yes."

"What happened to end the relationship?"

"I heard that he wasn't just 'fining' these people who were stealing from their employers," she said. "He was actually receiving stolen merchandise and then selling it off. He had a whole network set up to do it."

"Did you report him for these crimes?"

Pardo shook her head. "I should have, but I didn't."

"What did you do?"

"I told him he had to stop or I was going to leave him."

"What was his reaction?"

"At first he didn't believe me and just laughed. But when he saw I was serious, he got angry. He pointed out that I'd made a lot of money under the table, which was true."

"Did you stick with your ultimatum?"

"I did."

"And?"

"And he chose the money."

"How did that make you feel?"

"I was devastated. I thought he loved me, but all he wanted was a young woman on his arm and in his bed."

"Did you follow through?"

"Yes, I broke off the relationship and gave him his ring back."

"How'd he take it?"

"Not well. He'd always been possessive and jealous. I thought it was cute, the way he'd get upset if another man looked at me or I spoke to one. But now he started getting scary. He accused me of breaking it off because I had another boyfriend, and that I was sleeping around. He stalked me and showed up unexpectedly both at work and at home."

"How long did that behavior last?"

"Months. He called every day, sometimes several times a day. He'd be angry and shouting, calling me a whore and threatening me and anybody I met in the future. Other times he'd cry and tell me how much he loved me and wanted me back. The first couple times he did that I said I'd go back under one condition: he had to shut down his company. But it was always the same. I didn't understand, he needed the money; it was always about the money. I told him to stop calling me and stop stalking me, or I was going to go to the brass at the department."

"How'd he take that?"

"He said that if I did, I'd be the one who paid the price. I'd lose my job and be prosecuted and then go to prison. But he'd get off because of his friends high up."

"Did you turn him in?"

"Not then, no," Pardo said. "I never went out with him again and wouldn't take his calls. But I didn't do anything, either. I believed him when he said I'd be the one who was punished and that he'd get even for me leaving him."

"And did he?"

Pardo reached for the glass of water, which Karp stepped forward and refilled after she set it down. "Yes. One day I got back to the precinct after my shift and the sergeant said they wanted to see me in Internal Affairs."

"What about?"

"Somebody had reported Gary, probably someone who got tired of paying him off, but Gary thought it was me. He denied the criminal stuff, but he told them about me cheating on the academy test."

"What happened?"

"I told them the truth. I cheated. I thought it wouldn't be that big a deal if I just came clean. After all, I was a good cop. I had several commendations, and I knew my sergeant liked me. I thought I might get written up, maybe even put on administrative leave without pay."

"Was that what happened?"

Pardo bit her lip. "No," she said, shaking her head sadly. "They said they would drop the criminal investigation against my part in Gary's schemes, but I had to resign from the department. So that's what I did."

"What about Proust?"

Pardo laughed bitterly. "Apparently the investigation went no-where. I heard from my sergeant later that Internal Affairs wanted to charge him but they were told to drop it. The union had stepped in and so had some higher-ups."

"Is he still with the department?"

"No. I heard he retired a few years later, but I don't know much more than that."

"What sort of an impact did losing your job with the NYPD have on your life?"

Pardo started to answer but then choked up and buried her face in her hands. As she let out a loud sob, Karp walked up and offered her a tissue from the box on the rail. "Thanks, I'm sorry," she said.

"It's okay," Karp said.

"Do you need a few minutes?" Judge Kershner asked, leaning forward.

Pardo smiled at the judge through her tears. "No, I'm fine. This was bound to happen." She sniffed a couple more times and wiped at her nose before looking back at Karp. "In some ways, my life ended the day they took my badge away."

"How do you mean?"

"It wasn't all at once, more of a long, slow downward spiral, but eventually I got to the bottom of the barrel and stayed there."

"Were drugs involved in that downward slide?"

"Yes."

"How did that start?"

"Actually before I became a cop," Pardo said. "Gary liked to

party, and he was into coke and sometimes speed. It was pretty rec-
reational and I didn't like it much. I stopped doing all of that when
I got hired by the department. But after I got kicked off, I went to
this party with a guy I was dating, and he offered me heroin."

"Did you snort it or shoot it?"

"This was the kind you snorted, shooting would come later."

"Was it a problem right away?" Karp asked.

"No," Pardo said. "Some friends in the department hooked me
up with a private investigation firm. The money was decent, though
the work was pretty boring—mostly catching husbands cheating on
their wives and insurance fraud. Easy work and a lot of partying in
my off-hours. I snorted a lot of heroin and drank a lot of booze—I
think to disguise how miserable I was inside."

"At some point did you start shooting heroin?"

"I was at a party and somebody offered it to me," she recalled.
"They told me it was a better, more intense high. So I tried it. And
they were right."

"How else does the heroin you snort compare to heroin you
shoot?"

"It's not even close. One you want but can live without if it's not
available. The other you *need*, and you'd swear you don't want to
live if you can't have more. Your body, your mind crave it. The only
time you don't want more dope is when you're high, and as soon as
that feeling is gone, all you can think about is getting more."

"Did you become addicted all at once?"

Pardo shook her head. "No, there is a gradual buildup, and there
were times when I realized what was happening and I'd force my-

self to go cold turkey. Sometimes I could go a few weeks, but the entire time all I thought about was how much I wanted it."

"How did you support this habit?"

As he asked the question, Karp moved so that Pardo's eyes had to stay on him. He knew this was going to be the toughest part of his questioning, and he didn't want her to be concerned about the jury or spectators looking at her, judging her.

"I had my job as a private investigator," Pardo said. "But heroin has a way of taking over your life. At first, you can function, it even gives you energy and a feeling of being on top of the world. Like I said, the highs are intense, but there's a flip side to that. One of the common side effects of heroin withdrawal is severe depression. I'd already had issues with depression since my teens and this just intensified that. Some days, unless I had heroin, I couldn't get myself to get out of bed, or even answer the phone. Another side effect is paranoia, not a good thing for a private investigator.

"I lost that job then every other decent job I got after that, even minimum-wage jobs flipping burgers. You stop eating when you're a heroin addict, and you don't care, all you want is that next hit."

Karp could almost feel the spectators in the gallery hold their collective breath, waiting for the next step in Pardo's fall from grace. He knew she could sense it in the air, too, and felt for her.

"I did anything for a few bucks," she continued. "Went through the trash barrels in the parks for aluminum cans, shoplifted, and then I started . . ."

What she said next was inaudible. "I'm sorry," Karp said, meaning it, "but I'm going to have to ask you to speak up so that the jurors can hear you."

Pardo let out a deep breath and nodded. "I became a whore," she admitted. "I let men use my body for money. At first, I charged a lot, when I was still young and not too far gone to seed. But the more heroin I did, the worse I looked, and the less men would pay. I'd do anything—oral sex, sex in cars, sex in alleys, sex in restroom stalls. There was nothing I wouldn't do, no place I wouldn't go, for the money to buy heroin."

The witness looked deflated, beaten. Karp wished he could have held back at this point, but he needed this kind of honesty out of her now. He believed it would help the jury understand how far she had fallen and what it took for her to testify today, as well as blunt the edge of the defense attacks that were sure to follow. "Where were you living by this point?" he asked.

"On the streets," Pardo said. "Occasionally, I'd get a cot and a hot shower at one of the shelters. Sometimes a john would let me sleep it off if he sprung for a room. But I spent a lot of nights curled up on a park bench or under a bush."

"Wasn't that dangerous?" Karp asked.

Pardo shrugged. "I guess you could say that. I've been raped, robbed, and beaten unconscious."

Karp let the matter-of-fact statement sink in before he went on. "Were you ever arrested or charged with a crime after you left the police department?"

"Yes, all misdemeanors for prostitution and drug possession. I've spent more than a few days and nights in jail. But like we say on the streets, at least you get three hots and a cot, and in the winter, it can be like going on vacation to the Caribbean."

"You have family in New Jersey," Karp pointed out. "Why not go to them?"

Pardo looked at him for a long moment. He purposely had not told her every question; the jury needed to see her honest reactions.

"And let them know what I had become? No way. I'd have rather died. I wouldn't even talk to them for months at a time, afraid that I'd break down and beg to come home."

"How did you explain that?"

Pardo shrugged. "That I was busy, that I was working undercover as a cop. I never told them I got kicked off."

"When did they find out?" Karp said, turning to look out at the gallery.

"A few months ago, when the press showed up at their front door and told them." Pardo looked angry when she said it, but then her expression turned sad. "My mom found out that her daughter wasn't a cop, like she thought, just a washed-up, drug-addicted prostitute, from some man she'd never met who showed up with a camera and the horrible truth."

As some members of the media shifted uncomfortably on the benches, Karp turned toward the reason she was on the stand. "Did there come a time when you stopped prostituting yourself?"

Again the bitter laugh escaped Pardo's lips. "When you're a heroin addict, there comes a point when no one wants to pay for what you have to offer. No one with money, anyway. The others just take what they want. So I guess you might say I was involuntarily retired."

"So how did you survive?"

"Well, the good news is I rarely had enough money for heroin. And I was fortunate to meet a sort of street preacher, I guess you might call him, though his name is David. He spent a lot of time talking to me about God and that no matter how far I'd gone down the road, I could always turn around and go back the way I came." She shook her head. "He gave me and a lot of other homeless people a place to stay and hope. I don't know how he does it, he doesn't have a nickel himself, but he just has a way of making even people like me feel better about themselves.

"What about heroin?"

"One of the rules if you want to stay at his place is no drugs, but the thing is, I didn't want it anymore."

"But how do you eat?"

"Sometimes soup kitchens, but usually Dumpster diving."

"Explain 'Dumpster diving,' please."

"It's like it sounds," Pardo said. "You crawl into the big Dumpsters you see all over the city in alleys and behind buildings and scavenge for anything useful, like aluminum cans, clothing, or cigarette butts, and of course, food. You'd be surprised how much food gets thrown away that street people think of as a feast."

Then Karp brought her to the evening when Ricky Watts was shot. As he talked, he walked over to the prosecution table and picked up three photographs.

"I was in Harlem going through a Dumpster in an alley next to a tenement," she said.

"When you say 'going through,' where were you physically?"

"I was inside the Dumpster with the lid closed, having lunch."

Gasps and groans escaped the spectators. Kershner banged her gavel once.

"Did something interrupt your meal?"

"Yes. I heard voices near the entrance to the alley—"

"Excuse me for interrupting," Karp said, "but how far was the Dumpster from the entrance?"

"Maybe twenty feet."

"All right, please continue. You heard these voices . . ."

"Yes, so I lifted the lid a little to peek. You can never be too careful in some of these neighborhoods."

"What did you see?"

"Three black males. One very large man who appeared to be in his mid- to late twenties. A second man, tall and thin, who also appeared to be in his mid to late twenties, maybe thirty. And what I'd describe as a pudgy teenager; he wore glasses and just seemed out of place with these other two, who were rougher."

Karp walked up to the witness stand until he was within arm's reach. "Ms. Pardo, did there come a time when you were asked if you could identify the three individuals you saw that evening?"

"Yes, you showed me several photo lineups."

"And were you able to make positive identifications of these individuals?"

"Yes, I was."

Karp held out one of the photographs. "I am handing you what has been marked People's Exhibit 32 in evidence," he said. "Is this one of the individuals you identified?"

"Yes, this was the largest of the men. He was probably six-four, three hundred pounds."

Karp smiled. "You sound like a police officer."

"Old habits die hard," Pardo replied with a shy smile of her own.

"Let the record reflect that the witness has identified the largest of the individuals as George Parker," Karp said, and held out a second photograph. "I'm handing you People's Exhibit 33 in evidence. Do you also recognize this person as one of the individuals?"

"Yes, that's the teenager."

"Let the record reflect that the witness has identified Ricky Watts." Karp handed her the last photograph. "This is People's Exhibit 34. Do you recognize this individual?"

Pardo's eyes flitted to Johnson and back. She nodded. "Yes, this is the tall, thin male."

"Do you see this man in the courtroom?"

Pardo looked straight at Johnson. Their eyes locked, but he was the first to look away, smiling and shaking his head like it was all a joke. "Yes, he's right there," she said, pointing.

Karp strode across the courtroom until he reached the defense table. He, too, pointed. "This man, the defendant, Anthony Johnson?" he asked.

"Yes, that's him."

In the silence that followed the accusation, Johnson dipped his head and could be heard to say, "Lying bitch."

Karp stopped and stared at him, and then continued. "You said you could hear their voices. Could you understand what was being said?"

"Some. I missed whatever they said initially because the lid was down. And after that, I had to be careful, so some of it was hard to hear. But I heard him," she said, pointing again at Johnson, "tell the teenager, 'They won't be expecting you.'"

"Let the record reflect that the witness indicated the defendant in her previous statement," Karp said. "What else did you hear?"

"The kid sort of stuttered, like he was afraid. 'You . . . you . . . want me to shoot them?' But Johnson said something about wondering if he'd picked the right man for the job. The kid said, 'No, I'll do it.'"

"Did the defendant, Anthony Johnson, give anything to Ricky Watts as they were talking?"

"Yes, he handed him a stainless steel revolver with an ivory or mother-of-pearl grip."

"Could you tell what caliber?" Karp asked.

"Not a hundred percent," Pardo said. "But it was a large revolver, not a little Saturday-night special."

"What happened next?"

Pardo again nodded at Johnson. "The defendant told the boy to go into the building and wait. Some of that was muffled. I was afraid they were going to turn around and see me, so I kept ducking. But I heard Johnson say, 'Boom boom and it's over. If they're still moving, shoot them in the head. Then get your ass out of there and we'll meet you.'"

"Then what?"

"They walked off toward the front of the building."

"What did you do?"

"I got out of the Dumpster. I was going to run away before they came back . . . but I didn't . . . I stayed."

"Why?"

"Because they were talking about shooting people. I . . . I couldn't just turn my back. So I crept to the entrance of the alley and peeked around the corner. The two older guys, Parker and Johnson, were hanging out near a parked car. Then I heard two gunshots."

"You're sure? Two gunshots?"

"Absolutely. They were almost one on top of the other—*ba-bang*—but they were different caliber, so I could differentiate them. One sounded like a nine . . ."

"A nine?"

"A nine-millimeter semiautomatic. The other was bigger . . . a forty-five or maybe a forty."

"What happened next?"

"The teenager came out the door. At first I didn't think there was anything wrong, but then I saw the big red spot on his chest. He made it to the curb and then crumpled to the ground."

"What about Johnson and Parker?"

"They walked over to him. They said something, and he"—again she pointed at Johnson—"took the revolver out of the boy's hand. Then he looked up and saw me. He yelled for me to stop, but I ran down the alley."

"Where did you go?"

"One of the abandoned buildings on the far end has an open entrance to the basement. There's a tunnel system. It used to be used for hauling coal for the furnaces, now it's mostly abandoned. I heard him running after me, but he stopped and didn't come down into the basement. He knew that wouldn't be safe."

"When did you see the defendant again?"

"Not until you showed me the photo lineups."

"Sorry, I meant in person."

"Oh, you asked me to come down and see if I could pick him out of a standing lineup through a one-way mirror."

"And did you?"

"Yes. Immediately."

Karp walked over to the prosecution table and picked up the evidence bag containing the revolver. He pulled it out and showed it to her. "Is this revolver consistent with the type of revolver you saw the defendant, Anthony Johnson, hand to Ricky Watts?"

"It is," Pardo answered. "It looks just like it."

Karp placed the gun back in the bag. "Thank you. No further questions."

Judge Kershner looked at the clock on the wall. "Let's take our afternoon recess. When we return, the witness is yours for cross-examination, Ms. Nash."

"I look forward to it," Nash said coldly.

"Very well, we'll reconvene in fifteen minutes," the judge said to the jurors.

When the judge and jurors were gone, Karp and Katz went over to talk to Pardo, who'd remained silent and thoughtful on the witness stand.

"Once a whore, always a whore, ain't that right?" The voice was Johnson's, who remained sitting next to Nash. "And fuck you, Karp," he added. "Too bad that guy, what was his name, Oliver Gray, yeah, right, Oliver Gray, too bad he was such a poor shot. Next time, I hope somebody puts you down like a dog. Just like they're gonna do that bitch."

The court officers jumped up and surrounded the defendant, but Karp told them to relax. Hoping to bait Johnson, he said, "Not to worry. He's a coward who sets up kids to do his dirty work."

When Kershner arrived back in the courtroom, the chief court clerk told her what had transpired. The judge looked at Karp. "Is that true?"

"Yes, Your Honor."

"Mr. Johnson, any outburst from you will be dealt with severely in this courtroom," Kershner warned.

Johnson started to retort, but Nash put a hand on his shoulder and stated plaintively, "Your Honor, he's under attack for a crime he didn't commit."

Kershner raised her hand. "Stop right there. I stated precisely the behavior I expect in this courtroom. Don't test me."

"I know my rights," Johnson spat.

"You have the right to take the stand in your defense," Karp retorted, egging him on again.

"That's enough!" Kershner yelled. She glared from Johnson to Karp and back again. Satisfied that order was restored, she asked for the jury to be brought back in. She addressed them when they were seated. "When we left off, the district attorney had finished his direct examination of the witness. Ms. Nash, you may now proceed with your questioning."

"Thank you, Your Honor," Nash said, striding out from behind the defense table and up to the witness stand. "That was quite the story, Ms. Pardo. But it seemed a little self-serving. I mean, do all dyslexic children end up drug-addicted prostitutes who will perjure themselves on a witness stand?"

"OBJECTION!" Karp thundered. "Has counsel no sense of redemption, sensitivity, or civility?"

"Sustained. Both counsel will please try to stay focused on the evidence."

Nash's mouth twisted into a smirk. "Of course, Your Honor," she said, then turned back to Pardo. "If I understand your testimony, you've admitted to committing crimes while working for Gary Proust, a New York City Police Department detective?"

"Yes."

"And you cheated to become a cop, which makes you a liar. Correct?"

"That's correct."

"And after you became an officer with the NYPD, sworn to uphold the law, you knew that your boyfriend, also a sworn officer, was committing crimes?"

"Yes."

"Did you turn him in?"

"No, I did not."

"Why not?"

"I loved him. I wanted him to stop of his own volition."

"Did that happen?"

"No."

"Did you turn him in then?"

"No."

"No, instead you continued to date him. You were his fiancée."

"That's correct."

Nash crossed her arms. "Would you say that the NYPD is a corrupt organization?"

"No, I wouldn't say that."

"But you testified that your boyfriend said 'everybody' has some sort of racket going."

"That's what he said. That wasn't my experience."

"Ms. Pardo, are there a lot of racist police officers at the NYPD?"

"I'm sure there are some. But I never witnessed any acts of racism by a police officer."

"None whatsoever?" Nash asked, as if she found this hard to believe. "Just black and white officers working together, treating everyone on the streets with dignity and respect?"

"As I said, I never witnessed any acts of racism, either between officers, or officers interacting with the community."

"Yet three officers were indicted last summer for murder and the attempted murder of black activists."

"I don't know anything about that except what I've read in the newspapers, the same as anyone else."

"So this was just a one-time event."

"To my knowledge, yes."

Nash rolled her eyes and began walking along the jury box rail. "Let's talk about you for a minute. So you're a heroin addict?"

"I was. But I've been clean for five months."

"Five months? Do you still crave it?"

"Every day."

"Every day?"

"Yes, every day is a battle to stay clean and sober."

"I see. And some of the side effects of long-term use of heroin are memory loss, paranoia, and depression. Is that true?"

"I believe that's correct."

"So you don't always remember everything that happens to you?"

"Depends. If I was high, maybe not. But my memory is pretty good, at least for those times I was sober."

"But you testified that heroin affects memory?"

"It can."

"And were you high on heroin on the evening when you allegedly saw three men at the entrance of this alley in Harlem?"

"I don't remember," Pardo said, "but probably not. I didn't have much money at that time."

"And nobody wanted to pay to have sex with you, correct?"

Karp saw that the question stung. But Pardo smiled. "I don't think I could have given it away."

The humor caught Nash off guard as the gallery tittered with laughter. The defense attorney scowled and set her jaw. "I believe you testified that you were willing to do anything for heroin, is that right?"

"Pretty much."

"Commit crimes?"

"Yes."

"Perform sex acts in filthy alleys and restroom stalls?"

"Yes."

"And that you violated the oath you took as a police officer?"

"Yes."

"Lied and cheated."

"Sometimes, yes."

"Well, basically it sounds like you've lied, cheated, committed crimes, done drugs your entire adult life?"

"Yes. Pretty sad, isn't it?"

Again, Nash was caught off guard for a moment, as if she didn't know how to answer that response. Then her face hardened. "You sold your body for drugs."

"Yes."

"Isn't that like selling your soul?"

"That's not a bad analogy."

"I think it's a rather good analogy," Nash retorted. "So I have to ask you, have you sold your soul to the prosecution?"

"What do you mean?"

"Well, let's look at the evidence. Eight months ago, you were prostituting yourself, sleeping on park benches, and eating in Dumpsters. Now here you are, wearing nice clothes, living in a women's shelter where I assume you're safe, warm, and well fed. And you're taking courses at a community college. It would seem that your life took a sudden, miraculous turnaround after you went to the district attorney with your story."

"Yes, my life is better. But I'm the one making it better, with the help of people at the shelter."

"Or was it the district attorney who came along and told you what to say?"

"Objection!" Karp shouted as he stood. "Ms. Nash is making wild accusations without one scintilla of evidence to back them up. If she has it, she should put it before this jury now."

"Sustained," Kershner said, shaking her head. "Ms. Nash, you must know better."

Nash's face was pulled into a sneer. "No further questions."

Kershner shook her head and looked at Karp. "Anything more?"

Karp, who had remained standing, nodded. "Just a couple more questions," he said, and looked at Pardo.

"Ms. Pardo, you told me once and testified that as a young police officer, you dreamed of taking a bad guy off of the street."

"Yes."

"Is this the way you imagined it?" he asked.

"What do you mean?"

"I mean, was it your dream to appear on the witness stand and be exposed as a liar, a drug addict, a cheater, and a whore?"

Pardo shook her head. "No. This isn't a dream, it's a nightmare."

Karp nodded. "I'm sure. So I want to ask you, why should this jury believe you when you testified that you saw the defendant, Anthony Johnson, and his associate, George Parker, as well as Ricky Watts in that alley? And why should they believe that you saw the defendant hand Ricky Watts a stainless steel, forty-five-caliber revolver with a mother-of-pearl handle and say, 'If they're still moving, shoot them in the head'?"

Pardo looked over at Nash and then at Johnson. "Because why would I have put myself through this if every single thing I've said today wasn't true?"

"Now that," Karp said, "is a good question. Nothing further, Your Honor."

23

THE NEXT MORNING, KARP WAS FINALLY ABLE TO RELAX, knowing that the toughest part of his job was done. Step-by-step, piece by piece, the evidence had been laid out in damning order, drawing the noose tighter and tighter around the defendant's neck.

Now all that was left of the People's case was tying up some loose ends.

Karp first called Patrolman Brad Nickles, who had responded to the scene of the Watts shooting and taken a statement from George Parker. The officer identified People's Exhibit 32, the photograph of Big George, as the man he interviewed and later arrested for disorderly conduct and resisting arrest.

Karp wasn't sure if Nash had missed that particular memo book entry made by Nickles immediately after questioning Big George at the scene. There'd been a mountain of paperwork surrounding the shooting and subsequent investigation. Nash kept her head down and hardly looked up during the officer's testimony. "No questions," she mumbled when Kershner invited her to cross-examine the witness.

Putting the finishing touches on the attempted murder charge, Karp called two residents who lived in the tenement where Kim and Watts had their fatal meeting. The first, eighty-two-year-old Martha Motumbo, was the woman Kim had seen in the doorway with her grandchildren as he pursued Watts down the staircase. "I heard two gunshots," the woman testified, "and looked to see what was happening."

"You're sure it was two?" Karp asked.

"I may be old, but I ain't deaf," Motumbo scolded Karp, who was as amused by her cantankerous testimony as was the rest of the courtroom. "Same thing I told that investigator who said he worked for the defense attorney. He kept trying to get me to change my story, but I heared what I heared. It was two shots. You don't live as long as I have in the projects without knowing what a gun, or two guns, sound like. Now can I go?"

Nash released the witness without asking any questions. Nor did she challenge the testimony of the second resident, Elmira Jenkins, who had solved the one great mystery to the whole Kim and Watts confrontation: the absence of a spent bullet fired from the revolver, or bullet fragments, or even a mark left by a bullet in the wall of the staircase.

Several times in the days leading up to the trial, Karp had pulled out the photograph Fulton had given him of the building taken after the shooting. The only other place a bullet could have gone was out the window, but the window was closed and intact in the photograph. Then he recalled Kim's statement that as he approached the landing where he would find himself challenged by Watts, he'd seen a woman duck back from the hallway into her apartment. A thought crossed his mind and he decided to check it out in the company of Fulton.

They'd located the woman, who admitted she'd been in the hall when she heard the officer approaching from the stairs above her. But she was reluctant to say much more than that.

"You're not in any trouble here," Karp assured her as they led her out into the hall. "But was there any chance that window was open when you went back inside?"

"Oh, no, sir," Jenkins said. "The building superintendent doesn't let us open those windows. He says it lets in dirt and bugs . . . not like this place is so clean."

Karp nodded. "Well, okay, if you're sure. It's just that I need to know the truth. It would explain a lot, and there are some people's lives at stake here."

As he and Fulton turned to walk back down the stairs and leave, Jenkins called after them. "Wait. I can't live with the lie if you put it that way."

She explained that she lived with her daughter and son-in-law, and they wouldn't let her smoke in their apartment. "I'm afraid to go down to the streets to smoke," she said. "So I sneak out here and open the window to get some fresh air and smoke. When I heard the police officer coming down the stairs, I thought it was the superintendent. I panicked and ran inside, but I forgot to close the window. Then afterward, I was worried I'd get in trouble, so I sneaked back and closed it before the police got here."

The woman hung her head and began to cry. "I guess I better start looking for a new place to live," she said.

However, Karp and Fulton put their heads together and came up with a plan. Fulton accompanied the woman to the superintendent's office. "Mrs. Jenkins here is a star witness in our case," he said gruffly. "She has provided us with very valuable information involving the window in the hallway outside her apartment. But she is concerned that you may retaliate because of a small infraction of the rules. So I'm here to ask you, nicely, if you would overlook this small infraction—if she promises not to do it again—and in return, I'll make sure that no one troubles you about the smell of marijuana that permeates this building."

"Of course," the superintendent said. "Mrs. Jenkins is one of my favorite residents, and I would never want to cause her any trouble."

Jenkins had then happily testified about the open window. "I watch a lot of *CSI* on the television," she said when Karp talked to her afterward. "I've always wanted to be on the witness stand." There was no way of proving that the bullet fired by Watts had gone out the window, but "common sense and logic," as Karp intended to point out during his summation, would indicate that was what happened.

Following Motumbo and Jenkins, Karp had called Rose Torres, who talked about the party the night Officer Tony Cippio was murdered. "I know it was then, because the shooting was all over the television news the next morning," she said. "I remembered that Big George and Ny-lee was acting crazy, like they'd done something but wouldn't say what it was. Then Nat X—"

"The defendant, Johnson," Karp interjected.

"Yes, that fool sitting right over there." She pointed. "He showed up and everybody was treating him like the 'big man.' Ny-Lee and him was cousins, but he got real mad when Ny-Lee called him 'Tony' instead of Nat X."

Torres laughed at Johnson. "What kind of fool name is that anyway?" she said, eliciting an objection from Nash.

"Sustained. The witness is instructed to stick to just answering the question," Kershner said.

"Yeah, all right," Torres replied. "But I ain't afraid of him. He was only tough as long as he had George and that big ol' gun of his to wave around. But you know what they say: 'Big gun, small—'"

"Could you describe the gun?" Karp interrupted as the spectators laughed and Johnson scowled.

"Yeah, silver, sort of like a cowboy gun."

"A revolver?"

"Yeah, with a shiny handle. Not the sort of piece you usually see in the hood, especially with some no-account like him."

Torres identified the gun when Karp showed it to her. She then verified that she'd picked both Parker and Johnson out of photo lineups, and Johnson again after the defendant was extradited from California. "I didn't need no one-way mirror," she declared. "I'd a told him to his face. 'You that dumbass nigger who talked tough all the time, but when the heat was on, you turned tail and ran away to California with my baby sister.' But she's dumb as a stick, too, so they deserve each other."

Recognizing that Torres was a bit of a loose cannon, Karp got her off the stand as soon as he could. She was upset that she wouldn't be allowed to talk about her belief that Parker had killed Ny-Lee on Johnson's orders. He wasn't going to risk her blurting it out because he asked one too many questions.

Nash tried without success to challenge Torres's recollection of when the party happened. "And if you knew all this, why didn't you come forward and say something to the police?"

"Snitches get stitches and end up in ditches. I wasn't afraid of him," she said, nodding at Johnson, "but Big George was something else. Now, he was a scary man."

Noting that Torres had a criminal record for drug possession and sales, Nash asked if her coming forward was to "rack up some get-out-of-jail-free points for the next time you get in trouble with the law?"

"Ain't gonna be no next time," Torres retorted. "I got a new man and he don't abide drugs. He got himself a good job working at a bank, and I ain't gonna mess that up for him. We going to church every Sunday and everything."

After Torres stepped down, Karp called Mike "Moto Juku" Sakamoto to the stand to recount the sudden appearance and overly long stay of Anthony Johnson and his girlfriend, Lupe Torres. "My girlfriend wanted him gone and so did I," he said. "But he made sure we knew he was armed, even after he pawned the revolver."

Giving away how she planned to explain the events in San Francisco during her summation, Nash intimated that the revolver was

Juku's. At best, it was a flimsy attempt to deflect the blame, but considering all the testimony from the New York witnesses about the gun, it was all she had. And when Juku left the witness stand, both the defense lawyer and her client were taking on the appearance of a thoroughly beaten football team.

It didn't help when Karp wrapped up the People's case with Clay Fulton. Providing a final overview from New York to San Francisco, the detective particularly seemed to enjoy talking about his ruse to get Johnson out of Moto Juku's apartment.

"We were worried about the two young women in case he tried to shoot it out if we kicked in the door," he said. "So I got one of the San Francisco PD guys to get some forty-five-caliber dummy bullets used for training purposes. I then removed the four live cartridges and two empty shells from the chamber and bagged them for evidence."

"So how did you get the defendant to come out of the apartment?" Karp asked.

"I pretended to be breaking into his car. And as planned, Mr. Sakamoto pointed this out, which caused the suspect Johnson to exit the building and confront me."

"Did you then identify yourself as a police officer?"

"He sort of recognized me from a television newscast, but yes, I identified myself as a police officer and told him that he was under arrest."

"And did he come along peacefully?"

"Well, no," Fulton replied, playing his role to the hilt. "He pointed the gun at me and pulled the trigger."

"Did he know at that time that the gun was loaded with dummy bullets?"

"No, I'm sure he thought it was loaded with the real thing."

"So he tried to shoot you?"

"That's about the size of it."

"No further questions."

Nash rose tiredly from her seat but stayed behind the defense table. She asked a few perfunctory questions to remind the jurors that it was Moto Juku who attempted to retrieve the gun from the pawnshop.

"When Mr. Johnson approached you, as you were breaking into his car, did he believe that you were a criminal?"

"I believe he did. At least until I identified myself."

"Did you show him a badge at that time?"

"I didn't really have the opportunity," Fulton replied, "before he pointed the gun at my head and pulled the trigger."

"Because he thought you were a criminal. No further questions, Your Honor."

That brought the People's case as well to an end.

After admonishing the jurors not to discuss the case or view media coverage, Kershner released them until the next morning. When they'd left, she asked the lawyers if there was anything else that needed to be done.

"Your Honor, the defense moves to have the case dismissed," Nash said. "The People have failed to show enough evidence that taken in a light most favorable to the defendant, which is the law, would prove him guilty beyond a reasonable doubt."

"Denied," Kershner said, shaking her head. "I'll see you all in the morning, and Ms. Nash, be prepared to call your witnesses if you intend to present a defense."

Now morning had arrived, and Nash, who'd today chosen a powder blue pantsuit, called Dr. Cleve Schofield, her DNA expert, to the stand to repudiate the testimony of Dr. Offendahl.

After being qualified as an expert witness, Schofield, the director of the GenTest Laboratory in Park Hill, Maryland, began by testifying about several national scandals involving DNA laboratories that had either falsified results or rendered unqualified opinions in criminal cases.

"And did these major scandals literally result in the imprisonment of potentially thousands of innocent men and women?" Nash asked in seeming outrage.

"Yes, they did," answered Schofield, who looked somewhat like a nearsighted owl with his round face and eyes magnified by circular eyeglasses.

"These were certainly times when technology was used to violate the due process rights of those thousands of individuals, am I correct?"

"You are correct."

"And isn't it true that on a seemingly daily basis we hear about some new case in which DNA was misused to frame an innocent person?"

"I don't know about frame, or daily basis, though I suppose it happens," Schofield said. "But certainly it is an imperfect science, or, rather, the science is good but sometimes performed by imperfect scientists."

"Imperfect scientists or, perhaps, scientists who are given tainted evidence to work with?"

"Yes, that's a possibility, too."

Nash approached the witness stand with her head down as if in deep thought. She looked up. "Dr. Schofield, you just mentioned that there are limitations to DNA testing, or at least human variables. Would you say that so-called touch DNA is relatively new?"

"The entire science is fairly new. DNA testing only started in the mid-eighties and became generally accepted in the late nineties. And our ability to develop accurate profiles for touch DNA has only come about in the past few years."

Turning to face the jurors, Nash asked, "What are some of the ways DNA evidence might be rendered inaccurate or falsified?"

"Well, if improperly gathered, stored, and disseminated, it can be contaminated, either by other DNA—such as someone carelessly handling the sample—or by exposure to some other material or chemical. A DNA sample can also deteriorate on its own, such as over time or if exposed to sunlight. There are a number of ways a sample can be rendered inaccurate or falsified."

Nash moved over to stand in front of the prosecution table. "And would it be possible for someone to purposely contaminate an object—such as the shirt from Officer Tony Cippio that you were asked to test—with the defendant's DNA?"

"Yes, it would be possible if, say, someone transferred some DNA content taken from the defendant, even a few skin cells or drops of blood, and planted it on the shirt."

"When did you test the shirt?" Nash asked.

"About a month ago," Schofield said.

"A month . . . so approximately seven months after Officer Cippio was shot?"

"Yes, I believe that's correct."

"Are you aware of the findings of the prosecution's DNA expert, Dr. Offendahl?"

"Yes, I've reviewed them."

"Is there anything about those findings that, perhaps, raised a red flag?"

Schofield hemmed and hawed a little bit before clearing his throat and answering. "Well, if someone leaned over the victim in order to turn him over, I might have expected there to be more touch DNA than just skin cells."

"Such as?"

"Such as skin cells over a wider area or maybe a drop of sweat. I understand it was a warm evening."

"Given these variables and . . . possibilities, is it possible that Dr. Offendahl's conclusions were incorrect, even fraudulent?"

Again, Schofield seemed uncomfortable with the question, but he answered anyway. "Yes, it's possible."

"And this has happened in thousands of cases throughout the United States?"

"Yes, that's true."

Nash looked at the jury and raised an eyebrow. "No further questions."

Karp rose from his seat. "Good morning, Dr. Schofield. Let's begin with these 'thousands of cases' in which DNA results were allegedly falsified or the scientist was not qualified to render conclusions."

"Okay," Schofield said, and took a drink from a glass of water he poured for himself.

"Is it true that in spite of the number of cases, the erroneous or false conclusions were caused by a couple of individuals, as opposed to thousands of DNA scientists rendering thousands of false or inaccurate results?"

"That's true. In one instance, it was someone who lied and claimed to have the credentials when she was hired, and in the other case, it was a misguided individual who believed that she was helping the police convict guilty defendants."

"Simply, these cases of inaccurate or falsified reports are singular instances caused by an individual, not a widespread condemnation of DNA profile testing or the laboratories that conduct this testing."

"That's, uh, true."

"And is it also true that these 'scandals' cited by defense counsel resulted in more stringent guidelines both for law enforcement agencies that submit material for testing and the laboratories themselves?"

"That's very true. Laboratories have to be certified and are regularly subjected to inspection."

"And as the director of a laboratory that tests DNA profiles for criminal cases, would you say that it is common or uncommon for honest mistakes to be made?"

"Uncommon."

"How uncommon?"

"Very."

"And would you say that instances of some individual falsifying results is common or uncommon?"

"Very uncommon. Especially with the amount of double checking that goes on now."

Karp picked up a sheet of paper from the prosecution desk. "Doctor, are you familiar with Dr. Offendahl's work?"

Schofield nodded emphatically. "Yes, of course."

"And what is his reputation in the field of DNA profiling, in particular touch DNA profiling?"

"He's one of the leading, if not the leading authority in the field," Schofield said. "I guess you'd say he's the godfather of touch DNA testing."

Karp glanced over at Nash, who was frowning. She didn't look far enough, he thought, and now she's going to pay. "Doctor, is your lab certified to render results for law enforcement agencies throughout the nation?"

Schofield smiled. "Yes, I like to think we're one of the best."

Handing him the sheet of paper, Karp asked, "Do you recognize this document?"

Schofield studied it for a moment. "Yes, it's, uh, our certification."

"And whose name is signed on the bottom of the document?"

"It's, um, signed by Dr. Offendahl."

"So he certified your laboratory?"

"Yes."

"Are we to understand from your testimony that you are challenging the conclusions reached by the man who certified your laboratory?"

Schofield grimaced. "I don't know that 'challenging' is the right word. I would call it more of a slight professional difference of opinion."

"Slight? How slight?"

"Well, I, uh, agree that the touch DNA found on the victim's shirt was a match to the defendant," Schofield said. "I guess we might differ on what I said was my surprise that if the incident occurred as it was described to me, there wasn't more DNA material present from the defendant."

"A drop of sweat or more skin cells?"

"Yes."

"So it's not the conclusion but the sample size you question?"

"Yes."

"But isn't that precisely the same kind of issue as finding a partial fingerprint as opposed to a complete fingerprint?"

"What do you mean?"

"Well, a partial so-called latent fingerprint left at the scene still means the defendant touched the object. Correct?"

"Yes."

"But because of various circumstances, such as weather or time, it goes from a full to a partial fingerprint. But that doesn't mean the defendant didn't touch the object. Correct?"

"I see what you're saying. Yes, you're correct."

"So the sample size of the specimen is only relevant in respect to whether there's enough to create a DNA profile?"

"Yes, that would be true."

"Dr. Schofield, you agreed to a lot of 'possible' scenarios put forward by the defense," Karp said. "What would you say is the probability that Dr. Offendahl's conclusions are wrong?"

Schofield looked at Nash, who was turning red. He shrugged. "Slim to none."

"Your Honor, I offer into evidence the certification of Dr. Schofield's laboratory signed by Dr. Offendahl, authorizing Dr. Schofield's laboratory to engage in these analyses."

"So received."

"No further questions."

Kershner looked at the defense table. "Ms. Nash?"

"Nothing further, Your Honor."

"Very well. Call your next witness."

Nash stood back up. "We call Morton Feldinghaus."

When the defense witness, a fashionably dressed young white man with a shock of curly black hair and dark-framed hipster glasses, entered, Karp felt a wave of resentment pass through him. In a way, he held Feldinghaus, or more accurately the people he worked for as well as the complicit press, responsible for the deaths of Tony Cippio and even Ricky Watts.

A "policy wonk," Feldinghaus was a senior analyst at the U.S. Department of Justice. He frequently appeared on news programs and was quoted in newspapers propagating the narrative that unjustified police shootings of young black men were "epidemic," a word he'd used just the Sunday before on one of the morning talk shows. He was a favorite of the Black Justice Now movement and progressives with a willing ear in the White House.

However, Feldinghaus only went where his masters told him to go. The fact that he was appearing on behalf of Anthony Johnson was proof of how important the radical ideologues considered this trial. Not so much for any altruistic feelings for the defendant but for the propaganda opportunities of his arrest and trial.

"Their agenda is why we're here," Karp had said to Katz that morning when they met in his office before heading to the courtroom. "That's the money, that's the political will, for the ambushes, the cold-blooded executions, and the biased, bought-and-paidfor media that either ignores the truth—that law enforcement is under siege, not the other way around—or makes it appear that the murder of police officers is unfortunate but somehow understandable."

He's just a mouthpiece for the cowardly, disingenuous wizards behind the curtain, Karp thought as Feldinghaus, smarmy and selfassured, took his seat on the witness stand like he'd been invited onto a game show. He smiled at the jurors and then the gallery and finally at Nash, who blushed and smiled back.

Feldinghaus was well prepared with his statistics and spiel; after all, he'd given this dog and pony show a hundred times in the past year. Nash hardly had to prompt him as he made his case that law enforcement was carrying on a war against young black men.

"The statistics don't lie," Feldinghaus said, looking earnestly at the jury, especially the two young females and the black jurors. "Whites are sixty-two percent of the population and blacks make up just thirteen percent. And yet . . . and yet . . . twenty-six percent of the victims in fatal police shootings last year were black, and almost all black males. That's twice as many as their total makeup of the population would account for . . . unless the police are racially motivated to kill black men."

Feldinghaus leaned forward as if the conversation was between just him and the jurors. "And did you know that more unarmed black men are killed by police than unarmed white men, who outnumber them fivefold . . . that's five times more than can be explained by anything except institutionalized racism in the law enforcement community?"

On and on he went, repeating himself for emphasis as he quoted from different studies and reports until at last he finished and shook his head. "Racism is a sad historical fact in our culture and perpetuated by our institutions, especially the police. It hurts me to say this as a member of the Justice Department, but the police are the front line for people who want to keep black males in line."

It took Nash a moment to realize that Feldinghaus had finished his speech as she leaned against the jury rail captivated. When she did, she blushed like she'd been caught peeping in bathroom windows.

"Thank you for that, Mr. Feldinghaus," she gushed. "One last question. Given that sort of institutionalized oppression, would it surprise you that three police officers have been indicted for murder and the attempted murder of black activists in New York? In fact, one of the officers has pleaded guilty and will be testifying against his fellow conspirators."

"No, it doesn't surprise me at all," Feldinghaus said. "These activists are a threat to the power structure. There would be a perceived need to silence them by any means possible."

"Would it then surprise you," Nash added, "that the defense

in this case maintains that my client, Anthony Johnson, has been framed by the New York Police Department and the New York District Attorney's Office in an effort to silence him?"

Feldinghaus shook his head sadly. "I'm afraid that wouldn't surprise me at all. In fact, the DOJ is seriously considering launching an investigation into the NYPD. It could expand from that to include other agencies."

"Thank you, Mr. Feldinghaus. No further questions."

"Mr. Karp?"

"Thank you, Your Honor." Carrying his ubiquitous yellow pad, Karp stood in front of the witness stand, looking down at Feldinghaus, who smirked up at him.

"Mr. Feldinghaus, you began your testimony by telling the jurors that statistics don't lie." Karp's voice was even but firm. "Is that correct?"

"It is."

"But statistics can be manipulated and twisted, can't they, Mr. Feldinghaus? And they can be taken out of context, isn't that correct?"

Feldinghaus scoffed. "I'm not quite sure what you mean. I'm sort of a math guy, and to me, numbers are numbers."

"Really? All right, let's look at some of those numbers. I believe you noted that blacks make up thirteen percent of the population but are victims in twenty-six percent of fatal police shootings?"

"That's correct."

"And that the victims in fifty percent of fatal police shootings are white?"

"Yes, compared to being sixty-two percent of the population."

"But isn't it also true that there's more criminal violence in minority communities than in white communities and therefore police are more likely to encounter a disproportionately higher number of armed and violent offenders in the minority community?"

"That depends on the composition and behavioral disposition of members of the community."

"Well, are you aware that here in New York City, blacks commit seventy-five percent of all shootings, seventy percent of all robberies, and sixty-six percent of all violent crime, but they make up only twenty-three percent of the population?"

"I wasn't aware of those statistics. But I think they are probably a reflection of white oppression of the black community that encourages criminal activity due to poverty and other socioeconomic factors."

"Whatever the reason, there's more criminality, so don't you agree that officers are more likely to use force in areas where there are more violent criminals and armed suspects?"

"I guess that stands to reason," Feldinghaus agreed. "Though there are many factors at work here."

"Well, you're the numbers guy," Karp said. "If blacks commit, oh, let's round it off and say seventy percent of the violent crime, wouldn't you expect that blacks would account for more than twenty-six percent of fatal police shootings? In fact, shouldn't it be higher, or at around seventy percent of fatal police shootings?"

"Well, again, there's more . . . a lot more . . . to it than that." Feldinghaus was now looking less self-assured.

"Well, here are some more numbers with respect to homicide." Karp looked down at his pad. "Of all homicides committed against whites and Hispanics, the police were responsible for twelve percent. However, of all homicides committed against blacks, the police accounted for only four percent."

"No one is doubting that black-on-black crime is a serious issue . . . very serious," Feldinghaus said.

"But you deliberately make it sound as if it's the police, working for some omnipotent, evil power structure, who are waging a war on black males."

"You're talking apples and oranges, Karp," Feldinghaus retorted.

"Am I?" Karp walked along the jury rail, every juror's eyes on him now. "You also made it a point to say that unarmed black men are more likely to die at the hands of police than are unarmed white men."

"That's an absolute fact," Feldinghaus shot back.

"But doesn't some of that have to do with unarmed blacks in violent, crime-ridden communities being more likely to be violent criminals and try to resist arrest or even attempt to take the officer's weapon?"

"Maybe they have more reason to fear the police and to fight back."

"Nevertheless, it's one of those cases where statistics can be taken out of context, correct?"

"I wouldn't say that," Feldinghaus replied, now starting to squirm a bit in his seat.

Karp again referred to his legal pad. "And didn't a report from your own agency about a study conducted in Philadelphia demonstrate that black and Hispanic police officers were more likely than white officers to discharge their weapons?"

"We're going to revisit that report."

"Why? Because it didn't fit your narrative? Because it backs up a study conducted by a University of Pennsylvania professor who concluded that black cops were more than three times more likely than white officers to fire their guns?"

"We believe that studies would show that black officers have been co-opted by the white power structure in such a way that they actually overreact to members of their own community."

"Well, what about FBI data that shows that forty percent of convicted cop killers are black? And that cops are eighteen and a half times more likely to be killed by a black man than an unarmed black man is to be killed by a cop?"

"Again, it's not taking into account the gestalt of all that is occurring," Feldinghaus said, shooting Nash a get-me-out-of-here look, but the defense attorney sat slack jawed and useless in the face of Karp's attack.

Karp walked over and sat on the edge of the prosecution table. "Isn't it true, Mr. Feldinghaus, that people like you, and your pals in the media, have essentially made a dangerous job—being a cop—even more dangerous?"

"I think a case can be made that they've brought it upon themselves."

"And what about the rest of us? Haven't you made our streets, *especially* in the minority community, more dangerous because the police are afraid to do their jobs in violent neighborhoods for two basic reasons: One, because gutless politicians, demagogues, and the media will rush to judgment and not support them. The second reason is that it's simply more dangerous for the officers. Due to the political climate, they may hesitate to shoot or act, and that could cost them their lives. Isn't that a big part of what's behind that 'serious issue' of black-on-black violence?"

"I don't understand your point."

"My point is this: policing the streets has been irrevocably altered. For example, a routine, legitimate police stop is more likely to end in a deadly ambush. So aren't you, and the people you work for, who advocate a false narrative, a serious part of the problem, not the solution?"

Feldinghaus stammered for a moment and then set his jaw angrily. "I've got nothing more to add to this conversation."

Karp walked over to him and asked, eye to eye, "Mr. Feldinghaus, this isn't some feel-good encounter session that you can end when it becomes uncomfortable for you. This is a search for the truth and, frankly, that's something you can't handle."

24

"**Fuck this, I'm testifying!**"

The words shot out of Anthony Johnson's mouth like bullets from a gun. And his defense attorney recoiled as if ducking their impact.

"You can't," Nash argued. "Karp'll tear you apart."

"I can handle his white ass," Johnson said. "Hell, if those mother-fucking jurors can get all choked up by that old whore's bullshit story, I'll give them one that will leave them sobbing."

The pair were speaking in the holding room for prisoners off the courtroom following the disastrous appearances of Schofield and Feldinghaus. The latter had stormed out of the courtroom, slamming the doors as he left.

Watching the theatrics with arched eyebrows, Judge Kershner had looked at Nash and drily asked her to call her next witness. The defense attorney had called Lupe Torres to the stand to repudiate her sister's testimony and claim that Johnson had been with her when Tony Cippio was murdered, as well as during the attempted murder of Bryce Kim.

After Lupe stepped down, giving Johnson a smile and a wiggle as she walked past the defense table and out of the courtroom, Kershner again asked for the next witness. But there was no one else left, just Johnson.

"Just a moment, Your Honor," Nash requested, and engaged in an animated conversation with Johnson, who hissed, "Put me on the stand."

Nash rose and addressed the court. "Your Honor, Lupe Torres was our last witness. However, my client, Mr. Johnson, is contemplating whether to testify to counter these outrageous accusations and fallacious testimony brought forth by the People's case. As you know, this is a very serious decision, and I ask that he be given the rest of the day to confer with me and make a reasoned choice when the stress of today's testimony has diminished."

Kershner, who had seemingly grown less and less amenable to defense requests as the trial went on, furrowed her brow and looked at the clock. "It's noon," she said, "and I'm not inclined to delay these proceedings any more than necessary." She nodded to the jurors. "These good people have put their lives on hold long enough without this court asking them to give even more so that your client can think about this. We'll take our lunch recess, during which you can confer, and I'll expect your decision when we return."

After the judge recessed the court, Johnson and Nash were escorted to the holding pen area, where he refused to hear her out.

"They're laughing at me," he snarled. "Nobody laughs at me and gets away with it!"

"Can't you see that Karp's been egging you on? He set up those witnesses, like Rose Torres, and called you a coward, to get under your skin so that you'll take the stand. If you do, you'll expose yourself to questions not just about this case but also your criminal history."

"Fuck him," Johnson ranted. "I ain't no coward. I'm a stone-cold gangsta from the hood. I'm a motherfucking cop killer!"

Johnson saw the look on his attorney's face and smirked. She'd never asked him if he'd really done it. He'd told her that he was a victim of police lies, and she'd worked with that ever since. *These white liberals*, he thought, *with their little games and political remedies and agendas, are a joke.* They didn't live in the real world—not like him and even Karp.

"Yeah, that's right, I killed that motherfucking cop while he was begging me for his life so he could go home to his little white wife and little white kids." He laughed, enjoying the moment of truth. "I shot him down like a dog, and then I turned his ass over just like they said I done, and I looked him in the eye, listened to him beg me for his life, and then put a hot one in his head. Now, what are you going to do about that?"

Nash closed her eyes for a moment and then let out a sigh. "I'm going to do my job," she said. "None of that matters. I'm going to make the State prove you're guilty beyond a reasonable doubt. That's how the system works."

"The system," Johnson said, contempt in his voice. "The system is all about keeping the black man in his place. Make him be a good little house nigger, and if he gets uppity, shoot him or put him in the joint. Well, fuck that. If I'm going down, I'm going down fighting. But first I'm going to see if I can talk my way out of this after that shit show defense you put on."

Nash looked at him coldly. "I did the best I could with what I had to work with. Like you just admitted, you're a cop killer, and that's what the evidence says. But I'm still going to do my job because this isn't just about you, it's about a bigger picture."

"Fine." Johnson laughed. "Do whatever you want so you can go to your little white liberal cocktail parties and fund-raisers, and tell your friends how you tried to save the bad black man from hisself. Now let's get this done. You ask the right questions, and I'll come up with the right answers, and maybe one of them dumb motherfucking jurors will buy it."

After Nash left the room, Johnson dropped the tough façade. He felt a chill, and a voice in his head started telling him that he was going away for a long time, the rest of his life. There'd be no more Lupe Torres or any other bitch to pass the long nights with. His world would be defined by prison walls, steel bars, a community of broken, angry men and prison guards. He'd have a certain cachet as a cop killer, but that in itself would also add to the danger. Prisons were all about pecking order, and taking down a cop killer might be considered a step up for somebody.

As Johnson's fear grew, so did his anger. He was angry at Big George for not taking care of Tyrone and Maurice Greene. Without them, Karp would have never been able to place him at Marcus Garvey Park. And he should have taken care of DeShawn Lakes and his old man himself, before they could put him with Ricky Watts. But it wasn't just Big George who had failed him. His old friend Martin Bell, from San Quentin, messed up by not killing Judy Pardo. He sneered. Nash was a fine one to talk about the system when she'd been the one to pass him Vansand's note about where to find the women's shelter.

"She knew what she was doing," he said aloud to himself.

Relying on Moto Juku and pawning the revolver was his mistake. But he'd needed money, and the gun was the only thing of value he had.

"Too many loose ends," he said to the wall.

Vansand and the rest of the media had abandoned him, too. He could see it in their eyes whenever he turned around in the courtroom. The smiles and nods when he was their meal ticket were now cold-eyed stares and frowns. "Well, fuck them, too. And fuck Hussein Mufti."

The reverend had come to visit him at the jail only once, and it had ended on a bad note. "What I want to know is what you're going to do to get me out of this," Johnson had demanded over the telephone as they'd sat across from each other, divided by Plexiglas and watched by a guard.

"Get you out of this?" Mufti asked.

"Yeah, out of this," he'd repeated, pointing to his surroundings.

"Get you out of the Tombs?" Mufti said incredulously, and then he'd laughed. "Son, I don't know what you been smoking, but nobody gets out of the Tombs unless they let you out or, like my man Imani Sefu, they take you out in a body bag."

Johnson had suggested maybe an attack on the courtroom to spring him. "I'll give you some names of some of my homies who'll help." But Mufti had laughed even louder.

"Boy, you been watching too much television. You better hope that your attorney can convince one of them jurors to save your black ass, or you going to be singing the Attica blues, and there ain't nothing I can do about that."

"Are you dump-trucking me?"

Mufti shook his head. "Oh, I'll continue to speak out about the injustice. And I'm sure somebody in the press or one of the white liberals will take up your cause and demand a retrial. And maybe, if you're lucky, when enough time goes by you'll be able to talk some lifer into taking the fall for you. But that's down the road a ways. Until then, you'll be doing hard time."

Johnson realized then that he was on his own, the way it had always been. The only person he could trust was himself. That meant that he was going to take the stand and find the one juror he could con.

There was a knock on the door, and one of the court security officers entered. "It's time," the man said.

"You got that straight," Johnson said, standing up.

A few minutes later, he was seated at the defense table when the judge asked if he'd reached a decision on whether to testify before he brought in the jury.

Nash stood up. "Yes, Your Honor. My client has decided to take the stand and testify in his defense. I'd like the record to note that I am opposed to this and find it ill-advised. I believe that the district attorney has overstepped his authority and purposefully needled and insulted and backed Mr. Johnson into a corner until he feels that he has no choice but to defend himself. It is my opinion that this treatment has caused Mr. Johnson to suffer from a mental breakdown that renders him incapable of properly understanding the ramifications of testifying. So I'm requesting a continuance of this trial until such time as Mr. Johnson's mental state can be evaluated by a psychologist."

Kershner looked over at the prosecution table. "Mr. Karp, your response?"

Karp rose from his seat. "My response is that's utter nonsense. It is certainly Mr. Johnson's right to take the stand, and while defense counsel is correct to caution him, in the end it is his choice. As for counsel's concerns about anything I've said, I'd remind her that this is a murder trial of someone accused of the heinous, brutal execution of a young police officer who had been doing nothing worse than playing basketball with some children. The evidence clearly shows that he is guilty of this crime, and we're confident the jury will agree. As for the request for a mental health evaluation, one was already conducted at the beginning of this process and the defendant was found competent, meaning he understood the nature and consequences of the charges against him and was capable of assisting counsel in his defense. It is the People's position that this is nothing more than stall tactics to delay the inevitable."

Kershner nodded and looked at Johnson. "Is it my understanding that you wish to testify?"

"That's right."

"And you are making this decision after discussing the potential risks of exposing yourself to cross-examination by the district attorney?"

Johnson looked at Karp and sneered. "I ain't afraid of that man."

"I'll take that as a yes," Kershner said. "As for your other comments, Ms. Nash, you may argue those on appeal if you wish, but I don't find that Mr. Karp overstepped. Also, your request that these proceedings be continued until such time as the defendant can undergo another mental evaluation is denied." She looked at the chief court clerk. "Please bring in the jury."

"I'd ask that Your Honor admonish the jury regarding Mr. Johnson's right to decline to testify, and that if Mr. Karp introduces his criminal history, my client is only on trial for these charges," Nash interjected.

Kershner looked at Karp, who shrugged. "I can do that," the judge said.

When the jurors were seated, Kershner addressed them. "Before we broke for lunch, I asked defense counsel if the defendant wished to testify on his own behalf, and she requested time to confer with him. That has been accomplished, and the defendant, Mr. Johnson, has decided to testify from the witness stand. But before he is sworn in, I want to remind you that he was under no obligation to speak, and had he chosen differently, it should not have been taken by you as an admission of guilt. As it has been since the beginning of these proceedings, the presumption is that he is innocent and that it is the State's obligation to prove that he is guilty beyond a reasonable doubt. That presumption remains even after he is called to the stand. Is that clear?"

The jurors nodded. "Good." The judge continued, "It may or may not occur today, but when a defendant takes the stand, his history, including any prior criminal convictions, which would normally be off-limits, become fair game for the prosecutor to examine. However, I remind you that the defendant is currently on trial only for the two charges before you. While the prosecutor is free to address these issues in order to help you determine the defendant's credibility, truthfulness, and motivations, it is not to imply that because he was convicted of another crime that makes him guilty of these crimes. Is that clear?"

Again, the jurors nodded as one. Kershner turned to Nash. "Please call your witness."

"The defense calls Anthony Johnson."

Johnson rose, assuming what he thought of as a look of righteous indignation and noble purpose. He walked purposefully over to the chief court clerk, who waited by the witness stand to swear him in; afterward, he sat down in the witness chair.

Nash took a deep breath and let it out. She walked slowly into the well of the court. "Mr. Johnson, I'd like to begin by having you talk a little bit about your upbringing . . ."

Johnson thought the initial questioning had gone well. He thought he'd seen some of the jurors actually tearing up when he recounted growing up fatherless, poverty-stricken, and beset by all sorts of dangers in a neighborhood rife with crime and violence. The police were no better than the criminals. "They were all either on the take, or couldn't have cared less about a little black kid. I had to learn to fend for myself."

Nash then moved on to his criminal record. He explained that he broke into the old woman's apartment to steal "so that I could eat" and had not intended to wake her. He denied sexually assaulting the victim. "She said I did, but it wasn't true," he claimed. "White women know that if they claim a black man raped them, the cops will come down on him even harder. I only agreed to plead guilty to sexual assault because the cops said they were going to pin some other stuff on me if I didn't."

Johnson neglected to mention that the "other stuff" was strangling the woman to death. And he contended that all he took from the apartment was "some jewelry and a little television that I sold."

When Nash asked him about going to prison on the burglary and sexual assault convictions, he said it changed him forever. "I know it sounds funny, but it was probably the best thing that could've happened to me. I was living on the streets, committing crimes and hanging with the wrong people. But I met some people in prison who talked to me about my responsibilities as a black man, and I turned my life around. I found God and a calling to help other young black men."

"Was prison where you learned about and indeed picked up the banner of black nationalism?" Nash asked.

"Yes. Some experienced long-timers who had been screwed over by the system taught me what it really means to be a black man in white America. And I did a lot of reading, such as about Malcolm X and Martin Luther King."

"But doesn't black nationalism envision separation between white America and black America?"

Johnson looked thoughtful for a moment before he turned to the jurors to, as he said, "speak from my heart."

"I wish we lived in a world where all men were treated equal no matter what the color of their skin or their ethnicity. But unfortunately that's not the way it is. This country has been racist since the slavery days, and while some progress has been made, it's not enough, and if we wait for the white man to change things, it ain't gonna happen. I hate to say this, but I think we'd all be better off if we were separated by race. Then we could be more like two friendly countries than white masters and black slaves."

"And would that include better policing, do you think?"

Johnson nodded. "Yeah, each race would have police officers that come from their communities and understand the culture."

"And after you got out of prison, did you share these beliefs with others—white and black?"

"Yes. I didn't seek the spotlight, but I guess my words got some folks thinking. I was even asked to speak at events on college campuses."

"And how were your views received?"

"By the audience or the authorities?" Johnson asked.

"Well, first by the audience."

Johnson smiled. "Very well. They could see that I wasn't advocating violence, or nothing like that. I talked about building a better, separate world where we could interact as equals and partners."

"Was it during this time that you began to call yourself Nat X?"

"Well, actually Nat X is the name of several black activists, not just me," he said. "The idea was that we aren't speaking as individuals but as one for the black community."

"Where does the name come from?"

"It's a combination of Nat Turner, a slave who led an uprising in Virginia during the 1700s, and Malcolm X, who also advocated a separate black nation. It's our attempt to draw a line to connect the slavery days of the past and the slavery days of the present."

"So your audiences were receptive to your message. What about the authorities?"

"The authorities didn't like what I had to say, and as they always do, they sent the police to let me know I wasn't going to be tolerated," Johnson claimed. "I don't even really blame the police, though some are worse than others. Most are just pawns like the rest of us; they represent the white power structure that prevents all of us from treating each other as brothers and sisters. But they tried to silence me, just like they did with Malcolm X and Dr. King."

"How did they do that?"

"Well, at first they just followed me around and showed up where I was speaking. But when I didn't take the hint, they started getting more aggressive." He looked at the black men on the jury. "Some of you have probably experienced the police reaction to 'driving while black,' but try 'driving while black and taking on the white establishment.' It seemed like I couldn't even get in a car without getting pulled over and hassled."

"Was there a particular incident last spring that told you they were ramping up their efforts to silence you?"

Johnson nodded. "It was in the evening and I was returning from the cemetery where I laid some flowers on my mother's grave, when I got pulled over in a sort of deserted part of Oakland. I thought it was just another traffic stop, but it went to another level."

"What do you mean?"

"They hauled my black ass out of the car and put me on the ground. One of them put a gun to the back of my head and told me if I didn't shut up, the next time they'd say I had a gun so they had to shoot me."

"Did you report this incident?"

Johnson laughed. "To who? The police? They was the ones putting a gun to my head. Look, they ain't all bad, but they go along to get along and they don't cross that blue line they like to talk about. If there'd been a next time, I'd have had my head blowed off and no one would have said nothing as far as the police."

"Mr. Johnson, what brought you to New York City last summer?"

Johnson laughed again. "Well, the situation was getting dangerous in the Bay Area, so I thought it might be a good idea to go somewhere where I wasn't so well known. I hadn't seen my cousin Ny-Lee Tomes since we was kids. So I called him and he invited me to stay with him."

"After you arrived, did you continue to speak out about your political thoughts?"

"Well, not much at first," Johnson said. "To be honest, I was scared and planned on laying low for a while. But Ny-Lee said there was a lot of police brutality going on in the black communities here and that young black men needed someone to look up to who knew what they were going through. He asked if I would be willing to speak to some teens and young men he knew."

"And did you?"

"Yes, of course. Sometimes you have to do what's right even if you is scared. Like I said, I think of my philosophizing as a calling and that God wants me to be a voice for the black community."

"So at some point in these talks you gave, did you meet Maurice Greene, DeShawn Lakes, and Ricky Watts?"

"I believe that's probably true. But to be honest, I spoke to a lot of young men after I got here. Ny-Lee started seeing himself as my manager, like I was some sort of rap star, and he was getting me gigs. But while those names are familiar, and I sort of recognized them two boys when they testified against me, I don't have particular recollections of speaking to them directly."

"What about Big George Parker?"

Johnson shook his head and laughed. "George, he was sort of like a big kid. Like me, he'd had it rough growing up, but he was so big most people didn't realize that he was hurting inside. I met him through Ny-Lee and he just started tagging along with me sometimes."

"On the day that Officer Tony Cippio was shot, were you at Marcus Garvey Park?"

"Yes," Johnson acknowledged. "Only it was earlier in the afternoon. I was there hanging out with Big George and Ny-Lee. Then I had some things to do with my girlfriend, Lupe, so I left them there."

"So you weren't there when the police officer was shot?"

"No, I wasn't."

"What about Big George and Ny-Lee?"

Johnson shrugged. "I don't know," he said, looking troubled. "I mean, I hate to think that my cousin and my friend might have got mixed up in something like that, but like I said, I wasn't there. And I don't know if the cop said something or tried harassing somebody and it got out of hand."

Nash stopped and their eyes met. He could see the word "liar" in hers and he smiled slightly, but there was nothing she could do about it. "What about the party Rose Torres testified about?" she asked.

"There was a little party, but it had nothing to do with no shooting," Johnson said. "At least not from my perspective. I was thinking about it after I heard Rose testify, and Big George and Ny-Lee was kind of acting funny, like they was suddenly real tough or something. But I was excited about something else."

"What was that?"

"I was going back to San Francisco. I decided that I'd been gone long enough, and New York isn't my home; it's not where my momma is buried or where my friends are that I grew up with. And the best part is Lupe had said she'd go back with me. I'd asked her to marry me, and while she's a little young and we're going to have to wait to make it legal, I was happy she'd said yes."

"That's it?" Nash asked. "No celebrating shooting a cop? No threatening anybody with a gun?"

"No." Johnson scowled. "I didn't even have a gun. That's just some shit someone made up to get the police off their back. At least that's what I think."

"So you left New York City. Do you know if that was before or after Ricky Watts was killed by Officer Bryce Kim?"

"Before. I remember calling Ny-Lee from the road, and he said, 'It happened again.' And I said, 'What happened?' And he said, 'A cop shot an unarmed black kid in cold blood, but they is trying to cover it up and say the kid shot first. But he didn't have no gun.' That's what Ny-Lee said."

"And where were you at the time?"

Johnson shrugged. "I think Denver, Colorado. We was tired of driving my old junker, and I got some old homies that live there, so we stopped for a few days. That's when I called Ny-Lee to let him know we was okay, and he told me about that kid getting shot."

"Eventually you reached the San Francisco area and moved in with Moto Juku?"

"Yes, I'd met him a year or so earlier when I first got out of the joint. He was a DJ at one of the clubs. He liked to hang out with me; I think it made him feel tough to kick back with an ex-gangster. He invited us to stay."

"What about the gun we've heard so much about—the silver forty-five-caliber revolver?"

"That was Moto Juku's. He was real proud of having such a fine piece."

"But we've heard testimony that you pawned it."

"Yeah, Moto needed some money, but he's not very streetwise. So since he was letting me stay there, I told him I'd take it to a pawnshop and get him the best price I could. So that's what I did.

I didn't even know he went to get it back until he showed up at the apartment with it."

"So why was it in your possession when you were arrested by Detective Fulton?"

"Moto said he saw someone breaking into my car," Johnson replied. "I have to admit that old habits kicked in. I grabbed the gun off the counter where Moto put it and went to scare the dude off. I didn't even know if it was loaded or not."

"Did you point the gun at Detective Fulton?"

"I pointed the gun," Johnson admitted. "I saw this big black dude going through my car, but like I said I was just trying to scare him."

"Did you pull the trigger?"

Johnson looked at his lawyer as if she'd asked a stupid question. "Hell, no. Why would I kill somebody over a beat-up old Lincoln with a radio that don't even work? Now what kind of stupid shit is that?"

"Did Detective Fulton identify himself as a police officer?"

"Not at first. And when he did, I put the weapon down and surrendered. But he threw me to the ground and said I was being arrested for murdering a cop in New York."

Johnson stopped and looked at the jury. "And here we are."

"What about the testimony of Moto Juku and Detective Fulton?"

"Lies," Johnson said.

"Why would the detective lie?"

"Same reason the cops in Oakland stuck a gun to my head. They want to shut me up."

Nash strolled over to the jury box and looked at their faces as she asked her next questions.

"Did you kill Officer Tony Cippio?"

Johnson shook his head and addressed his answer to the sole black woman on the jury. "I did not kill the officer."

"Did you collaborate with Ricky Watts and give him the gun to kill Officer Bryce Kim?"

"I don't even really remember Ricky Watts. I wasn't there."

Nash nodded. "Thank you, Mr. Johnson. No further questions."

Johnson braced himself for what he believed would be an onslaught of questions by Karp. He almost looked forward to showing the jurors and the press his disdain for the man. But then the district attorney surprised him.

"Mr. Johnson, I'm not going to dignify most of this nonsense by asking you questions so that you can repeat your lies," Karp said, picking up a sheet of paper, as well as the evidence bag holding the revolver, and walking over to the witness stand. "I'll let the jury decide in their deliberations who was telling the truth, the People's witnesses with their corroborated, dovetailed, comprehensive mosaic of your crimes, or a desperate killer trying to thwart justice."

"Objection!" Nash shouted. "I didn't realize we'd already moved on to summations. This is an extremely improper cross-examination."

Kershner tilted her head and arched an eyebrow as she looked at Karp. "Sustained. Mr. Karp, save your ad hominem remarks for your summation. Do you have any questions for this witness?"

"Well, I think just a few, Your Honor. Mr. Johnson, I want to ask you about your conviction for burglary and sexual assault."

"Go ahead, I got nothing to hide," Johnson shot back. "I paid my debt to society and I'm a changed man."

"Really? I guess we'll see about that," Karp said. "In your testimony, you claimed that all you took from the apartment of Mrs. Clare Dupre was, and I quote, 'some jewelry and a little television,' which you then sold."

Johnson frowned. "Yeah, that's right."

"Were you aware that Mrs. Dupre's son, Robert, gave the police a list of items removed by you from the apartment?"

"Yeah, my defense attorney showed me a list. Like I said, some jewelry and a television."

"You are aware that none of the items you took from the apartment were recovered?"

Johnson shrugged. "Like I said, I sold them so I could eat."

"Did your defense attorney later inform you after your plea agreement that there was a supplemental list added to the official list of missing items, or actually one item, provided for the record by Robert Dupre?"

Johnson scowled and shook his head. "I don't know nothing about no supplemental list."

Karp turned to the judge. "Your Honor, permission for ADA Katz to set up an easel in front of the witness stand so that the jurors can also see it."

"Go ahead, Mr. Katz."

With a nod from Karp, Katz got up and grabbed a folded easel that was lying behind the prosecution table. He set it up where Karp indicated, then returned to the prosecution table, where he picked up what appeared to be a large photograph, though it was covered by a blank sheet when he placed it on the easel.

Frowning, Nash got up from her seat and walked over to the end of the jury box so that she could see the demonstration as well.

When everything was set, Karp gave the piece of paper to Johnson and announced, "Your Honor, the witness has been handed People's Exhibit 42, a certified copy of the aforementioned supplemental list that was dated and signed by both Mr. Dupre and the receiving court clerk the day after Mr. Johnson's plea agreement for the burglary and sexual assault of Mr. Dupre's mother."

"Very well," Kershner said.

Karp turned back to the witness. "Mr. Johnson, would you please tell the jurors what item is listed on the supplemental police report."

Johnson was already looking at the paper. His hands began to shake. "This is bullshit," he said.

"Bullshit is not what's on the list. In fact," Karp said, walking over to the easel and revealing the photograph beneath it, "this is what is listed on the report."

The jurors' eyes turned to the photograph. "For the record," Karp said, "this is an enlargement of the certified, dated supplemental police report, People's Exhibit 42, Mr. Johnson is holding in his hand. Mr. Johnson, would you please read the report and tell the jurors what item is listed there."

Johnson sat back in his seat and crossed his arms. "This is a lie, and I ain't reading nothin'."

"Let the record reflect that the defendant refused a legitimate request from the People to read from the supplemental report," Karp said. "With the court's permission, I'll do it for him." He turned to the easel. "The item listed is a forty-five-caliber, stainless steel Smith & Wesson Model 460 with an after-market mother-of-pearl grip. Is that correct, Mr. Johnson?"

Johnson refused to answer, which Karp remarked on for the record. He then handed Johnson the gun. "Let the record reflect that the witness has been handed People's Exhibit 43, a forty-five-caliber, stainless steel Smith & Wesson Model 460 with an after-market mother-of-pearl grip."

As he looked down at the gun, Johnson could be seen mumbling but not loud enough to be heard. "Mr. Johnson, would you please look on the left side of the gun and locate the serial number above the trigger guard."

When Johnson didn't comply, Karp continued. "Would you agree that the serial number on the gun is"—he turned to the easel and read—"according to People's Exhibit 42, SW 952-3?"

Johnson just kept mumbling and turning the gun over in his hand. He flipped open the empty chamber and snapped it shut.

"Your Honor, let the record reflect that the defendant is unresponsive," Karp said.

Kershner addressed Johnson. "Mr. Johnson, please answer the district attorney's questions."

Johnson looked up at Karp, his eyes filling with hatred and malice. He raised the gun, sighted down the barrel at Karp's head, and began to pull the trigger. *Click. Click. Click.*

The court security officers reached him about the same moment he pulled the trigger for the sixth time. One wrested the gun from his hand, and they were about to haul him down when Karp interceded. "Hold on a second."

Johnson didn't speak. He just glared at Karp, who didn't react except to turn to the judge. "The record will reflect, Your Honor, the defendant continued to be unresponsive except to point a gun at me and repeatedly pull the trigger."

Karp moved toward the defendant. "Mr. Johnson, thank you for showing the jury how you used your forty-five-caliber, mother-of-pearl-handled revolver, loaded with cop-killer bullets, to execute Officer Tony Cippio as he pleaded for his life."

Johnson lunged out of the grasp of the court officers and tried to climb over the witness box rail to reach his antagonist before he was restrained again. "I'm not done with you, Karp," he screamed.

"But I am done with you," Karp replied mildly. "No further questions, Your Honor."

25

KARP GRIMACED AS HE LOOKED OUT OVER THE SPECTATORS who'd packed the gallery in anticipation of the summations of *The People of the State of New York v. Anthony Johnson.* Eight months after the fact, he still, occasionally, felt where the bullets fired by Oliver Gray had broken his ribs, the impact of the first round stopping his heart.

He didn't remember much about the shooting. A young black man calling out his name, raising the gun, and then a blow like someone had kicked him in the chest. After that it was all a dream.

As he lay on the exam table, he dreamed he stood in a courtroom, alone except for the men, and a few women, who crammed the jury box to overflowing. He recognized them as the killers—the sociopaths and terrorists, the brutal, evil animals of society—that he'd tried and convicted in the past. Their bright, glittering eyes were filled with hatred and malice as they mouthed voiceless threats. The young black man, Oliver Gray, was there, too; he stood with a gun in his hand and pointed it at Karp.

Click. Click. Karp twisted to avoid the expected bullets, but there was no sound of gunshots, no impact like being kicked in the chest. Instead, he looked up and found himself facing the gallery, only now it was filled with men, women, and children he recognized as the victims of the killers sitting in the jury box. They were smiling and one at a time stood and began applauding.

Karp left his place at the prosecution table and, opening the gate, moved past the rail separating the well from the gallery and began walking down the aisle. Although they didn't speak, the victims continued their applause as he passed them, heading for the closed double doors at the back of the courtroom.

Light filled the edges around the doors. He felt drawn to it, at peace, but just as he reached for the handles to leave the courtroom and step into the light, he heard a voice call out behind him. Turning, he saw Marlene standing in the well of the court, their children—Lucy, Zak, and Giancarlo—as they had been when young, clutching at her legs.

Tears rolled down Marlene's cheeks as she held out her hand. "Butch, don't leave me." He took a step toward her . . . and that's when he'd come to on the table in the emergency room at Bellevue Hospital. A bright light glared above his head, making him squint. "We have a heartbeat," a voice shouted triumphantly.

Someone else squeezed his hand and his eyes shifted to that side, where he saw Marlene, her face wet with tears. "Oh, God, thank you," she cried out, and pulled his hand to her mouth, kissing it repeatedly.

Later the doctor had told him that he had Fulton to thank for insisting on his wearing the Kevlar vest under his shirt and jacket, so while the bullets had broken ribs, turned his chest the color of a ripe eggplant, and stopped his heart, they had not penetrated. He continued to feel the occasional twinge, which the doctor had attributed to the healing process, "as well as the physical and psychological trauma, which can cause 'phantom sensations.'"

One of those twinges had grasped him for a moment now, then released its grip as he looked out over the gallery, waiting for Judge Kershner to invite him to address the jury for the last time. Nash, who had already given her summation that morning, sat looking off into space, dressed entirely in funereal black, including her stiletto heels. Her client brooded next to her, lost in his own thoughts.

On the defense side of the gallery, the benches were filled with solemn black faces and a smattering of white "community activists." Reverend Mufti had taken his customary seat in the row behind the defense table with bodyguards on either side. The disposition of those sitting on that side was muted, like fans of a baseball team that had just been crushed in the World Series. Only the scores had been so lopsided, the outcome so evident from the first pitch, that there was no point complaining about the umps or even that the games had turned on this play or that at bat and only a few twists of fate had decided the outcome. Just the humiliation of knowing that their heroes had been beaten by a much better team.

On the bench behind the prosecution table, Vince Cippio Sr.

sat next to Ricky Watts's father, Robert, both men finding solace in each other while coping with the loss of their sons. Marlene was next to them, and on her other side was Judy Pardo, who'd asked if she could attend the trial after she had testified.

Karp had requested that she wait until the defense rested its case in the event there was a reason to call her back to the stand. "But if you want to attend the summations, and be there for the verdict, that'd be fine," he'd told her. "But can I ask why you want to, after having to deal with those thugs who attacked you, and then what the defense attorney put you through?"

Pardo had shrugged. "I told you that when I was a young cop, I dreamed of putting a killer behind bars. This isn't the same, but it's as close as I'm going to get. I'd like to be there until the end."

Now she sat dressed in the sweater and skirt she'd worn on the day she testified. Her head was up, and it seemed to Karp that her posture was straighter, more self-assured than he'd remembered. He'd heard from Marlene that she was back in touch with her family and was planning on joining her parents in Florida, where they'd moved. She saw him look at her and smiled shyly.

Much of the rest of the gallery behind the prosecution side was filled with cops, both in uniform and plainclothes. Their faces were grim, and when they looked at Johnson the hatred was palpable. But they didn't engage with the opposition on the other side of the gallery in spite of the glares they received.

Among them was Officer Bryce Kim. He'd been disciplined for withdrawing his weapon from its holster in violation of department policy as he walked down the stairs, but otherwise he'd been cleared of any criminal wrongdoing and reinstated to the job he thought he'd lost forever.

"I can't thank you enough," Kim had told Karp in a meeting before the morning's session.

"I'm just doing my job," Karp replied. "Like you were doing yours."

The only other seats were occupied by the media and the few court buffs who'd managed to arrive early enough—hours before the courts building even opened—to be at the front of the line. Many others, disappointed not to get a ringside seat, joined the crowds outside braving the bitter February wind to wait for a verdict.

Pete Vansand was sitting with other members of the media, though Karp noticed the journalist seemed to be a pariah among his own. *How quickly they turn on a wounded member of the pack*, he thought. There'd already been a thinly disguised reprimand of Vansand in an editorial in the *New York Times* calling for "more restraint in the coverage of high-profile and controversial cases."

Karp had read the duplicitous column that morning after getting the newspaper from Dirty Warren, who'd teased him for "channeling Jack Nicholson as . . . whoop whoop . . . Colonel Nathan Jessup" at the end of his cross-examination of Feldinghaus.

"You can't . . . crap balls . . . handle the truth," the news vendor chortled as he danced from foot to foot in the cold.

"I see your inside intel is as good as ever," Karp replied drily as he turned to go into the Criminal Courts Building. "But your impression of Jack still leaves a lot to be desired."

The suspicion was that Pete Vansand had followed Marlene and Judy Pardo to the women's shelter and then that information had "somehow" been passed to the defendant. It was one of those suspicions that might never be proved. One man who knew the truth was lying in the city morgue, and the other two weren't talking . . . yet. But if the day came, Karp would be ready to investigate the newsman and those with whom he acted in concert to kidnap Judy Pardo. In the meantime, he had an exclamation point to put on the end of this trial.

Those in the gallery who were hoping for fireworks would be disappointed. With her client sitting sullenly in his seat, Nash began her summation by excusing Johnson's outburst as "a natural reaction after sitting here day after day listening to the lies and distortions, as well as the insults hurled in his face by the district attorney."

Karp looked at the jury as Nash rambled on, and although they were listening, he could tell they weren't buying it. Their glances at Johnson were unsympathetic.

As expected, Nash's summation was essentially a repeat of her opening statement with a few added details and invective. "She's got nothing else," Karp had said to Katz when they went over his closing one last time. "She has no evidence, she has no case; her only option is to try the district attorney and the police."

And that's what she did by trying to pull the prosecution's case apart into its individual pieces, hoping that whatever small inconsistencies or blanks she could turn up would confuse the truth for at least one juror. She invoked the ghosts of wrongful convictions, citing statistics on the percentage of innocent prisoners in American

penitentiaries—"most of them black"—and decrying the DNA profiling "as fraught with fraud and mistakes," thus denying thousands
of defendants their constitutional rights.

The witnesses were misguided, or liars, she claimed, and
"whether knowing or unknowing were part of a conspiracy to
silence the voice of my client because he's black, because he's a
threat to their racist power structure, and because he was a conve-
nient scapegoat when they needed to sweep the police shooting of
an unarmed black teenager under the rug."

Calling on the jurors to find her client not guilty, Nash did
her best to strike a note of righteous indignation. But her words
sounded hollow, and she sat down with an air of defeat about her.

As the jurors now filed into their seats, Karp was ready.

He carefully reassembled the People's case as he'd promised
during his cross-examination of Johnson into a "corroborated, dovetailed, comprehensive mosaic" of his crimes, depicting "a desperate
killer trying to thwart justice."

All that was left was for him to put it into perspective. He talked
to them about the Big Lie of the frame defense and how "if a lie is
repeated often enough, even those who know better can no longer
separate fact from fiction."

He pointed out that during the Russian Revolution, the Bolshe-
viks' numbers were small but they were violent, more organized
and focused than their opponents, and by using the Big Lie to further their cause as the cause of all Russians, they were able to take
over the country. "And from there they exported the Big Lie so that
even a brutal mass murderer like Che Guevara was romanticized

as this cigar-chomping, heroic revolutionary. I wonder how many young people wearing T-shirts with CHE LIVES over a photograph of him are aware that he advocated murder as a means to an end."

He pointed out that the fallacy was no different than when considering the defendant, Anthony Johnson, who, speaking to impressionable young black teens, advocated the murder of police officers. "The goal of terrorists like the defendant, and those who support him, is to remove the barrier between you and their vicious, exclusionary worldview."

Karp left that image in their minds as he asked why Vince Cippio and Eddie Evans and every good cop would want to frame an innocent man "knowing that the killer of their son, their partner, their colleague is out there walking the streets ready to kill again. Such venal arguments are ludicrous and fly in the face of reason and common sense, as well as decency."

With his own voice rising in genuine indignation, he pointed out that Johnson had victimized many more people than Tony Cippio ever had, among them the slain officer's wife, Fran, "and their three children, including an infant who will never meet his father."

Picking up the gun from the prosecution table and holding it up, he added to the list of victims Vince Cippio, who had two sons "sacrificed by terrorists, some crashing airliners into buildings filled with thousands of innocent people, and the one who sits at the defense table and used this stainless steel, forty-five-caliber revolver with a mother-of-pearl grip."

There were also the teenagers to whom Johnson had told the Big Lie, especially Ricky Watts, "who just wanted to be accepted in his own community and respected because he and his family value education and trying to make something of oneself."

"And let's not forget Officer Bryce Kim, who had to shoot a teenager to defend his own life. It's not something he wanted to do, but it's something he will have to live with for the rest of his life. All of these lives devastated by one man with a gun and a cause."

Finally, after Karp had gone through all of the evidence and tied it back together and made his points about the Big Lie and the frame defense, he wrapped up with a story that had come to him several months earlier. He'd been going through some old mementos from his past, when he came across a yellowed envelope addressed to him many years earlier. He knew then how he would end the People's case.

As he told the jury, the letter was written by Victor Dubensky, his best friend when growing up in Brooklyn. Since kindergarten they'd done everything together—from street stickball to basketball, pinochle to blackjack, and on late summer nights as teens, talking about girls, the Yankees, and their dreams of the future.

Then shortly after high school graduation, Victor called him. "I've been drafted," was all he said, but they both knew what that meant in those days. There was a war raging in Southeast Asia, and young American men were being shipped off to fight it by the thousands.

Some who received an induction notice were running away to Canada. Others didn't have to worry as they protested the war on college campuses; their status as students kept them safe from the bombs and bullets. But not Victor, who reported to the induction center and from there to boot camp.

After receiving his orders that would send him to Vietnam, Victor came home on leave. He and Karp had done their best to cram a year's worth of beers and reliving their past together into a few nights. Then on the last night before he was to report, Victor handed the envelope to Karp. "Don't open it unless . . . unless I don't come home," he said. In the morning he was gone.

"Victor Dubensky came home from the war," Karp told the jurors. "But it was in a flag-draped coffin, and he was buried at Arlington where so many other fallen heroes lie in honor. I flew to Virginia from California, where I was going to college, safe from the bullets and bombs, to attend his funeral. Then afterward I returned to Brooklyn, where I opened this letter I'd now like to read to you."

Karp knew that reading the letter would be difficult for him, even after all the years that had passed, but he believed that the jurors would understand if his voice cracked and he had to pause from time to time. And so he read the words that started by thanking him for his friendship but moved inexorably on to the last paragraphs that told him not to mourn too long.

"We all have to die at some point," Victor had written, "and I can't think of a better way than for my country. It's not about whether this war is just, that will be on the politicians' consciences. For guys like me, we put on the uniform and answer the call because we're Americans and that's an ideal worth fighting and dying for. So don't dwell on how my life ended. Pay me back by becoming a basketball star and putting a law school degree to good use. Get married, have kids, grow old, enjoy your freedoms. That's what I answered the call of duty to ensure. So if you remember me, remember the good times and know that I died for something worth believing in. Love you big guy, Victor."

Fighting back the tears, Karp folded the letter and put it back in the envelope, giving him enough time to regroup so that he could finish.

"You don't have to wear a uniform to be a hero in our society," he said as he strolled along the jury rail. "Every one of you who gets up in the morning and goes to work, and sees your children get good educations and become productive, law-abiding citizens is a hero for the part you play in our society. And sometimes, heroes are asked to sit where you're sitting now and perform their civic duty for long hours and listen to all the horror and visceral emotions that a murder trial can invoke in a solemn, sacred search for the truth. And then, without fear or favor to either party, render a just verdict. You are also owed a debt of thanks and are heroes even if you don't wear the uniform of our armed services or that of the police officers and firefighters who serve the community."

Then his jaw set and his voice grew angry as he drove to the finish. "There is a movement afoot in this country," he warned, "that would have you believe that this country and its institutions are broken, that they no longer serve a purpose, and that the people you rely on to protect you and those who also serve the ends of justice are no longer trustworthy. There's a lot of money and a lot of energy being spent to convince you of that from this courtroom to the halls of Congress and the White House. But you know what?"

He paused and looked from juror to juror. "You can send a message that the Big Lie stops here. You can send a message that you see through their banality that is represented by this evil man sitting right there," he said as he walked over and stood facing Johnson, "and let the world know that he is not some heroic revolutionary the so-called system is trying to silence. He is a desperate, cold-blooded, and ruthless killer trying to escape justice. And every last one of you is more heroic than he could ever have imagined himself to be."

And finally Karp said, returning to his place in front of the jury, "I'm not asking you to find the defendant, Anthony Johnson, guilty beyond a reasonable doubt for the crimes of murder and attempted murder.

"When this is all over, when you've deliberated and reached your verdict, I want you to be able to go home and, when your family, your friends, and your neighbors and co-workers, who have been reading and listening to the distortions and lies of the media and the demagogues, ask you how you reached your verdict, you will be able to say you know that Anthony Johnson, from all of the evidence, was guilty beyond any and all doubt. And with that you will send a message that will be heard from coast to coast across this great country of ours. Our shared traditional values remain inviolate."

One last time, Karp paused to look each juror in the face, and then he nodded. "I thank you for your service."

EPILOGUE

Something startled Pete Vansand from a deep sleep in the bedroom of his fourth-floor walk-up in the Village. He held his breath and lay completely still, listening, though all he could hear was the pounding of his heart through the comforter and the sounds of the city outside his window, which seemed unusually loud.

Then he noticed that the night-light in his bathroom down the hall must have burned out. He couldn't see anything past the doorway, just an empty blackness like the maw of a cave. The only light in the bedroom came through the window from a weak streetlight down the block and was diffused by thin white curtains.

Letting his breath out, he wondered what had awakened him so abruptly. He inhaled, and that was when he noticed the odor. It was horrible . . . the stench of something rotten and putrid. Had a rat died in the wall? *Or a bunch of rats*, he thought as the odor grew nauseatingly stronger. Maybe the building manager put out a bunch of poison and now dozens of furry bodies were decaying on the other side of the paneling.

Casting about for the source of the stench, he noticed the curtains flutter slightly. *Funny, I don't remember leaving the window open*, he thought. Then he realized the smell was wafting in on the breeze. *Is there a garbage strike I haven't heard about?*

Then again, he hadn't been paying much attention to the news lately. It had been two weeks since the jury in the Johnson case had come back with a verdict. Guilty on both counts. A cheer had gone up from the police officers and court personnel in the courtroom, while the defendant's former supporters sat mute and disgusted. There weren't many left. After Johnson's meltdown on the witness stand and then Karp's evisceration of the defense, most of those who hadn't already jumped ship did so, he among them.

Really the only excitement left when Karp finished his summation was when Johnson attacked his defense attorney immediately after the verdict was read. He'd actually gotten her to the ground with his hands around her throat before the court security officers could pull him off.

Sentencing wouldn't take place for another eight weeks, but no one doubted Johnson would get life for the murder of Officer Tony Cippio plus twenty-five years to life for the attempted murder of Officer Bryce Kim. And if that wasn't enough to make sure he never got out of prison, he'd also been charged with the attempted murder of a police officer by the district attorney in San Francisco County for pointing a gun at NYPD Detective Clay Fulton and pulling the trigger.

Johnson and Nash weren't the only ones disappointed by the verdict. The case had been Vansand's ticket back to the big news programs, but only if the story line was wrongfully accused black activist won against the Nazi district attorney. A cop killer getting what he deserved was nowhere near as sexy.

The national news desk had stopped taking his calls. Adding insult to injury, the twentysomething news director at his station had called him into her office to tell him he was being reassigned to "soft features." The Action News Team spot was being given to Eric Mason, the enterprising young reporter who'd responded to the police call when thugs attacked the prosecution witness Judy Pardo and the district attorney's wife, Marlene Ciampi. It was the story of the year, and Vansand had been in the courtroom twiddling his thumbs when he knew the location of the shelter and that something was likely to happen.

Vansand felt a little guilty about passing that note to Johnson through his attorney about where to find Pardo. But he reasoned that he thought the accused killer just wanted to intimidate her, and if he had, the verdict—and Vansand's future—might have taken a different turn. But apparently the two women had been more than three criminals could handle.

Nash was another person who wasn't taking calls. But she was probably dealing with her own failures. This had been a big case— a real career maker if she'd pulled it off—and a lot of money had gone into making it happen. She'd heard that protesters and even the rioters had been paid in an attempt to influence the jury pool.

Mufti, too, had disappeared off the radar. The verdict seemed to take the wind out of his sails. His last statement to the press had been that he was going to take some time "for reflection before resuming my dedicated efforts on behalf of the black community." Of course, his silence might have been more tied to rumors that he and other New York City Council members were being investigated by a federal grand jury for fraud and accepting bribes. So his treading lightly around the authorities might have been in the hopes that they'd go easy on him.

The stench filling his room prompted Vansand to get out of bed to close the window. But he'd taken only two steps when a large shadow passed across the light from the streetlamp. "Who's there?" he called out in fear. The window led to the fire escape, but only residents of the building should have had access to it, and there was no good reason they'd be outside his room at that time of night.

When there was no answer, he wondered if maybe he'd imagined the shadow and started to move toward the window when the light was again blocked off by an enormous figure. This time a bear poked its furry head in through the window, parting the curtains.

"Who are you?" Vansand asked, backing away, his voice choking with fear.

"'ooger," the bear said.

Vansand was too frightened to scream. *This has to be a nightmare*, he thought. *There are no bears on fourth-story fire escapes in New York City.* But he didn't wake up as the bear began trying to fit his massive bulk through the window, bringing with him the foul odor.

"Go away," Vansand pleaded, but 'ooger kept coming.

Then he heard a sound coming from behind him. He whirled and peered down the pitch-black hallway. "Who's there?" he cried out.

"'at's 'avid," the bear said behind him.

A shadow separated itself from the black of the hallway and stepped toward him. A hooded and robed figure appeared, the light just illuminating his pale features and glittering in the eyes that burned in the darkness beneath the hood.

"Please, what do you want?" Vansand begged.

"Repent," the ghoul whispered.

The scream died in Vansand's throat.